MAXWELL'S DEMON

Also by Steven Hall

The Raw Shark Texts

MAXWELL'S DEMON

STEVEN HALL

Grove Press
New York

Typeset in Minion by Sharon McTeir, Creative Publishing Services.
All visual text elements created by the author.

First published in Great Britain in 2021 by Canongate Books Ltd

Printed in the United States of America

First Grove Atlantic hardcover editon: April 2021

Library of Congress Cataloging-in-Publication data is available for this title.

ISBN 978-0-8021-4920-6
eISBN 978-0-8021-4922-0

Grove Press
an imprint of Grove Atlantic
154 West 14th Street
New York, NY 10011

Distributed by Publishers Group West

groveatlantic.com

21 22 23 24 10 9 8 7 6 5 4 3 2 1

For Mighty A,
and my Second Stanley

MAXWELL'S DEMON

PART I

I Don't Believe in God, but I Miss Him

The world is barely there at all. Don't we all secretly know this?
It's a perfectly balanced mechanism of shouts and echoes
pretending to be wheels and cogs, a dreamclock chiming
beneath a mystery-glass we call life

—Stephen King

1

Roses

When I was little, my father was famous. Dr Stanley Quinn was a man of letters, a man of words, a man who'd built himself from clattering keys and spooling ribbon – and a firm yank on his own bootstraps – to become the greatest poet, journalist and war correspondent of his generation.

In real terms, this meant that I grew up without my father around, although as I remember it, he always seemed strangely present. Throughout his many absences, my father endured as an active part of my life – his picture in the press, his thoughts in broadsheet black ink that rubbed off on my fingers, his disembodied voice from inside our kitchen radio.

To a child of perhaps three or four, it seemed as if my father only ever left home by degrees. His name, his voice, his picture were always there for me, always around to watch over us. Even now, almost thirty years later, my father returns, although far less frequently. His voice comes back in television documentaries about the old conflicts. Beirut, Suez, Muscat.

Live sound recording, original tape says the caption, and then he's in the room, reporting through hiss and static, my father still.

And it's no small thing, you see, the way a child sees a parent. The world comes in through our mothers and our fathers like light through a stained-glass window, and our infant selves can't help but be coloured by it, then and for ever. To me, Dr Stanley Quinn was always a man dismantled, and Alexandra Quinn – well, she was always a woman fading away.

As a child, it never occurred to me as strange that my mother spent all of her days in bed. Not until years later. At the time, I simply assumed that it was how things should be and, to tell you the truth, I liked it. The mornings and evenings of my very early life would be spent upstairs with her in our home in the country, talking and listening to her read from one of the many books that filled every corner of our house.

My mother was a beautiful woman, pale and delicate, with the kind of hair that lights up like a halo in the sun. Even as an adult, I've never been able to equate the knowledge of what was happening to her, that her illness was growing ever more severe, with how I remember the changes she underwent. She simply became softer, paler, lighter. More *other* somehow, more somewhere else. As far as I can remember, there were no bad days, no coughing fits, no unpleasant deterioration, simply the impression of her becoming less of one thing, and more of another. She spoke quietly, and read to me every day in that gentle voice; we soon exhausted all the children's books we had in the house, and moved on to the heaped shelves of my parents' collection. Before long, I was a child of Greek tragedies, Darwinian struggles and of bright, burning tygers. She read aloud the words of great thinkers, writers and artists from all across history and, as she did, she read them into me.

Oh, don't misunderstand me when I say this – I know I'm nothing special. What I am, I've often thought, is a little garden shed, a rickety box of old, reclaimed planks lifted from the great houses of Dickens and Darwin, topped off with cracked and fallen slates from Herman Melville's home. My latch doesn't work, my window doesn't open, and if it rains, everything inside me gets wet in less than half an hour. And, well – that's okay, you know? That's just how it is, and I mind it a lot less than I could. Because here's the thing – learning and growing were never what kept me climbing up those creaky old stairs with the next heavy hardback clutched tight to my chest all that time ago. All that mattered were the quiet hours with my mother, sitting on the bed, listening to her gentle words as they came. It was only years later that I understood how the stories that she read had become a part of me, worked into my skin and my blood by the quality of her voice, and the uncomplicated love that illuminated and defined those times.

o

I remember two seasons from this very early part of my life, a summer and a winter, although, of course, there must have been an autumn in between. That summer was an extraordinary one, because Dr Stanley Quinn made one of his rare extended visits home.

I remember how the physicality of my father seemed magical to me. I'd become used to him as a picture, a voice, as the smell of clothes in a wardrobe, and as a hundred other single-sensory avatars. But now, it was as if some force had pulled all of him together, as if, for the shortest of times, these fragmented elements had condensed to make a man, and that man could suddenly exert his physical will upon the world. The simplest of things – that my father could respond to spoken words, could move from one part of the house to another, could cut back the roses, could be touched and felt and had a real hand that could hold mine – these things were miracles, magic, amazing events that left me full of wonder.

I have a clear memory of one specific conversation with my father from this time.

The memory starts with roses in a basket.

‘Why are you doing that?’

My father glanced down at me, a freshly cut rose stem in one hand, a pair of bright silver secateurs in the other.

‘So we can take them inside to your mother. She loves the roses.’

‘She likes the red ones best.’

‘That’s right.’ My father clipped another stem. ‘She does.’

‘But they’ll die now they’ve been chopped off.’

I must have sounded very serious as I said this because Dr Stanley Quinn stopped what he was doing and knelt down in front of me.

‘But if they weren’t chopped off, how would your mother see them?’

I thought.

‘We could take her a picture,’ I said.

‘And would that be the same?’

I thought again.

‘No.’

‘No,’ he said. ‘The roses are bright; they’re beautiful, but they don’t last very long. And that’s all right; it’s an important part of what they are.’

We took the roses inside.

o

My next memory is of the following winter, of being led into my parents’ bedroom to see my mother’s body, to *say my last goodbyes*.

I remember snow piled up against the windowpane and the blizzard blowing outside, but the room itself was still and quiet. Dust particles hung like stars, fixed points in unchanging space. My mother’s head looked so light on her pillow; she seemed to be barely there at all.

I walked across to her bedside, unafraid.

I felt no sudden pain of separation. Like my father, though in a different sense, my mother had always been leaving home by degrees.

I remember feeling that it was not as if her life had ended, but more that she'd arrived at the natural conclusion of some motherly process. Since the beginning of time, her voice had been growing steadily quieter and her movements more slow. In the last few weeks she'd read to me in a barely audible whisper, and in the last few days she had read in silence, her mouth forming words I'd been unable to hear. She moved less and less until her movements became imperceptible, until, finally, there were no movements at all. One thing becoming another – this was how it had always been, and in the end, it was no more complicated than that.

I stood quietly beside the bed, my hand on my mother's, watching the snowflakes swirl and pile against the windowpane. I could feel snow falling inside me too, I realised, a settling white blanket that made my thoughts quiet and edgeless, a cosy sort of numb.

After a little while, my eyes drifted down and found a large book, *Broten's Encyclopaedia of British Plants and Trees*, sitting on the edge of my mother's bedside table. We'd read this book together and the hundreds of descriptions, etchings and colour plates were all very familiar to me. I hauled myself up onto the mattress beside her, reached out and heaved the encyclopaedia onto my lap, and then opened it.

It fell open, and there, between two pages of text, was something I couldn't remember having ever seen before.

A real, red rose, pressed completely flat – flat almost to transparency.

I put out a hesitant finger and found that I could move it.

Carefully, very carefully, I slid the rose loose from the lines of type.

I stayed like that for a long time, sitting quietly, just holding it in my hand.

2
Thirty Years Later

Broten's Encyclopaedia of British Plants and Trees is the first book on my bookshelf, but you wouldn't know what it was if you saw it. It's cocooned in bubble wrap and the sort of UV-resistant plastic that keeps old Superman comics from falling apart in the sun.

The thirty-year-old rose inside is only slightly the worse for wear. One petal is gone, plucked from it by my scruffy-haired sixteen-year-old self. The idiot. He felt the need to carry that petal around and show it to girls at the sort of parties where they're always playing The Cure. Eventually, of course, he gave it away to one of them as they sat in a locked park, late one summer night.

There are other, lesser, damages. A leaf folded and split accidentally here, a thorn come loose and picking at the book's bindings there. With each exposure, these things build up. That's why, nowadays, my mother's rose stays firmly pressed between its pages, safe in the pitch-black care of etched hawthorns and hyacinths, swaddled in its bubble wrap and Superman's special plastic.

The next book on my bookshelf – and this is assuming we're travelling east, as all young readers here learn to do ✤ – the next book is a big hardback edition of my father's *Collected Works*.

✤ In English, the literary arrow of time travels to the right. This is our law of pages, lines, words and letters. Left is a past left behind, and right is an unknown future. Of course, you know this. You're travelling along with that arrow at this very moment. But be careful, these words might appear to be rattling by like scenery glimpsed from a train window but – just like that scenery – nothing on this page is really moving at all.

The inscription on the title page reads, '*I'll always be here for you, Tom*', and if you asked me to, I could reproduce every curl and line of that note from memory, even now. It's a solid book with a lot of wear, pages thumbed, corners folded, passages underlined. A collector's bookshop might describe it as 'heavily used', but if it were a teddy bear, you wouldn't hesitate to call it 'well loved'.

After the *Collected Works*, we come next to three books from my early teens. A handsome hardback of *Don Quixote*, a paperback of *It*, and a dog-eared copy of *The Warlock of Firetop Mountain*.

These books are survivors, remarkable because they still exist. At the age of thirteen, on one long-forgotten day in July, I took each one down from its shelf in our country home and put it into a suitcase (along with *Collected Works* and the encyclopaedia of plants and trees, which went everywhere with me) to take to my aunt's place by the sea for summer holiday reading. Because of this, these books were not in our house when my father's second wife, the poet Margery Martin, burned it down and destroyed everything else that we had.

Let's move on.

After the survivors, there's another book by my father, *The New Collected Writing*. This is a thin, black book, a line of soot and desolation dividing the shelf like the K–T boundary. Its inscription reads '*To Thomas, my son*'. Dr Stanley Quinn left room for more words to follow, but must've reconsidered, or never got around to adding them. The rest of the page is untouched. And marks an ending, this book, a scarred and blasted Maginot Line between me and my father. A line that neither of us would reach across for the many long years that followed.

The books continue along the shelf, more than a decade passing with them, until finally we arrive at *The Qwerty Machinegun* by Thomas Quinn, my own first novel. I posted this particular copy to my father on publication day, only to have it come back a week later with a curt note from someone I'd never met – '*Too little, too late*', it said.

Too little, too late. The obituaries began to appear a few days later. My timing has always been lousy. My father – my talking, speaking, moving, breathing, hand-holding father – had come apart for good.

o

Just beyond *The Qwerty Machinegun*, standing behind my own first novel like the Empire State Building stands behind that little church in New York, is another first novel – *Cupid's Engine.*

This huge book sits at the absolute centre of my shelf like a great, dark keystone, every inch of its creased and battered cover plastered with praise: 'The crime novel of the decade', 'An intricate puzzle-box of delights', 'addictive and astonishing', 'a feast for whodunit fans', 'flawless', 'remarkable', and somewhere in amongst it all, '"A uniquely talented writer" –Stanley Quinn'. My father rarely supported other writer's books in this way, but then, *Cupid's Engine* is remarkable in at least half a dozen different ways. The book's author, Andrew Black, barely gets a mention on this particular cover, but that hasn't stopped the name looming large in the imaginations of the literary press and reading public in the nine long years since *Cupid's Engine* first found print. 'A mysterious and elusive mastermind' says the quote from the *Independent*. And they would know. They, like everyone else, had been unable to land an interview, or even an author picture to run alongside their five-star review. No details about Andrew Black were available at the book's publication; nobody talked to Black; nobody met Black, and that remains the case even to this day. Conspiracy theories, hoaxes, blurry author photos and doctored documents all did the rounds and were debunked and dismissed in turn. Black's publishers offer nothing but coy smiles and upturned palms when questioned, knowing that that mystery does nothing to hurt book sales, and Black's agent, Sophie

Almonds, continues to issue the exact same statement, year on year, in response to any and all enquiries: 'Andrew Black is not available for comment or interview, but he thanks you for your interest in his work.'

One of the few concrete details to be unearthed and verified by Black hunters concerned that unusual cover quote from my father. I hadn't been the only one to find a quote from Stanley Quinn surprising, and pulling on that particular thread yielded results for those hungry for details on the mysterious author.

Andrew Black had been my father's assistant and, later, his protégé.

Chosen one. Heir apparent. Disciple. Take your pick from the press clippings. I'd seen *spiritual son* a few times too, which stung just that little bit more than the others, as you can probably imagine. My father was immensely proud of Black, and Black – by several published accounts – idolised my father in return. They were a team, a unit, a literary family of two. My father never revealed a single additional detail about Black, no matter how often he found himself pressed, but he happily confirmed the basics. *Assistant turned protégé. Proud.*

And here's the thing – my father was *right* to be proud of Black. And yes, it sometimes hurts my insides a little when I think about it, but what does that matter? He was right.

Cupid's Engine became a global phenomenon, and continues to sell in huge numbers, year after year after year. And it should; *it should.* Andrew Black is a genius. The book is – there is no way to deny it – an out-and-out masterpiece.

This particular copy has been read almost to destruction: the spine is a mass of white fracture lines; its glue is cracked; and dozens of yellowing, dog-eared leaves poke out of it at odd angles. It's an arresting object, a great, shabby monolith that's so big, so dominant in fact, that you could easily miss the book behind it.

Tucked away on the far side of *Cupid's Engine*, sitting so far back on the shelf as to half vanish into the shadows, is a second copy of my novel, *The Qwerty Machinegun.* This one's damaged, its spine horribly buckled from a collision with something hard.

If you were to take this copy down from the shelf and open it, you'd discover that its pages were crammed almost to obliteration with changes, crossings-out, and hundreds and hundreds of neat, handwritten notes and corrections made with a fine black pen. Flipping to the front, to the title page, you'd find a small, equally neat inscription:

Thomas,
You asked me what I thought of your novel.
Andrew Black

3
Why Knocks An Angel?

The books on the bookshelf stand in silent, dusty rows.

They stand, and stand, and stand.

Nothing happens. Nothing changes.

Within certain parameters, this could be any day at all.

The books are the books. The dust is just – dust.

Do you know what dust is? Have you ever really thought about it?

Dust is everything and nothing happening all at once.

It's the smoke and exhaust from the breathing city; it's the Great Fire and the Blitz, the Elizabeth Line and the braziers in the Temple of Mithras. It's the life and times of Thomas and Imogen Quinn, the fibres from their tissues, tights and Christmas jumpers; it's skin particles sent swirling from scratched heads, rubbed eyes and rough hugs, from high fives, DIY, stupid dancing and handjobs, from yanked-down knickers and pulled-up socks, from arm waving, shouting, crying and itches that are *up a bit, up a bit, up a bit more.* It's an intermingling of all those things, events, and all the different people we have been as we've lived together in this space, it's a mixing together of almost everything to create – almost nothing.

Just dust.

'Do you ever think about the stories it could tell?' my aunt said to me once, as she batted great plumes of the stuff from the rug straining the knots of her washing line. Well, I've thought about it a lot and the answer is – no stories at all. You see, the dust doesn't know *and* or

how or *when* or *but*. It has no understanding of *so*, or *then* or *because*. Even if it could speak, its stories would have no unfolding of events, no beginnings or endings, just one senseless, single-syllable cacophony of middle.

With dust, the medium is the only message.

Sometimes, the way it gathers around the books on the bookshelf, it makes me think of those first mammals, the tiny prehistoric proto-mice, watching the dinosaurs, waiting for their time to come.

'Fuck.'

And just like that, it *couldn't* be any day at all.

Just like that – it's now.

That *fuck* came from me out in the hallway, the moment I discovered that my iPad, and also, wait for it – 'Oh, fucking hell' – my iPhone were both busy installing updates, leaving me with nothing to entertain myself with, even though I was absolutely desperate for the toilet.

I shoved the spare bedroom door open and shuffled quickly across the room. I grabbed my big, battered copy of *Cupid's Engine* from the middle of the shelf and headed towards the door.

Two minutes later, and I was sitting in our tiny little bathroom, pants down, flicking my way past the book's publisher notes and the yellowing title page for the first time in years.

That was when the landline started to ring.

I glanced helplessly across the hallway to the living-room door. I was still very much occupied on the toilet and in no position to answer it.

What if it's Imogen? I thought. *Well, if it is, the answerphone will pick it up. You can call her back in a few minutes. It's not the end of the world.*

Turning back to my book, I barely noticed when the ringing stopped and the answerphone gave out its loud beep.

Then, gradually, I became aware of the voice coming from the speaker.

I recognised it subconsciously at first, I think, the familiarity of it, and it drew me partway out of my thoughts. The words were muffled, however, and a low-priority message filtered through to the edge of my consciousness – they were playing one of his old recordings on the radio again: an interview, or an old battlefield report. I didn't exactly try to hear what was being said, and as a result, barely caught anything but the last few words.

'. . . Why knocks an angel in Bethlehem?'

There was a brief pause, and then his voice said:

'Are you there, Tom?'

My head snapped up.

What?

I dropped *Cupid's Engine*, loose pages spilling out all over the bathroom floor.

What?

Cu-clunk. Buuuuuuuuuuuuurr.

Pants still around my ankles, I raced across the hallway towards the living room.

The other person has cleared.

The other person has cleared.

The other person has cleared.

I pushed the door open and stood in the doorway, heart thumping, staring at the phone.

The other person has cleared.

My father had been dead for almost seven years.

4
Analogue

You have no new messages.

You have no new messages.

You have no new m—

You have no—

You have. One. Saved message. From. 11 May . . .

'Hey, it's me . . . Me, Imogen . . . your wife. Are you there? . . . Are you there? . . . No? All right, fine. I hope you haven't forgotten to eat and died. Love you. Call you later. Love—'

Message saved.

1471

You were called yesterday at. Fourteen. Thirty—

100

'Hello. Operator.'

'Hi, yeah. Could you tell me the last time someone called this number, please?'

'Yes – the last call made to this line was at 2.36, yesterday afternoon. Would you like the caller's number?'

'No, that's all right. It was, er, a PPI bot or something. And there's been nothing else after that?'

'That's correct, sir.'

'Only, the phone was just ringing.'

'Oh. Well, there's nothing showing up on the system.'

'Okay. So—'

'You probably had a crossed line.'

'A crossed line?'

'That's right, sir. You do still get them from time to time. Would you like me to put you through to the BT helpdesk? They can test the—'

'No, it's okay. Thanks.'

'All right sir, thank you.'

[Clunk]

HELLO 30TH SEPT

You have no new messages.

You have no new messages.

o

The whisky rolled around the tumbler, and I stared out of the window at the old church spire rising from the oranges and yellows of the tree canopy on the far side of the park.

It's strange to get an honest peek inside yourself, to have some event come along and – for the briefest of moments – knock the lid off and allow the light to shine down inside. A few hours ago, I'd heard a muffled voice coming from the answerphone in the other room, and not only was I instantly convinced that this voice was my dead father's, but also, that he'd been trying to tell me something. It only took a single word for me to jump to this impossible conclusion.

Tom. A word that, in the cold light of day, was probably another word altogether – something half-heard and through two walls, a hallway and a living-room door. Nevertheless, I'd been so certain in the heat of the moment that I'd gone racing across the flat, chasing after that voice with my trousers around my ankles.

When you get right down to it, what do we really know about ourselves? All those years apart from my father, the resentment, the distance, the funeral in Spain that I didn't attend and the graveside I've never seen, even though I kept telling myself I'd visit one day, even though I'd always known that I wouldn't. All of that water rolling on under the bridge, water that only rolls down and past and away and never, *never* comes back and yet, despite all of it, some dark part of my brain had been biding its time, waiting for him to pull off that old magic trick – to reassemble himself from a scattering of words and old recordings and come back home to me, just like he did when I was a child.

Google confirmed what the operator said about crossed lines – they do happen from time to time. It's something to do with all the old analogue cable still out there in the network. Old wires wear thin during the long years in ragged winds, or go brittle in the sun, or rot away in leaky junction boxes. This means you can be minding your own business and the phone will ring – you'll pick it up, and there'll be two strangers talking about a garage door, or booking the car in for a service, or about someone called Alison's new boyfriend. These calls are not really calls, they're pseudo calls, un-calls, and they do all sorts of weird things to answerphones and caller data records. It's odd, it's unusual, but it's nothing more dramatic than that. Bugs in the system are inevitable, because all systems are corrupting systems to a greater or lesser degree. As Max Cleaver, the detective hero of *Cupid's Engine*, puts it: *The only thing necessary for the triumph of chaos is for the repairmen to do nothing.*

It seemed poetic to me that an analogue fault would be at the heart of things though, my father being such a resolutely analogue creature himself. An analogue ghost down an analogue wire. Except, of course, there was no ghost. Dr Stanley Quinn had no time for zeros and ones. He trusted in ink and he trusted in paper. He always carried a pen and he never traded his typewriter for a computer, not even when lightweight laptops became something that everybody just had. I remember him telling the *Paris Review* that he'd 'never liked the damn things and wasn't about to start at his age' (I would read interviews with my father from time to time; they'd sneak into the house amongst the papers and magazine subscriptions, another inky aspect of a man who was never, ever in just the one place).

I rubbed my eyes, drained my glass, and I headed to the kitchen to fix myself another drink.

o

By the time I went to bed that night, I felt altogether better about things.

If there'd been anyone around to tell the story of the phone call to, I probably would have done it with a can-you-believe-it smile and a slightly red face. That is, if I'd said anything at all. I definitely wouldn't be telling Imogen, I decided, not least because I had no interest in a rousing rendition of 'Cabin Fever' every time I picked up the phone.

And this is how it is sometimes, isn't it? When the pendulum swings especially high in one direction, its momentum carries it back to swing high the other way. Love becomes hate, shame becomes anger, shocked disbelief becomes – some sort of embarrassed, comic incredulity.

I decided, on the whole, not to worry about it.

Tomorrow's another day.

I heaved the duvet up to my chin and went back to reading *Cupid's*

Engine, and soon enough, the novel's current began pulling and tugging at me, demanding my full attention. I was only too happy to let go of things and be carried away by it, racing off downstream, disappearing into the distance like a small boat on the rapids.

o

Cupid's Engine begins with a tall, scruffy man in a white fedora and crumpled linen suit. He's propping himself up in a doorway, covered in blood. Although we don't know it yet, this man's name is Maurice Umber. He has a bloody knife in his right hand, and a telephone receiver pressed to his left ear.

'*Police*,' he mumbles into the phone. '*You're going to have to send somebody*.'

As my eyes tracked towards the end of that first paragraph, a wholly unexpected wave of emotion rose up inside me: a sudden, overpowering force of words and worlds revisited, a return to another time. The depth and strength of it – it felt like a tight hug with someone you never thought you'd see again, or like throwing on your old self like a faded old hoody; not lost after all, only misplaced for a few years in the bottom of the wardrobe. This is one of the great powers of books, isn't it? And one that's easy to forget these days, with everything else that's going on.

So anyway, I was lying in bed, still feeling a little strange but mostly just silly about the phone call, and allowing myself to relax into this deep, nostalgic haze, when an idea came to me for a script I'd been struggling with for months.

That's how I made my living, you see. I wrote stories and scripts. I know what you're thinking, but no, we're not talking movies and we're not talking novels. The manuscripts for my last two novels were neatly stored in manila envelopes at the bottom of the linen box at the end of the bed. My agent hadn't been able to convince anyone to publish either one of them after the lukewarm performance of *The Qwerty Machinegun*, and so – after years of plodding on regardless – I got up from my desk one ordinary afternoon and in the midst of a long struggle with a particularly tricky passage, I just turned the computer off.

Click – and that was that.

When I say I made my living writing stories and scripts, what I mean is that I made a pretty poor living, and that I wrote digital, downloadable short stories and audio scripts for existing intellectual properties. I created what the industry calls *auxiliaries*, or *officially licensed story products*, or, in language an actual, real person might use, tie-in material.

For some admirers of Dr Stanley Quinn, this was an unthinkable, abhorrent thing. It made me the tone-deaf kid who'd jump on stage and belt out 'Ten Green Bottles' at the end of a virtuoso piano recital. These people always got the same look in their eyes when they heard what I did for a living. *For the love of God*, it said, *if you can't do it properly, don't do it at all. Don't you know who your father was?* It hurt me, of course. It hurt me every time. It still does, though mostly in a dull, itchy-scar-tissue sort of a way, as the years have rolled on by. Truth is, I'm not so bothered any more. These people are not the gatekeepers, judges and tastemakers I once saw them as. They're refugees from my father's time, a bunch of ageing Bruce Willises from *The Sixth Sense*, who can't see that their whole world has ended, and who don't have the first clue about the world we're living in now.

Here's a question: how many writers do you think spend their days working with new stories, with new characters and new plots? My guess is: a tiny number, compared to how many are working with the old ones. And that's not just the case at the bottom of the food chain where

I make my living; it's the same at the very top – think about those big brand writers creating big brand book sequels – more James Bond, more *Hitchhiker's Guide to the Galaxy*. And it's the same story times a million in the film industry – a whole generation of filmmakers working on *Star Wars*, *Captain America* and *Batman*. A whole raft of us – at every level you can imagine – are investing our writing lives into the continuation of stories that were new when we were kids, or when our parents were kids, instead of creating new worlds of our own. And these stories tend to be children's stories; you've noticed that, right? Now don't get me wrong; I'm no snob. I might love Herman Melville and B.S. Johnson, but I also love *Star Wars* and Harry Potter. Of course I do, we all do, so we roll up our sleeves and we service the IPs. I'm certainly not complaining, and even if I was complaining, there's really no point burying your head in the sand and hoping that any of it will go away, because – let me tell you – it absolutely won't. It's a hard rule of late-stage capitalism – big, established brands dominate, and start-ups find it harder and harder to get a foothold in the market. There's no changing it. This is our world, and it's a world of sequels, prequels, remakes, remakquels. This is our age, and it's the age of the hyperlink and the shared universe, where all the stories are interconnected and everyone takes a turn at being the author of everything.

I don't let it keep me awake at night.

Not that anyone has ever asked me to write *Star Wars*.

On the night of the answerphone message, I was thirty-three years old, married but temporarily living alone in our small flat in East London, and in dire need of a shave and some natural sunlight. I'd published one book seven years earlier, written two more that nobody wanted, and thereby managed to pull off the impressive feat of having a failed literary career in my mid-twenties.

And, you know, that is what it is.

I had written new adventures for *Thunderbirds*, *Stingray*, *Doctor Who*, *Sapphire and Steel*, *He-Man*, *The Tripods*, *Thundercats* . . . I took these projects seriously, and though I wasn't the best writer in the field, and I certainly wasn't the quickest, I was quietly proud of several of the audio plays I'd helped to create. By and large, I enjoyed the work, and the fans of the old shows generally liked my stories more than they hated them – which is a bigger deal than you might perhaps imagine.

And now I had an idea for the *Captain Scarlett* script that'd stumped me for months, a genuinely good idea, the first good idea, in fact, in God knew how long. I jumped up, jotted down an enthusiastic page of notes, then climbed back into bed and turned off the light.

I lay there for a while, listening to the distant traffic and the hum of the city.

'Why knocks an angel in Bethlehem?'

What does that even mean? I thought. *Why knocks an angel? It's nonsense. It's nonsense and that's probably because it isn't what the voice was even saying.*

Alone in the dark, I shuffled across to Imogen's side of the bed.

Don't worry about it. Just let it go. Tomorrow's another day.

Imogen's pillow felt icy cold and had stopped smelling of her a long time ago, but I pressed my face against it anyway, eyes shut tight, waiting for unconsciousness to rise up like dark water.

5

Imogen in Green

Ten hours later, on the morning of the following day, I was one of 927 people watching my wife sleep.

If that seems like a very specific number to be quoting, it's because the website had a viewer counter under every camera window, so I could always see just how many people had clicked through. If the number was a big one – and 900-plus was pretty big – I'd make a note on a Post-it.

I'd been watching Imogen sleep for most of the morning, through the fuzzy green night vision of Dorm Cam Two. All that time, she'd been lying on her side, facing out, with the duvet pulled up under her chin. That's how she always slept, although when she slept like that at home, she'd usually do it turned away from me, facing the wall. This meant that by watching Imogen on a computer screen and from 8,383 miles away, I'd learned more about how my wife looked sleeping than I ever did from lying next to her in bed. Something about that made me think of the trouble scientists have studying very small things in laboratories.

I drained my 'I ♥ coffee' mug and glanced across at the answerphone on the desk.

It just sat there being quiet and unremarkable.

I set the mug down and scrubbed my fingers through my hair.

On-screen, the duvet rising and falling with my wife's breathing and a slight digital fuzzing were the only things to give the image away as a live feed and not a flat, dead picture. And, as none of the webcams had sound, the scene was utterly silent too.

In every traditional sense, nothing at all happened.

The counter clicked up to 945 viewers.

I crossed out the old number on the Post-it, added the new one, and then pinned it up on the board.

It's both compelling and reassuring to watch a person living in real time. The long pauses. The stillness. Sleeping, staring, thinking, reading – all played out in their vast and blank entireties. Putting those familiar little islands of talking, arguing and laughing that we always think of as *what people do* into wide, empty oceans of context. And then, at the other end of the scale, the opposite of those stillnesses – the rare, powerful, private things – the truthful, the revelatory, the sexual. Those one-in-a-million moments that probably won't happen while you're watching, but just might, just might, just might . . .

The phone rang, loud in the quiet flat.

I jumped, grabbing the handset before it could ring again.

'Hello?'

'Hello, Euston,' said Imogen. 'This is Eagle One.'

On the screen, my wife's green body slept soundly. 'Hello, stranger,' I said. I half-expected the tremble of adrenaline to come through in my voice, so the hardness I heard there instead surprised me.

'Don't be like that, I haven't got long.'

'No, I wasn't. I didn't mean it like that.'

'I did say I didn't know if I'd be able to call.'

'I know, that's fine. I'm not. I wasn't meaning anything.'

'Promise?'

'Yeah. It's just the first time I've said anything all day. I'm . . . strange.'

'Ah, that'd do it,' Imogen-on-the-phone said. 'I did want to call when I got back, but we ended up being on site longer than I thought and it would've been like three a.m. or something over there.'

Imogen-on-the-screen showed no signs of waking up. She just carried on taking her slow, deep breaths – in . . . out . . . in . . . out . . .

'It's fine, I'm just feeling a bit weird, a bit . . .' The word I wanted to use was *flat*, but I didn't. '. . . abstract. Hello?'

'Hello. I'm here. Hello?'

'Hello. I can hear you.'

'What did you say? Abstract?'

'Yeah, like, as in, not all here.' I looked down at the phone. 'It's not seeing people, I think. I should probably go out later, walk around a bit.'

'That sounds like a good plan. You should definitely do that. Get some sun and have some fruit.'

'I think I will.'

'Sun and fruit stop a person from being abstract, that's a well-known fact.'

'I did not know that.'

'Oh yeah, there's nothing better for it.'

'I'll take action.'

'You should. Hey, so. Did you get your *Thunderbirds* off?'

'*Captain Scarlett*?'

'Yeah, that one.'

'Yeah, all good. Script's in and the cash should be through next week.'

Not true. The script wasn't in. The cash wasn't coming. I hadn't written a single usable word of it. Still – this was my mess, and my job to fix it. Imogen didn't need to know how bad the mess had become.

'Good stuff, Quinn,' she said. 'So what're you doing now?'

Good stuff, Quinn. A twist of guilt grabbed my stomach. I pushed it away.

'Hello?'

'Sorry. I'm here. What did you say?

'What are you doing now?'

'I'm watching you sleep.'

'Oh God, you're not, are you? Am I thrashing around? I've been having the weirdest dreams.'

'No, you're just lying there. All still and serene.'

'That's something, then.'

'You're really very calm. And you had a nine-four-five a minute ago.'

'Jesus. How many?'

'Nine hundred and forty-five.'

'Hang on, I'll write that one down. Nine-four-five. And I'm not doing anything?'

'No. Nothing. You're breathing. But, no.'

Imogen-on-the-phone thought for a moment.

'It's funny,' she said. 'It only bothers me when you tell me the numbers; the rest of the time it's like the camera thing isn't, well, I don't mean it bothers me really, but you know.'

'Yeah.'

'Actually, it is bothering me now I'm thinking about it. I'm waving at them.'

'You should.'

'I'm doing it right now.'

Imogen-on-the-screen lay fast asleep. In . . . out . . . in . . . out . . .

'I'll wave back when it comes up,' I said.

'You're lovely.'

'Thanks.'

'I do miss you, you know.'

'I miss you too. How's it going?'

'God. Slowly.'

Imogen had been on the other side of the world for almost six months. She was working as part of a research team looking for one small spot on a very remote island, where the single most important act in the entire history of humanity might have taken place. Because this was the twenty-first century, the research facility had webcams.

'But you're still getting a good general movement, right?'

'In patches,' she said. 'But it's not like they just went from east to west or something.'

'I suppose that would've been – oh, hang on.'

'What?' Imogen-on-the-screen moved her sleeping green head as if to shake something away.

'You're dreaming.'

'Told you. Very weird dreams.'

'I think you're going to wake up in a minute.'

'I am. Listen, I've got to go. I'll try to call tomorrow, but if not, I'll call Wednesday morning.'

'Okay.'

'My time.'

'Okay. And get them to sort out your video calls.'

'I will. But Johnny says my laptop's killed itself.'

'Nice.'

'I know. Shit, right. I really need to—'

'Okay. Love you.'

'I love you too. And go out.'

'I will.'

'All right, bye.'

'Bye.'

'Bye bye bye . . .'

The line cut to a flat buzz.

I kept the handset to my ear for a moment then clicked it back into the dock.

Imogen-on-the-screen frowned in her sleep and tugged at the duvet. The viewer counter had been falling steadily, but once she started to dream it stabilised. Now it climbed back up in ones and twos towards the 900 mark.

I waited, watching, arms folded.

Imogen jolted awake, eyes flashing about in a panic before she realised where she was. She relaxed as she got her bearings, rubbed her face with her palms, propped herself up on an elbow and then looked around the dorm. Seeing she was alone, she leaned out of bed and flicked on the lights.

The greenscreen image instantly flared to a white blank, then the facility's familiar dorm room re-emerged in full colour. Eight beds, wardrobes, tables, lamps, mess – all the signs of human habitation, of a group of people living packed in together.

My wife climbed out of bed and walked out of shot in her pyjamas.

I waited.

Almost four minutes later, she came back carrying a glass of water and an industrial-looking phone with a long cable trailing behind it. She sat down at the far side of her bed, facing away from the camera, tapped numbers into the phone and put it to her ear.

I could only see the back of Imogen's neck and jawline, but it was enough to tell she was talking to someone, speaking into the phone and then listening. After a little while, she turned, looked straight at the camera in surprise and silently mouthed, *Jesus, how many?*

She listened for a second. Her mouth made all the shapes for . . . *Hang on, I'll write that one down.* Cradling the phone in the crook of her neck, she reached and made a note. *Nine-four-five*, her lips were saying, then she turned away from the camera again so I couldn't see what came next. Almost straight away, she turned back and I caught *. . . now I'm thinking about it.*

I lifted up my hand to the monitor, the palm flat.

Imogen waved at the camera. Her lips made, *I'm waving at them.* She listened, still waving, and replied, *I'm doing it right now.*

I waved at the screen.

Imogen smiled.

You're lovely, she said to the camera without a sound; then she turned away and carried on talking into the phone.

'I'm trying,' I said to myself.

Not long after that, Imogen-on-the-screen finished her call. My wife took the phone from her ear and pressed a button. With only a glance towards the camera, she stood up and walked out of shot.

I'd made it half out of the desk chair when she suddenly reappeared.

Close up this time, she leaned in towards the camera, smiled and mouthed *go out*.

Then she was gone.

6

Only Entropy Comes Easy

I waited for a few more seconds, but Imogen didn't appear again on Dorm Cam Two.

Her words stayed with me though.

Go out. Good advice.

Wandering through to the kitchen, I balanced my mug on top of all the other dirty crockery in the sink, then poked about inside the washing machine for something vaguely clean to wear.

I looked around, taking in the pile of plates in the sink, the remains of cooking, curry pots, jammy bread crusts, fish and chip papers, baked beans tins, empty Pot Noodles. *The phone cables might have their rough spots*, I thought, *but this, my friend, is a total systemic collapse.*

The only thing necessary for the triumph of chaos is for repairmen to do nothing.

Imogen had always been the organised, tidy, well-prepared one. Without her around, things tended to go south pretty quickly. Written on the fridge door in multicoloured, magnetic plastic letters is an old message from her:

St y Alert: Entropy Wants th s Kitch n.

Just before we went to bed one night, I'd plucked the 'a', the 'i' and the 'e' out of their respective words and arranged them at the bottom of the door, making it look like they'd fallen down in a heap. I remember lying in bed the next morning and hearing her call out *oh, how we laughed* as she opened the door to get milk for her tea.

Question: do you know why time works the way it does?

It's all down to entropy.

To see why, I'll need you to imagine that my kitchen is the universe. Or, if you'd rather, you can imagine your own kitchen is the universe – it doesn't really matter. But pick a kitchen.

So. There are only a relatively small number of ways for this kitchen to be tidy. Only a relatively small number of ways for the boxes to fit in the cupboards, the bowls to fit on top of the plates, the bottles to stand up in the fridge door, all those things. Relatively small, I mean, against the countless billions of different ways the same kitchen can be messy. If the Rice Krispies are *anywhere else* but in the Rice Krispies box, the kitchen is messy. If the milk bottle is *anywhere else* but standing upright in the fridge (with the milk still in it), the kitchen is messy. If one or more of the bowls are on the worktop, on the floor, on the table, smashed in the sink, *anywhere else* but stacked neatly away in a cupboard – then the kitchen is messy.

You get the idea. Messy is more likely than tidy. But in order to see the full picture, we need to understand just how much more likely messy really is.

To get a good look at the massive improbability of tidiness compared to messiness, let's empty all the plates, cups, bowls, food, drinks, cutlery, cloths, sponges, towels, powders and cleaning products out of our kitchen, then put just a single item back in – the butter. Now. Let's say the butter can be in maybe five hundred different places around the empty kitchen that we would call messy and maybe five places we would call neat. So there's a one in a hundred chance that the butter is somewhere we would describe as neat. Let's move up to two items – the butter and a butter knife. Assuming the butter knife has the same number of messy and neat positions as the butter, the chances of them *both* being in a place we could call neat goes from one in one hundred to one in ten thousand. At three items – the butter, the butter knife and a slice of bread – the chances of all three being in a place we would describe as neat are now one in a million.

Already, *messy* is a million times more likely than *neat* – and this is a kitchen with only three objects in it. Three. Now go ahead and put back all the many hundreds of other objects into your ordinary, everyday kitchen and you start to get some sense of just how very unlikely *neat* is versus *messy*.

Of course, the universe is a lot bigger than a kitchen, and made of a lot more things. And those things are made up of things, which are also made up of things, all the way down to a basic, atomic level. There's also an added complication – the universe does not have the benefit of someone coming along once in a while to tidy the place up. Taken together, what all this means is that when a thing – the butter, the butter knife, a brick, a stone, a screw, an atom – happens to move into a new position somewhere in the universe, it is a countless billion times more likely to move into a messy position than into a neat position.

Without someone around to tidy and fix it up from time to time, the kitchen and the house around it would progressively get messier until the whole thing fell apart. Everyone knows this happens to old houses because they've seen it – uncared-for structures fall into disrepair and eventually collapse. This is common sense. *Why* it happens is simple: because there are countless billions of messy situations for all the things that make up the house – bricks, beams, nails, lintels, joists and all their atoms – to be in, *any* of which would cause it to fall down, and only a handful of neat situations where the house stays standing.

This ever-increasing movement towards messiness is called *entropy*.

But here's the thing. We wouldn't say 'the house fell down due to the gradual movement of its component elements from a low-entropy state to a high-entropy state' (at least, most people wouldn't). We'd say – the house fell down *over time*.

Entropy is what drives time forwards, and only forwards. It's the reason you can't un-stir the milk from your coffee, the reason you can smash but can't un-smash a glass vase, and the reason that if you did smash a glass vase then fixed it really well, somebody might say, 'it looks as good as new'. People get old and die *over time*, things get lost *over time,* stuff gets broken *over time*. Entropy is the inevitable sliding of all things from an ordered state towards disorder and meaninglessness; ice cubes melting, tea cooling, roofs caving in, glass vases smashing, people ageing, all manner of things we might casually associate with *time passing*.

And as everything gets messier, more and more things end up in the wrong places, until – eventually – there are no wrong places any more, because the bigger things that the smaller things were once a neat part of have also completely fallen apart. The more our universe moves towards a maximum entropy state of affairs – from a confusing jumble of broken and out-of-place things, to a heap of barely recognisable bits, to a heap of interchangeable particles – the less can actually happen, and the more slowly the arrow of time can move forward. To begin to get an idea of this, think about stirring a pile of sand with a stick. No matter how much you stir, it doesn't make the pile of sand any more disordered, because there's no order to the sand grains anyway – it doesn't matter where the individual grains go, it's still just a pile of sand. Because things can't get any messier within the pile of sand, entropy cannot increase and so there cannot be a discernible *before* or *after*, nothing can happen, nothing can change or, to put it another way, *time does not pass.* ❦

'Avoid the world,' Kerouac said, 'it's just a lot of dust and drag and means nothing in the end.' Well, the diagnosis might've been premature, but you can't fault the science. When entropy reaches a universal maximum, nothing can be anything, or do anything, or mean anything. Our universe will not see out its days by barrelling towards some big, climactic, Revelations-style ending, but by slouching through an increasingly meaningless jumble of dispersing elements, then limping on towards the most bland, uniform, entirely generic middle you can possibly imaginable, and dying there.

This is all a little bleak, I realise, but it's important to get the facts down on paper. It's also important, and maybe even a little heartening, to say that there's a speck of scientific fairy dust to be found amongst all this gloom and collapse. You see, entropy and the arrow of time are not driven by a hard constant – like, say, the speed of light – but by probability, and probability alone. What I mean is, there is no rule specifically saying that everything in the kitchen can't fall, bounce or somehow shift from a messy state to a neat state by sheer chance. It's just that the odds against such things are so astonishingly, incredibly, mind-bogglingly, unimaginably huge, compared to the usual 'neat to messy' movement, that for practical purposes we say it doesn't ever happen.

But it could.

You'd have to watch countless billions of kitchens for countless

❦ Our pile of sand is sitting inside a wider closed system (our universe) where entropy can still increase and time can still flow, however. You can walk over and clean up the pile of sand, write your name in it, make a sandcastle out of it, if you want to. But if the whole universe and everything in it (including you) had reached the same maximum entropy state as the pile of sand, then this would be completely impossible. There would be no outside looking in. Entropy could not increase, so there would be no possibility of real, meaningful change, and nothing could or would ever happen. The arrow of time would simply stop.

billions of years to glimpse even the beginnings of something like that, but – it could happen, in theory.

How would it feel to experience something like that?

The overwhelming sensation would probably be that something magical and impossible had happened – a visit from the fairies. But also, wouldn't there be a sense that you had somehow travelled back in time?

7
The Letter

Cleaning the kitchen in a kind of trance, entirely absorbed in the act of ordering and restoring, I took a deep satisfaction in matching up the plates, cups and pans, and in vanishing each set behind cupboard doors and drawer fronts. I'd just finished mopping the floor and was pouring grey water into the toilet bowl when there was a knock on the front door.

Danni Grayson from the flat upstairs stood in the doorway, her arms full of post, all of it for me and for Imogen, and all of it delivered to her flat by mistake at various times over the last three weeks. Her expression said *they have one job* and *for God's sake*, and mine said *sorry* and *tell me about it*. The problem had been going on for so long that we didn't need to discuss it.

I took the pile through to the kitchen and began to sort it. Junk mail, red bill, junk mail, junk mail, red bill, red bill, junk mail, bank statement, red bill, red bill, red bill. And then—

'Oh.'

The word came involuntarily, as my chest squeezed itself tight in surprise.

I stood dead still, the red bill in my hand still hovering above its pile on the counter.

A small, simple, handwritten envelope had emerged from the mass-produced, plastic-windowed heap. My name and address appeared in small, neat black capitals, and the whole thing was finished off with a perfectly aligned first-class stamp.

I knew the letter was from Andrew Black the moment I saw it.

'Oh,' I said, for a second time.

I thought I'd never see that neat black writing again.

The story was a fairly famous one. I knew it as well as anyone, probably better than most:

Six years ago, Andrew Black abandoned his writing career, *Cupid's Engine*, and everything else. He released one massive bestseller, and then he vanished. Even the few people who knew him, who had worked with him on his novel, never heard from him again. If you'd pushed me for a reason as to why he'd do such a thing, I might've told you that *certain circumstances* led to this decision, prompting him to sever whatever ties he had with the world, and his literary ties especially, but none of those things were down to me. I'd have said we were *acquaintances* – friends would be too much of a stretch – for a while after my father died, but even so, I assumed – I assumed that I'd hear something from him when things finally settled down. Or, at least, I assumed that *somebody* would hear something. But, as far as I knew, no one ever had.

Not until that moment.

I turned the envelope over in my hands.

The postmark told me that the letter had been sent weeks earlier. I ripped it open, feeling a stab of anxiety. Small talk, pleasantries, just saying hello – that wasn't Andrew Black. This meant that something was happening, or had happened, and I was only hearing about it now.

Inside, I found a single Polaroid picture and a small folded note.

The photograph showed a black sphere, resting on what I took to be Andrew's desk. He'd placed a ruler next to the object, and though the Polaroid was a little fuzzy, it seemed to indicate a diameter of around ten centimetres. I struggled to make out much more, partly because it was slightly blurred, but also because the sphere was so utterly black. The most diffuse crescent moon of light touching the thing's left side, and an equally faint shadow on the bench to its right, were all that gave it away as three-dimensional.

The object – whatever it was – looked as black as a hole.

And it bothered me.

I don't write that lightly. I've thought long and hard about whether to include my reaction here at all, but the facts are the facts. I didn't like the picture when I first saw it. As to whether we should set any store by this, whether it means anything – that's another matter altogether.

I put down the Polaroid and unfolded Andrew's note.

Only nine words, each one written in that same precise hand:

Thomas,
What do you think this is?
Andrew Black

8
The Mary Magdalene Treatment

'No,' said Sophie Almonds.

I'd barely had a chance to lay Black's letter and the picture of the black sphere out on the table between us. She glanced down just long enough to recognise the handwriting on the note, then her bright blue eyes flicked up and locked on mine, steady as a boat on a calm sea.

'But what is it?' I said, meaning the object in the picture.

'I don't know, a snooker ball? Why did he send you this?'

'Why does Andrew Black do anything?'

She didn't answer.

'Maybe it's – well. He doesn't have my father any more—'

Sophie folded her arms.

'We're not having this conversation.'

Sophie Almonds worked at Hayes & Heath as a literary agent. This meant that she got her clients – clients including me – contracts and cash advances for their novels, or whatever else she could get them hired to write. I took whatever she brought me, which wasn't much by then to be honest, but I always got the impression that it never stopped her from trying. Unfortunately, Sophie Almonds was also Andrew Black's literary agent, technically speaking, and that made talking to her about his letter a little . . . *problematic.*

Not only did Sophie make a point of never discussing one client with another – and doubly so if that client happened to be Andrew Black – but from a personal perspective, it was possible, in certain lights, to see her jaw tightening ever so slightly at any mention of the man's name. A little over six years ago, Sophie Almonds pulled off the book deal of the decade, only to have it come crashing down spectacularly because of Black's peculiar foibles (he would've said principles). If there had been anybody else I could have talked to about Black and his letter, I would have.

'I'm worried he might be in trouble,' I said, planting my elbows on the table and pushing on. 'I think this might be – not a cry for help, but . . . it's like he's being as intriguing as he can, just so I'll get back to him.' I waited, but Sophie didn't reply. 'I've been thinking a lot about it,' I said. 'I mean, why not say more? Why just send this? I haven't heard from him in years, and now . . . He's trying to make sure that I reply. This and this,' I waved a hand at the Polaroid and the note, 'it's a hook, isn't it? A pretty decent hook too.' I turned over the letter to show the address written on the reverse. 'He's letting me know where he is, and he wants to make sure that I'll write back.'

'And will you?'

'Yeah. Well. That's the plan.'

Sophie's big blue eyes were hard and bright as polished glass. I felt as if I were being unpicked, one stitch at a time.

'But you haven't written back yet, is that what you're telling me?'

'No, I haven't written back yet,' I said.

'Good.' Her eyes flicked away from mine, to the Thames rolling by outside the pub window. 'Then don't. It's for the best.'

Sophie Almonds stood around five foot four, with shoulder-length, dark brown hair, often tied back with a simple black ribbon, and increasingly threaded through with silver. She was a still, watchful woman, with big, expressive eyes, and the sinewy build of a long-distance runner. She reminded me of a small, wiry bird of prey, the kind that makes its living on blasted moorlands, and has to keep its wits about it to survive. I'd once thought – maybe because of the way she carried herself and those cool, unflinching eyes, or maybe because of her little black notebook that seemed to have half the world's secrets tucked away inside it – I'd once thought that this Sophie bird could've been a sphinx once upon a time, defeated by some great hero of legend and now living on vastly reduced means. Certainly, it always seemed to me that it would be deeply unwise to cross or underestimate her.

Sophie Almonds was in her mid-forties I thought, and possibly of Scandinavian descent. I didn't know these things for certain though, because she kept all personal information locked away as tightly as the affairs of her clients. And, as I've said, it was never wise to push her too far, except when absolutely necessary.

'I'm worried about him,' I said again.

'What I'm going to suggest to you now,' Sophie said after a moment, slowly knitting her fingers together, 'is that you put that picture, and that note, back into that envelope there, and then pass the envelope to me.'

'Why?'

'So I can take it home and burn it.'

I looked at her. 'Well, that seems extreme.'

'No, not really. For one thing, I don't think we should be leaving Andrew Black's address around where anyone might find it. My agency still represents his interests, and that means protecting his anonymity as well as we possibly can.'

I raised my eyebrows.

Sophie sighed. 'All right, look. You shouldn't respond to this. If you're asking for my advice, then that's the advice I have for you. *Do not respond to this.*'

'Okay.'

'Good.'

'No, I mean, *okay but*.'

'But what?'

'I know you don't like him.'

Sophie waited.

'And I don't blame you for not liking him,' I said. 'You got him an amazing deal for the rest of his series and he went out and did—'

Sophie looked at me.

'—what he did,' I finished weakly.

A tiny smile with no warmth in it broke through her composed expression.

'The rest of the series,' she said, and she let out a small sound somewhere between bemused sigh and bitter laugh. It was a dangerous sound; it had broken glass in it.

I waited a moment, let a little time pass.

The clock ticked and the river rolled by.

'Look,' I said, 'I know coming to you with this isn't ideal but I think he might be in trouble.'

'He's not in trouble.'

'Do you know that for sure?'

Sophie didn't answer.

'You see? Because he'd never just come out and ask anyone, would he, never just say what's on his mind. He can't do what normal people do, and there's an urgency to this—' I pushed the note towards her. 'I'm – concerned about him; I really am.'

'Why?'

'What do you mean, why?'

'Tom. You don't like him either.'

'That's. That's not—'

'Of course it is.'

I looked at Sophie.

'Of course it is,' she said again. 'And there's nothing wrong with it. Why *would* you like him? Why *would* you care so much about him and his fucking book, Tom? Maybe you should spend some more time with that, rather than—' She waved a hand at the note in from of her.

I held her gaze.

'I'm *concerned* about him,' I said. 'And this—' I slid the Polaroid up alongside the note. 'Whatever this is, I'm concerned about this too.'

Sophie stared right back at me. Then she folded her arms and began searching my face, my expression, picking her way inside.

'Is this about his thing?' she asked at last. 'His whole entropy, end of the world – thing?'

'Just look at it.'

It took a moment, but Sophie's eyes finally dropped from mine to the picture in front of her, perhaps seeing it properly for the first time. A pair of neat little frown lines appeared above her eyebrows. She picked up the Polaroid and took some time to look at the thing, like a jeweller with a stone. She tilted and turned it, this way and that way, held it up to the light, investigated the back, and then finally put it back down next to Andrew's note. She nudged the picture with her index finger – tap, tap, tap – until the two objects were perfectly aligned, then considered them both for a while in silence. When she spoke again, it was in a quiet, even voice, without looking up from the table:

'Tom, do you know what a raccoon trap is?'

'I – no, I can't say that I do.'

'It's really quite clever,' she said, eyes still on the photo and the letter. 'You start with a small cage, really small, say, as big as a teapot. Then you fasten the cage to the ground and you put something shiny inside it.'

'Something shiny?'

'It doesn't matter what – something with glitter, a crystal, a diamond, if you want. All that matters is that the shiny thing is too big to pull out through the bars of the cage.'

Sophie flicked a glance up at me.

'Okay,' I said.

'And when it's all set up, you go home, leave it there. And then along comes the raccoon. He sees the shiny thing and tries pulling it out through the bars. He tries and tries, because raccoons love shiny things, apparently, but he can't do it. He can't bring himself to give up either; he can't physically let go of the treasure he's found, so he just stays there, holding onto it. Even when you come back with a sack in the morning and he wants to run away, he can't make himself let go of the thing because it's too shiny and wonderful and intriguing.'

'And you've got him.'

'You have. You unfasten the cage, lift it up with the raccoon still dangling from it, and drop them both into the sack.'

'And that's what you think this is?'

'I wonder,' Sophie said, still staring at the objects on the table.

Moments passed. Sophie continued to stare, lost in thought.

'Sophie?'

'After that, you knot the sack and you throw it in the river.'

'What?' I said, and when she didn't answer: 'You are joking, right?'

When she looked up, her expression was quite serious.

'Can I show you something?' she said.

'Yeah. Yes. Of course you can.'

My agent reached down beside her chair and lifted a small black handbag onto the table. She took out her purse, opened it and removed a little square of greyish paper from one of its many pockets.

'Just read this, if you would,' she said, passing it to me.

The square turned out to be a neatly folded piece of newspaper. It folded out into a long, thin column of text. An old print review of *Cupid's Engine*.

I began to read. *Astonishing manipulation of expectation, countless twists and turns, flawlessly realised.* On and on it went, the words *masterpiece* and *genius* showing up, and pulled double, triple duty, the review text escalating through the excitement registers as it progressed, leaving any attempt at even-handed, critical assessment of what was, after all, a murder mystery novel, far, far behind.

'Wow,' I said, refolding the clipping and handing it back.

'Absolutely.'

'She liked the book, I think.'

'Absolutely,' Sophie said again. 'At the time, I cut that review out and kept it, just because I'd never seen anything like it. And because I was so pleased to be a part of something so special, you know? Now, I keep it with me as a reminder.'

'Of what?'

'To run,' she said simply. 'If a novel like *Cupid's Engine* ever lands on my desk again, I will run. Nobody can do this,' she held up the review, 'nobody can produce a book like this one and be anywhere approaching sane or normal. The work, the focus involved, do you have any idea?'

'I do.'

'Then you know that anyone capable of achieving what Black achieved is, potentially, a very dangerous person.'

'What? I don't think—'

'Oh, *come on*, Thomas,' she said. 'You've read that book. What is it – a thousand pages? – and not a single unnecessary word in the whole thing. The things he's able to achieve, the level of manipulation. He has you believing that up is down and black is white.' She pushed the picture of the sphere across the table towards me. 'You're right that this is a hook, but it's not *a pretty decent one*. It's a brilliant, and – I promise you – an extremely well-calculated one. What in

God's name makes you think it's a good idea to bite?'

I sat back in my chair, not really knowing what to say.

'I'm just telling you what I think,' Sophie said, 'and I think you should stay well away from this. A person with a brain like Andrew's, well, they're capable of anything. Can make you do and think anything, make you *be* anything.'

'Oh, come on,' I said, finding my feet. 'I mean, I'd never deny that he's a great writer, but—'

'What do you think the world is, Thomas? No, don't answer now. But I want you to take some time to think about it. Is the world you live in, each and every day, made more from rocks and grass and trees, or from articles, certificates, records, files and letters? Is it made more from soil and rivers and sand, or from thoughts and ideas, beliefs and opinions? Actually, let me ask you another question: is it the kind of world where nine words' – she rapped her knuckles on Andrew's letter – 'nine words presented in just the right way, can compel a normally well-balanced person to charge blindly off into the unknown, to an address they've never visited before in their life?'

'I didn't say I'd go.'

'Of course you'd go. This is what I'm trying to make you understand. With a person like Black, you might think he's your friend, like you're in it together, when all the time he's dancing you like a puppet off the edge of a fucking cliff.'

'–'

'Oh, don't look at me like that.' Sophie's cheeks flushed. 'You know what I'm talking about, or you would've just written back to him without coming to me for – for fucking permission.'

I started to respond but the words didn't come.

An awkward moment passed.

'Not a cliff,' I said quietly.

'What?'

'He mainly just told me I was a terrible writer, to be honest. He didn't dance me off a cliff. He did that to you.'

Sophie stared at me, big bird eyes searching my face for meaning, as if meaning were a frightened mouse seen darting away through the heather. And then – she laughed. It was a tired laugh, a release of tension, an *oh-fucking-hell* and slumping-into-your-chair sort of a laugh.

'I'm sorry,' I said.

'Oh, Tom. Listen, can you just drop this, please? I'll sleep better knowing he's just – gone.'

I looked at the objects on the table. I nodded.

'Is that a yes?'

'It's an *I'll do my best*.'

Sophie Almonds sighed a long, deep sigh. She picked up the note.

'I wouldn't be at all surprised if these are the most words he's written since *Cupid*,' she said. 'I suppose you know that this text belongs to his publishers technically, under the terms of his contract?'

'I do.'

'You do.' She held up the single sheet of notepaper, as if testing its weight. 'What do you think? The long-awaited second Andrew Black novel?'

I stared at the small piece of paper dangling between her finger and thumb with its nine neat little words.

'You'd be looking at some very generous typesetting,' I said.

'I'm not entirely sure that they wouldn't try.' She folded the letter and put it back into the envelope. 'But let's save them the trouble.'

'I think that's probably for the best.'

She slipped the Polaroid into the envelope as well, and slid it across the table to me. 'You should save yourself the trouble too,' she said. 'I mean it.'

I picked up the letter and tucked it into my jacket pocket.

A flutter of old memories came back to me then. They hovered in the back of my mind, loitering around this meeting with Sophie, just like they always did, each one distilled down to a single movie frame from heavy use – *The Open Leather Satchel Memory, The Water Dripping Down Gloss Paint Memory, The Shards Of Glass On The Doormat Memory* – each one fluttering and batting at the edges of my thoughts, drawn to the light of our conversation.

I lifted my glass and took a long, deep drink, mentally shooing them away.

'Would more have made a difference?' I said, putting the glass down. 'To what you think of him, I mean?'

'More books? No,' Sophie said. 'But it would've paid off the mortgage. So, you know, it's something.'

'My father thought a lot of him.'

Sophie held my gaze.

'Your father, who we're not going to talk about, thought a lot of his *talent*.'

She took her purse from the table, unzipped it and slipped the newspaper clipping back inside. She was about to put it back in her bag when she noticed my nearly empty glass.

'Another?' she said.

o

'Tom, have you ever heard of Frederick J. Klaeber?'

Sophie had returned from the bar with a round of drinks. I'd been staring out of the window, watching the river, lost in thought.

'What? Sorry – who?'

'Frederick J. Klaeber,' she said, passing me a glass and sitting down. 'Great academic. Early translator of *Beowulf*.'

'Sorry. I don't know much about *Beowulf*.'

This was true. For whatever reason, my parents had never owned a copy of *Beowulf* and I'd never felt the need to track one down.

Sophie looked surprised. 'Really?'

'I mean, I know the story, but nothing about the business end.'

'Would you like to?'

'Sure.'

'All right then. So, the problems with Mr Klaeber's translation of *Beowulf*,' Sophie said, 'begin with the Old English word *aglæca*'.

'What does—' My mouth lost its nerve, like a horse at Becher's Brook.

'*Aglæca*.'

'Yeah, what does it mean?'

'Well, that's the thing. Nobody knows. The meaning of the word is lost, so we can only make an educated guess based on the way it's used in the story. But Klaeber's educated guess back in 1922 was a little . . . suspect.'

'How so?'

'Well, the word appears several times in *Beowulf*. For instance, it's used to describe Grendel, Grendel's mother, and the dragon at the end.'

'Okay, so it means something like "monster"?'

'Aha. This is what Mr Klaeber says too. In his book, which is considered the gold standard of *Beowulf* scholarship by the way, he translates *aglæca* as . . . hang on.' Sophie dug her little black notebook out of her bag and thumbed through it until she found what she was looking for. 'Monster, demon, fiend. In the case of Grendel's mother, the word is modified to *aglæc-wif*.'

'Female fiend?'

'Klaeber charmingly opts for "wretch, or monster of a woman", and where Klaeber's translation goes, all the others follow.' Sophie turned a page. '"Monstrous hag" is Kennedy's definition, "ugly troll lady" from Trask, "monster-woman" from Chickering, "woman, monster-wife" from Donaldson. Even Seamus Heaney translated *aglæc-wif* as "monstrous hell bride", can you believe it?'

'I can,' I said. 'I mean, I can't see why he wouldn't. What's the problem?'

'The problem is that *aglæca* also appears in the poem to describe Beowulf himself.' Sophie closed her book with a theatrical snap. 'What do you make of that?'

I thought about it.

'Beowulf wasn't a monster, was he?'

'No, and when the word appears in reference to Beowulf – the exact same word, remember – Mr Frederick J. Klaeber translates it as "warrior, hero".'

'Hmm.'

'Yes.'

'Sounds like Mr Klaeber was making it up as he went along.'

'Doesn't it just? A professor by the name of . . .' the notebook again '. . . Sherman Kuhn makes the very sensible suggestion that *aglæca* should be translated as "a fighter, valiant warrior, dangerous opponent, one who struggles fiercely".'

'You're about to make a point.'

'I am. You see, Grendel and the dragon are clearly written as monsters, but there's nothing in *Beowulf* to suggest that Grendel's mother is a "monstrous hell bride" or a "troll lady", or anything of the sort; quite the opposite, in fact. She's a female warrior, an accomplished, powerful woman who's every bit the equal of Beowulf.

Then our Mr Klaeber comes along – this one man sitting alone at his writing desk, and with a few flicks of his pen, a few scratches of ink, he changes her. Turns her from one thing into something else. He reduces her into "a wretch". *A wretch.* He steals her from every schoolgirl, from every young woman growing up in this world trying to understand what they can and cannot be, for the best part of one hundred years. Maybe for ever, because words have power once they're written down.'

'The Mary Magdalene treatment.'

Sophie nodded. 'The Mary Magdalene treatment.'

I stared into my drink, unsure of what else to say. A Paul Auster line floated into my mind – *a word becomes another word, a thing becomes another thing* – but I didn't speak. The second hand ticked around the large clock over the bar, the Thames rolled on, and the entropy of the universe steadily increased.

'Why do you have notes on *Beowulf*? Is there going to be a book?'

I didn't say 'is one of your clients writing about *Beowulf*?' but it amounted to nothing more than a slightly obscured version of the same question, and when I heard the words coming out of my mouth, I knew Sophie wouldn't answer.

'Someone has to keep track of these things.' She shrugged. 'Frederick J. Klaeber wasn't really Frederick either, he was a Friedrich.'

'In 1922? Well, we can't blame him for that.'

'No, we can't.' Sophie fixed me with her steady blue eyes. 'But we can observe that he was a man who was fully prepared to rewrite the narrative, when he deemed it necessary.'

I took a sip of beer then set the glass down on the table between us. The head had completely collapsed by now, leaving a ring of white bubbles and a few little islands of foam gently fizzing themselves out of existence.

'Sophie?'

‘What?’

‘What are we talking about here?’

Sophie leaned forward on her elbows.

‘Take it home and burn it,’ she said, quietly.

9

The Leaves of Autumn

I left the pub around nine p.m. and spent the next ten minutes standing outside a bus shelter on the opposite side of the road, happy to be outside despite the cold, my chin tucked deep into the zipped-up collar of my coat. A strong, wintry wind blew up from the river, gusts buffeting and breaking against me, full of the scent of rain.

Autumn had come early this year, the leaves turning quickly in the frosts. The change had taken me by surprise, as it usually did. I spent so much time inside the flat, and inside my own head, that I'd barely noticed summer running out of steam until I stepped out of my door that afternoon and found I had to go back for a jacket.

It felt good to be out in the world again, to be pushed about by the blustery wind. It felt good to be an anonymous small cog amongst the countless streetlamps, headlights, cars, passers-by, buildings, roads and noises of the city at nighttime. It felt good not to be talking to anyone, not to be thinking at all.

Is the world you live in every day made more from rocks and grass and trees, or from articles, certificates, records, files and letters?

I pushed Sophie's question away, focusing my attention on *things* – on the hundreds of things made of matter, of chemical elements, of sound waves and light waves, standing or driving or strolling or rolling on all around me. Gloriously, none of it – in this city of millions of lives, and bricks, and lights – none of it had the slightest interest in me. None of it depended on my thoughts or ideas. The buildings and the traffic couldn't care less if I replied to Andrew Black, or finished my *Captain Scarlett* script, or got a call from Imogen, or if there was a crossed line that sounded like my dead father talking nonsense from the answerphone. It didn't matter. In the big, magnificent, busy scheme of things – it didn't matter at all. I closed my eyes, felt the cold wind on my face and smiled deeply into the depths of my collar.

Minutes passed.

A light, ice-cold rain rolled in on the wind, stinging my cheeks and forehead. I didn't mind at all. A group of teenagers passed by. I watched them weaving their noisy, flirty way off up the road. They were laughing and joking despite the worsening weather, happy and drunk, finding excuses to touch each other – shoving, tripping, fake pushes into the oncoming traffic. I thought about Imogen laughing, the way she'd suddenly leap on me in bed when the alarm went off, screaming *think fast* at the top of her voice. I remembered her breathless laughter and wild thrashing when I pinned her down and tickled her when we fought, and her hysterical giggling at a YouTube video of a dog called Fenton chasing a herd of deer. I saw her laughing until her eyes were bright and shiny and she couldn't catch her breath to speak. Then – like an uninvited guest at a party – I saw Sophie's bright and shiny eyes, her serious expression, saw her knuckles coming down on Andrew Black's letter.

Knock.

Knock.

Knock.

The knocks were slower and louder in memory, like a Victorian ghost story, like the Ghost of fucking Christmas Yet-to-Come.

Jesus, I thought.

Sometimes, my brain won't let me have anything.

A little way up the street, one of the boys had picked up one of the girls and was running off through the rain with her – *'Fuck off, Craig! Craig, fuck off, you fucking, fucking . . .'* she screamed, punching him but not really punching him, as the others trailed behind, laughing.

I smiled and dug my hands into my pockets.

He didn't dance me off a cliff. He did that to you. That's what I'd said to Sophie.

Fucking hell.

I felt the familiar fluttering in the back of my mind, the old memories stirring again. *You could tell her*, said their fat, furry bodies and the *bat, bat, bat* of their dry, leafy wings in the dark. *You could tell her, you could tell her, you could tell her, you could tell her.*

After all these years, they still hadn't given up on their freedom.

I scribbled my fingers through my wet hair to shut them up.

Before meeting Sophie that day, I'd spent the afternoon touring the bookshops. In every single one, I'd picked a book that shared a shelf with *Cupid's Engine*, pulled it out, then posted it over the top of the others, so that it dropped with a *thunk* into the dark, hidden space at the back of the shelf. I'd been doing this for years and usually I chose a Borges to take the fall, if one was available. I'd always thought that he, of all writers, wouldn't mind it so very much. Anyway, with a single book removed like this, there's more room on the shelf. I would use this room to create a book-sized gap between *Cupid's Engine* and the next book along to the right. It'd become a ritual over time, I suppose. In every bookshop I went to, I'd make a book-sized space, a gap big enough for Andrew Black's second novel. I don't know why I started it. Maybe I thought that one of us – Andrew, me, my father – had to publish *something*. Time's arrow had to keep making us a past, present and future, and as my father wouldn't be writing anything else – oh, I don't know. For years, I made those gaps in every bookshop all over London, even after I became sure that a second Andrew Black book would never come. Recently, I think I've come to understand that creating those spaces was less about the giving of room, and more about the recognition of a hole.

I stamped my feet to bring some warmth back and watched the teenagers disappearing into a bar some way up the road. I let out a long sigh that escaped as steam through my collar. Six years ago, Andrew Black sent Sophie Almonds over a cliff, and it was clear that she'd never forgive him for it. The sheer force of her reaction took me by surprise though. And what she'd said about my looking for reassurance from her, that took me by surprise too. Was I really looking for permission to contact him? I didn't know. When I asked myself that question, I got nothing back but the vague mental image of wading through a patch of brambles. The brambles had no malicious intent as far as I could tell – no hint of Sophie's raccoon trap – they were just brambles, but it was a dense and thorny tangle nonetheless. *And once in,* the image seemed to be saying, *you might not find it so easy to get yourself back out.*

I sucked air in through my collar and fixed my attention on the hypnotic, endless parade of headlights travelling along the road towards me. Before long, a bus rounded the corner at the far end of the street, and I joined the shuffling, rain-glittered queue forming to meet it.

o

Maybe I wasn't ready to be back inside our empty little flat so soon, maybe I wanted to be out in the world of things a little while longer, or maybe I'd been half planning it all along. Whatever the reason, I got off the bus a couple of stops early that night and struck out on my own to walk the rest of the way home.

My route took me along the edge of Victoria Park, where the wind whipped up great shoals of fallen leaves and sent them tumbling and hissing in racing waves, swirling past my legs as I walked, then spiralling up in tornado spouts, up and up, under the streetlamps. On such a quiet and empty street, the noise was incredible.

As I pushed forward through the leaf storm, head down and blinking, I found myself thinking of a story that Sophie had told me a few months earlier. Almost every time I saw her, Sophie's little black book would make an appearance, its pages holding the specifics of some new story, a new set of names, dates and technical terms that she'd keep referring back to while telling me something remarkable. Once, she told me about Johann Fust, the shady business partner of Johannes Gutenberg, inventor of the printing press. Apparently, Fust betrayed Gutenberg, got himself arrested for witchcraft, and became – according to some historians – the inspiration for *Doctor Faustus*. Another time, she told me how a man named Thomas Harvey stole Albert Einstein's brain, kept it in a beer cooler for thirty years, and studied it by cutting bits off in his spare time. Harvey became drinking buddies with William Burroughs, and Burroughs liked to brag to friends that he could get hold of bits of Einstein's brain any time he wanted to. There were lots of others too, from how duelling algorithms led to a book about fly DNA going up for sale for $23,698,655.93 on Amazon, to the origin of the word 'ampersand' and the brief period where '&' appeared in the alphabet after 'z'. The story that came back to me on that particular night though, the one I remembered as I made my way home through the swirling, whirling leaves, was about a mathematician named Barbara Shipman.

Shipman was a researcher at the University of Rochester in New York State, and she studied 'manifolds', that is, exotic, theoretical shapes described by complex mathematics. Bizarrely, manifolds can be shown to exist in many more dimensions than the three that we are able to perceive. Specifically, Shipman had been working with a six-dimensional shape known as a 'flag manifold'. How does a three-dimensional human attempt to comprehend a theoretical, six-dimensional shape? Well, she doesn't. What you need to do is find a way to visualise the shape in a form that the human mind can actually grasp, and this is generally achieved by the detailed study of shadows cast onto a flat surface such as a wall (*to the delight of Plato fans everywhere*, Sophie had said). Just as a three-dimensional cube might cast a shadow that appears as a two-dimensional square, so a flag manifold can be made to cast its own complex two-dimensional shadow that the human brain is able to comprehend and work with. I imagine that a fair number of mathematicians have calculated and projected the shadow of a flag manifold, but when Barbara Shipman did so, her life as a mathematician collided unexpectedly with another part of who she was – it collided with her life as the daughter of a beekeeper, of all things. Because of this collision, Barbara Shipman saw something in the shadow of the flag manifold that no one else had ever seen before.

You see, while the mathematicians have been studying their manifolds, the beekeepers have been baffled by a mystery of their own. For millennia, they've been puzzled by an odd little routine that bee scouts perform when they return to the hive. Known as the waggle dance, this strange performance sees the scout moving through series of loops and figures of eight, while vibrating the back half of its body at various points in the process. This seems to provide the other bees with strikingly accurate directions to the best sources of pollen, though how on earth the scout bee is able to transmit such complex data through such a simple little dance has always been a mystery. A mystery, that is, until Barbara Shipman looked at the shadow of her flag manifold and saw in it not the complex geometry of a theoretical six-dimensional shape, but the familiar waggle dance of her father's bees.

It's easy to forget in the midst of day-to-day life, but logical conclusions needn't always be boring, pedestrian things. Sometimes, a logical conclusion is so wild, so wonderfully bizarre, that only the fact that it *is* a logical conclusion allows any sane person to imagine it in the first place. The logical conclusion to be drawn from Barbara Shipman's observations is this: though we as human beings live our lives entirely in the familiar three dimensions, bees do not. Bees are fully aware of, and see and communicate in, six-dimensional space. What does that mean, practically speaking? What does the world look like to a bee? What do we look like, going about our three-dimensional business? It's impossible to say because the human mind is completely incapable of comprehending the answers to these questions. There are some things out there that we simply cannot understand.

Running my fingers along the cold park railings as I walked on through the leafy night, I imagined Barbara Shipman waking up on the day of her discovery, cleaning her teeth, getting dressed and having her breakfast, all as usual, and then preparing to face what seemed like another ordinary day. The truth is, none of us have the slightest idea what we're in for when we get up in the morning. A phone rings, a shadow dances across a wall, a plane falls out of the sky, a letter arrives out of the blue and, before we know it, the world is a different place.

I stopped at a windy junction on the lonely road home, the blowing leaves tumbling all around me. Turn left, and I'd be back at the flat in less than five minutes. Carry on along the park-side road, and it'd take me to the red post box opposite the old, boarded-up church at the end of the street.

I unzipped my coat pocket and pulled out Andrew Black's letter. The hungry wind pulled and tugged at it, but I kept my grip tight.

Take it home and burn it, Sophie had said.

I stared at my name and address on the front of the envelope as it flapped wildly between my fingers, trying to get free. I could feel the edges of the Polaroid picture inside.

What do you think this is?

You're right that this is a hook. What in God's name makes you think it's a good idea to bite?

I reached inside my coat on the other side, and pulled out a second envelope. This one was addressed to Andrew – my reply, already written, stamped and ready to post.

You shouldn't respond to this. If you're asking for my advice, then that's the advice I have for you. Do not respond to this.

The wind sent a breaker of leaves roaring past me, skittering and crashing away towards the old church with the post box outside. Stuffing both hands – and both letters – into my coat pockets, I put my head down and made my way after them.

o

I stood in front of the post box, for two, three, four minutes.

Just put it into the slot. It's just a letter.

My hand didn't move.

'Fucking hell.'

I didn't want to stand there like an idiot for another five minutes, so I crossed the road, climbed over the old fence and sat myself on the steps of the boarded-up church, Black's letter in one hand, my reply in the other.

'Fucking hell, Sophie,' I said.

That's another thing I should've told you about Sophie Almonds – whenever she gave advice, it was almost always right. The longer I'd known her, the harder it had become to dispute this one simple fact.

'Fucking hell.'

There were more trees by the church, the fallen leaves even more plentiful, and swarms of them whipped and tumbled as the icy wind threw its weight around the little graveyard.

I stretched out my arms, holding both envelopes up to the wind and they fluttered and shook violently, trying to get free. It would've been the easiest thing in the world to let them go. The leaves were so deep, they'd probably lie forgotten amongst the weathered headstones until they mulched down in the cycle of winter snows and thaws. The thread of this whole story would simply blow away and be gone. Nothing would come next: no answers, no problems, no decisions, no nothing. *Turn off the computer – click, and that would be that.*

I held my hands up a little higher. Sophie had done all she could to convince me to let this whole business go, and with the slightest movement, I could do exactly that.

The entropy of a closed system tends to a maximum, I thought, picturing those coloured plastic letters on the fridge back home. I thought about Imogen, away from home for so long, and about what our marriage might be, or not be, when she came back. I thought about frayed phone cables and crossed lines over empty fields, and about all the silence and all the noise between my father and me. I felt the envelopes in my hand and I thought, *'clue' is an old-fashioned word for a ball of twine, promising guidance through the labyrinth.* Was Black's sphere photograph a clue? I thought, *of course it's a hook* and *beware raccoon traps promising answers.* I thought, *there is no labyrinth, no grand plan. Only chaos and collapse. Things just fall apart.* I thought, *'I talk to God, but the sky is empty.'*

I closed my eyes, focusing on the thunder of leaves all around me. *The entropy of a closed system tends to a maximum.*

10
Another Name for God

The Second Law of Thermodynamics states '*the entropy of a closed system tends to a maximum*'. Einstein believed that the Second Law of Thermodynamics was the one law in all of science that would never be revised or amended, and astronomer Arthur Eddington put the case even more strongly: '*If your theory is found to be against the Second Law of Thermodynamics I can give you no hope; there is nothing for it but to collapse in deepest humiliation.*'

It's funny, I suppose, that the law of entropy, the law of unavoidable corruption, is itself considered by science to be almost uniquely incorruptible. Einstein felt sure that no scientist in all the generations to follow him would break down its walls, or even so much as scratch a name into the plaster. If the great man is right about that, then the Second Law's architecture is never to crumble, its gilding will never flake, its statues will stand unweathered and untouched, unchanging and always, for ever. As everything else falls apart, the Second Law itself will endure. In the realm of scientific theories, the Second Law of Thermodynamics represents something quite remarkable – a perfect, perpetual paradise.

And like any good paradise, it does tend to attract snakes.

Before we go on, I should say that when we talk about entropy we're not just talking about the messying-up of the material world. Entropy is also concerned with the ability to do what scientists call 'useful work'. This means that a charged battery or a wound-up clock can be said to be in a low entropy state, just like a tidy kitchen. As the clock winds down, or the kitchen gets messier, its entropy increases. It's all the same process; the rules do not change whether we're talking about a tightened spring or a tidy cupboard. And, in fact, the Victorians weren't looking to unearth some fundamental mechanism of time when they stumbled upon these principles; they were attempting to achieve something much more practical. Their intentions can be seen to this day, preserved in the names of the laws themselves, like fossilised ferns preserved in coal: thermodynamics. Heat, motion, *power*. They wanted to make their machines more efficient.

The First Law of Thermodynamics states that energy cannot be created or destroyed, only transformed from one state to another. The Victorians discovered the Second Law while trying to understand why these transformations were never 100 per cent efficient, why every change – coal to heat, heat to steam, steam to motion – meant losing some energy along the way.

The bottom line is this – ordered concentrations of *anything* are all subject to the effects of entropy. Ice cubes melt, batteries run down, stars shine themselves out and your cup of tea goes cold. Probability alone dictates

Lang
uage p-
aradoxes a
re considered
to be the most
basic and easily
solved form of paradox
by modern thinkers. A
good example of a language
paradox is 'this statement is
false', which asserts that if the
statement is true, then it is actually
false, and if it is false, then it is actually
true, which would seem to be impossible.
Actually, the solution is simple – language
is a product of human thought and the inner
workings of the brain; it is not a discrete part of
the external, logical, physical universe at all, and
therefore is not required to adhere to, or reflect the
laws of science or mathematics. Ergo a statement
can be both true and false, or neither true or false,
because the human brain is a wildly contradictory place,
fully capable of feeling and thinking many inconsistent
things simultaneously. The fact that we still struggle to
see the obviousness of this in the modern world gives some
idea of how powerful an idea like the Two Books must have
been in ages past, and how huge and powerful the
underlying notion of unified physical/linguistic truth or
falsehood was, and continues to be, in Western Culture. It
appears likely to me that human beings have some cognitive
predisposition towards the idea of linguistic–physical interconnectivity (more of that soon), but this seems to have been
much amplified and hardened into a unified form in the West
by the victory of proto-orthodox Christianity over other early
sects such as the Gnostics in the second century. Victory of
proto-orthodoxy ensured that the Bible – and by extension,
all other books – would be interpreted literally rather than
figuratively, with the understanding that the word of God
(and therefore all words and sentences employed in the
Bible, and – because these words and sentences were
not unique to the Bible – elsewhere) was meant to be
taken as read and to be considered divine, flawless
and absolutely true. The victory of proto-orthodoxy eighteen hundred years ago is currently
having a huge effect on how you read and
interpret the words on these pages.
If the Gnostics' standpoint had
prevailed, then our relationship with text – and by
extension, language
and thought –
would
be
qui-
te
diff-
ere-
nt
to-
day.

that your tea was warmer in the past and will be colder in the future, as its heat goes from a neat position (entirely concentrated and contained within in your cup), to an increasingly messy position (spreading out into the air as steam, seeping into your desk and hands, and eventually dissipating across the universe).

The Second Law of Thermodynamics insists that you cannot make your cup of tea warm again without expending additional 'neat' energy from elsewhere to do so (electricity from the microwave, for example). Just picture a cup of tea spontaneously sucking its steam back in and becoming hotter – it looks an awful lot like a film playing in reverse, doesn't it? Like the tea is moving backwards through time. We know that doesn't happen in real life. Time doesn't run any which way it pleases, because our old friend, the Incalculably Gigantic Weight of Probability, is always driving the universe from neat to messy, and the arrow of time from past to future. The Second Law of Thermodynamics has that vast weight of probability backing it up, and that makes 'messy to neat' and 'future to past' so astronomically, mind-shatteringly unlikely that we might as well – and usually do – consider such things impossible, and we never, ever, *ever*, see them in observations or experiments. Never. *Entropy only ever increases.* Tea, left to its own devices, only becomes tepid. If you want your tea hot (or neat) again, you pay for it, and you always get a little less back than you paid out. No exceptions, no cheats. The rules of this scientific paradise are absolute, unbending. Einstein told us so, and seeing as Einstein looks a little bit like God on his day off, we might want to take a moment to picture ourselves walking across the Second Law's perfect lawns at the great man's side, as he explains yet again that trying to break the Law can only end badly. 'Collapsing into the deepest humiliation,' he says, before ambling away under the apple trees. Once he's gone, we're disturbed, though not surprised, to hear something slithering towards us through the grass . . .

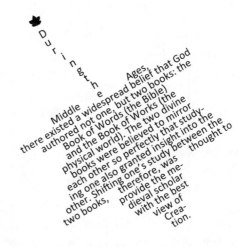

A little over a decade after Rudolf Clausius composed the first expression of what would come to be known as the Second Law of Thermodynamics back in 1850 a Scottish mathematical physicist named James Clerk Maxwell presented a simple thought experiment as part of a public lecture. This thought experiment would go on to become a thorn in the side of physicists for almost eighty years, because it seemed to demonstrate that it *was* possible, under the right conditions, to simply and regularly break the Second Law and make your cup of tea hot again without expending one single joule of energy to do so. Without any identifiable cost, Maxwell proposed a process that could reverse the effects of entropy, and that meant, to all intents and purposes, reversing the flow of time.

This snake in the grass came to be known as Maxwell's demon.

During the Middle Ages, there existed a widespread belief that God authored not one, but two books: the Book of Words (the Bible) and the Book of Works (the physical world). The two divine books were believed to mirror each other so perfectly that studying one also granted insight into the other. Shifting one's study between the two books, therefore, was thought to provide the medieval scholar with the best view of Creation.

Just like the sciences, stories have laws. The notion of a reflective, even interactive, relationship between scientific/physical systems on the one hand, and narrative/linguistic ones on the other is a very old way of understanding the world, though one that both the Modernists on the side of words, and any sensible scientist on the side of works, will happily tell you has had its day.

This is how the thought experiment works: imagine a box with two compartments.

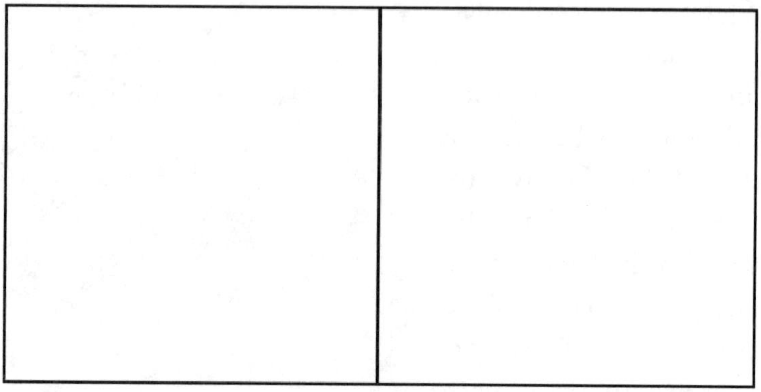

The box is full of regular room-temperature air, and each compartment is completely sealed. Not a single molecule can get in or out.

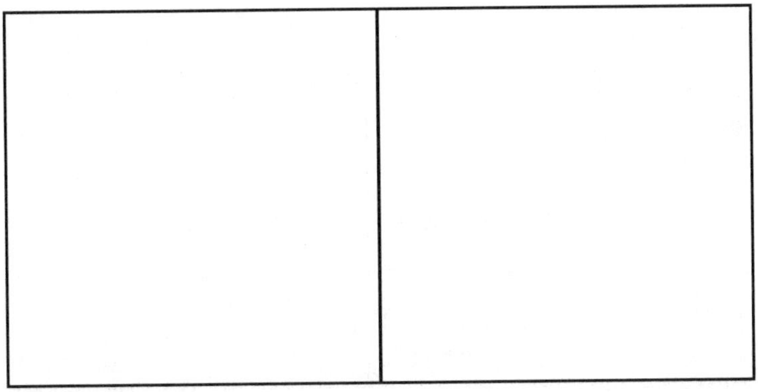

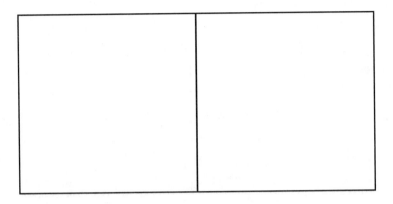

Actually, wait. We need to talk a little more about air here, before we go on.

Air is a mixture of gases, which basically means it's empty space sparsely populated with molecules, and these molecules are all zipping around, doing their own thing.

Some of the molecules have more energy than others, and these ones zip around faster. The overall temperature of the air is dictated by how many fast-moving and slow-moving molecules it's comprised of. If you have a lot of fast-moving molecules, the air is going to be warm. If you have a lot of slow-moving molecules, it's going to be cold. Thanks to entropy, the air molecules don't like to stay neatly concentrated in hot or cold areas – they want to mix, move, dilute, towards a maximum-entropy, middle-of-the-road sort of temperature. You can see this easily enough by leaving your freezer door open for a few hours, or opening your living-room windows on a cold day. Messiness increases, which in the case of air temperature means a jumbling up and mixing of fast and slow molecules until the temperature is flat and uniform.

Okay, let's get back to our sealed box:

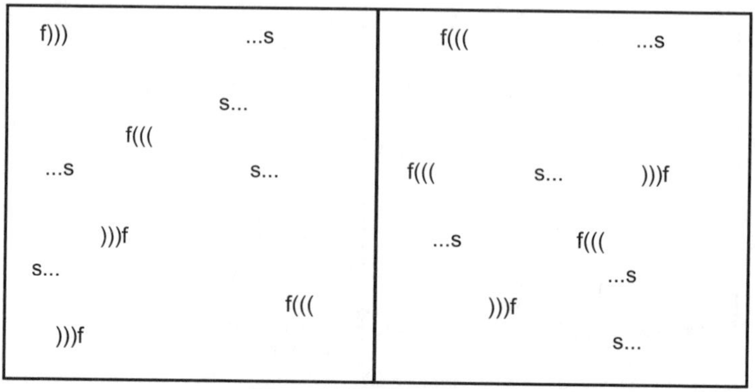

f(((= *fast, high-energy molecule.* s... = *slow, low-energy molecule.*

The box contains the same evenly mixed, room-temperature air, but separated in two airtight compartments. There is no temperature difference between the two spaces. Entropy is at a maximum in both – no further change is possible because any further mixing-up cannot make the air any messier.

Now imagine a trapdoor in the dividing wall between the two compartments:

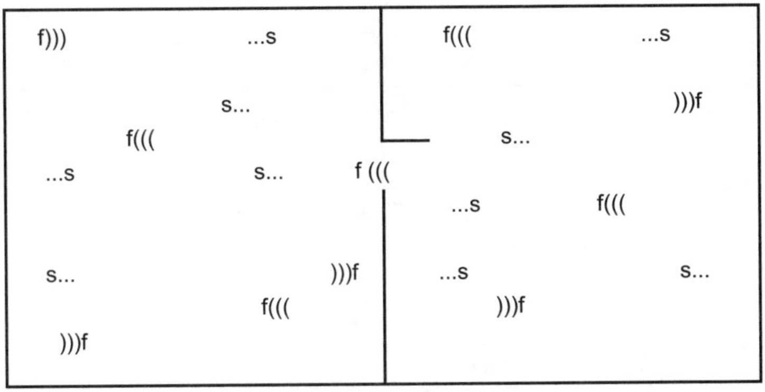

The trapdoor is so tiny, and it opens and closes so quickly, that only a single air molecule can pass through at a time. In our first test, the trapdoor opens and closes randomly. Sometimes an air molecule will pass through, moving from right to left, sometimes from left to right. Sometimes it'll be a fast, high-energy molecule, sometimes a slow, low-energy molecule.

As you'd expect, this makes no difference to the temperature inside the two compartments, as molecules are as likely to move in one direction as the other, and no energy is being spent to reverse the entropy inside (it's important to note that the trapdoor does not add energy into the system, it merely opens and closes, sometimes allowing a molecule to pass through, and isn't acting on the air molecules inside). So far, no surprises and no controversy, everything is exactly as the Second Law dictates.

Now we'll add our demon:

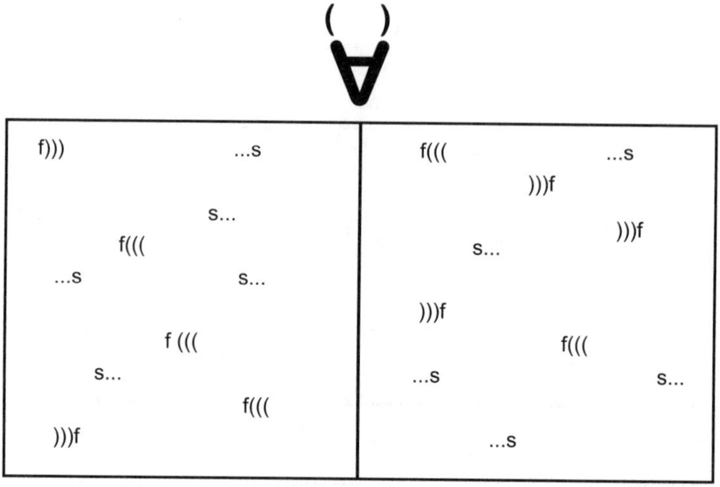

Let's run the experiment again – sealed box, two compartments filled with air, a trapdoor – but this time, the trapdoor does not open randomly. Instead, its movement is dictated by the mind of a tiny demon. Maxwell's demon is so small, and its eyesight is so good, that it can see the individual molecules as they approach the trapdoor. The demon only allows the trapdoor to open for slow-moving molecules if they are moving from the right to left, and for fast-moving molecules if they are moving from left to right.

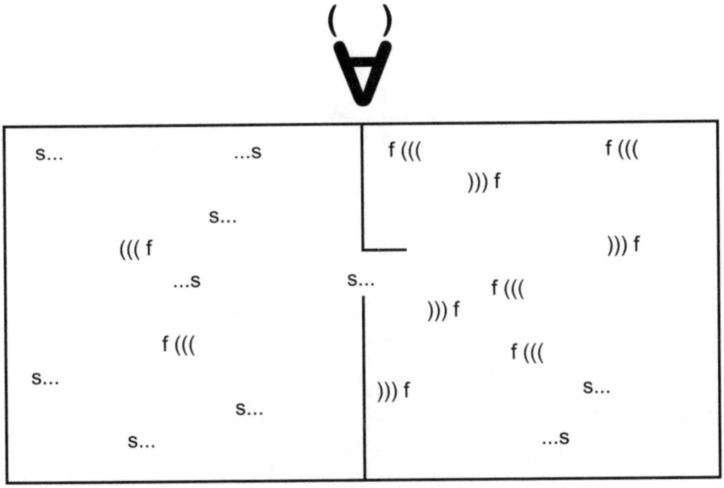

And that's it. That's all it needs to do. The temperature will begin to drop in the left-hand chamber, as the percentage of slow-moving molecules inside there increases, and it will rise in the right-hand chamber as the fast-moving molecules collect there. The trapdoor still opens the exact same number of times as it did in the first experiment, so no extra energy is being added into the system, but Maxwell's demon seems to be achieving something that should be fundamentally impossible – it is making the left-hand compartment cold, and the right-hand compartment hot. It is literally creating heat and cold (and order) out of thin air. To put it another way, it's causing the entropy of a closed system to *decrease*, and to decrease for free. This is something that the unbreakable Second Law says can never happen. But still.

Maxwell's demon looks a lot like it's increasing the sum total of order in the universe, which means it's moving things from a messier state in the past to a neater state in the future.✱ Or, to put it another way, it is reversing the arrow of time.

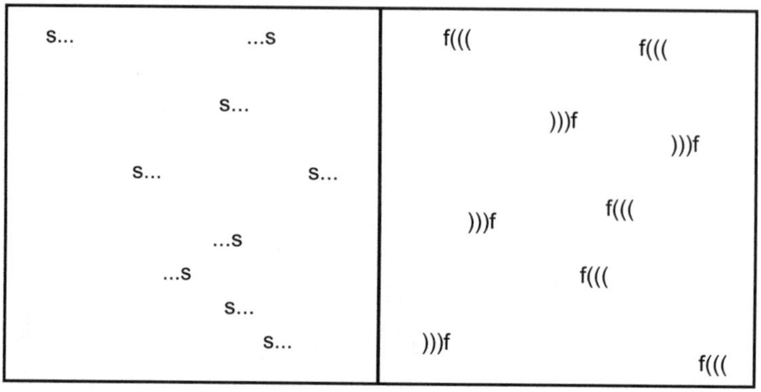

For over a century, scientists tried to resolve the problem of Maxwell's demon without success. Hard science insisted that the demon simply could not be doing what it appeared to be doing. The Second Law never bends and it never breaks.

Scientists learned over the years that when the Second Law appears to be contradicted, what's usually happening is that the closed system isn't as closed as it appears to be – things are getting in from outside.□

I remember finding Genesis 1:2 disturbing and compelling as a child, filled as it is with powerful, dreamlike imagery and – it always seemed to me – illogical and contradictory information, hinting at some strange, ungraspable mode of existence.

Interestingly, the God of the Old Testament goes about His acts of creation in an eerily similar way to Maxwell's demon. That is to say, God doesn't tend to magic things into existence so much as bring them about through acts of dividing, sorting and arranging. For example: '*God divided the light from the darkness*' (Genesis 1:4), '*And God said, let there be a firmament in the midst of the waters, and let it divide the waters from the waters*' (Genesis 1:6), '*And God said, let the waters under the heaven be gathered together unto one place, and let the dry land appear*' (Genesis 1:9). Genesis even provides a brief description of the primal universe as a strange, high-entropy un-place: '*And the earth was without form and a void; and darkness was upon the face of the deep. And the Spirit of God moved upon the face of the waters*' (Gen. 1:2). God divides this high-entropy nothing space to create the lower - entropy elements of heaven, earth, day, night, sky, land and sea.

□ Holes in seemingly closed systems can be devilishly difficult to identify. Occasionally, causing the problem. Creationists have been known to take the name of the Second Law evolving life forms should be impossible inside a closed system like the Earth. This is wilful mation. Anyone with the intelligence to put together such an argument must surely know that of our entire food chain (and all our fossil fuels too), absorb their energy directly from the sun. entirely from beyond our borders.

There's another fascinating and regularly repeated characteristic of God's creating-through-sorting which may be of interest here, not least because it provides numerous early examples of (or perhaps some early inspiration for) our tendency to believe in scientific–linguistic interconnectivity. Throughout the early books of the Bible, God tends not to work on his world directly (physically), but through the use of words; more specifically, through names. Genesis 1:3 is one of the most famous verses in the Bible: '*And God said, Let there be light: and there was light.*' But have you ever noticed how the word 'light' is created first, with the light itself only coming into existence later, as though it has been summoned into being by the use of the word itself? The pattern is repeated several times in the book's early going. Later God seems to be continuing this process on a smaller scale, as we see him tinkering with his people through the modification of their names: '*God also said to Abraham," As for Sarai your wife, you are no longer to call her Sarai; her name will be Sarah."*' (Gen.7–15).

As a species, we seem instinctively drawn to the idea of the 'true name' – the belief that knowing or controlling something's real name grants mastery or control over that thing. The small child reciting 'tyrannosaurus, stegosaurus, triceratops' is no different in this respect to the Stone Age artist drawing mammoths and … on the c…

My uncle's name was Edward, though everyone called him Ned. I remember asking him about this when I was young – not why people called him Ned, but about where the N at the start of his name had come from. I must have been quite young, because I'd been watching Sesame Street, probably at my uncle and aunt's house by the sea (I spent a lot of time there after my mother died), and I had come to believe that letters and numbers could exist in physical forms – that when a big, blue, foam rubber '3' appeared on screen, for example, I thought what I saw was 100% pure, real, actual three. I suspected vaguely, I think, that Grover or Big Bird had visited their house at some point in the past and brought my uncle the N (which was definitely orange) and that he had somehow decided to fix it to the front of his name. 'It's just what people call me,' my uncle had said. 'Like we call you Pip even though your name is Thomas Philip.' I tried to explain that I already had the letters for Pip in Philip, so it was a different matter altogether, but my uncle was a very practical man, and we often struggled to understand each other. Many years later, I learned that my uncle's N was actually the product of a form of language evolution that linguists call 'rebracketing'. Up until the 1700s, people would denote ownership with the words 'mine' and 'thine' before any noun beginning with a consonant sound, and 'my' and 'thy' before any noun beginning with a vowel. So there were a lot of people going around saying 'mine Ed' or 'thine Ed'. Try saying that aloud and you'll see how it sounds a lot like 'my Ned'/'thy Ned'. Over time, the N became detached from 'mine' & attached instead to the beginning of various vowel-nouns, making many Eds and Anns into Neds and Nans in the process.

however, it's not the hole but the investigator
in vain, claiming that the increasing complexity of
ignorance for the purpose of spreading misinfor-
the Earth is not a closed system – plants, the basis
For the last 3.4 billion years, we have been fuelled

But how can anything be getting in? The demon's knowledge of molecules is the only thing causing the decrease in entropy. The demon doesn't need to do anything, doesn't need to lift a finger. Simply by knowing the difference between a fast-moving and a slow-moving molecule, the demon increases neatness and reduces messiness inside the box, reversing the effects of entropy.

Many great minds spent years pulling apart the language, trying to find some flaw, but no one could. And the reason no one could is because there *is* no flaw in the language. The solution to Maxwell's demon isn't hidden, it's right there in plain sight. But the solution is so remarkable and shocking that it would take the better part of a century and an especially brilliant mind to identify it. In 1929, a man named Leó Szilárd finally solved the puzzle.

Szilárd realised that only a demon capable of observing and understanding the properties of the molecules it sorted could reduce the entropy of the air inside the box, whereas a demon lacking those abilities could not. So, given that we know that the orderliness of the air can be made to increase, and given that the demon's knowledge is the one variable dictating its success or failure in the task, this increase in order and decrease in entropy can be fuelled by one thing, and one thing only – *knowledge.*

Not gas, or electricity, but the very *knowledge* of the demon is reducing the entropy inside the box. The demon doesn't need to act – it just needs to know. To see how an abstract concept like knowledge can possibly have any impact on the hard, physical world of zipping molecules and thermodynamic principles, it helps to picture the demon's mind functioning like one of those Victorian machines. Instead of coal, the demon must receive nourishment to function, as all living creatures must, and it must also take in the learning necessary to complete its task. This information is then stored neatly inside its head, bringing its brain into a low entropy state – the intellectual equivalent of a charged battery or wound-up alarm clock. Naturally, these things happen before the experiment begins. Once the demon gets to work, the low-entropy information inside its brain dictates the ranges of movement available to the molecules, and reduces their entropy by arranging them into two compartments. As many suspected, the system is not closed after all – once the energy necessary to fuel, educate and order the demon's mind is taken into account, the overall entropy of the process can be shown to *increase*. The Second Law remains unbroken, but the fact that the well-fed and well-educated demon's mind could be causing these changes through nothing but the orderly quality of its knowledge is remarkable.

In 2010, one Dr Shoichi Toyabe at Chuo University in Tokyo succeeded in creating a real-world Maxwell's demon in the laboratory. Instead of two sealed compartments, Shoichi developed a minute staircase with an equally minute polystyrene ball. The demon takes the form of a camera hooked up to a computer system. The staircase and ball are so tiny that the ball is subject to something called Brownian motion – it can be jostled around by zipping air molecules. All things being equal, these air molecules would usually knock the ball down the stairs, but occasionally the impact is sufficient to knock the ball up a step, and this is where the demon comes in. The computer system is programmed to watch the ball and activate a small electromagnetic field behind it every time it jumps up a step. And so, entirely as a product of the demon's observation and knowledge, the ball moves up, and only up. At the top of the staircase, it falls down through a tiny turbine back to the bottom to the stairs to begin again.

Shoichi has created a machine that actually converts information into energy.

He calls his creation *an information–heat engine.*

❦ A wealth of further 'true name' examples are available, here are just a few. According to European myth, fairies could not cast spells over children without access to their names, and children who were not baptised – and therefore had no names – could be stolen away and replaced with changelings. Rumpelstiltskin could only be banished once his name was known, and his comic book cousin Mister Mxyzptlk could only be sent back to the fifth dimension if Superman could trick him into saying his name backwards. In many cultures, women are expected to give up their last names when they marry, a custom that is increasingly rejected by modern women. In Genesis, Adam is →

→ permitted to name the animals, and at one and the same time gains dominion over them. Mathematician Alexander Grothendieck said 'he saw the act of naming mathematical objects as an integral part of their discovery, as a way to grasp them even before they have been entirely understood.' Luke Skywalker cannot defeat the masked and mysterious Darth Vader, but triumphs when he knows his man is Anakin Skywalker, his father. Likewise, in Genesis 32:22–32, Jacob is outwrestled by an angel who learns Jacob's name but is careful to withhold his own. Batman, Spider-man & many other superheroes have secret identities, and go to great lengths to conceal their real names →

→ from their enemies. The divine nature of logos is emphasised by Judaism, and later the Gospel of John (more on that later) and either as a separate matter or as an entirely connected one, we must include the true name of God Himself: YHWH, the Tetragrammaton. Ancient Jewish people believed that speaking or writing the true name of God gave the speaker so much power over creation that it could only ever be spoken by a very few, and even ↲

↱ then, only with extreme care and respect. By the time of Jesus, the name was only used once a year, only by one man, and only in the holiest of all holy places. Religiously observant Jewish people are forbidden from writing or pronouncing the Tetragrammaton. When necessary, they replace it with another name – 'Adonai'. Though it is not forbidden, in Christianity the Tetragrammaton is still omitted from the Bible, replaced with a capitalised translation of Adonai: ↲

↱ 'LORD'. Compare this statement by Russian Symbolist Andrei Bely – 'Language is the most powerful instrument of creation. When I name an object with a word I thereby assert its existence.' To our old friend, Genesis 1:3 – *'And God said, Let there be light: and there was light.'* To 'summon' is to demand attendance by name, with a suggestion that the object of a summons is compelled to do so. Likewise, to 'invoke' involves the specific use of language to bring something to oneself (traditionally a higher being – a god, spirit, or muse, now more usually a law, a rule or the work of a respected expert), with the express intention of bringing the power of that thing in line with one's own cause.

O

11
The Church

A huge horse chestnut leaf hit me square in the face.

I gasped from the shock of it, my eyes shooting open. I almost lost my grip on the two fluttering letters in my hands as I scraped and fumbled with my jacket cuffs to get the thing off me. It took flight again immediately, rejoining its rattling mob as they roared off and away through the empty graveyard.

For a few seconds I just sat there, on the steps of the boarded-up church, breathing heavily and staring with incomprehension, like a sleepwalker shaken awake in some strange land. I stared down at the two envelopes, at my reply to Andrew, all sealed and stamped and waiting for nothing but my resolve to post it.

I climbed to my feet, telling myself I'd do just that.

I'd made it most of the way across the little graveyard and was heading for the fence and the road, when I heard a sound that stopped me dead in my tracks; a sound barely loud enough to register amongst the whirlwind of brown and red and yellow and orange going on all around me, but there nevertheless. I stood still, listening. A moment passed, and then – yes, *there* – there it was again. A sound at the very edge of my hearing – the sound of a baby crying.

That can't be a baby, I thought. *There's nowhere for a baby to be out here, not in this weather.* But at the same time, an older, deeper part of my brain – the part formed by books and my mother's gentle voice – began to whisper, *Moses, Oedipus, Tom Jones, Heathcliff. If there's one thing we know about babies, it's that they turn up where you don't expect them. And people really do abandon babies, don't they? Not just in books. They abandon them in churches, on graves, by roadsides, in parks.*

And if it is a baby, I thought, *it won't last long on a night like this.*

And so I stood there in the windy old graveyard, turning my head this way and that way, trying to hear the sound through the roar of the leaves, trying to figure out where it could be coming from. I took a few steps towards the road and, when that didn't help, I took a few more steps back towards the church – and, yes, the crying seemed a little easier to hear there – a few more steps in the same direction and, sure enough, the crying got a little louder still.

I wrapped my arms around myself and stared up at the great, dark block of the church in front of me, its spire disappearing into a canopy of wildly swaying, rocking trees. It seemed an awful lot like the cries were coming from inside. Standing with my ear pressed against the church's old oak door a moment later only confirmed it.

The cries were *definitely* coming from inside.

'Hello?' I shouted, trying to make myself heard above the wind.

Nothing.

'Hello? Is anyone in there?'

Still nothing.

I looked around helplessly, then – not knowing what else to do – I took hold of the heavy, black metal ring that served as the old door's handle and tried to turn it. *Clunk.* I couldn't have been more surprised when it *did* turn. With a painful creak, the heavy door popped open, just a few millimetres. After that, it wouldn't budge, much of its weight now rested on the worn flagstones, rather than on the rusted brackets that once held it in place. I put my shoulder to it and shoved. The door gave a little ground with every push, until finally I'd forced it wide enough to be able to squeeze myself inside.

The space beyond was deep and dark. After being out in the gale all that time, the reduction in the noise made my ears ring, but it wasn't quiet. I could hear the crying clearly now, and . . . and there was something wrong with it. It was a something that hadn't registered amongst all the wind and noise outside, but something that became skin-crawlingly obvious inside, in the quiet of the church.

I felt my stomach drop.

The cries were too long. What I mean is, some of the individual moans and wails went on far longer than any real, human baby could have ever possibly managed, even with all the air in its lungs.

The effect was deeply unsettling.

'Hello?' I tried to keep my voice steady. 'Is someone in here?'

Nothing. Nothing but my own thumping heart and those long – *much too long* – wailing cries. I forced myself to stand still for a few moments, to take slow breaths that were supposed to be calm, but that pulled in all ragged and rough anyway, and let my eyes adjust to the darkness. Every little part of me wanted to run, but somehow I managed to hold my ground. Gradually, objects began to form in the gloom. I found myself standing in a vestibule area, and the space wasn't entirely dark. I could make out a doorway up ahead, drawn in the faintest of flickering yellow light. Somewhere inside the church, a candle burned.

'Hello?' I said again. 'I'm not the police.' *Stupid thing to say.* 'Is your baby okay?'

I took a few steps forwards.

'Hello?'

Nobody answered. Taking another deep breath, I made my way carefully around upturned furniture and debris towards the doorway and the faint glow of yellow light.

o

A single, small candle flickered far away, at the foot of the altar.

As I walked down the long, dark aisle towards it, I moved between dozens of tall stained-glass windows. Many of these had been partly boarded over, turning them into strange, half-made jigsaw puzzles. I passed by a disembodied hand reaching for an apple, six sandalled feet, part of a halo, a palace on a cloud, and Jesus's left arm, nailed and bleeding, sticking out on its own. These odd, redacted scenes had just enough gaps and cracks in their coverings to allow a few leaves to sneak through, and to make the wind whistle and moan as it found its way inside.

Was that what I'd heard as a baby crying? Just the wind screeching and wailing between those old boards? It could've been; certainly I couldn't hear anything else now.

It must've been, I thought. *It must have.*

But I didn't feel entirely sure.

I continued down the aisle.

Chunks of grit and plaster crunched and popped beneath my feet as I walked. The battle to keep the church roof repaired had been lost years ago, the place shut up indefinitely.

Shut up but not locked *up, apparently.*

Which was odd.

'Hello?' I tried again. 'I'm just . . . I'm here to help.'

Only the wind answered.

I kept walking.

The little candle stood on the floor, directly in front of the altar.

Someone had cleared a two-foot circle around it, carefully sweeping all the plaster, grit and leaves outwards to create a spotless space surrounded by a neat ring of tiny debris. The candle wasn't alone in that space, however. I knelt down to get a better look. Standing in front of it were three small pottery figurines – the remains of the church's nativity set. On the left, an angel with a missing wing. On the right, a big, brown, indifferent-looking ox. And in the centre, a manger, completely empty, with no Baby Jesus in sight.

There was something deeply sad about the whole thing. The depleted nativity, the empty crib, the little candle, the meticulously swept circle with its ring of plaster, leaves and junk acting as a perimeter. The candle had burned down about halfway.

'Hello?' I called again. Again, nobody answered.

Then something caught my eye: a small, folded sheet of paper tucked into a crack at the base of the altar. I pulled it out, tilted it towards the candle, and began to read:

> *I was walking, and I walked not. And I looked up to air and saw the air in amazement. And I looked unto the pole of the heaven and saw it standing still, and the fowls of the heaven without motion. And I looked upon the earth and saw a dish set, and workmen lying by it, and their hands were in the dish: and they that were chewing chewed not, and they that were lifting the food lifted it not, and they that put it to their mouth put it not thereto, but the faces of all of them were looking upward. And behold there were sheep being driven, and they went not forward but stood still; and the shepherd lifted his hand to smite them with his staff, and his hand remained up.*

Something terribly sad had happened here. I could feel it in the air, in the candlelight that carried no warmth, in the cold radiating from the fallen plaster and the old stones, in the wailing cries of the jigsaw saints behind their boards and planks at the gloomy edges of the place. Something terribly sad had happened, and this tiny little clearing with its broken figurines and its weak little candle was a memorial.

I folded the paper and put it back where I'd found it, then looked again at the small, empty crib in the flickering candlelight.

I'd started to climb to my feet when something began tugging at my thoughts.

I paused, waiting. The *something* felt significant, though I couldn't pull it into the light for a moment or two.

Then, suddenly, there it was:

Why knocks an angel in Bethlehem?

But what if this wasn't what the answerphone voice had been saying?

What if I'd misheard through two walls and a door?

What if the real question was . . .

Why an ox and an angel in Bethlehem?

I stared wide-eyed at the old pottery figures in their circle of candlelight, the broken angel and chipped ox, the skin creeping and crawling on the back of my neck.

I scrambled up to my feet. *How could that be? How could that possibly be?* I cast around wildly as if the answer might be painted in huge letters on the walls, and then—

Bang.

A noise from nearby, from inside.

I froze.

Breathe.

Breathe, just breathe.

And then – *bang, bang, bang.*

I became aware of something inside me, something under the raging fear – a want or a need or an ache-shaped thing. I forced myself to move, to run, to chase down the origin of the sound with all the strength I had.

In a small vestibule off to the left, I found a small window still swinging back and forth on its hinges – *bang, bang, bang* – opening out into the night, as if someone had forced it open to get outside. Someone, or *something*, had been in here with me all along, watching, listening, not answering when I called out to ask if anyone was there.

That's when my nerves finally gave up on me.

I backed away – step, step, step.

I turned, and I ran.

o

There's a pub at the edge of the park that does a good line in burgers, taxidermy and Herman Melville memorabilia. I crashed in through the door that night trying not to look like the frightened sheriff in a western, and felt the slightest sense of relief when the whole place didn't whirl around to stare at me. Unnoticed, shaking and shocked to my bones, I shuffled towards the bar. The place was busy, an even bigger relief, and bustling with all the normal goings-on for that sort of bar at that sort of time – dating couples, a few suits and those older, well-heeled pseudo-hipsters that mean 'up and coming' has all the way up-and-come.

Under the bright lights at the bar, I did my best to look casual, but the look the bartender shot me as he worked the pump, and the fragments of a pale, haunted face floating in the picture frames behind him told a different story. Thankfully, Londoners don't ask many questions. Taking my drink, I found a table near a window looking out over the dark park and the leaf-rattled street. From there, I'd be able to see anybody who came along the road from the church.

Nobody came.

For one minute, two minutes, three minutes, the street remained empty.

Of course it did.

What did I think would happen?

Who did I think would come?

I felt too foolish to admit the answer, even to myself.

Come on. I knocked back my drink, embarrassed by my shredded nerves even as they kept up the squeeze on my chest. *You're being ridiculous, and you know it.*

I did know it. But still, I found myself looking up every time the pub door swung open. It didn't matter that the person I looked up expecting to see didn't come through the doors any more. *He does not arrive,* I thought, *does not sleep, does not cry or drink or piss or sing along with the radio. He doesn't do anything. He's nothing now but bones and old tape recordings, a finite arrangement of letters on a finite number of pages. And that's all he ever will be. Full stop, the end.*

But I looked up anyway, every single time.

Ridiculous. And you know it.

A little while later, I took Andrew's letter out of my pocket, read his note again and studied the Polaroid of the black sphere.

What do you think this is?

'I don't know, Andrew,' I said quietly to the picture. 'Why don't you go ahead and tell me?'

o

My letter to Andrew Black disappeared into the post box. The wind blew, swirling the fallen leaves. Brown, yellow, orange, red, brown, brown, yellow, brown, orange, gold, red, green.

Walking home, I thought about my father, about the ox and the angel and the empty manger. I thought about all those gaps I'd made on bookshop shelves over the years, and I thought about the gaps in the wardrobe in our flat, all the gaps in drawers and cupboards, and all the things missing from Imogen's toiletries shelf. I thought about the bed on Dorm Cam Two, and about an electronic demon willing a tiny ball of polystyrene up a tiny spiral staircase.

As I turned onto our street, I thought about reaching out an arm from the warm side of the bed late at night, only to find the other side freezing cold.

o

Factoring in time for collection, sorting, the overnight train, more sorting and then delivery, I imagined that my letter to Black on the mysterious sphere – *Dear Andrew, I've no idea. What is it?* – might just make it to him by the following day, but most likely, it'd arrive the day after. If I'd had any reason to think more specifically about it on the walk home, I'd have been able to calculate that Andrew Black could be reading my words in something like eighteen to forty-four hours' time.

It took me all of ten minutes to walk from the post box back to the flat.

When I opened the front door, I found a new letter from Andrew waiting on the doormat. I ripped it open and the first line read:

Dear Thomas,
Thanks for asking.

PART II

Gutenberg and Faust

'And now,' said he, cheerily, 'I suppose you want to see our great machine . . .'

—Herman Melville

12
Andrew Black

I first met Andrew Black on a cold February morning, a little over six and a half years ago. Another time, and another letter dropping into my life out of the blue. This one arrived in a nondescript white envelope with a strip of tape fixed neatly across the back, making absolutely sure that it wouldn't pop open in the post. I tore it open and pulled out the note inside. My eyes skipped down to the signature, then widened with surprise.

Andrew Black.

Andrew Black, my father's spiritual son, a man whose bestselling book was *everywhere*, while he himself was nowhere to be found – was inviting me to speak to his creative writing class at the University of Hull. *And they all think my name is Mike Mondegrass,* the note added casually, *so please play along.*

Andrew Black.

My first thought when I saw his name – *my father has sent him.*

And then, half a second later – *no, he hasn't, because my father is dead.* That unlikely fact was still new and strange to me then, still becoming a part of my mind, like an invasive species that hadn't quite taken hold.

And now this, from his protégé.

'Well,' I said, just standing there, staring at the letter. 'Well.'

The Qwerty Machinegun had been published a few months earlier, but the book hadn't sold very well, so under ordinary circumstances I'd have been delighted to grab a reading copy, jump on a train to wherever, and speak to whoever it was who wanted to listen. But this wasn't that, was it? No, surely not. Surely this was something else.

But what sort of something else?

Did he want an excuse to talk about something, tell me something? Was he asking me to read from my mostly unloved book as a show of power, a plain old act of cruelty? Maybe he thought that Stanley Quinn's ledger needed some balancing out in that respect, now the man himself was gone. Then again, maybe he thought nothing of the sort. Wasn't it just about possible that he didn't even know that Stanley Quinn *was* my father? Because, surely, there have been stranger coincidences in the world than a writer being asked to speak to a creative writing class, haven't there?

Of course there have.

But still.

Standing there with that letter in my hands, I got the uneasy feeling that some sort of reckoning had just announced itself. And now it had, I knew I wouldn't be able to rest until I looked Andrew Black in the eye and met the man face to face.

Andrew Black.

Andrew fucking Black.

'Well,' I said again.

I replied the same day, accepting his invitation.

o

Andrew Black had been sitting on the low wall outside the campus reception when my taxi pulled up. I didn't know it was him at the time, but the man on the wall caught my attention, and I couldn't help looking him over as I waited for the driver to write out a receipt.

He was an odd, thin man, all knees, nose and Adam's apple, folded down onto the wall like a spider. He looked wiry, with thick black hair that looked wiry too, with great masses of it hanging down over his shoulders. He seemed totally absorbed in the paperback in his lap – all except for a left knee that powered up and down like a piston – and totally untroubled by weather that was cold enough to have groups of students hurrying by in winter coats, trailing steam plumes.

The man didn't look up as I got out of the cab and I'd almost passed him by on my way to reception when he lifted the book he'd been reading to turn the page and I caught sight of the cover. *The Qwerty Machinegun.*

I stopped.

'You're not out here in the cold because of me, are you?'

The knee stopped jiggling, but he didn't look up. I thought he hadn't heard me.

'Excuse me.' I made my way back down the steps. 'Are you waiting for me?'

The man finally lowered his book, and he *glared* at me.

The unexpected force of it, the furious, out-and-out incredulity lighting up his eyes took me completely by surprise. I had no idea how to respond, and when I didn't speak again quickly, his irritation only intensified.

He even turned up his palms at me. *Well?*

'I'm Thomas Quinn. I'm here to speak to a creative writing class.'

The glare broke into a teacher's *thank you.*

His face said *eureka* and *finally.*

'I can't answer if I don't know, can I? Yes, I am waiting out here in the cold because of you. What was the other one?'

'That, I think. I just said it twice.'

'You just said it twice.'

'Yes. Not the same, but . . . yes.'

He looked down at my novel, carefully folded over a corner to save his place.

This is it, then, I thought. *This is what we're doing.*

'Thanks for coming out to meet me,' I said, trying to keep my voice even.

'Well,' he replied, not so much to me as to a large, redbrick building in the middle distance.

Then, a hand swung out on the end of a long, wiry arm.

'Andrew.'

'Thomas.'

'Well,' he said again, 'there's time before your star turn, if you want to get a drink.'

o

I drank a cup of coffee with Andrew Black in a smallish, underground university café with plastic chairs and bright strip lights. He didn't say much, and what little he did say between the painfully long pauses tended to be directed towards inanimate objects and more statement than conversation – *it's a boring journey, on the train,* to the empty chair to his left, or *don't drink it if it's too disgusting,* to the cup in my hand. These sparse pronouncements only required the occasional 'uh-huh' or 'hmm' of agreement from me, although I did try, a little, at least. Ultimately though, he'd been the one who wanted this, to bring us together, for – for whatever this was supposed to be. I felt determined to sit on my hands and let him get to wherever he was going on his own.

I sipped my coffee, and I waited.

In the far corner of the café, a young blonde woman sat typing on her phone, a cup of tea untouched on her table. I watched her for a moment; then I watched the woman behind the drinks counter make three cups of coffee, then two teas and two coffees, then a tea, a coffee and a cheese sandwich. Then I watched a man in overalls arrive with a stack of boxes on a pallet truck and I watched him unload them one by one, by one, by one.

Eventually, I cracked.

I asked Black how his writing was going – *yeah* – I asked him how long he'd been teaching – *few months now* – I asked him if he enjoyed it – *it's fine* – and finally, because he hadn't stopped thumbing the cover and because I needed *something* to happen, I asked him what he thought of *The Qwerty Machinegun*.

He stopped fidgeting.

'What do I think?'

'Yeah. What do you make of it?'

Black gave me a puzzled look, and then he gave my novel another. He turned it over, reading the blurb as though he had no idea what the book might be about, even though he was well into the final third. He looked up, and spiked me again with that glare of his. I saw irritation, disbelief, and also – a hint of desperation.

Desperation?

Suddenly, I had an overwhelming sense that I'd missed a fundamental *thing* about this meeting with Andrew Black, or maybe about Andrew Black himself. What sort of thing? I had no idea.

With growing unease, I watched as he turned the book over again. He pulled back the cover and quickly skimmed some of the earlier pages. He continued on like this, skimming, skipping and flicking forward through the book, until he arrived at the page with the folded corner. Then he carefully unfolded the little paper triangle, smoothed it down with his thumb, and began to read to himself.

Seconds passed. More seconds. After nearly a minute, I realised that Black wasn't going to answer my question about the book at all. He was just going to read it.

'You're a very strange man,' I said, not quite keeping the edge out of my voice.

'I'm entirely straightforward,' he replied to the page.

'Right. But. Fine. You asked me to come here to do a job and I'm—'

'You asked me what I think of your book. How can I tell you until I've read it?'

'I meant, what do you think *so far*?'

'What are you talking about?'

'Of the parts you've read—'

'I can't know anything until I'm at the end, can I?' He flicked back to the beginning. 'Is this a good opening? How would I know? How would I know if it's the best opening or the worst opening ever written until I've read it all?'

'Well, did you enjoy it?'

'What does that matter? Look – what do I think of this sentence? What do I think of this word? Is this foreshadowing as well tuned as it could be? Is this' – he stopped at a page and tapped it – 'is this reveal running properly? How can I know?'

'For God's sake. It's a novel, not a engine.'

'How can it not be a engine?'

This pulled me up short. I was about to fire back, to demand to know *what the hell that's supposed to mean* – but I didn't. It was such an unexpected statement, such an unexpected shape to drop into the conversation, that I found myself falling silent.

We stared at each other across the table.

Black gave *The Qwerty Machinegun*'s pages a final flick, then set it down between us. 'That's what I think anyway,' he said quietly, looking at the book.

I sipped my coffee.

We left it at that.

o

Black's creative writing class assembled outside, on a circle of plastic chairs at the edge of the sports field, because Black didn't like to use the classrooms, apparently. Everyone looked cold, bundled up in scarves, gloves and hats. I'd been digging through my bag on the chair next to me, looking for my reading copy of *The Qwerty Machinegun*, when a voice beside me made me jump.

'Hey.'

I looked up to see the young woman from the café, her blonde hair so dazzlingly bright in the winter sun that I found myself squinting.

'Oh,' I said. 'Hey.'

'Anyone sitting here?'

'No, no.' I hauled my bag onto my lap. 'Go ahead.'

'Thanks.' She dropped into the seat and we watched Andrew Black going around the far side of the circle, handing out stapled sheets of A4. 'Mr Mondegrass,' she said, without taking her eyes off Andrew.

'Yes.'

'Were you two having fun earlier?'

I felt my eyebrows go up.

She laughed. 'Well, at least you don't have to pay to be here.'

She smiled. I smiled.

An awkward moment began, but didn't pass.

Say something, Quinn.

'And there's all the difference in the world between paying and being paid,' I said. *Oh wow*, I think, *you horrendous fucker*.

'Yep.'

'It's a—'

'Yeah, from *Moby-Dick*.'

I nodded. 'Nice work.'

Nice work?

I'd been fumbling in my bag the whole time, then at last I found my book and pulled it out. When I looked up, Black was suddenly in front of us, handing over two small piles of stapled pages, before moving on. The girl watched him retreat around the circle for a few seconds, then extended a hand.

'Imogen.'

'T—'

'Thomas Quinn,' she said. 'I know. Exciting young writer, brilliant debut novelist, and son of the legendary Dr Stanley.'

I can't imagine how my face looked.

'Psychic.' She grinned. Then she pointed down at my lap. 'Also, it's written on your book.'

The class started a few moments later, with an older student reading her story out to the group, while we followed along on Black's printed handout. I felt bad for her, the student. Her story was clearly autobiographical but the sadness and loneliness that were all too evident in her as a human being hadn't made their way onto the page at all. The story felt flat, empty, dead on arrival.

Once the reading ended, an awkward group feedback session took place with Black's contribution amounting to a handful of *I see*'s, a couple of *I suppose so*'s and a particularly crushing *well, if that makes sense to you*. The older student cracked under the weight of this last comment and, in a loud, uneven voice, said that she knew her story wasn't right, but that she 'couldn't get the feelings she wanted to go into the words coming out of her pencil'.

To my surprise, Black wasn't rude or dismissive of this. Instead, he thought for a little while, then said:

'Words, like atoms, are mostly empty.'

Atoms, for the record, are ninety-nine, point nine, nine, nine, nine, nine, nine, nine, nine, nine, nine, nine, nine per cent empty space, made solid only by the magnetic pull and push of their tiny nuclei and spinning electrons. Likewise, Andrew Black explained to his group, most letters can be considered to have an infinitesimal weight of meaning on their own, but in coming together – in electron constants drawn to proton vowel cores with their inevitable, silent-letter neutron baggage – their pull and push upon one another creates the immense solidity of words.

'The word is the atom of the mind,' Andrew Black said.

I thought – *write that one down.*

Black's lecture didn't stop with atoms and words though. Finding his rhythm, he moved on up the scale to discuss the emergent properties of molecular sentences, then up again, and up again, through paragraphs, pages, chapters and parts, up to the great orbital curve of plot and character arcs as they each roll around a central theme, then up one last time, to discuss the concept of a complete and perfect closed system, the universe between two covers – the printed book.

The whole speech took about fifteen minutes and by the time he finished, I was smiling from ear to ear. Honestly, I felt so delighted, so swept along by the sheer meticulous lunacy of the whole thing, that I forgot briefly about book engines and spiritual sons, and the reckoning I'd been expecting to face up in the north. I felt nothing but pure admiration, finding myself thinking: *to have the sort of mind that can throw a thing like that together*. But then I watched Andrew

Black adjusting the creases in his trousers, making them run perfectly down the middle of both his knees, and I knew, I just knew, that this man had never thrown a thing together in his life.

I turned to Imogen and she flashed her eyebrows at me. Her look says *quite something, huh?* and *welcome to crazyville* all at the same time.

I could only stare back at her, wondering what the hell I'd just seen.

o

By the time I finally boarded my train back to London that evening, I'd decided to draw a line under the whole day. The reading, the meeting – whatever that was and whatever it was supposed to be about – I'd showed up and I'd got myself through it. I'd met Andrew Black just like I said I would, looked him in the eye, and now it was done. The time had come to leave the man, his word-atoms, book-engines and all the rest of it back in the north behind me.

Only – I couldn't.

A question mark, an inky little fishhook, had snagged itself in my mind and I couldn't work my thoughts free, no matter how hard I tried. Throughout the journey home, I found myself replaying events, sifting through Andrew Black's various strange responses and proclamations, searching over and over again for the single, unifying *thing* behind all of that odd behaviour that I felt sure must be there, but that I'd somehow managed to miss.

As a first guess, I wondered if Black didn't have some chronic need for things to be complete. It made good sense, up to a point – his frustration outside the reception had been caused by my not giving him all the information he needed to answer my question; then, in the café, I'd asked if he liked my book and he couldn't answer because his reading wasn't complete. And, well, yes, this *completeness* sort of worked with the *how can it not be an engine* part too, if you were generous, or squinted – engines need to be complete to run, don't they? And, yes, wanting to meet me after my father's death – didn't that suggest a need for completeness too? But how about *the word is the atom of the mind*? *The universe between two covers* part at the end might slot in nicely, but what about all of that business before it, all those orbits and emergent properties, molecules, protons and neutrons? Those things were about more than completeness, they were about complexity too, moving parts, working systems, technical stuff, in the same the way that engines are technical stuff. And his pedantic, uncomfortable way of talking to people, that was *technical stuff* too, wasn't it? Yes, somehow, *somehow*, all of it was connected.

I sat back in my seat, letting out a long breath that I didn't realise I'd been holding.

Completeness wasn't the answer. What the answer was, I had no idea.

I stared out of the train window for a long time, watching dusk falling across wide empty fields. Little towns hurtled by, a rattle of yellow streetlights and glimpsed moments through living-room and bedroom windows, life stories clipped into single movie frames. I bought coffee from the onboard shop. I searched around for my charger to power up my dying phone and, after unpacking my entire bag onto the seat next to me, had to conclude that I'd left it on the train north that morning. Finally, I put my forehead against the glass, closed my eyes and let the vibrations rumble deep into my skull.

I slept, woke up, half-slept again.

The train skimmed the edge of a pine forest, its trees planted out in long, perfect rows. I watched their silent ranks and the dark spaces between them flicker past through half-open eyes. And that's when it hit me:

Andrew Black's thing wasn't completeness, it was *order*.

I sat up.

Machines, atoms, orbits, engines, a full and complete question to receive a full and complete answer, even those damn creases over his knees – all of it pointed to some chronic dependency on, or compulsion towards, *order*. And when I say *order* here, what I'm talking about is order in its full, nineteenth-century, top hat, handlebar moustache, grand old Newtonian finery – the right things happening in the right parts of the right framework at the right time, predictably and systematically, always and for ever.

I found myself smiling.

Order. That's it. That's the thing.

Even better, I realised that I could test my theory.

When the train gets to King's Cross, I thought, *I'll head straight for the station bookshop. If I'm right about Black, his novel will tell me so.*

And it did. It really, *really* did.

Despite its length, *Cupid's Engine* is an economical marvel, a tight, beautifully balanced whodunit, where every moment, every twist, every clue, is delivered exactly at the point it's required. From first word to last, from first scene to last, the book's workings shift and turn to what Inspector Cleaver himself calls '*the tick and tock of cause and effect*'.

As I sat up reading late into the night, the book reminded me of nothing so much as a Victorian orrery – one of those miniature, mechanical solar systems, with its array of brass planets and moons all whirring and ticking around their burnished sun with faultless, mathematical precision. The image was partly seeded during my time in the north, of course – atoms and orbits, the novel as a machine – but still, I couldn't shake it. More than any book I'd ever read, *Cupid's Engine did* feel like a machine, and an intricate and beautifully engineered one at that.

I'd never read anything like it.

13
Cupid's Engine

Cupid's Engine begins with a tall, scruffy man in a white fedora and crumpled linen suit. He's propping himself up in a doorway, covered in blood. Although we don't know it yet, this man's name is Maurice Umber. He has a bloody knife in his right hand, and a telephone receiver pressed to his left ear.

'*Police,*' he mumbles into the phone. '*You're going to have to send somebody . . .*'

Unusually for a murder mystery, we open on the character who'll eventually prove to be the killer, standing at the scene of the crime, holding the murder weapon, and we're given every possible reason to believe that he has just stabbed a man to death.

Sounds like the shortest whodunit in history, but the point is, we're misled by our own expectations from the get-go, blinded by what we think we know about the type of book we're reading. *This is a murder mystery,* we think, *so there's bound to be some sort of twist or trick. Come on, I wasn't born yesterday. There's no way this guy really did it.*

In this way, we let Maurice Umber in.

The charming, likeable and incredibly persuasive Maurice Umber. When he talks, the ridiculous begins to sound reasonable, the improbable, plausible. Not whiter-than-white by any means, Umber comes across as a loveable rogue, a slouchy Han Solo in a hand-me-down suit. We know he's not altogether good, but we like him and we're happy to believe that he's not, you know, actually *bad*.

It's hard to spot what's really happening here, in these early pages, hard to see how thoroughly we're being played. At first glance, Black seems intent on making life as difficult as possible for Umber, even to the point of giving him a background as a stage-magician-turned-preacher. Think about that for a minute – *a stage-magician-turned-preacher.* For a character in a crime novel, it's difficult to imagine a more outrageous and less trustworthy CV, and yet, when Umber reveals this information to the arresting officer in Chapter One, he does so with such a weary sense of irony that we can't help but see what a perfect scapegoat a man like that would actually be. Once this notion has occurred to us – or rather, once it's been carefully nudged into our field of vision – a subtle, psychological trick is deployed to make sure that it sticks. During hours of police questioning, Maurice Umber never explicitly makes the scapegoat plea for himself, thereby inviting his audience to mentally step forward and make it for him. As any good fraudster will tell you, the best way to sell a mark a lie is to have them sell it to themselves. And, as any whodunit fan will tell you, the mark in this case is not only the investigator – it's the reader too.

As an opening gambit, it's bold, elegant in its simplicity and beautifully pitched. Not only does Umber turn that suspicious past into a tool to encourage the police to believe him, but he's also using it in conjunction with our expectations of the genre – never trust the obvious – to con us into believing him as well. It's the first shot in a great barrage of tricks, illusions and psychological manipulations that keep Umber's various marks – both fictional and non-fictional – exactly where he wants them to be. The control throughout is exceptional, and the complexity of the cons only increase the deeper into the book you travel.

Maurice Umber is a tall man, handsomely dishevelled, with a firm handshake and a lopsided smile. He lives in a handful of expensive, ever-so-slightly threadbare suits, and he never leaves home without his old white fedora, a hold-over from his stage days, which is peppered with scorch marks and has a semi-circular chunk burned out of the brim. Early in the book, Umber explains that it's his lucky hat, a hat he's worn every day since it prevented him from being blinded by a dangerous stage trick, back when he was young and careless. A little later, he admits that he also wears it to explain the faint smoky smell that surrounds him, which is actually caused by the cheroot cigars that he's still struggling to give up. There's a third, very different, explanation for the hat at the midpoint of the novel. By now, Inspector Maxwell Cleaver – our investigator and hero – has uncovered evidence of a powerful, shadowy conspiracy seemingly linked to whole series of murders, including the one for which Umber was arrested in the book's opening pages. Despite this seeming to clear his name, Cleaver has summoned Umber to the station yet again for more questioning. Umber is travelling in a police car with an apologetic Dan Wayburn (our arresting officer from Chapter One, who is reluctantly evolving into Cleaver's sidekick) and they're pulling into the station car park when, out of the blue, Umber says something *off*, something that felt like icy water running down my back as I read it. Dan has been asking questions about the most dangerous magic tricks, when Umber confides that it wasn't a trick at all that damaged his trusty white hat, but holy fire from the burning bush, when he received his divine orders from God. We're jolted – not just by the realisation of how much we've come to like and side with Umber, but by the fact that we find ourselves wanting to ignore or rationalise this pronouncement, so we can like and side with him still. We're relieved when his serious expression cracks:

'I'm screwing with you, Dan,' he smiles, laying a friendly hand on the officer's shoulder (which feels a lot like a friendly hand landing on our own). Wayburn laughs, we laugh, and the story rolls forward. Only, something is different now. Doubt has been reintroduced. The novel began with doubt of guilt, now we're moving towards doubt of innocence. From this point on, *Cupid's Engine* is all about peeling away the layers of pseudo-conspiracy that have accumulated in the first half, unmasking dozens of tricks, lies, cons and deceptions – some fiendishly cunning – until we're shocked to arrive back exactly where we started – with Maurice Umber, the clearly guilty, cold-blooded killer.

And there you have it. That should be the end, shouldn't it? When our detective hero, Inspector Cleaver, finally unravels the complex plot and solves the case, we should have reached the end the story, but we haven't – not quite. Umber's incredible powers of persuasion come into play yet again, allowing him to escape from police custody at the last possible moment. To be clear, this shouldn't happen. It's a breakout to end all breakouts – it's as if Umber's final gambit is an escapology act from traditional murder-mystery structure itself, as if the villain managed to slip out of the inescapable 'last page reveal' that has locked down and ended the stories of all other mystery villains since the genre began. In the end, it's only a remarkably cold act from our hero in an unexpected extra chapter that finally brings matters to a close. As a direct result of Inspector Cleaver's inaction, Maurice Umber is struck in the throat by snapping steel cable and robbed forever of his greatest weapon – the power of words. The book's final page contains nothing but Umber's failing attempts at speech as he lies wounded and bleeding on a warehouse floor and, as those attempts degenerate in garbled sounds with no vestige of meaning remaining, *Cupid's Engine* ends.

Now, at this point you may be wondering – *how could an intense and awkward person like Andrew Black possibly create a character as charming and charismatic as Maurice Umber?*

Well, the bottom line is – novels are tricksy, even the simple ones.

Very little about a novel is exactly as it appears, and if you think about it, very little appears at all. If you read *The Lord of the Rings*, you don't see Frodo, you don't hear Gandalf say anything. You think you do, but it's a trick. All you really see are rows of dark symbols on a light surface, all you really hear is nothing at all. You also get the impression of time passing in a novel. This is another trick. There is no time in a novel. There is no time because entropy doesn't increase between the first word on the first page and the last word on the last. For instance, if a character smashes a valuable vase on page 78, it remains unbroken on page 77, and you can visit it there on that page any time you like. Page 77 is as present and as accessible as page 78 at all times. Of course, you probably won't do that, you'll probably go to 79 after 78, because that's the way we read books – always travelling east – but should you ever find yourself going back to reread a passage, you can be certain that the vase will be whole and unbroken in the first 76 pages of the book. Time only *seems* to pass within a text. This is an illusion created by the temporal actions of the reader and the writer as they interact with it. And here's the thing – and this is, partly, how a character like Maurice Umber can be created – a passage that takes the reader ten minutes to read might take the writer ten hours, ten weeks, or even ten years to write.

I know. Relativity.

It's an unsettling business, when you really look at it.

Unsettling to think that when we read a novel, we're burning through years of a writer's life in a matter of hours. Unsettling too, though in a different way, the realisation that a reader will rarely have any sense of the temporal disparity at all. From the reader's perspective, the words invite movement across the page at an obvious pace, sometimes racing, sometimes ambling, sometimes moving with a slow, deliberate creep, and for all the world as though the writer is right there alongside the reader, that the two are in this together, tiptoeing, then sprinting, then pausing for breath at one another's side. But none of that's true. That's not what's happening at all. The truth is, it took me forty-eight minutes to get from writing the words 'It's an unsettling business' to here, to build that little road with its various curves, slopes and rises. To work it over, to stamp its surface as flat as I possibly could, to do my best to ensure you wouldn't trip or stumble along the way. How long did it take you to go from there, to there, to here?

The writer is setting the pace for the reader to travel at, but the writer *does not travel at that pace*. It's another trick. The reader's and writer's temporal relationship with the text are different by many orders of magnitude – as far as their relationship with the book is concerned, they're moving through time at vastly different speeds. So while it might seem to readers that a character has delivered a sharp and witty response off the cuff, we must remember that the author may have taken months to write and rewrite that single brief phrase, taking all the time necessary to get every letter and punctuation mark exactly right.

Time, then, is the secret ingredient that allows a socially awkward, difficult author to create an effortlessly likeable and charming character – the artfully concealed application of a shitload of time.

o

But anyway, while we're talking about *Cupid's Engine*, it's important to say a few words about its protagonist too.

Cleaver is an unusual hero. Put simply – no one likes him. Not his colleagues, not his family, and – at least initially – not the reader. A little bald man in a dull grey suit, he is pedantic, prickly and fixated with rules and procedure. Everything in its place, everything at the right time, everything as expected, no exceptions, no excuses. He has no interest in basic social niceties, has no imagination, no sense of wonder. And, of course, this is what makes him the only person able to see through Maurice Umber. At first we dislike him all the more because of that – Umber has a magnetic personality and Cleaver, well, Cleaver is kind of an arsehole, but slowly, things begin to change.

I was surprised at just how much I warmed up to Maxwell Cleaver in the novel's second half, especially as the detective does very little warming up of his own. Cleaver doesn't go on what Hollywood scriptwriters like to call *an emotional journey*; in fact, we get no explanations, no backstory, no excuses for the character's behaviour at all. Maxwell Cleaver simply does not fit into the world, and nor does he want to. For all his dreary unpleasantness, Maxwell Cleaver behaves as if he has a keen moral compass; acting in a way he personally feels is right and honest at every turn and being perpetually appalled, wounded even, by the vacuous dizzy-headedness of the population at large. He has a job, a house, a wife. Beyond the basics, however, you get nothing. Cleaver is a blank and it becomes increasingly difficult not to respect and even admire the fact that at the heart of this great, intricate machine of a novel, is a short, bald, obstinate character *who does not want you to love him*. Gradually, you start to cheer for the bastard, and when you do, Maurice Umber's sticky double-talk begins to taste so sugary and filled with empty calories that he starts to make you sick.

The brass planets spin and cross, the machinery whirrs. You're always exactly where the book wants you to be, and it is magnificent.

o

I sat up until ten a.m. the following morning reading Andrew Black's novel. He'd written a book that was every bit as good as people said, that much was clear. But *Cupid's Engine* also seemed to confirm much of what I'd suspected about the man himself. Order, order, order – and more than that too. I found myself digging and sifting through the text like an archaeologist, looking for shapes, imprints, casting marks, brushstrokes – signs of the maker in the shape of his work.

Cleaver, most obviously, appeared to be a proxy for Black himself. On the face of things, the characters seemed to be Black's *here I am, I don't care if you like me or not* howl at the world, but when I looked a little closer, I thought I saw an exercise in self-justification, even a bid for personal approval on the part of the author in there too. After all, Max Cleaver is the hero of the story. He wins out on the final page because of all the things he is, not in spite of them.

So whether consciously or not, I thought, *Andrew Black wants the world to like him.*

But what about Maurice Umber? Another, more complex, self-portrait, I decided. Umber was a negative of Andrew Black, a Rachel Whiteread sculpture where all the empty spaces, all the things the author *wasn't* had been filled up with magic plaster of Paris and brought to life. Umber was Andrew White then, a character who personified everything that Andrew Black rejected, everything he hated, a monster intended to act as a chilling illustration of why he did so.

In fact, once you recognise this, I wrote in my notebook, *it's possible to see the disproportionate fears of the author preserved in the reversed impression that is the character. Look carefully at the persuasive power of Umber's rhetoric for example, and you'll see a ghost of the mould that cast it – some deep and corresponding sense of powerlessness within Andrew Black that has allowed him to mould his villain so very convincingly.*

Wow.

What a smug, self-assured prick I could be sometimes.

o

One more thing before we move on. I've said that Maxwell Cleaver is a cold and impenetrable character in *Cupid's Engine*, but that's only 99 per cent true. Two very short scenes appear in the book that feature Max Cleaver and his wife, Olive. Both are brief, simple and domestic. These are the only moments in the novel where Cleaver feels even slightly more open, ever so slightly more than the locked box we get everywhere else. These dining-table chats – the only times that Olive appears – are also the only moments in the novel that seem to serve no narrative purpose at all. But then, we're told that Olive Cleaver is a beautiful, dark-haired woman with a mysterious s-shaped scar on her cheek. She also happens to be an amnesiac who stumbled into Cleaver one night and has never recovered her memories. *So, okay,* we think, *this is the author seeding a future mystery, another story for another book*. That's what I thought anyway. With every other ticking brass planet in the orrery having an elegantly defined path and purpose, I thought I knew what I was seeing as I read these two little sections. Two tiny little moons, sitting motionless at the back of the grand machine, going nowhere and doing nothing at all.

I didn't pay them the attention that I really should have.

14
Annotated Edition

As you can probably tell, I got a little obsessive with my readings of *Cupid's Engine*. My meeting with Andrew had been so loaded with emotional weight for me, and his behaviour on the day so very strange, that I suppose I caught a little detective fever myself.

Detective fever. Huh, I'm being flippant.

The truth is, this bizarre and mysterious not-brother, Dr Stanley Quinn's spiritual son, haunted my waking thoughts. What I wanted to do, maybe more than anything, was to use his book to figure him out, crack him, just like a detective cracks the case in a mystery. I felt that doing so would grant me, I don't know, some sort of power, some sort of restored authority and family standing, at least in my own mind. When I think about it now, the whole thing reminds me of how children feel strengthened and empowered by learning the names of dinosaurs.

Anyway, I spent a whole lot of time and energy exploring *Cupid's Engine* for clues and accidentally preserved information, carefully constructing theories about the author from the text. After a week though, the trail began to go cold. Once Umber spluttered and died on the book's final page, there were no more letters, no more words, nothing else to dig at and unpick. And, to be honest, I'd started to question the healthiness of the whole business by that point too, so I put *Cupid's Engine* up on the bookshelf and attempted to let the whole encounter slip away into the past.

The package arrived three days later.

I ripped it open to find a copy of *The Qwerty Machinegun*. On the title page –

Thomas,
You asked me what I thought of your novel.
Andrew Black

– and beyond that, a deluge of handwritten notes and amendments that all but swamped the book's original, printed text. The margins of almost every page were filled to bursting with the tiny letters, footnote after footnote, suggested additions and line rewrites. Whole pages were crossed out. All of Chapter Eleven had been removed with no explanation other than a circled and double-underlined 'NO', and in what space remained on the back cover, Black summed up the major deficiencies in my work in handy bullet points before signing off with – *I hope this is useful. I'll be in London next week, if there's anything you would like me to explain further.*

The book hit the floor hard, then skittered away up the hallway as I kicked it, shooting under the shoe cupboard like a frightened mouse. Storming into my office, I drafted a long and furious letter to Black before deciding that I really wanted to say all the angry things in it to his face. I screwed up the first letter and wrote another:

Dear Andrew,
Yes, I would like to talk about this very much.
When are you in London and where should we meet?
Thomas

I stuffed the letter into an envelope and posted it straight away.

It frightened me to pick up that book again, but I wanted to stay angry, so a few hours later I dug *The Qwerty Machinegun* out from under the shoe cupboard and began to read. It did the trick. I can't tell you how much I wanted all those notes to be worthless, for him not to have understood my novel at all. But the changes were good. He'd taken my book apart and remade it into something better, something much, much better.

I hated him for it.

For the next forty-odd hours, I did nothing but read and reread those changes and rehearse exactly what I'd say to the self-righteous bastard about every single one. The longer I spent with the notes, however, the more I came to see what Black had done for me and I knew there was one thing that I should say to him before anything else. When I walked into the pub to meet him that Friday, I forced myself to say that one thing before any one of a thousand other things could rush up and take its place:

'Thanks.'

'Right,' he said. 'It wasn't. Well. I made it to the end, so, you know.'

I stared at him.

He opened a satchel, pulled out a couple of books, and handed them to me. I took a look: *The Hero with a Thousand Faces* by Joseph Campbell, and *The Writer's Journey* by Christopher Vogler.

'I think you should read these,' Black said, 'to help you get better.'

I looked at the books.

'Fucking hell,' I said.

I bought us both a beer.

The hero may have to be brought back from his supernatural adventure by assistance from without. That is to say, the world may have to come and get him.' – Joseph Campbell.

The freedom to pass back and forth across the world division, from the perspective of the apparitions of time to that of the causal deep and back – not contaminating the principles of the one with those of the other, yet permitting the mind to know the one by virtue of the other – is the talent of the master.' – Joseph Campbell.

The herald calls the hero to adventure. The herald can be a character or creature, like R2-D2 bringing the message from Princess Leia, or it can be an event, like the phone call in the middle of the night that begins Auster's City of Glass.

'Shapeshifting is also a natural attribute of other archetypes such as Mentors and Tricksters. Merlin, Mentor of the King Arthur stories, frequently changes shape to aid Arthur's cause. The goddess Athena in The Odyssey assumes the appearance of many different humans to help Odysseus and his son.' – Vogler.

Though, as a Victorian woman, Jane's relationship with power and money is very different to that of many male heroes, and this difference causes significant changes to her hero's journey. The notion of an altered monomythic structure for female heroes is explored further in Murdock's The Heroine's Journey, and Schmidt's The Feminine and the Masculine Journey.

The Romans also believed that every man had a guardian spirit or Ally, his "genius," and every woman had a "juno." ... Each person made offerings to their genius or Juno on his birthday, in return for guidance and protection, or a little extra brain power.' – Christopher Vogler.

In *The Hero with a Thousand Faces*, Joseph Campbell argues that a single, underlying narrative structure can be seen again and again in both ancient myths and modern stories from all around the world. He calls this structure the monomyth, or the hero's journey. The stories of Moses and Christ have been described in monomythic terms, as have the adventures of Frodo Baggins, Luke Skywalker and Jane Eyre. Campbell gives this overview of his monomythic structure: 'A hero ventures forth from the world of common day into a region of supernatural wonder: fabulous forces are there encountered and a decisive victory is won: the hero comes back from this mysterious adventure with the power to bestow boons on his fellow man.' In other words: the hero goes, faces challenges and ultimately wins a great victory. Then, the hero returns and brings something back. Campbell goes on to break down this journey into 17 stages, including: The call to adventure, refusal of the call, crossing the First Threshold, The Belly of the Whale, Atonement with the Father/Abyss, Apotheosis, Rescue from Without, Master of Two Worlds. Campbell also proposes that every character encountered on the hero's journey maps to one of eight basic character archetypes, each of which fulfils a specific role within the story. The eight archetypes are: hero, mentor, ally, herald, trickster, shapeshifter, threshold guardian and shadow.

'Shapeshifters change appearance or mood, and are difficult for the audience to pin down. They may mislead the hero or keep them guessing, and their loyalty or sincerity is often in question . . . The Shapeshifter serves the dramatic function of bringing doubt and suspense to a story. When heroes keep asking, "Is he faithful to me? Is she going to betray me? Does he truly love me? Is he an ally or an enemy?" a Shapeshifter is generally present.' – Christopher Vogler

The belly of the whale is the stage where the hero is swallowed up by the quest, well and truly leaving the ordinary world behind, and being reborn as something new as they embark on their journey proper. Jonah is swallowed by the whale; a tiny Millennium Falcon is dragged into the gigantic Death Star. Campbell writes: 'The hero, instead of conquering or conciliating the power of the threshold, is swallowed into the unknown . . . The disappearance corresponds to the passing of a worshipper into a temple . . . The temple interior, the belly of the whale, and the heavenly land beyond, above, and below the confines of the world, are one and the same. That is why the approaches and entrances to temples are flanked and defended by colossal gargoyles: dragons, lions, devil-slayers with drawn swords, resentful dwarfs, winged bulls. The devotee at the moment of entry into a temple undergoes a metamorphosis.'

When the call comes, a hero will often refuse it, either out of fear, or because of their mundane commitments and responsibilities in the ordinary world. The hero may see the adventure as reckless, or just too damn crazy – a step into the unknown that they are simply not prepared to take. Luke Skywalker initially refuses to help Obi Wan Kenobi, claiming that he can't just go running off across the galaxy, as he is needed at home to help run the family farm. Luke only commits to the adventure when his home is burned down and his aunt and uncle are killed.

thre… ardian sta… the first thresho… attempts to prevent the… moving out of the ordinar… and into the special worl… adventure. Sometimes, … old guardians are low le… that must be o… part of the stor… *Stardust*, or the … in the Mos Eisley … be concerned pa… advise against th… to ban the hero f… at all. A thresh… mettle… to pr… impo… ho… lis…

The threshold guardian stands at the first threshold and attempts to prevent the hero moving out of the ordinary world and into the special world of the adventure. Sometimes, threshold guardians are low level opponents that must be overcome in the early part of the story, like the Wall Guard in *Stardust*, or the pair of thugs Luke encounters in the Mos Eisley spaceport, but equally, they may be concerned parents or friends who strongly advise against the path of adventure, or seek to ban the hero from setting out on their journey at all. A threshold guardian exists to test the hero's mettle, and to challenge their determination to proceed with their quest. Perhaps the most important part of the threshold guardian's job, however, is to inform us – the reader, the listener, the audience – of the risks of undertaking the journey in the first place. They are there to sell us on the stakes, to inform us in either broad or detailed terms: '*this is a risky course of action,*' or even '*our hero may not come back from this thing at all.*'

15

Mighty A, Greedy C and Missing Q

As the months passed, and as Black found himself coming to London more and more for meetings about his career post-*Cupid*, there'd be times where one of us needed someone to talk to – about writing, or publishing, or about having to deal with the world at large – and we'd find ourselves with no one else to lean on at that particular moment but the other.

And so, in this difficult, roundabout way, we became, no, not friends, not even something adjacent to friends really, but it seemed as if we were drawn together. Death can create an odd kind of gravity, I suppose. A hole, an absence, something like that can move you around without you fully realising, creating a pull you don't even know is there. Not that Andrew Black ever spoke directly to me about my father, about his time as his assistant, or the origin of that quote on the cover of his book. Dr Stanley Quinn was not on the table for discussion for either one of us. That was the one big, unspoken rule of our meet-ups and drinks. After all, *close to* is not the same as *contact*, and there's all the difference in the world between an orbit and a collision.

Black turned out to be much more open when it came to discussing his own parents, and the events of his childhood. *Open* and *discussing* might be the wrong words, actually. Whenever drink factored into the equation – as it increasingly did after meetings with his publisher – it was as if some deep valve would relax in him, and all of these memories – some clearly stored under very high pressure – would simply force their way out.

o

Andrew Black was born to Ursula Marie Black and Newhall Anthony Black. His early life seems to have been an idyllic time, full of warmth, love and encouragement. Black was a naturally bright child who quickly developed a love of language thanks in large part to the dedication and infectious enthusiasm of his mother. The daughter of a history professor, a linguistics graduate and a life-long reader, Ursula Black wasted no time in immersing her young son in the world of books – books with baby-friendly thick card, then books with windows to open and tabs to pull, then books for bedtime story readings, then books to be read together, then books to attempt himself – the little boy's finger travelling across countless words and sentences, travelling miles, travelling great Roman roads of text, to new worlds and across uncharted seas, a diminutive pink Columbus, halting, yes, stumbling, yes, struggling through thick jungles of 'ph's, 'gh's 'kn's, but never stopping, marching on, letter to letter, word to word, sentence to sentence, page to page, over long afternoons spent sitting alongside his mother at her desk.

By the age of two and a half, Andrew could identify all twenty-six letters of the alphabet (along with half a dozen others that had slipped in and out of the pantheon over the years) and could conjure up a shaky, scrawly approximation of each one. He could even surprise adults by delivering a potted history of the letters when asked, because – at her son's request – Ursula began reading to him from her own collection of books and essays, and adjusting what she found there to suit the curious little boy. This meant that, in addition to *Chicken Licken* and the Three Blind Mice, Andrew knew the story of Mighty A, who was

once a great, ferocious bull before he was tricked into rolling on his back and his horns got stuck in the mud; as well as Mr Tickle, Mr Tall and bandaged-up Mr Bump, little Andrew Black knew all about the Long Lost, Long S, and naughty, Greedy C, who stole a whole bag full of the other letter's sounds, and hasn't given them back, even to this day.

By the time he was eight years old, Andrew and Ursula had developed a complementary reading routine – lying together on the sofa through the long school holiday afternoons, or eating dinner in quiet companionship over their respective paperbacks. Newhall Black worked late most nights, so the TV wouldn't be switched on until he got home at 7.30, kicked off his shoes, and put his smelly feet up to watch *Coronation Street*.

Listening to Andrew talk about his father, it was as if mother and son had shared a house with a grizzly bear rather than a man. Not an especially dangerous bear, not despised or feared, but closer to a natural phenomenon than a human being and, as a result, day-to-day interactions with it were no more complex than feeding, making way for its habits, and adopting a sensible level of deference whenever the situation required. The Newhall Bear was *just a thing that happened*, and sharing thoughts, feelings or achievements with it made about as much sense as sharing them with a sudden downpour, or an especially high tide.

Andrew's world revolved around his mother.

Reinventing the alphabet as a host of storybook characters came easily to Ursula – language was her passion. The histories and mechanisms of letters, words and syntax fascinated her, as did the origins and evolutions of stories. Ursula had a strong grip on half a dozen languages, living and dead, and deployed them in the untangling of bad translations and corrupted transcriptions of old texts, occasionally on the payroll of museums and universities, more often simply because she loved the work.

Back in her early twenties, Ursula made a steady living on the road, visiting churches around the country and lecturing on key biblical passages and their history in translation. Her popular talks focused on the deeper meanings, lost allusions and buried nuances that could be revealed through a linguistic excavation of the text, all the way back to the original Greek. Ursula's good sense and understanding of her audience kept these talks primarily fixed on the familiar language of the canonical books, though her interests extended well beyond the regular gospels and acts found in every Bible today, reaching back to the lost, the fragmentary, the missing parents of these texts, to the earliest of early examples. As a matter of fact, her interests extended well beyond these too, into the apocryphal, the heretical, into a deep, black hole in the Egyptian desert in 1945, and into what a man with the unlikely name of Muhammad Ali found buried at the bottom. But that's another story for another time. For now, all we need to know is that Ursula made a living talking to Christian congregations about their holy book, and was careful not to say anything that they wouldn't want to hear.

After a particularly well-received lecture at Holy Cross Church in Ashton-under-Lyne near Manchester – on a cold night in October, with fallen leaves swirling in the car park outside – she met Newhall Black. The pair soon discovered that they shared a very specific passion and hit it off in a big way, talking for hours in the shabby little church hall under the peeling magnolia paint, talking until the tea was stone cold and the free biscuits all packed away. Talking until Reverend Dean finally got sick of pointedly looking at her watch and started to turn off the lights. Talking about what? Well, as it happened, both Newhall and Ursula were fascinated by a long-lost, long-speculated biblical text known as The Q Source, or more simply as 'Q'.

Q's existence was first speculated as early as 1801, though more thoroughly and convincingly identified by Christian Hermann Weisse

in 1838 when he proposed what came to be known as the Two Source Hypothesis, now a key element in modern academic study of the four canonical gospels of the Bible.

One of the many interesting things about the Bible's four gospels – Matthew, Mark, Luke and John – is the way they relate to each other or, sometimes, the way they don't. You see, the Gospel of John is surprisingly out on its own. In John, for example, there is no Sermon on the Mount, the Kingdom of Heaven is barely included, and the Second Coming isn't mentioned at all. Thomas does all of his doubting in John, and another apostle, Nathaniel, exists in John and nowhere else. In the Gospel of John, Jesus doesn't talk in parables, though he performs a lot of miracles not recorded in the other three books and is generally much more forthcoming about his own divinity. Only in John do we get the famous line 'In the beginning was the Word, and the Word was with God, and the Word was God', a verse most commonly interpreted to present us with a Jesus who is not only the Son of God, but also the divine Word, the Logos – a Greek philosophical term for reason and cosmic order that is also perhaps related to the mysterious personification of Wisdom (Hebrew *hokma*, a feminine noun) who shows herself several times in the Old Testament and, according to Proverbs, is present alongside God at the creation of all things.

Actually, there is no hard evidence to support the idea that *logos* is intended to be read solely in its philosophical context in John. *Logos* is derived from *lego*: 'I say'; *legein*: 'to speak' and, stripped back to its basic meaning, may be translated as 'word', 'speech', 'account', 'story' or 'narrative'. Therefore, we may present a perfectly valid translation of John 1:1 that reads – '*In the beginning was the narrative, and the narrative was with God, and the narrative was God.*' Which changes things considerably. It also brings us once again into the realm of true names and offers a dramatic progression of the interactive relationship between the linguistic and the physical that we've encountered several times before – now God uses and manipulates words to change things within the biblical narrative, because God *is* the biblical narrative. In this reading, there is no external Book of Works. Everything is language. The physical world is made in our imaginations by a Creator whose true identity is revealed to be the story we are reading.

Greek grammar and context both strongly suggest that the last portion of John 1:1 should be translated as: 'the Word was *with* God, and the Word was *a god*.' For a monotheistic religion, it's surprising just how often other gods seem to crop up. '*Thou shalt have no other gods before me*' doesn't say there are no other gods; in fact, it implies quite the opposite, and in Psalm 82 we meet a whole congregation of them: '*God stands in the congregation of the mighty; / He judges among the gods. / How long will you judge unjustly, / And show partiality to the wicked? Selah / Defend the poor and fatherless; / Do justice to the afflicted and needy. / Deliver the poor and needy; / Free them from the hand of the wicked. / They do not know, nor do they understand; / They walk about in darkness; / All the foundations of the earth are unstable. / I said, "You are gods, / And all of you are children of the Most High."*' God seems to be in a position to judge the other gods here, and also invokes 'the Most High', who the Gnostics believed to be a different and more powerful entity than the God of Genesis.

John, then, is a gospel apart, with around 90 per cent of its text appearing nowhere else. In contrast to this, Matthew, Mark and Luke, known collectively as the synoptic gospels, bear a much closer family resemblance. I say family here, because the Two Source Hypothesis is concerned with the narrative genealogy of these three texts. It's generally believed that John's gospel is the youngest, having been written in isolation somewhere around 90–110AD, and of the other three, Matthew and Luke come in at 80–85AD, with Mark being the oldest, at 65–70AD.

The Two Source Hypothesis suggests that, because the three synoptic narratives are so closely related, sharing identical lines and verses, the two younger gospels, Matthew and Luke, must have taken much of their material directly from the older gospel, Mark. But here's where it gets interesting. Matthew and Luke also have *other* material in common, material not found in Mark. This indicates a second source for Matthew and Luke – a lost gospel known as Q.

Rather than a traditional narrative, Q is believed to have been a collection of the sayings of Jesus. *The Lord's Prayer, love your enemies, judge not lest you be judged, the house on the rock, the blind leading the blind* – all these heavy-hitters are found only in Matthew and Luke, and are believed to come directly from the missing Q. Even more interesting is the proposed age of Q. Some scholars estimate that parts of the Q text were written as early as 30AD, as much as forty years before Mark. At 30AD, you're intoxicatingly close to the period of time described in the New Testament itself. How could such an important text be lost? In 2001, the editorial board of the International Q Project gave this answer: 'During the second century, when the canonising process was taking place, scribes did not make new copies of Q, since the canonising process involved choosing what should and what should not be used in the church service. Hence they preferred to make copies of the Gospels of Matthew and Luke, where the sayings of Jesus from Q were rephrased to avoid misunderstandings, and to fit their own situations and their understanding of what Jesus had really meant.'

Rephrased to avoid misunderstandings. Jesus wept.

The authors of Matthew and Luke tinkered with the wording of Q as they incorporated it, corrupting the language, and because copying out a manuscript is a long and laborious job, and because the meat and potatoes of Q appeared in Matthew and Luke anyway, more or less, the scribes didn't feel the need to make more copies. And so the Q text itself – potentially the oldest of the gospels, and the closest we might hope to come to the actual, uncorrupted words of any real, historical Jesus Christ – has been lost.

How could something like Q not fascinate a woman like Ursula? How could she not find Newhall Black's knowledge and passion for it hopelessly attractive? Ursula's personal life had been a vaporous, drifting thing until that point, shaped by the preoccupied whims of distant, academic family. Newhall seemed impossibly solid to her at first meeting – sure, grounded and determined in all he said and did. To Newhall, Ursula was a dazzling, incorporeal being – incomprehensible, the way he believed angels must be, a creature of light and firecracker thoughts. Neither paused long enough to see that having a shared interest, even one as unusual as Q, is not the same thing as two people being compatible – not until it was too late.

They were married three months after they met.

Newhall Black was a Christian and devoted Bible scholar. It'd be unfair to say that the man had no imagination, I think; all the religious people I've ever met possess the capacity for wonder, and clearly he *was* passionate about the history and deeper secrets of the Bible, but what fired him up most of all was the idea of the absolute – the divine truth. For Ursula, the Q was a puzzle, a tantalising missing piece of a great, cultural narrative. For Newhall, it was the closest thing possible to the actual word of God.

It didn't take them long to realise their mistake, to see that their connection had been a mirage, a flukey overlapping of wildly different worlds, but Andrew Black was already growing in Ursula's belly by then and marriages were made of more resistant material in those days. They got on with it as best they knew how.

As the years passed, the sharper, more interesting edges wore away from Newhall, and he became a more blunt and simple creature, as some people do. Work on Monday to Friday, TV in the evening, church on Sunday, and not much more than that. Newhall loved his family a great deal, despite often feeling like an outsider in their quiet, bookish world, and if there were times when he lashed out at them for excluding him, he rarely saw himself clearly enough to understand that this was what he was doing. But if life in the Family Black wasn't everything that it could have been, it certainly wasn't terrible either.

And then, one ordinary afternoon in late January, Ursula Black pulled out of the local supermarket car park, turned right down a small slip road, then pressed her foot to the brake pedal to halt her car at a set of traffic lights. Ursula had made this same trip almost every week for the previous six years, and performed this same, simple manoeuvre hundreds of times. But that day was different. A tiny hole had formed on the car's brake line, and when Ursula pressed down on the pedal, the car did not stop. The sky-blue Audi 80 slid out into the road and into the path of a ruby-red Leyland-DAF 95, a truck that'd been riding its overheated brakes down the steep Pennine A road from Sheffield. Ursula's car suffered a high-impact collision on the passenger side, and was sent spinning from the road into the churning black water of the old mill's watercourse. She was pronounced dead at the scene.

Andrew Black was nine at the time.

When Auntie Elsie, the next-door neighbour, came to collect him from school instead of his mother, he showed her his copy of *The Iron Giant*, brand new from the school library, and – halting his explanation of the book's plot to look closely at her eyes – asked if she'd been chopping onions.

Dark times followed. Newhall Black became a drifting, cellophane wrapper of a man and Andrew felt the deepest and darkest of holes open up under his feet. Only the arms of neighbours and visiting grandparents – arms he was constantly slipping through, that were always letting go too soon, always having to *get back now* to their proper places in the world – slowed his tumble into the pit, and that imminent tumble, that halting, faltering, slipping drop – one centimetre, another centimetre – towards a black hole with no net, persisted over the months, years and decades, to become one little boy's life.

The story stayed with me after Black told it one drunken afternoon, and I thought about it a lot over the six years that followed.

Andrew Black never stopped fighting to avoid that hole, I decided, never stopped trying to cover it over with a lattice of logic and structure and order, the more complex the better. He never stopped trying to make something like solid ground under his own slipping feet, to keep them from sliding down into the apocalypse.

o

I'm coming to realise, perhaps a little late, that I never really stopped trying to crack Andrew Black. I never really stopped approaching him in the same way that I approached his writing – with careful attention to the details, and an unspoken understanding that nothing whatsoever had found its way into the narrative by accident. If you'd asked me six years ago why that might be, I'd probably have avoided saying a single word about my father, and told you that it's just a stubborn neurological tic, a product of association settings in my brain – I knew that in Andrew Black's novel, everything that first appears chaotic or tangential is ultimately shown to be relevant, as the clockwork of the plot is revealed and A leads to B leads to C leads to D, and so I found myself looking for that same pattern in real life too. It's just a crossed line, I would've assured you, a wiring fault caused by the way that we make sense of the world through narrative. We can't help ourselves in this, I'd say. We're hopelessly committed story-builders, we are tidy minds making sense of the great noise of our experience by bookending, selecting, sorting, sifting, ordering, arranging and contextualising it into a clear list of cause-and-effect plot points. That's just who we are, that's just how we work, and if the process goes wrong once in a while, if it throws up an odd knot of false associations around a person like Andrew Black, then that doesn't mean anything at all.

If you asked me that same question now – well. I'd say that maybe the brain is smarter than the conscious mind gives it credit for, and that maybe I'd just been waiting all those years, knowing that something big was going to happen.

PART III

The Ox and the Angel

The gold and scarlet leaves that littered the countryside in great drifts whispered and chuckled . . . as if they were practising something, preparing for something . . .

—Gerald Durrell

16

Thanks for Asking

Factoring in time for collection, sorting, the overnight train, more sorting and then delivery, I imagined that my letter to Black on the mysterious sphere – *Dear Andrew, I've no idea. What is it?* – might just make it to him by the following day, but most likely, it'd arrive the day after. If I'd had any reason to think more specifically about it on the walk home, I'd have been able to calculate that Andrew Black could be reading my words in something like eighteen to forty-four hours' time.

It took me all of ten minutes to walk from the post box, back to the flat.

When I opened the front door, I found a new letter from Andrew waiting on the doormat. I ripped it open and the first line read:

Dear Thomas, thanks for asking.

It'd be easy to say that reading those words staggered me, but *staggered* isn't quite right. *Untethered* would be better, or *unhooked. Cast adrift.* I'm not sure if I can explain it properly, but imagine being lost at sea, imagine being entirely out of sight of land, so that all thought of direction becomes not only useless, but meaningless. Imagine the great depths unseen below you and the vast dome of the sky overhead, imagine a distant ring of horizon all around, unbroken and identical on every front – and nothing else at all.

I felt the fuzz of adrenaline rising, the hot thump of my pulse in my tongue and at the back of my throat. I think I laughed – an incredulous little *ha*.

I'd posted my letter to Black ten minutes earlier and here, already waiting for me, was his reply.

Except, it wasn't.

Another few seconds, and the paradox collapsed in on itself.

Thanks for asking. This was Black being sarcastic because he hadn't received a response to his previous letter. That was all. That first letter had been sitting upstairs in Danni Grayson's flat for what, two weeks, maybe three? In that time he'd grown frustrated and written another one, with all of his typical grace and diplomacy. When I checked the postmarks on the two envelopes, they backed up the theory.

A coincidence. Just a coincidence, and nothing more.

Pulse slowing, I dropped onto the living-room sofa and, controlling my breathing, found the focus to read on through the rest of Black's letter. After 'thanks for asking' there was a chunk of white space that felt a lot like a glowering silence, and then:

> *Something else you should have asked:*
> *The day we met, you wanted my opinion on your novel before I'd finished reading it, do you remember? You said 'it's a novel, not an engine', and I said 'how can it not be an engine?'*
> *You've never asked the obvious question:*
> *If a novel is an engine, then what is it for?*
> *What does it drive?*
> *What does it do?*

The letter ended there.

I didn't have the first idea what any of it might mean.

I read it through again, more calmly and carefully this time. There was an uncharacteristic hastiness to it, I saw now, a raw impatience in its wild spacing and hard-scored underlining.

He wants a response, I thought. *He's angry because he hasn't heard back, because, oh God* – the penny dropped – *he's angry because he's scared.* Yes, that felt right, that's what the tone of the letter was trying to tell me. *He's angry because he's scared, or because he really needs someone to help him, but he's never going to come out and say that, so he's pulling out all the stops – all of his best hooks – to make me get in touch.*

It felt so totally, obviously, like something Andrew Black would do.

But scared of what? Needing help why?

I had no idea. I started to push the letter back into its envelope. After trying for a few seconds without actually thinking too much about it, I realised that it wouldn't go in and after some investigation, I discovered that the reason it wouldn't go in was the small, square *something else* still sitting inside. I poked my finger in and pulled it out – a small newspaper clipping, a little browned with age, about the size of a book of stamps.

I unfolded it, and read its smudgy text:

> *Readers downloading George Eliot's* Middlemarch *from Barnes & Noble's Nook Store this week may have noticed something strange about the famous novel. English student Robin Mitchell was surprised to encounter the following passage:*
>
> 'There is no question of liking at present. My liking always wants some little kindness to nook it. I am not magnanimous enough to like people who speak to me without seeming to see me.'
>
> *'It did seem a little odd,' Mitchell said, 'and then I found another one.'*

'He was a vigorous animal with a ready understanding, but no spark had yet nooked in him an intellectual passion . . .'

Mitchell later compared these passages to a printed copy of Eliot's classic, discovering that the word 'kindle' had been replaced with the word 'nook' in every instance.

At the bottom of the story were two small words in Andrew's familiar black script:

It's happening.

I left the sofa and dropped down into my desk chair. Minimising the browser window showing Imogen's empty bed, I pulled up another and Googled the story. All that came back were variations of the same chirpy little report. Barnes & Noble had messed up the text of their *Middlemarch* ebook, a few people noticed at the time and had a quiet little laugh about it. That was it. *Still tilting at windmills, Andrew*, I thought. But the last remnants of panic refused to let me go.

It's happening.

I searched for '*novel*' and '*engine*', but nothing remotely useful came back.

I shut down the browser.

I got up.

I walked around the room.

I put Black's letter and the clipping back into their envelope, and the envelope on the mantelpiece. I stared out of the window at the dark street, at the leaves blowing through pools of streetlamp yellow. Somewhere in that deep, ink-black space beyond the houses at the end of the road, the old church spire rose from the tree line, up and up into the moonless night. I glanced across at the phone, the answermachine light not lit, not blinking, not doing anything at all.

Why an ox and an angel in Bethlehem?

I dropped into the desk chair again, found a searchable online Bible and began to type.

Tap-tap, ox. *Taptaptap tap-tap,* angel. *Tap-tap taptaptap tap taptaptap*, Bethlehem.

Enter.

I scrolled down through the results.

Huh.

I scrolled up to the top of the page.

I scrolled down through the results again, this time more carefully.

I redid the search.

I replaced 'Bethlehem' with 'stable'.

I redid the search again.

I redid the search again on a different online Bible site.

I sat back in my chair, folded my arms and stared at the screen.

'Huh,' I said out loud.

o

Let me ask you a question. The traditional nativity set has an ox and an angel, along with a donkey, the shepherds, the wise men, a lamb or two, Mary and Joseph and the baby Jesus in the manger, right?

Of course it does, everyone knows that.

But of the four gospels, only Matthew and Luke actually have nativity stories, and they're really quite different. Luke has the shepherds visiting Jesus in the stable, and no one else; Matthew has the wise men and no one else. So this nativity set, the one we all know, the one in all those churches, shops windows and homes, along with the nativity play that all the little kids perform at Christmas every year – it's an amalgam, a fudging together of two different versions of the story. But that's not all: the amalgamated nativity seems to have picked up three extra characters along the way, three characters that were not present at the birth of Christ in either the Gospel of Luke *or* the Gospel of Matthew. These three characters are the donkey, the ox and the angel.

The donkey appears to be a simple elaboration. After all, though not specifically mentioned in Matthew or Luke, we shouldn't be surprised to find a donkey in the stable of an inn full of travellers. At the very least, it's entirely expected background furniture. You might also recall that this particular Little Donkey has an extended role in some Christmas songs and nativity plays, appearing in the stable only after fulfilling the important task of carrying a heavily pregnant Mary to Bethlehem in the first place. Again, not mentioned in Luke or Matthew but its inclusion is at least logical – a man and heavily pregnant woman having to travel away from home for several days are unlikely to set out on foot, and if they find themselves having to sleep in a stable, they'll probably be doing so alongside the animal that brought them there.

The angel's presence in the stable is a straight-up corruption of the narrative, albeit an understandable one. The angel appears to the shepherds in the fields in Luke, but never visits the manger. Still, we can see how the angel might be added to the stable ensemble – it's an easy thing to bunch all the nativity characters together, especially if you're trying to capture the whole narrative story in a single stained-glass window, for example. So another understandable addition really, when all's said and done.

All of this leaves the ox, which is where things get strange.

To put it simply – there is no ox.

There is no ox in the nativity of Matthew.

There is no ox in the nativity of Luke.

According to the Bible, there is no ox in the nativity at all.

And, when you really think about it, why on earth would there be? Why would this stable in Bethlehem – the stable of an inn, remember – have an ox in it? What would it be doing there? As modern people, we tend to miss the discrepancy of the ox because when we hear 'stable', we think 'farm', but this isn't a farm – finding an ox here is like finding a combine harvester in a Travelodge car park. It makes no sense. The ox plays no part in the nativity narratives and, unlike the donkey, there's no logical reason for it to have been added. Which rather begs the question: given that this creature is never mentioned, not once, in either account of the birth of Jesus Christ, why exactly is there an ox watching quietly in the background of every single nativity set you've ever seen?

17
Imogen in Red and Gold

The handsome, blond-haired angel stood on top of a battered old box on the coffee table in the living room. Below him, a scattering of assorted wise men and shepherds gazed with adoration and wonder at nothing in particular. A manger-shaped package sat on the floor, a half-wrapped donkey stood beside my 'I ♥ coffee' mug, and an ox and a magnifying glass lay side by side on the sofa, about six inches from my sleeping head.

I'd unwrapped the old nativity set that had once belonged to Imogen's grandmother, brushed off years of dust and removed the figures for inspection, paying extra special attention to the ox and the angel, even giving them a careful once over with the big old magnifying glass my aunt had used for reading. I don't know what I'd been looking for, but I found nothing. No clues.

Why an ox and an angel in Bethlehem?

I'd say *that's the question*, but the truth is – accepting that there'd actually been a question required a leap of faith towards all sorts of things (faith included) that were not really in my wheelhouse. Statistically, it was still far more likely that I'd heard nothing but garbled nonsense on the answerphone – a bag of half-heard words, halfway remembered and then squeezed and twisted until they matched the strange display I'd found on the old church floor – a self-generating revelation, or delusion, if you're feeling harsh. I'd misread Black's letter and scared myself witless with a phantom paradox already that night – ghosts and *messages from the great beyond* could take a number, frankly.

But then, why *were* they there? Why an angel, and most especially, why an ox standing beside that empty manger on the old church floor, and why an ox here again in the handsome old nativity set from Imogen's grandma, why an ox in every single nativity set all over the world, for God's sake?

The ox's enduring, familiar presence as a background player in all those childhood plays, Christmas cards, nativities and advent calendars masks its great secret – the ox is a free radical, a rogue element, an out-of-place animal, a big, bovine cuckoo in the nest.

Why?

I didn't have a clue.

Exhausted and overwhelmed by this long, strange day, I'd pulled up our wedding video on the iPad, sent it to the TV, and set it to repeat until morning. I did that sometimes. When watching webcam footage of Imogen's empty bed on the desktop felt too lonely, and our own bed felt too cold, I'd put on the wedding video and fall asleep on the sofa as it played through. I liked to see her. When I closed my eyes, I liked to hear her voice laughing and talking in the room as sleep came up. It helped, a sad melancholy sort of help for sure, but it did help.

The phone rang, impossibly loud in the quiet flat.

I jumped up, scattering nativity figures, scrabbling to grab the receiver.

Why an ox and an—

'Hello?'

'Hello, Euston.'

I let out a big lungful of air. 'Hello, Eagle One. I'm just watching you in the snow.'

'You're what?'

Imogen and I had been married in the Lake District in the depths of winter. Her dress was a brilliant red and gold, and when we went outside to take our wedding pictures, she stood out against the drifts and bare, black trees like a living, dancing bonfire. Watching her on TV right then, my wife was a giggling firework, ankle-deep in snow, twirling and laughing, fuelled by champagne and gin and tonic. Imogen-in-red-and-gold looked like the happiest woman in the world.

'Hello?' said Imogen-on-the-phone.

'Sorry.' I snapped out of it. 'Got the stares. I'm watching the wedding video.'

'Aw, are you? Have I fallen over yet?'

'Which time?'

'Ho, ho.'

'No, not yet, but you're about to.'

'We're doing the pictures?'

'We sure are.'

'It was so fucking cold.'

On the TV, Imogen-in-red-and-gold steadied herself and leaned in to whisper to her bridesmaid, Claire. The two of them collapsed into fits of laughter.

'And those shoes never recovered,' Imogen-on-the-phone said. 'I was going to keep them, you know. There was a plan.'

My sleepy eyes shifted from the TV to the computer screen. Imogen's unmade bed remained empty on Dorm Cam Two, no sign of her there at all.

'How come you're calling?'

'Oh right, nice.'

'No, I don't mean it like that. It's great, it's just . . .'

'What?'

'I didn't think—'

'We just got back. You were saying you felt abstract this morning, so I thought I'd check in again, see if you went outside.'

'I did, yeah. I saw Sophie.'

'Oh good. How is the beautiful and fascinating Ms Almonds?'

'Well. Beautiful and fascinating, obviously.'

'Obviously.'

'Listen,' I said. 'I've had a really strange day.'

'Oh right, sorry, do you want me to go?'

'No. No, not that. I mean – I've had an actually strange day. Not brain-strange, but weird, real-life strange.'

On TV, Imogen-in-red-and-gold leaned herself against a wintry tree, smiling, laughing, her cheeks glowing as she bantered with the crouching photographer.

'What happened? Are you okay?'

'Yeah, yeah,' I said. 'I got a letter from Andrew. Two letters, actually.'

'What does he want?'

'I don't know. I think he might be in trouble.'

'Did he say that?'

'No. He doesn't say things, does he? They were both bizarre. This morning there was a weird picture and this afternoon, something about *what books do*.'

'Don't get involved.'

'No?'

'One minute.'

'What?'

'Sorry, I was just, someone here. Just don't get involved with any of it.'

'Wait, hang on,' I said. 'You're going to—' Imogen-in-red-and-gold stumbles, spins her arms and falls backwards into the snow. I laughed. 'Snow angel.'

'I can't believe you don't get bored of that.'

'I never get bored of it.'

'Seriously though. The Andrew stuff, just leave it.'

'And there's—'

'Tom.'

'No, listen. There's something else. I think it might be properly weird.'

Imogen was silent for a moment. 'Go on.'

'Right. So . . .' *Just stick to the last bit.* 'Did you know that the ox and the angel are never actually in the stable in the Bible? At the birth of Jesus, I mean. There's no mention of an ox at all, but it's there anyway, this great big ox, in all the nativity sets and all of the plays.'

'Right.'

'Well. That's weird, isn't it?'

'Is it?'

'Yeah, of course it is.'

'Hmm. Maybe it is a bit.'

'It's really weird.'

'*Fear not said he for mighty dread had seized their troubled minds.* That's the bit that always seemed weird to me.'

'Really?' I thought about it. 'From the Christmas carol?'

'Yeah, but it's in the Bible too, I think. Like, why are the shepherds so scared of the angel? Sure, it's a guy with wings descending from the heavens, which would be a bit—'

'Unsettling.'

'Yeah, of course. But, *mighty dread had seized their troubled minds*? It sounds like they're terrified, like, they're practically out-of-their-minds frightened. It's a really weird bit in the middle of a Christmas story. *The* Christmas story. Angels are the good guys, aren't they? We like angels. Fluffy wings, tinsel halo. I was an angel in the nativity once.'

'And your Aunty Eileen made you a sub-par halo.'

'. . . and I had to hold it on the whole way through. All right, I know, I tell you every year.'

'I like you telling me every year. It's like a Christmas tradition.'

'Fuck off.'

'It is.'

'Fuck off.'

A moment of quiet came and went.

'When I was little,' I said, 'I used to pray to the angels. Have I ever told you that?'

Imogen thought about it.

'No,' she said. 'I don't think so.'

'I must've been really small. My aunt would say "ask Baby Jesus and his angels", but I didn't think Baby Jesus, being a baby and all, would be able to help too much, so I prayed to the angels.'

'Did they answer?'

'What do you think?'

'I don't know, what did you ask them for?'

'Well' – a small pause – 'I wanted my mum to come back. And for no one else to die.'

Silence again.

'Im?'

'I'm sorry.'

'It's fine.'

'It breaks my heart sometimes, to think of little you.'

'It's fine, honestly. It's just – that was what I asked for.'

'Uh-huh.'

'—that and maybe a bike.'

'Ha. Well. Did you get the bike at least?'

'I did actually.'

'Oh well, there you go then.'

'Yeah.'

Neither of us spoke for a moment.

'The Devil was an angel, you know,' Imogen said.

'I can honestly say that I never prayed to the Devil.'

'No, but . . . He's the one who has a history of giving people things when they ask for them.'

'Hmm. Not sure you'd call it "giving". I'm pretty sure I remember hearing about strings of some kind. Anyway, the bike came from—'

A sudden movement caught my attention on Dorm Cam Two. Imogen walked into shot, wrapped in a towel, wet hair brushed back and shining.

'Hey! Are you still there?'

'Yes. You just arrived.'

'Yeah?'

'Yeah. I'm expecting the numbers to start climbing any second.'

Imogen laughed, but a few moments later the viewer numbers did, inevitably, start to go up.

Oh, the internet, I thought.

On screen, my wife opened a drawer and found herself some underwear.

'Anyway, you were saying—'

'Wait,' I say.

'What am I doing?'

Imogen stepped into a pair of knickers and slid them up her legs, shuffling to get them up under her towel. The webcam numbers steadily increased.

'Some sort of live sex show?'

'Ha. World's worst one, maybe. You've been on your own too long if you think that counts.'

'I have been on my own too long.'

It just came out. A monumental chunk of honesty dropped right into the middle of the conversation. A full-on, dinosaur-killing asteroid.

Silence came back down the line.

I watched as Imogen pulled on a pair of jeans then dropped her towel. I stared at her bare back, her shoulder blades working under her skin as she slipped on a bra. The slightest curve of a breast appeared when she turned, then the bra pulled tight and she was all jutting elbows, her fingers reaching and feeling to hook the fasteners into place.

Back on the TV, Imogen-in-red-and-gold appeared in the background of a shot of her bridesmaids dancing, holding a champagne flute, leaning against the bar and talking to someone whose name I don't remember, one of her cousins, I think. Her hand swept out in front of her as she spoke, a big gesture, as if describing a landscape, or a flat sea, or maybe a clear view or the whole of something. Truth is, I have no idea. It's my wedding day and both of us are right there in the building, laughing and speaking and being together, but—

'Sorry. I'm not having a go at you,' I said into the silence. 'I just – I didn't mean it to come out like that. I just miss you.'

'I feel really bad—'

I fought back the urge to say *so come home then*. 'Don't feel bad.'

'The worst part is, a lot of the time I don't actually feel – I'm just getting on with it here, you know, so I don't always. I mean, I do, but—'

'Yeah.'

'And then that makes me feel even worse.'

'I don't want you to feel bad. It's just hard. We knew it would be hard—'

'You know I love you, but if I'm going to be here, doing this, I need to be here.'

'I know.'

'Like, in-my-head here. Or else, it's. Just.'

'I know.'

'I feel fucking awful now.'

'Don't,' I said again, but I couldn't quite give it the weight it needed.

Neither of us spoke for a while. On the computer screen, Imogen walked back into shot carrying the big, chunky satellite phone.

Look, I thought. *That woman's about to call her husband because she cares, and she's worried about how his day went. Be nice to her because you love her, and because she's a good person doing her best, and because she's a very, very long way away.*

'Come on, don't feel awful,' I said, finding a decent chunk of conviction. 'I don't want you to, and you don't need to, honestly.'

'Thanks.'

'Honestly.'

'Thanks. I still do though.'

Imogen-from-the-shower dialled and waited for an answer. I saw her smile and mouth the words *Hello, Euston*.

'Would you maybe say that mighty dread seized your troubled mind?'

Imogen laughed. 'It actually has.'

'Don't let it. Say *fuck off mighty dread*.'

'What *is* that though? It's just like, I wonder if some older version of the story is showing through, like with the Brothers Grimm, where original versions are darker and scarier and it shows through a bit. I'm talking about the angel and the shepherds again now.'

'Yep. I caught up.'

'Sorry.'

Some little memory bubble broke free from the sludge of years then; it rose up and popped on the surface of my conscious mind.

'I think that – only the lowest ranks of angels looked like people with wings,' I said.

'Ranks? There are ranks?'

'Yeah. I can't remember it properly, but there are all these different levels of angel, nine or twelve, I think, and only the bottom few look like how you'd imagine an actual angel to look.'

'What do the others look like?'

'I can't remember, but really weird. Scary. Lots of arms and heads and wings and hundreds of eyes, I think.'

'Yeah?'

'Yeah, they get weirder and weirder the higher up you go too. The highest ones are really strange. Geometric shapes, abstract forms within other abstract forms that don't make much sense. It's all very unsettling.'

'*Fear not said he for mighty dread had seized their troubled minds.*'

'Yeah, maybe that's why. If it was one of the important ones—'

'If a giant, hundred-eyed triangle descended from the sky—'

'Those shepherds would be rightfully fucking terrified,' I said.

'That *is* unsettling.'

'I know. If we're talking about the old versions wearing through, the original nativity probably looked like a H.P. Lovecraft.'

Imogen laughed. 'Isn't a kid in the *Love Actually* nativity dressed up as an octopus?'

'You see?' I said. 'It's all right there.'

A guy appeared in-frame, holding a couple of bottles of beer. Imogen looked up and mouthed *just a minute*.

He nodded, grinned, and was gone.

'Do you need to go?' I asked.

'What?'

'A guy with beers just came to get you?'

'Oh, shit. It's been that long already? We're all supposed to be having a few drinks and going over the – it doesn't matter, but I should probably—'

'Yeah, of course. Don't miss it.'

'No.'

'Go on,' I said. 'Drink beer.'

'All right. I'll call you soon.'

'Okay, I love you.'

'Love you too.'

'Have fun, and don't worry.'

'Okay. Bye.'

'Bye.'

'Bye.'

'Bye.'

The line cut to a flat buzz.

Imogen-on-the-screen continued her conversation into the phone, but she looked stiff now, on edge. The guy on the screen was Johnny. *Fucking Johnny.* I tried not to let his stupid, over-familiar grin bother me, telling myself that the fact he'd been holding exactly two bottles of beer – not one, not four, not six – meant absolutely nothing at all.

o

I wandered through to the kitchen and was momentarily surprised – for the third time that night – by how clean and tidy it was. I filled up the kettle, trying not to look at the still-unopened stack of red bills piled up on the worktop, then clicked it on and started digging through the cupboard for coffee.

Here's something important. No matter how messy this room gets, and no matter how thoroughly I tidy it when I can't take it any more, there's an object on the kitchen worktop that never, ever moves – not even a millimetre.

It's a mug with 'I ♥ tea' printed on the side.

Imogen's mug.

She placed it very carefully on that spot, just in front of the kettle, almost six months ago, on the morning that she left.

'I'm putting this here,' she said. 'Don't move it.'

I must have looked confused.

'Don't move it,' she said, 'and then when you make a drink in the morning, it'll be like I'm here too.'

I kissed her.

'No, look. Look,' she said, pulling away and trying to make me pay attention, 'there's a teabag in here and everything. I've set it up now, so that when I come home, I'll be able to walk in through the front door and drink it. This is a cup of tea with my name on it,' she said. 'Remember that, okay?'

We wrapped our arms around each other and stayed like that for a long time.

'Love you,' she said, into my shoulder.

'Love you too. How long d'you reckon until I pour water in and fuck it all up?'

'Ha. Three days.'

Very carefully, I placed my 'I ♥ coffee' next to the dusty 'I ♥ tea'.

As always, I made sure not to so much as tap Imogen's mug. Nothing and no one had touched 'I ♥ tea' since my wife put it there. She touched it last, and it felt important that she would be the one to touch it next, when she came home.

A cup of tea with my name on it.

I made myself a drink.

For the hundred and sixty-eighth consecutive day, I did not fuck it all up.

o

An hour later, around half past one in the morning, I was sitting at my computer, staring at a mostly blank script document titled CAPTAIN SCARLETT as our wedding video – now on its third loop of the night – played on the TV in the corner.

Imogen-in-red-and-gold was partway through a toast.

'I *have* read parts of the second one,' she said. I didn't look away from the blinking cursor onscreen; I didn't need to. I'd seen the video so many times that I could picture the scene perfectly. Imogen standing at our top table, nervously pinching at the stem of her champagne flute as she stood in front of the quiet, listening room. She'd just paused to glance down and smile at me, sitting there in my tuxedo. Imogen-in-red-and-gold looked happy, nervous, excited, a little drunk and very, very *proud.*

'I have read parts of the second one, and all I'm going to say is' – she spoke directly to me now – 'we'll remember you all when my *husband* . . .' – cheers from the guests – 'has won the Booker Prize and we're horribly rich and living in a great big castle.'

I picked up my mug and swallowed a mouthful of lukewarm coffee.

Brilliant, brilliant Imogen. I thought again about how her own project, conceived some four years after we were married, was utterly inspired, and how her determination to make it happen – to have a thought and push against the world until she made it real – filled me with awe, and pride. It filled me with something else too. Something that felt like cold rain on fields, like a river running underground, like a long, empty train track.

Brilliant people have to go and do what brilliant people have to go and do.

On screen, the cursor blinked in and out of existence:

Tick-tock.

Tick-tock.

Tick-tock.

Once, the two of us were bright and focused and hot. We were private and fierce and close-as-close-could-be. But a slow dispersal had been underway for a while, only an idiot wouldn't be able to see it. My Imogen was becoming the world's Imogen, spreading out, cooling, dividing up amongst all those viewer numbers written up on the Post-its above the desk. Once, Imogen was whole and here and everything, but now—

Now I'm losing her. I'm losing her and if I don't do something soon she'll be nothing but seven billion little pixels, blinking off and on, off and on – a sky of electric stardust and never solid and real and coming home again.

The cursor streaked and wavered, but it wasn't until the first drops tapped onto my desk that I realised I was crying.

I stood up, walked into the kitchen.

I looked at the stack of unopened red bills.

Back in the living room, Imogen and I were beginning our first dance.

'See the pyramids along the Nile,

Watch the sunset from a tropic isle . . .'

I began to rip open the letters.

Court, bailiffs. Bailiffs, bailiffs, fine, court. Foreclosure, proceedings, repossession.

Jesus.

Bailiffs, fine, fine, court, bailiffs.

Jesus, Jesus, Jesus.

Bailiffs, foreclosure, proceedings, repossession.

They were coming to take our things.

They were going to take everything away.

I stumbled back into the living room.

We were dancing now, holding tight to one another, Imogen's head pressed against my chest.

'See the market place in Old Algiers . . .'

I'm going to lose her.

Tears made our dancing bodies slide and blur into meaningless, streaking colours.

'Send me photographs and souvenirs . . .'

I felt empty, and utterly powerless as the world unravelled.

And then—

They came to me.

They came suddenly.

They came with the *tap-tap-tap* of urgent wing beats and the bumping thump of fat furry bodies in the dark, they came fluttering up and out from the back of my mind. *Now, now, now, now. Time, time, time.* Up they came and they wouldn't hear no, those old memories. Sensing a chance for freedom, they came flapping and battering into the light.

For the thousandth time, I remembered Andrew Black raging about his publishers in the doorway of my flat after that career-ending meeting. For the thousandth time, I remembered Andrew throwing the glass of vodka I'd given him against the wall, the drips running down the wallpaper, glass shards in the doormat.

I picked up the phone and dialled.

For the thousandth time, I remembered Andrew thrusting his satchel towards me, and me catching a brief glimpse of what he had inside.

Bur-burr, bur-burr. The phone rang and rang.

Finally, after a long time, someone answered—

'Hello?'

'Sophie,' I said, 'there's another book.'

'What?'

'It's Tom. There's another Andrew Black book.'

Silence.

'Sophie?'

'Are you sure?' she said.

'I've seen it.'

Me catching a brief glimpse of what he had inside – the thick block of white manuscript pages. Black's name and the title of the novel on the front sheet: ***Maxwell's Demon****.*

'You've seen it?'

'Yes.'

On the TV, Imogen looked drunk, unsteady; she grabbed a chair to keep herself upright.

I took a breath. 'Would there be . . . Could you get me some sort of finder's fee on it?'

The line was quiet for a few seconds.

'Let me see what I can do.'

o

The weak dawn light, watery as skimmed milk, had begun to seep in around the edges of the living-room blind when a clattering sound from the kitchen woke me up.

I jumped up from the sofa, putting one foot on a small pottery wise man as I did – *agh fuck* – then went hopping and staggering out into the hallway to investigate.

One of the magnetic letters had fallen off the fridge door, scattering its paper load of takeaway fliers and appointments notes all over the tiles. I gathered up the various menus and finally found the fallen letter under the kitchen table – it was a little green plastic 'i'. I tried to reattach everything, but there wasn't enough magnetic grip from the small 'i' to hold it all in place. With an exhausted sigh, I put the scruffy stack of menus on the edge of the worktop, and put the little letter back onto the fridge door where it belonged. It dropped lifelessly to the floor. I picked it up, brushed it against my T-shirt and tried again, but the exact same thing happened. For some reason, the magnet had completely lost its power.

When I came back through to the living room, I saw the beginnings of dawn leaking in around the blind and, despite being unbelievably tired, I lifted it up and stuck my head underneath, to get an early look at the new day.

That's when I saw him.

He was leaning against a wall at the far end of the street, the autumn leaves dancing and twirling all around him.

He seemed to sense me looking, and slowly turned his head in my direction.

I felt all the heat leave my body.

The man's features were lost in the bluish gloom of the early dawn and in the deep shadows of his broad-brimmed hat. As I watched, a tiny ember of bright orange flared in the depths of that dark place and, a moment later, a huge cloud of smoke billowed out from under the brim, churning and whirling away in the wind.

I stared, feeling him staring straight back at me.

The impossibility of it gnawed at my insides, fixing me to the spot.

I watched as a hand came up to touch the brim of that infamous burned white fedora. In a slow, tiny movement – a movement filled with concentration and malice – Maurice Umber tipped his hat towards me.

18

About Five Hours Later . . .

Bang bang bang bang bang.

The sound of someone hammering on the flat's front door woke me. *Jesus.* My head pounded. Sitting up on the sofa, I stared at the empty whisky bottle on the floor and worked my knuckles into my temples.

Bang bang bang bang bang.

'All right, all right. Jesus Christ.'

I found my jeans in a heap and dragged them on, then I scrabbled my fingers through my hair in front of the mantelpiece mirror.

I checked the time on my phone. 11.23 a.m.

On the computer screen, Imogen slept in the fuzzy green night vision of Dorm Cam Two. I hadn't seen her come to bed, even though I'd stayed up until—

I remembered the man at the end of the street.

Bang bang bang bang bang.

Jesus Christ.

By carefully lifting the very edge of the living-room blind, I was able to peer out at the person banging on the door. Well, at his back at least. I had no idea who the man was, but he wasn't wearing a Maurice Umber outfit and didn't look like a bailiff either – though I'd never actually met a bailiff and so I decided to err on the side of caution.

Bang bang bang bang bang bang bang—

'Yes?' I called through the letterbox, behind the door, on my hands and knees.

A second's pause and then a pair of blue eyes came down to my level, peering in at me.

'What are you doing down there?' said the eyes.

'I'm looking at you,' I said.

'I see.'

'And – I'm wondering who you are.'

'I'm here with a business opportunity,' said the eyes.

'I don't think I'm interested in a business opportunity.'

'Oh, you definitely are,' said the eyes.

'What makes you think so?'

'Mostly, because it was your idea.'

'What?'

'I believe there was some question about a finder's fee?'

Ohhhhhh.

'*Maxwell's Demon*.'

'Beg pardon?'

'Sorry. The second Andrew Black novel.'

The eyes winced and looked quickly from left to right. 'It would be really great if you could open the door now, Mr Quinn.'

I opened the door.

The man on the doorstep stood around five-ten, five-eleven, with a trim, sporty build. He had a strong nose and narrow face topped off with dirty blond hair artfully cropped short and pushed around in a playful, messy style. At maybe thirty-eight or thirty-nine the hair seemed a bit young for him, but a broad, boyish grin and something I want to call *his general bounciness* helped him get away with it. The clothes he wore – understated white trainers, dark blue jeans, a light blue shirt and a simple, charcoal grey jacket – were all the sort of expensive that doesn't want to draw too much attention to itself, or advertise the wearer as a *gentleman of means*.

'Mike Chesapeake,' the man said, thrusting out a very straight hand for me to shake.

'Thomas Quinn,' I said, shaking it.

The hand felt very cold.

'Excellent,' said Mike Chesapeake.

I led him into the living room and quickly started gathering up blankets, plates and nativity figurines, all too conscious that the room smelled like a grown man had been living and sleeping in it for the last twelve hours. I crossed to the window, rolled up the blind, unlocked the sash and pushed it wide open. Light and cold air flooded in.

'My goodness, you're the spit of your father, aren't you?' Chesapeake said.

'So they tell me.'

'How is he? Heard from him lately?'

I stopped what I was doing, turned around to stare.

Chesapeake looked back with a polite and curious expression, though perhaps I detected the faintest trace of a smile haunting the corners of his mouth.

'He's dead,' I said. 'He's been dead for seven years.'

Chesapeake's eyebrows shot up his forehead.

'Oh good God. So he has, of course he has. What a terrible thing to say. How are you going to forgive me?' He held out his hand again. 'I mean, seriously. Please do forgive me. I'm an out-and-out idiot.'

'These things happen.' I shook the hand with controlled enthusiasm. 'What sort of book publisher doesn't know that Stanley Quinn is dead?'

'Oh, only a very bad one, I would've thought.'

'But – okay.' This stumped me. 'Sorry, I thought – I *assumed* that you're here from—'

'Oh, for our purposes, yes. I most certainly am. I'm not down in the trenches with the literary geniuses though, I'm more—'

‘Up?’

This time, there was definitely a small smile.

‘The parent company,’ he nodded, allowing the smile to blossom in a way that was mostly graceful and only a little bit smug. ‘I can provide identification if that helps?’

‘It’s okay,’ I said. ‘Just tell me about—’

Chesapeake held up a long white finger.

‘Might I check your apartment for bugs before we speak openly?’

‘Bugs?’

‘I know. It’s ridiculous. There are never bugs. But’ – he rolled his eyes – ‘company policy. If you’ll humour me? It won’t take long.’

o

I made us both a drink in the kitchen while Mike Chesapeake wandered around the flat with something that looked like a selfie stick attached to a squealing Geiger counter for ten minutes.

When he’d finished, he called out from the living room.

I went through, carrying the drinks.

‘Clean as a whistle,’ he said when he saw me. ‘They always are. It’s a bloody stupid rule. I’m sorry I have to do it.’ Mike Chesapeake sat in the middle of the sofa, with something that looked like an old, bulky laptop balanced on his knee.

‘What’s that?’

‘Mr Quinn,’ he said, ignoring the question. ‘We have a proposition for you.’

‘Oh yeah?’ I said, putting the mugs down on the coffee table and taking a seat in the armchair.

‘You know that Andrew doesn’t like us, don’t you? His publishers, I mean.’

'I did get that impression.'

'Do you know why?'

'I think so.'

Mike Chesapeake weighed up my reaction.

'You do know he signed a contract with us? That he made certain commitments?'

I didn't say anything.

'Anyway,' Chesapeake said. 'How much do you know about what happened afterward? Once he took himself off and – disappeared into the ether?'

'Not very much.'

'Thought not.' Chesapeake drummed on the top of the old laptop with obvious pleasure. 'Would you like me to tell you about it . . . ?'

o

According to Mike Chesapeake, Black had taken the money he'd already made from *Cupid's Engine* – which must have been a considerable amount – and opened his own small press in a tiny seaside town on the East Yorkshire coast. Perhaps him taking matters into his own hands like that shouldn't have been so surprising, given his spiralling frustrations with traditional publishing and the way the industry seemed to be headed, but what might surprise you is the fact that Black didn't use his brand new publishing house to release more Max Cleaver mysteries – by which I mean sequels to *Cupid's Engine* – and the reason he didn't do that was very simple: it was because he couldn't.

Black had signed an extremely complicated and lucrative contract with his publishers six months earlier, a dream contract, a set-for-life contract, but a contract with one major downside. In exchange for the guarantee of princely advances against any and all future output, Andrew Black signed over exclusive rights to all of his past and future work. This meant that nobody but Black's publishers could legally print old or new adventures featuring Maxwell Cleaver, Dan Wayburn, Maurice Umber and the rest. In fact, nobody but Black's publishers could print a single word of Black's writing on any subject whatsoever. In the days following the bust-up, Sophie Almonds tried to help Black buy himself out of the contract, but the break-up had been a bitter one. The publishers refused to cut him loose at any price, and because Andrew Black was Andrew Black – a man immune to compromise and wholly without a reverse gear – this effectively amounted to a lifelong gagging order. Black would never work with his old publishers again, and he couldn't legally work with anyone else either, and so, as a result, the world would never see a new story, sentence, or even a solitary word from the imagination of Andrew Black. Not one. Not ever. Black's life as a writer was over.

What was this titanic, career-ending bust-up about, you might ask?

It was about ebooks.

As far as Black was concerned, a book needed paper, it needed ink, and it needed pages, real, physical pages that were fixed, ordered, and complete in and of themselves. A book also needed covers to separate everything inside – the book – from everything outside – the not-book – a barrier, a line, a bell jar, I suppose, to protect and preserve the intricacies of the work within. Andrew hated computers, tablets, mobile phones, any phones, but he *really hated* digital editions, electronic text, ebooks, he hated them – yes – obsessively. Andrew's publishers on the other hand, they, well – most of them hated ebooks too, Chesapeake had admitted in a conspiratorial whisper – but back then, the industry was in something of a panic over digital media. They saw the red-inked sales charts and the shifting figures, they saw year-by-year forecasts, predictions of catastrophically declining print and swiftly rising ebook sales, they worried endlessly about pirates, blanket digitisation of texts and whatever else Google and Amazon might secretly be cooking up, and they spent a lot of time talking frantically about 'getting out of the dead tree business'.

'Of course, it all turned out fine, more or less,' Mike Chesapeake said. 'The sky didn't fall in, and people still spend money on their Dan Browns and Andrew Blacks.'

But nobody knew that at the time. At the time, Andrew Black's publishers feared for their very existence, and were fanatically focused on getting *Cupid's Engine* onto as many Kindles, iPads and other devices as humanly possible, to help survive the fast-approaching future.

A meeting was set. Black listened, looked at the charts, heard the dire predictions on the death of paper, and when the marketing assistant's e-reader was passed over to him, he carefully held it between finger and thumb and dropped it into the litter bin like a dead rat. Black said *no*. Things deteriorated. Black's publisher said *we don't legally need you to say yes*. Black said he'd never write them another fucking word, whether they had sales lined up for his next novel in thirty-six languages or not. And since any word he wrote for the rest of his life technically belonged to them, he said that he wouldn't write so much as a shopping list again until the day he died. And that was that. The publisher released a digital edition of *Cupid's Engine* six days later. Until I'd made that call to Sophie in the middle of the night, pretty much everyone – including Black's publishers – believed there would never be another novel. Now, of course, they knew differently. A sequel to one of the bestselling books since the Second World War actually existed, it legally belonged to them – and they wanted it.

'Our publishing arm publishes books, Mr Quinn, lots and lots of books. That's what it's there for.'

‘That and making money.’

‘Well, yes, obviously. I thought that part went without saying.’ Mike Chesapeake considered for a moment, he smiled. ‘Although—’

He left the word hanging, a clear note of *oh dear* trailing in the air behind it.

‘Although what?’

Andrew Black’s small press also published books, Chesapeake explained, truly beautiful books. Only, Black being Black, he became disillusioned and dissatisfied with even the highest quality products his various suppliers could deliver. This is why Andrew Black started to make his own paper. This is why Andrew Black made his own ink. This is why Andrew Black bought his own printing press, and when that didn’t measure up, this is why Andrew Black built his own by hand. This is how Andrew Black became a maker of things, a creator of some of the most beautiful books available to modern book-buyers. This is how Andrew Black made himself practically bankrupt.

‘Bankrupt?’ I said. ‘How can he be bankrupt?’

‘I said practically bankrupt.’

‘Answer the question.’

‘He signed a contract,’ Chesapeake said for the second time, as if that explained everything.

I thought about it, and came up with nothing.

Chesapeake sighed. ‘If one fails to live up to one’s contractual obligations, there may be certain penalties.’

‘You took his royalties away.’

‘There is an ongoing fine in place.’

I shook my head.

‘We are not the bad guys here, Mr Quinn.’

‘Oh, I think you probably are.’

Chesapeake considered. 'I'm going to tell you something now,' he said. 'I wasn't planning to, because it's something we try to keep out of the official story as much as possible.' He thought. 'It plays extremely badly with the investors. But anyway, this is what happened.'

'Okay.'

'Mr Black was very unhappy about the idea of a digital *Cupid's Engine*.'

'Yes.'

'So we pulled it.'

'What?'

'The board pulled it. *Okay,* we said, *if it means that much to you, Mr Black, we won't do any non-paper editions of your work. No electronic. No audio. We'll take that hit so you can be happy*.'

'What happened?'

Chesapeake folded his arms and leaned forward on the old laptop.

'I can tell you this part for certain, because I was there.'

'So what happened?'

'Black demanded that we pull *all* our digital books. Not just his – but every single one.'

I stared at Mike Chesapeake.

'And if we didn't . . .' He drew a thumb across his neck.

'Did he say why?'

'As a matter of fact, yes, he did. He said it was *to prevent the apocalypse*.'

I heard Sophie's words from the day before:

Is this about his thing? His whole entropy, end of the world, thing?

'Mr Quinn?'

'Right,' I said.

'Mr Quinn. This thing on my knee here isn't really a laptop. Andrew Black needs you to save him from himself and the world needs you to save that manuscript. I suppose you know that Kafka wanted all his work burned after his death? In cases like this, good people have to act. You'd be doing an immeasurable service to literature. And for the service you'd be doing us, we'd be prepared to offer you a fee of five hundred thousand pounds.'

19
And a Monster Made of Eyes

'*Option one*. He said that?'

'Yes, he did,' Sophie replied.

I swapped the phone to my other hand. 'So what's his option two?'

'I don't know.' Sophie thought about it. 'I had no idea that he'd show up at your home like that, Tom. I may have mentioned to him that I thought it was unprofessional.'

As I wandered into the small train station bookshop, I found myself in the strange position of feeling sorry for Mike Chesapeake.

'But it definitely checks out?'

'It does. They weren't happy with us taking two days to make sure, but yes. The contract is solid, all signed and submitted.'

Five hundred thousand pounds.

I found *Cupid's Engine* on the bookshelf, then pulled out a copy of *The Da Vinci Code*, which happened to be a few books further along.

'He wanted me to set off there and then.'

'Thankfully they rarely come out of the woodwork, these nasty little executives.'

'Sophie?'

'Yes?'

'I don't know if it's right.'

'No,' she said, after a moment. I waited for more, but nothing else came.

I posted *The Da Vinci Code* over the top of the other books, hearing the solid *thunk* as it landed in the dark space behind them.

'You do have a walk-away clause, remember.'

I shuffled the book along the shelf, using the gap left by *The Da Vinci Code* to create an empty space next to *Cupid's Engine*.

'I'm—' Sophie began, but then she stopped.

'Sophie?'

'I don't know if it's right either,' she said, 'but I definitely don't think it's *wise*. You're bringing him back into both of our lives. You've thought about that, I suppose?'

'Five hundred thousand pounds,' I said. 'And another book.'

'A book that he doesn't want anyone else to have.'

I stood back from the shelf, looking at my work.

'I know,' I said. 'I know.'

What else could I say?

'Why do you think he showed it to you?' Sophie asked after a moment. 'The manuscript, I mean?'

I thought about it then, realising with a creeping little panic that I hadn't asked myself the question before. 'He was angry,' I said, after a few seconds.

'He was so angry that he showed you that he'd written a second, secret manuscript?'

'I think—'

'All I'm saying is, let me worry about Mike Chesapeake. I'd like you to keep both of your eyes on Andrew Black.'

'All right,' I said. 'Deal.' Shouldering my bag, I made my way out of the little bookshop and out into the hustle and bustle of King's Cross Station. 'I'll report back when I can. Keep me posted on developments?'

'Of course I will. You do the same.'

'I will do.'

'Okay.'

'All right, talk soon.' I ended the call and made my way towards Platform 5, where the 09.48 First Hull Trains service to Hull had already begun to board.

o

When all you want is to sit quietly, the universe tends to notice and take it as a personal challenge. I walked through carriages full of arguing siblings, football fans, a hen party and a group of salesmen shouting into their phones, before dropping down at a table seat opposite a guy with ginger hair and thick mutton-chop sideburns, who was intently studying a huge pile of pages in a big, green A4 binder. I chose the seat because the guy looked like he wanted to be quiet and focus, but I guessed he must've been studying for a medical exam because we'd barely left the station before he started mumbling away, trying to memorise tongue-twisting medical terminology without looking at his page.

'Hippocampus, thalamus, paleomammalian cortex, hippocampus, thalamus, paleomammalian cortex . . .'

He recited these phrases like incantations, mumbling each one under his breath over and over again, all the while tugging on his long ginger whiskers and screwing up his eyes in concentration.

I lasted for the best part of an hour before I had to change seats. The student looked up at me as I pulled my bag down from the overhead rack. I pretended to be getting off at the next stop, gave him a nod, then moved into the next carriage along.

Finally, I found something that looked a little bit like peace – a window seat in a quiet spot near the train's front end.

I settled in as we pulled into Grantham. I watched the few dozen passengers disembarking, all pulling their coats tight and hurrying off, heads down, dashing away across the blustery platform. One of the billboards near the exit advertised a deluxe anniversary edition of Dan Brown's *Angels and Demons.* The blown-up book cover on the poster carried an image from the film adaptation. You probably remember it – it's a statue. On the right side, it's a beautiful, traditional angel, all long hair, gentle features and cut-glass cheekbones, while on the left, those features have warped into the grotesque mask of a leering demon, complete with a long, curving horn sprouting from its forehead.

Dexter and sinister, I thought, wriggling the fingers on one hand and then the other as I shuffled down deep into my chair. When nobody from Grantham came to sit on the seat next to mine, I screwed up my coat and pressed it up against the window. Resting my tired head against it, I quickly fell asleep.

o

I dreamt, and in the dream, I woke up on the sofa at home.

Andrew Black was in our flat, sitting cross-legged on the living-room floor, fiddling with the various nativity figures we'd inherited from Imogen's grandma.

'I'm sorry,' I said, but he didn't seem to hear me. 'Andrew. I'm sorry about all of it.'

No response.

As I watched, he turned the little pottery ox over in his hands, pressing on one small, specific location at the back of its neck. To my surprise, the animal's head came loose with a well-engineered *clunk*. Next, he took the angel, turned it around and clicked the ox head onto the back of the smiling, human one. Finally, he began to rotate the combined heads, which made the well-oiled ticking sound of a bank vault's safe as they turned, until the ox's head pointed forwards.

As soon as it did, the angel's wings separated as if spring-loaded, and two additional pairs sprang out, clicking into place both higher and lower than the originals.

'You never asked – what does it do?' Andrew said, holding up this six-winged, ox-headed angel. 'What's it for? What does it drive?'

Oh my God.

I jumped awake, sitting bolt upright with a gasp and rifling through my pockets for my phone almost before I knew where I was. I practically hummed with off-kilter certainty, that irrational sense of knowing – and needing to act on that knowing – that can occasionally spring fully-formed from a dream. I yanked out my phone and tapped open the browser.

Why an ox and an angel in Bethlehem?

What if the ox isn't an ox at all?

Ranks of angel. Search.

As it turned out, there were nine.

The most detailed article I could find ran through them from lowest to highest – from the two-winged human-looking angels on the bottom rung of the ladder, to the identical but superior archangels, one place above them, then up through 'Thrones' and 'Powers' and 'Principalities', to the second-highest rank, the cherubim.

Now, when you hear the word 'cherub' you probably imagine one of those little fat babies with wings, but let me tell you – that isn't a cherub. That's a *putti*, an adorable, chubby creature from Renaissance art that's somehow found itself confused with the real deal over the past few hundred years. No, true cherubim are something else entirely. I scrolled down through the description – terrifying creatures covered in eyes, with four wings and four faces: the face of a man, the face of a lion, the face of an eagle . . . and the face of an ox.

Gotcha, I thought.

Fear not, said he, for mighty dread had seized their troubled minds.

Dream-fuelled and fierce, I forced myself to take a moment – to map waking logic over my sleeping certainties: why *an ox and an angel in Bethlehem?* Could the question really be driving at the fact that we include a separate ox and angel in modern nativities, when really, we shouldn't . . . because they're actually the same character? If we entertain that crazy-seeming possibility for a moment, then the terror of the shepherds seems perfectly rational – it makes little sense when we picture a handsome, benevolent angel descending from heaven, but it makes all the sense in the world if the earlier versions of the story – or even the earlier readers' understanding of it – featured a four-winged man-, lion-, eagle- and ox-faced cherub in the role. *Could the ox and angel really be one and the same?* It's not nearly as out there as it sounds – the ancient Minoans were obsessed with the holy bull, and the Egyptians too, and then there's the sacrificial calf, the Hindu holy cow, and the golden bull the Israelites turned to when Moses was up the mountain—

My God, I thought, opening search window after search window, *what if there's actually something here?*

Okay. So here's the surprising thing.

I think I actually solved this one.

Why an ox and an angel in Bethlehem? I think I found an answer. I mean, I don't claim to be an expert and it's possible I got something wrong along the way, but I don't think so, I really don't. Nevertheless, I'd encourage you to jump online and spend a little time checking my findings for yourself. I suspect that when you hear what I've got to say you'll probably want to do just that.

All right then. Here we go . . .

What if our ox-faced cherub has another name: a secret, true name that – once we learn it – allows us to see something quite remarkable, something that's been right in front of us from the very beginning?

I spent a long time googling cherubim and following my searches down some very dense and strange pathways.

Here's what I found:

In Genesis, cherubim are guardians of the tree of life in the Garden of Eden, and appear in the strange, unsettling visions of Ezekiel, who refers to them both as 'cherubim' and '*hayyoth*' (Hebrew, 'living creatures'). They also appear in Revelation – the apocalyptic, final book of the Bible – as part of the prophet John's own world-ending vision:

> *Around the throne, on each side of the throne are four living creatures full of eyes in front and behind: the first creature like a lion, the second creature like an ox, the third living creature with the face of a man, and the fourth living creature like a flying eagle* (Revelation 4:6–7)

Again *living creature(s)* – it's very specific. John uses the Greek *zoa*, which corresponds exactly to the Hebrew *hayyoth*, and although *hayyoth* may be mistaken for a simple descriptive term, it's actually much closer to a name in this context – so much so that several writers have chosen to clarify the point with capital letters. ♠ All of which is to say, '*hayyoth*' and 'cherubim' can be taken as interchangeable names for our purposes.

Now, not nearly enough has been written about the Book of Words and the Book of Works, about true names, or about the old belief that the physical universe can be affected, changed or reshaped by the use of words. Because the fact is, the more you look for this sort of thing in holy texts, and in ancient and mystical writings, the more examples

♠ As Borges does in *The Book of Imaginary Beings*, referring to 'the *Hayyoth*' and 'Living Beings' in every instance.

of it you start to see. Psalm 33 couldn't be more clear, for example: *'By the word of God were the heavens made'* (Ps. 33:6). R. Judah bar Ezekiel, a Talmudic sage, states that the Biblical architect Bezalel succeeded in building the Tabernacle because he *'knew how to combine the letters by which the heavens and earth were created'.* The secret knowledge of the manipulation of these letters might be gleaned from ancient, mystical/philosophical texts such as the foundational *Sefer Yetzirah* ('Book of Creation'), and according to the Babylonian Talmud, *'R. Hanina and R. Oshaia spent every Sabbath eve in studying the "Book of Creation", by means of which they created a third grown calf and ate it.'* So if God (and one or two cheeky wise men) could use words to bring about Creation, and if God used letters to build everything there is, what did God need to create first? Well, the *Sefer Yetzirah* gives us the answer very clearly: *'Twenty-two letters: he drew them, hewed them, combined them, weighed them, interchanged them, and through them produced the whole creation and everything that is destined to come into being.'* According to the *Tanna debe Eliyahu* however, it was the cherubim that were the first objects created in the universe.

Here's a question: what if these two claims don't actually contradict each other?

Another interesting aspect of this creation-through-letters is how the letters themselves tend to behave in these stories. According to one version of the text, when Moses brought the Ten Commandments down from Mount Sinai, the letters engraved into the tablets saw the golden calf and flew back to heaven, abandoning the heavy tablets and causing them to fall and break. Likewise, when the Romans wrapped Rabbi Ḥananiah ben Teradyon in the Scroll of the Law and set him on fire, he declared, *'the parchment is burning but the letters are soaring on high'*, and after this passage from Genesis – *'God also said to Abraham, "As for Sarai your wife, you are no longer to call her Sarai; her name will be Sarah*'" (Gen. 17–15) – we get this midrashic continuation of the story: '*the* yod *[letter i] which the Lord took from Sarai soared aloft before God and protested: "Sovereign of the Universe! Because I am the smallest of all the letters, Thou has withdrawn me from the name of that righteous woman!"*'

Soared aloft? Protested? What sort of letters behave like this?

Another question – who and what are the heavenly host – the seraphim, the powers, the thrones – all those strange celestial ranks with their great wheels, multiple animal heads, wings covered in eyes? God made his great choirs of heaven but what are they *for*? What do they do?

The *Sefer Yetzirah* presents '*thirty-two mysterious ways of wisdom*', these being the twenty-two letters of the Hebrew alphabet and the ten *sefiroth* (numbers). Though dense, elusive and very mysterious, these characters are illustrated at one key point in the text with a single, all-important word – *hayyoth*. Which is to say, cherubim, which is to say – angels.

Do you know what 'angel' means? It means 'messenger'. That is, transmitter of a message. That is, the exact same task the words and letters your eyes are passing over right now are performing for you. This is why the higher ranks of angels are so otherworldly and strange-looking. The ancient texts describe them as creatures made of multiple wheels, eyes, arms, wings, animal faces. Take a look back along the various letters in the words on this page, and see if you can figure out why that might be. Maybe that'll be enough for you to see it, but if you can't, remember that the ancient texts are very, well, ancient, and that writing often looked quite different back then:

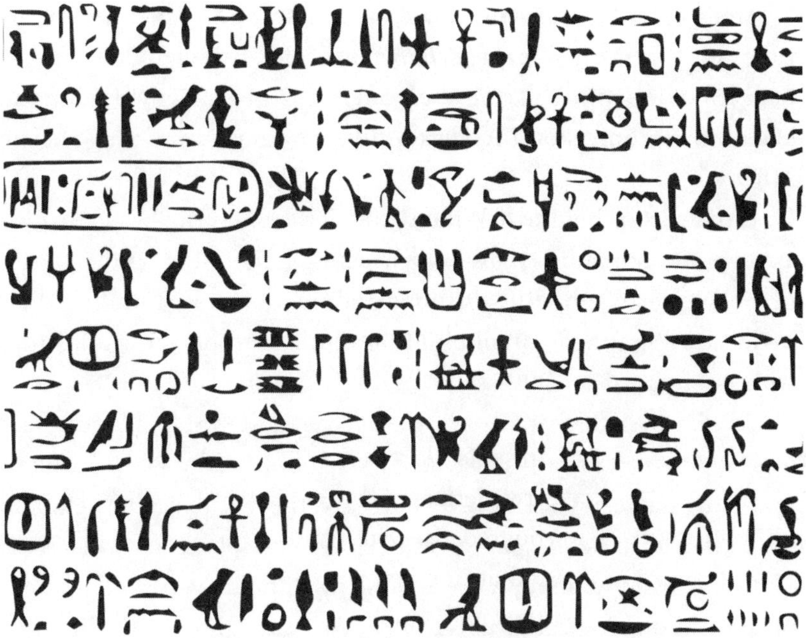

A chaos of animal heads, wings, arms, hands, eyes and wheels within wheels.

So what if our ox-headed cherub at the nativity had another name – a true name that we've known all along, or at least for the last 17,000 years, since early man began to write it up on the walls of caves? What if, as the ages passed, we've called this cherub *aurochs*, then *alph*, then *alpha*, but its true name – which was also its fundamental self, of course, as all true names are – has remained recognisable to anyone who knows how to look for it throughout the millennia:

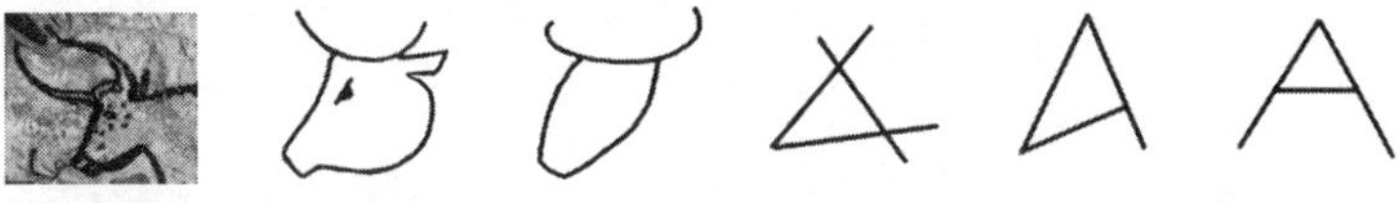

Magdalenian 17,000 BC | *Egyptian 3,000 BC* | *Sinai 1,850 BC* | *Phoenician aleph 1,200 BC* | *Greek alpha 600 BC* | *Roman 114 AD*

You've met this cherub before, of course; you've met him many times on every single page in this book. He's responsible for 8.137 per cent of the things you've seen and heard and imagined since you began to read my story. Andrew Black's mother called this cherub *Mighty A*.

If the theory holds, then the divine letters and the heavenly host are one and the same – *the angels are the letters* – singing the glories of God, transmitting the narrative and, by doing so, fulfilling their divine role as fundamental building blocks and bringing all things within it into existence.

So why 'in Bethlehem'? Well, 'bet' is a very old world for 'home', and was represented in early writings by a symbol that looked a lot like a house (or stable, if you like). That symbol, the 'bet', became 'beta' and 'B'. So the '*ox in Bethlehem*', gives us not only Alpha, but Alpha Bet.

Can you see them now, the angels? It's difficult, you need to focus on several ontological levels at once, you need to treat reading like some optical-cognitive magic eye picture, and understand that – as with Shipman's flag manifold – a fully rounded comprehension isn't actually possible. You can't bring the focus together; you can only conceptually understand that this focus is possible. But do that, and you'll see them, even if it appears you're seeing double. These angel-letters are quietly manifest at the heart of the nativity story, physical presences, subtly acknowledged amongst the shepherds and the wise men come to witness the birth of Jesus Christ, even as they're simultaneously singing the Good News of it across the page, bringing it to life in all their celestial chaos of wheels, arms, eyes, mouths, wings, swords, human and animal heads.

Fear not, said he, for mighty dread has seized their troubled minds.

o

Utterly absorbed, I didn't take my eyes off my phone until the train pulled in at Doncaster Station. As my carriage came to a slow stop, I clicked the screen black and stared out of the window with a vague bewilderment, managing the waves and troughs of travel sickness as I blinked my way back into the here and now.

Absentmindedly, I let my eyes wander over the crowded platform. All those people out there, all huddled and bundled down against the wind and the weather, every one sheltering and waiting for the moment when the digital LED listing for their train – that true name collection of letters and numbers – would move to the top of the Departures Board and summon a set of physical, squealing carriages to the boarding area of Platform Three, Six, Eight or Five.

And the LORD said, 'Let there be an 11.28 Hull Trains service to Hull' . . .

A couple of hoardings here also carried the *Angels and Demons* poster. My tired eyes settled themselves again on the split-faced statue as a line of new passengers, reflected and transparent in the rain-streaked glass, shuffled down the aisle behind me, cold radiating from their thick coats and bags as they went. I noticed something as I stared at the poster, something I'd always missed before, and in my vague state it took me a moment to realise what that something was. I sat up a little. The angel-demon was smiling. Both sides of its mouth held the exact same smile. Only a faint shadow on the angelic side to be sure, but most definitely there – a knowing, cunning, unifying sort of a smile. Rather than being a creature of two conflicting natures – good and evil, right and wrong, God and the Devil – the smile, once you spotted it, transformed the image into a more subtle and insidious suggestion of the concealed and revealed self.

In the back of my mind, I heard Sophie's voice: *the things he can do with words . . .*

I rubbed my eyes and sighed.

It's odd, isn't it, how something like that can snag in your mind like a thorn, and then subtly direct and inform all the things you notice, all the things that you see? I stared again at the poster, eyes fixed on that subtle, unbroken smile.

The things he can do with words, Sophie had said, and then, later, *is the world you live in every day made more from rocks and grass and trees, or from bank statements, articles, files and letters? Letters and words,* I thought, *always and again, letters and words.* I thought about all those open searches and documents waiting on my phone, about the divine letters who were also the heavenly host, the cherubim, the *Hayyoth*, Mighty A, Alph and Bet. *How can it not be an engine?* Andrew had said, the first day I met him. *You never asked what the engine did, what it was for,* said his letter. What does the engine do? I thought about Maxwell's demon sorting and dividing, creating something from nothing and seeming to reverse the arrow of time. I thought about God changing the letters in the names of his people, and about the *Yod*, angrily flying up in his face when he removed it from Sarah's name. I thought, *if knowledge is the hidden tightened spring that powers Maxwell's Demon, then what drives the creative acts of God?*

The split-faced angel stared out of Dan Brown's poster, giving nothing away.

As a last few stragglers found their seats, I thought about Andrew Black telling his publishers that digital text, ebooks of all things, would bring about the end of the world, and about that damnable weird, too-black sphere in the Polaroid he sent me – *Do you know what this is?* I thought about Black working for my father, my father's proud, parental quote on the cover of *Cupid's Engine*, and I thought again about the angel-demon's subtle smile.

But what did it mean? What did any of it mean? There were so many things to know, so many whirring, moving things. I had the sense of some vast mechanism that I couldn't quite grasp, of glimpsed cogs, ticks and tocks, gears that were really just shadows on the wall, huge, simplified shapes cast by some titanic, exotic manifold.

'How could it not be an engine?' *But what does it do? What is it for?*

'Of course it's a hook,' Sophie said, her steady blue eyes cutting into me.

Of course it's a hook.

I thought about Black's second letter then, the urgency in the writing, the palpable sense of fear. Naked emotion. *He needs me,* I'd decided, *he's frightened and he's pulling out all the stops, being as interesting as he can because he needs me.* But frightened of what?

Of course it's a hook.

Can nine words on a piece of paper make some normally level-headed person go chasing off to some place they've never even heard of?

And here I was, sitting on the train.

Of course it's a hook.

But frightened of what?

Why an ox and—

Or . . . I thought. *Or.* And I forced the whole careering brainstorm to a halt. *Or maybe, just maybe, you should actually take responsibility for some of what happens in your life.*

Because whatever else might or might not be true, Andrew Black wasn't responsible for Mike Chesapeake's visit and his offer, was he? I was. *I'd* called Sophie and Sophie had called his publishers. And it was them, them and their half a million pounds, that had finally put me on this train. Not Andrew Black. Because whatever Andrew knew, whatever put that tone of distress into his letter, whatever he feared and whatever he needed from me now, I was the one who'd sent myself on this little mission. I was the one who'd made the deal. I was the one who was going to steal his manuscript from him.

Whatever I might learn at the other end, this journey was entirely on me.

But anyway.

I picked up my phone again and was ready to go back to my search results as the train began to pull out of the station, but then – I saw a cloud of thick, blue-white smoke tumbling across the platform. Several travellers blinked with annoyance as it rolled over them, and a large woman in a knitted hat wafted a hand in front of her face theatrically, before turning to scowl upwind, her eyes searching the crowd before landing a disdainful stare on some fixed point at the platform's far end. I came forward quickly in my seat then as the train gathered speed, pushing my nose against the window, trying to look in the same direction as the woman and see what she saw, struggling as the angle between me and the platform grew ever more obtuse. And maybe, *perhaps*, I caught sight of what might've been a white hat down there, just for a moment, just for an instant, before the train pulled out of the station altogether and carried me off, off, off and away, like the literary arrow of time, travelling ever further into the east.

20
Signs and Wonders

It was a black and hooded head; and hanging there in the midst of so intense a calm, it seemed the Sphinx's in the desert. 'Speak thou vast and venerable head,' muttered Ahab, 'which though ungarnished with a beard, yet here and there lookest hoary with mosses; speak, mighty head, and tell us the secret thing that is in thee. Of all divers, though hast dived the deepest. That head upon which the upper sun now gleams, has moved amid this world's foundations. Where unrecorded names and navies rust, and untold hopes and anchors rot; where in her murderous hold this frigate earth is ballasted with bones of millions of the drowned; there in that awful water-land, there was thy most familiar home. Thou hast been where bell or diver never went; hast slept by many a sailor's side, where sleepless mothers would give their lives to lay them down. Thou sawst the locked lovers when leaping from their flaming ship; heart to heart they sank beneath the exulting wave; true to each other, when heaven seemed false to them. Thou saw'st the murdered mate when tossed by pirates from the midnight deck; for hours he fell into the deeper midnight of the insatiate maw; and his murderers still sailed on unharmed – while swift lightnings shivered the neighbouring ship that would have borne a righteous husband to outstretched, longing arms. O head! Thou hast seen enough to split the planets and make an infidel of Abraham, and not one syllable is thine!'

'Sail ho!' cried a triumphant voice from the main masthead.

'Aye? Well, now, that's cheering,' cried Ahab—

Buuzz.

I opened my eyes, lifted my phone, and hit the pause button on *Moby-Dick*. It'd been my comfort listen of choice for years by then, since a time before Audible and iPhones, from the earliest migration of unabridged audiobooks from their huge, expensive eighteen-CD boxes to the miraculous, tiny hard drives of MP3 players.

Jesus, how fast times change.

I closed down Audible, and when my home screen appeared, the little email icon had grown itself a bright red dot. *1 new message.*

I tapped it open.

> **BREAKING NEWS: Reclusive author Andrew Black missing after signs of a struggle.**

I stared. My peripheral vision dropped off and the rest of the world receded into a high-pitched, static whine. My heartbeat thumped in my ears. I could hear the dark whoosh of blood, the lightless, depthless currents of my interior.

I reached out a careful finger and scrolled down. The email came from the industry news website *Book Brief*, the body text containing little more than a repeat of the headline, and a link. I tapped, and it took me to a short news article on their website:

> *The reclusive author of the bestselling novel* Cupid's Engine *is said to be missing after vandalism to a property and 'signs of a struggle' were discovered by local police this morning. Black, who has successfully kept his identity a secret since his book's release, had retired from writing after a contractual dispute with his publisher. No further details are available at this time.*

Hands shaking, I unzipped my jacket pocket and took out the first envelope that had arrived from Andrew, turning it over to look at the address on the reverse. The train was still about twenty minutes out of Hull. I closed my browser, opened Google Maps and looked again at the route to the small, remote seaside town where Andrew Black was apparently living.

Or, *had been living*, I thought, *until this morning.*

There it was. Owthorne. A tiny dot of a place, perched on the very edge of the North Sea, and served by a single B road, on an otherwise white and empty square of map. I expanded the phone screen a few times, zooming out. Nothing new appeared, the map still showed only that single place, twenty more miles of lone, winding road, and the continuing jagged rip of coastline. Nothing else. The rest of my screen, the rest of the map, stayed completely white and unmarked.

The middle of nowhere.

I chewed on my nails and stared at my phone, wondering what the hell I was supposed to do now.

o

I jumped off the train in Hull and tried Sophie's number again. Through patchy reception on the train, I'd made it as far as her voicemail only twice in nine calls, and never as far as the beep. I'd thought about emailing, texting, but I was pretty shaken, and not entirely sure I should be putting anything in writing.

Sophie's phone went to voicemail again.

This time, the signal held.

Beeeep.

'Sophie. It's Tom. Call me back, please. It's urgent.'

I hung up. I thought about heading to the central police station in

Hull, but didn't want to do anything so extreme before I'd spoken to my agent. The article mentioned local police and, in my shaken state, I decided to head to Owthorne, and speak to the investigating officers there, if Sophie thought that was for the best. The long taxi ride would allow my agent plenty of time to call me back, I thought, or I could keep trying her, and we could come up with some sort of plan together before I arrived.

This was a mistake.

My phone reception dropped off altogether within minutes of my cab leaving the city. I rode on through miles and miles of wide flat fields under huge grey skies, cut off from everything, *untethered, unhooked.*

My phone wouldn't budge from *No Signal* for the hour's drive to Owthorne, and as the cab pulled up outside the little, squat police station building, the message refused to change.

I hung around for a few minutes outside, willing it to find a network. It didn't. What I should've done, what I could've done, was to walk into the police station and ask to use the phone there, or even better, find myself a pay phone, leave Sophie another message with the phone's number, and wait for her to call back. But, as I say, I was shaken, and worried about Black too. I could only stand around for so long. The worry, no, what I really mean is the guilt, was unbearable.

After five more minutes, I pocketed my phone and marched into the police station. I told the officer at the desk that I'd seen the news story, knew that Black had gone missing. I said I was a friend of his and that I wanted to help. Was I also going to tell them everything about Mike Chesapeake, about my deal and what I'd come here to do? Christ knows. Probably. But things never really got that far.

'Missing? What the hell do you mean, he's missing?'

This wasn't the response I was expecting.

'The article says he'd gone missing,' I told him, '*damage to a property* and *signs of a struggle*,' and as I said this, I pulled out my phone and tried to bring up the story, but with no signal, I got nothing but a white screen.

The officer slowly looked from me, to my phone, then back again.

'And what's your name, sir?'

'Thomas Quinn,' I said. 'What's yours?'

What's yours? Really?

Fucking hell.

The officer stared at me through narrow eyes.

'Sergeant Claybourn,' he said, and he reached for his desk phone.

I watched him dial, then wait for an answer.

Sergeant Claybourn was a heavy-set man with short, receding hair. He also had a yellow stain that was probably egg on the front of his shirt. I looked around the little station's reception area. Four plastic chairs. Fading posters about drink driving and rural crime on a mostly neglected noticeboard. A dusty clock on the wall behind the desk gave the right time, but the wrong date. It was the fourth, and the clock's little window to the right of its centre still housed a 3. I watched the red second hand sweep past it. *Tick-tick-tick . . .*

Then, Officer Claybourn spoke again, making me jump.

'Hello. I'm sorry to interrupt you, sir . . . It is yes, yes . . . I just wanted to give you a call. I've got a gentleman here who's concerned about your wellbeing.'

Claybourn's eyes settled on me. 'Thomas Quinn.'

He listened, more relaxed now. '. . . and I'm glad to hear you're absolutely fine, yes . . .' Claybourn looked at me again, listened, and then smiled. 'I will do.'

He hung up the phone. 'Well,' he said.

'That was him? Andrew? He's okay?'

'It was. He is,' said Claybourn. 'Mr Black is at his place of work, and is happy to report that he is absolutely fine.'

'Right,' I said. 'Good,' I said.

Not knowing what else to do, I turned to leave.

'Mr Quinn?'

I turned back.

'Mr Black asked me to tell you that he's glad you finally arrived. He said he wondered what the hell took you so long.'

o

Half an hour later, I was looking for Andrew Black's shop. Until a couple of days ago, I had no idea Andrew Black even had a shop, and now I was searching the windy streets of this little seaside town, trying to find it.

I stopped to get my bearings opposite a large, glass-fronted showroom selling fitted kitchens.

A full-sized kitchen had been mocked up in the window, realistic down to the large dining table with places set, and rows of glass jars filled with pasta, rice and dried beans. It felt like looking into somebody's home, and doubly so right then because a middle-aged couple were storming around inside it, arguing. Really arguing. Slamming drawers, banging fists, the woman jabbing her finger, red-faced, the man flinging arms wide, tipping his head back and yelling some appeal up to heaven. I watched the whole thing play out for what could have been minutes, I don't know. Eventually a tight-faced shop assistant stepped into the space and broke the illusion, for me and I think for the couple too; they looked embarrassed, shaken awake, as if suddenly remembering where they were.

I finally found Andrew's shop a few minutes later.

I'd passed it a couple of times already, and even stopped to look in the window, but I didn't realise the shop was Andrew's because the door didn't have a number and because I was looking for a bookshop. Mike Chesapeake said that Andrew Black published books. He'd been obsessed with books, of one sort or another, for most of his life, so of course his shop would be a bookshop.

Only, it wasn't a bookshop.

Andrew Black's shop stood almost in the middle of a tired and pokey-looking row. The window frames and door should've been a clue – they made this shop stand apart from the others, recently painted and varnished an immaculate glossy black. A sign above the shop window read 'PALACE' in simple white lettering that, anywhere else, might have looked a little sparse. Sparse worked fine here though, sparse worked great, because what attracted people's attention, what stopped them dead in the street, wasn't the signage, but the marvels in the window.

There were four of them on display – four remarkable doll's houses.

Even at a glance, the craftsmanship took your breath away. A thatched cottage with a roof painstakingly woven from real, dried grass; a very modern house made from steel and glass walls, allowing the viewer to see into various open-plan interiors; a wooden colonial farmhouse built onto a large jutting finger of real rock, its stony summit crowned in what looked like a wizard's tower, seeping real wisps of dry ice and flickering with mysterious lights. But it was the fourth house that truly dazzled me – a vampire's castle straight from Transylvania. I stared, amazed, at its array of haphazard turrets, bolt-on wooden walkways and the greening drawbridge lowered over a thick, muddy, liquid moat tangled with miniature reeds. The thing was astonishing. Despite being entirely impractical, having nowhere to put it, and no need whatsoever for a large, spooky doll's house, I surprised myself with how much I wanted to own the thing, to be able to buy it and take it away with me.

I pushed the door open and stepped into the shop, causing a small bell to jingle overhead. Then – *ah.*

I stopped.

Andrew Black's shop was full.

Not full of people. Like Black himself, this shop had very little room for people. No, this shop was full of things, and of immense amounts of storage for other things. Shelves covered every inch of every wall, and cabinets crowded almost every foot of floor space – tall, wood and glass cabinets, dozens of them in various shapes and sizes, seemingly slotted together by a Tetris grandmaster. Taking just half a step forward from the doormat brought me nose to glass with the first one, a cabinet filled with tiny chairs. Inside it, I saw easy chairs and sofas, wooden dining chairs, office chairs, highchairs, deckchairs, garden chairs, sun-loungers, barstools, kitchen stools, a number of wheelchairs (including an electric one), barber's chairs, and a perfectly formed steel and black leather pneumatic dentist's chair the size of my thumb.

Being up close to the cabinet of chairs like this also gave me a chance to look down its length and see that the space between the cabinets on my left wasn't quite as tight as it first appeared.

There was, well, I'd hesitate to call it a passageway over there, but at least some shuffling space, if you were careful.

With a deep breath and some delicate manoeuvring, I made it into the gap, leaving behind the cabinet of chairs, then passing a cabinet of doors, before arriving at a T-junction dominated by a much larger cabinet. A cabinet of rooms: a living room in '60s black and white, complete with Bridget Riley prints; a bathroom specially modified for an old or disabled person with tiny mechanical bath hoist, lowered sink and toilet; a whole range of kitchens, including one – the familiarity came before the recognition, but then I saw it – including one that was a miniaturised version of the showroom kitchen in the shop around the corner, a perfect replica in 1/28 scale.

'Thomas Quinn.'

Andrew Black's voice.

I bent down to peer through the glass panels of the various cabinets and I thought I saw a tall figure standing at the back of the shop.

'Yep. Just bear with me . . .' I pushed up on my toes, and found I could just about see over a cabinet full of tiny musical instruments. 'Hello.'

Black gave a slow wave. 'Are you lost, or stuck?'

'Both, I think, probably. How are you?'

'You need to go forward, then right . . .'

Black looked well. A little heavier, I thought, and this made his height seem much less severe. He'd also grown a beard, thick and bushy and shot through with grey. His old out-of-control hair still hung wild and wavy around his ears. He wore an overall filled with pockets for tools, and an old-fashioned brown warehouse coat over the top. He looked like a craftsman, leaning on his counter, like someone who made furniture. *That would be because he did make furniture*, I thought, *very small furniture. Because, surely, no one else could've made this stuff.*

'What were you doing at the police station?'

'Believe it or not,' I said. 'I read an article saying that you'd been kidnapped. Or gone missing, under mysterious circumstances.' I caught a glimpse of deep and wrinkled brow as I squeezed between two cabinets filled with miniature bookcases. 'Signs of a struggle,' I said.

'Is that right?'

'Yep, the whole nine yards.'

'Hmm.'

'But how have you been?' I asked when I finally made it to the counter. 'Other than not missing. What's all this? I got your letters. What's going on?'

Black sighed.

'What's all this?' I said again. 'There you go, let's start with that one. Aren't you supposed to be publishing books now?'

Black put his face in his hands and rubbed.

'Ahhh,' he said, quietly. Then, he looked up at me again.

'Come on,' I said, 'the second one was elaboration.'

'The second one was elaboration.'

'It was.' When he didn't answer, I leaned on the counter, copying his pose. 'I wanna buy fork 'andles.'

'For God's sake,' Black grumbled to the wall. I thought I heard the smallest hint of bemusement in there too though, almost buried, but detectable amongst the irritation and nervous energy.

A moment passed.

'Andrew,' I said, 'why are you behind the counter of a shop that sells doll's houses?'

Black seemed surprised. 'There are no assumptions in that question.'

'I know. That's because I'm genuinely hoping you'll answer it.'

Black began to soften after that. That's how it had always been with him – a period of banging your head against a brick wall, and then a gradual softening. His answers would get a little less rigid, letting out a few more words every time. He'd start to follow up with questions of his own and before you knew it, you were having something that – if you squinted – might just pass for a conversation. Still, he wasn't exactly forthcoming on the particular *why* of his shop. As far as I could gather – and this did involve a certain amount of speculation – Black had been teaching himself carpentry as a way to improve his book production. If a certain tool, joint or rack needed to be *just so*, then why not make it yourself? Black said he enjoyed the physical process of making and had spent some time *dabbling with a couple of chairs*. How did chairs become doll's houses? Beyond confirming that, yes, he'd made everything in the shop himself, Black didn't explain, though I could easily imagine that full-sized chairs were too straightforward to keep his attention for long, that he decided to test himself by going for something smaller, something more *intricate*. It seemed exactly the sort of thing Andrew Black would do, and once he'd committed to miniature things, he'd want to practise and get better and better. Hence there being so much stuff. Black did say that he'd been running his small press from the rooms above the shop for a couple of years, so when his landlord offered to throw the shop itself into the deal for next to nothing, he decided to make use of it *to sell off some of this stuff*.

I said earlier that I'd always approached Andrew Black in the same way I approached his writing, but looking back, I can see that I wasn't always as thorough as I thought I was being. To be blunt about it, I had a nasty habit of letting my own high opinion of myself – an inflated sense of my own abilities as a detective, coupled with a workman's knowledge of how stories work – get in the way of seeing what was right under my nose. It happened once with those two little moons I spoke about in *Cupid's Engine*, those two scenes with Cleaver and his wife that I convinced myself were nothing more than a set-up for the next book. *That's just something writers do in a book series*, I thought, and in doing so, I missed something big. The same thing happened again here. I jumped on this little run of events – making books to making chairs, making chairs to making doll's houses – because the progression of work seemed so very Andrew Black, so overwhelmingly like something he would do. The chain of cause and effect seemed so very obvious to me, in other words, that I didn't stop to realise how completely I'd invented it.

Black made us both a cup of tea and we talked for a while, about novels and about the state of the world, both of us leaning on his shopkeeper's counter.

I told him how much I loved the things he'd made, especially the vampire's castle in the shop window. This seemed to genuinely please him, and he offered to get the castle out *and show me around it*. I said that'd be great and so that's what he did.

It took a fair amount of time.

I wandered amongst the glass cabinets while he got everything together.

'I might need a ball of string to get back,' I called to him, when I realised I'd wandered a little too far.

'Did you know that *clue* is an Old English word for ball of twine?' he said, crossing the shop carrying something heavy, somewhere half-glimpsed and distorted beyond various glass cabinets. 'Because of Ariadne, and Theseus in the maze.'

'I did know that,' I said, and my stomach twisted a little as I realised that my father, who'd been the one to share that particular gem with me as a child, had probably been the one to share it with Andrew Black too.

For the millionth time, I thought about the two of them in a cosy study crammed with papers, talking late into the night about books, language, history, the way that stories work. Stanley Quinn and his spiritual son. The thought came with its familiar feeling – more of an ache than a wound now, the way a long-mended bone sometimes aches on a particularly cold morning. Our histories are written into us, aren't they? Do you ever think about that? The past is preserved in the pages of our bodies. We're walking stories with a thousand big and little chapters, and every chapter makes its presence felt, every chapter is *unquiet* once in a while, in its own special way.

By the time I made it back through the cabinets, Andrew had the vampire's castle set up on the shop counter in front of him. There were other things too: a graveyard, some kind of outbuilding and a mausoleum. I arrived just in time to see him placing a black carriage with four black-plumed horses onto the castle's cobbled forecourt.

It was incredible, and I told him so.

Black only nodded, his eyes travelling back and forth over the vampire's castle, a slight knot in his forehead. Then, without any introduction or explanation, he began removing the castle's walls. Ignorantly maybe, I had imagined that the back of the thing would simply lift away to grant access to the interior, but access to the spaces within proved to be a much more intricate process than that. Certain walls, or parts of walls, or roofs, or ceilings, or walls-then-roofs-then-ceilings, came away to reveal the various rooms and spaces. There seemed to be no way of knowing which parts of the castle were removable until Black removed them; the joins were always invisible and the extraction of each new surface a surprise.

There were wonders inside the castle.

Behind every wall, a new, miniature miracle: a great hall with an aged oak banqueting table, dozens of chairs and tiny silver tableware. Woven tapestries covered the walls, and the ceiling was hung with chandeliers made from the bones of tiny birds or mice. Next came a dusty library stocked with removable books, books that, despite being as small as your smallest fingernail, opened to reveal real paper or parchment pages. I spotted Aleister Crowley's *Magick* on the crowded shelves, and a remarkably bound *Necronomicon.* Black used a fingertip to tilt one book outward by a few millimetres, causing an entire bookcase to swing open on tiny, invisible hinges and reveal a greening stone staircase leading down into the dark.

'There are four secret passages,' Black said, but he didn't show me any others. Instead, we went on to discover bedrooms with draped four-poster beds and mirrors in which ghostly reflections could be seen from certain angles; bodies bricked into walls; a turret laboratory filled with steel and brass science equipment; a dungeon stocked with torture devices. One room contained a finger-sized door that opened into an impossible black corridor some twelve inches in length, impossible because the door was fixed to one of the outer walls of the castles and, viewed from the outside, there was simply no room for such a corridor to exist.

'Optical illusion,' Black said, 'false perspective.'

And still there was more. Black demonstrated the mechanics of the drawbridge and the real liquid moat. The miniature plants were not real after all, but handmade and lifelike. As we were exploring the edges of the moat, something moved in the water. The muddy moat liquid swirled and I found myself taking half a step back.

'The moat monster,' Black said. 'It's mechanical, on an arm.'

'I'd really like to buy this,' I said.

Black looked up at me then; as he did, something flashed across his face, something that might have been a shadow of panic.

'If,' I said, trying to chase after the look with my eyes, to draw it out, 'if that's okay. If it's for sale?'

'That's why it's in a shop.'

'No, I mean – if it's not display-only or something.'

'Everything's for sale. It's expensive though.'

'I don't care,' I said.

I hope it is, I thought. *I hope it's fucking extortionate.*

A part of me, an ashamed part deep down in my insides, knew that if my trip was successful and I managed to get hold of Black's manuscript, I could afford almost any price for the castle. The same ashamed part wanted to buy the castle, I think, because it needed to make at least some small amends – to give some portion of Mike Chesapeake's money to Andrew Black. Of course, the logical part of my brain knew that Black wouldn't need it – once Chesapeake had the second book, Black's royalties would come flooding through and he'd go from broke to rich in an instant – but it still felt important to me, very important, that – if I was able to take the book – I find some token way to pay for what I had done.

For what I had done.

What would Imogen think of me, if she knew?

My stomach turned at the thought, so I forced myself to picture the bailiffs cleaning out the flat, taking our things, taking our life together. I pictured Imogen's 'I ♥ tea' cup sitting quietly on the kitchen worktop next to the kettle, waiting for her to come home. I thought, *deep breath, Quinn*, and I thought, *the only way out of this is through it.*

'Are you listening?'

'What?' I said, looking at Black, pulling myself back into the here and now.

'I said it doesn't matter if you don't care how much it costs now. What matters is if you care how much it costs after you've heard how expensive it is.'

'Go on then,' I said, trying to look like I'd been there all along. 'How much?'

A moment of silence passed.

'Andrew?'

The smallest hint of that look, that panic, haunted the edges of his face.

‘There’s more I’d like to show you,’ he said, at last. ‘So you can decide if it’s worth it.’

‘Okay,’ I said. ‘I’m not in a hurry.’

Black considered, checked his watch, considered some more.

A few seconds of silence passed.

‘I could just . . .’ I pointed towards the door. ‘And come back later?’

Black nodded, with a hint of relief.

‘There’s something I need to do,’ he said. ‘Would you be able to come back in an hour?’

‘Sure,’ I said. ‘No problem at all.’ I turned to look at the maze of cabinets. ‘I might need directions though.’ I didn’t want to use the word *clue*.

o

I wandered Owthorne’s blasted and battered seafront to pass the time. The water turned out to be just at the end of Black’s road, and I liked the noise of the waves as I walked, the feeling of the sea spray rolling over me in a cold mist.

If you’d asked me what I felt most of all right then, I’d have to tell you it was curiosity. Andrew Black was doing something I’d never seen him do before. Andrew Black was stalling and, despite all of my confusion, mixed feelings and thundering guilt over the job I’d accepted from Mike Chesapeake, I wanted to know why.

A little further along the shore, I found a small parch of wavering phone reception and sent Sophie a text. *All fine. Some weirdness, but all fine. Sorry. Will call soon.*

I put my phone back in my pocket.

Do you know what a raccoon trap is?

The waves crashed, rolled back, crashed, and rolled back again.

I stared out at the horizon.

Here's what I do know, I thought. *I know that I'm finally doing something, not just sitting and waiting for the sky to fall in on my head day after day.*

I felt a rush of energy, of joy almost, at being a fully empowered agent of my own fate. With my own two hands, right there, right then, I had a chance to change things, fix things, undo my mistakes and failures and put everything back as it was, *even better* than it was – in a way that had seemed utterly unthinkable only six days earlier.

It's all to play for, I thought.

And all that time, Sophie's words came rolling in with the waves, *he's dancing you off the edge of a fucking cliff.*

It's all to play for, I thought again, this time more firmly. *And anyway, the only way out of this is through it.*

I marched on along the abandoned front.

As the minutes passed, I thought about the night at the church in the park, the tumbling leaves all around me, the two letters in my hands, the moment I'd chosen to bring Black back into my life. I thought about the half-made nativity inside the church, and the strange cries that I'd been so sure belonged to a baby. I thought about the banging window, about my father, and the voice on the answer machine that came and went without a trace. *Crossed lines.* I thought about the ox, the angels, the *Hayyoth.* I thought about Imogen on the green night vision of Dorm Cam Two; I thought about her freezing cold in her red-and-gold wedding dress; I thought about her naked and hot, her bright blonde hair darkened and sweaty. I thought about days spent having sex and watching movies and reading books, and *just being around each other like that* for weeks at a time, how we never went anywhere for those first few months because the bed, the little flat, those things were our whole living, turning universe, and the two of us didn't need to move or do anything or go anywhere at all. I thought *the entropy of a closed system tends to a maximum.*

I walked and I walked, until a burning smell came in on the wind, interrupting my thoughts.

My spine crawled.

Pin-pricks of cold jabbed at my cheeks.

I stopped, turned, looked around.

And there he was.

A tall man slouched against a lamppost on the seafront walk, his face hidden under the brim of a pulled-down, burned white hat. He stood some distance away, back down the path, a spot I'd passed maybe a minute earlier, but I knew him. To me, he was *unmistakable.* Without moving an inch, Maurice Umber let out a steady stream of thick grey smoke. It swirled and curled up from under his hat and whipped and raced away from him, tumbling, thinning, and finally breaking over me in another faint wave.

I just stood there.

I wanted to run back down the path towards him, find the strength to move as I'd done after that bang in the old, abandoned church, but I couldn't. I couldn't make myself do anything at all. A moment passed, and another plume of smoke swirled out from under the burned fedora. I had the sense of being evaluated, carefully weighed and measured, and that the figure in the hat made these calculations with a cold sense of amusement. As I watched, he slowly reached up and tipped the brim of his hat ever so slightly towards me, just as he'd done that night outside the flat. Then, he turned, and quickly disappeared amongst the seafront buildings.

Once I felt sure he'd gone, I found myself a bench to sit on, caught my breath, and – once it was back under control – looked around for somewhere to get a drink.

o

When I returned to the shop, Black wasn't at the counter. I rang the bell he'd set up there and when that didn't work, I shouted. Eventually, Black appeared, sleeves rolled, smelling vaguely of paint and hot glue.

'Come on through,' he said. 'I want you to see this.'

'More parts for the castle?'

Black looked confused for a second. 'Oh,' he said, seeming to remember the earlier part of my visit for the first time. 'No, this is something else altogether.'

I made my way around the counter to join him, which was difficult as a large pile of boxes had appeared there at some point since I left.

I asked Black if he'd packaged up the castle already but he mumbled about the boxes being 'for another project' without looking at me, and disappeared through a doorway into the depths of the shop.

I followed.

The downstairs back room of the shop had been crammed with freestanding and wall-mounted cupboards, many containing hundreds of small drawers, and all neatly labelled with intriguing titles like: 'chair legs', 'flex', 'wheels: small', 'wheels: extra small', 'cogs' and 'light bulbs'. Beyond these was a small galley kitchen – sink, kettle, hob, fridge – then a corridor lined with boxes that led to a set of wooden stairs going up to the first floor, where Black apparently ran his small press.

He climbed the stairs and I followed.

We emerged into a small room filled with bookshelves, the same beautiful books repeated over and over again across various cabinets. I didn't get time for a proper look, but clearly these were the books Andrew typeset, printed, bound, made – his stock. We passed from the first small room of books into another, and then another. By the third, we'd moved through too many rooms to fit within the footprint of Andrew's shop. The upper floors of several shops on the row must have been knocked together to make a bigger space above them, I decided. But these later rooms were a little strange.

Compared to the first room, which had been packed solid with books, the second room (a little) and the third room (a little more) had noticeable gaps on the shelves. These spaces must've been created when Black pulled out books to meet deliveries, I supposed, though the un-Black-like haphazardness of the gaps surprised me. The fourth room had even more spaces, whole chunks missing from rows of stock, some copies tumbled sideways on the shelves and even a couple left fallen on the floor. This room mostly held handsome copies of John Ketchum's *A Novel with One Hundred Characters* and I stopped to pick up one of the fallen books and return it to its shelf. As I did, the cover came open in my hands and I was shocked to see a whole chunk of it missing – only ragged stumps remained of the first fifty or so pages. I looked up at Black in surprise, but he was already disappearing through a doorway up ahead, so I slotted the damaged book back onto its shelf and followed.

The next room was *decimated*. Think of locusts on a farm. The shelves had been thoroughly picked over, with only a few dozen books still in place, and all the others lying in heaps on the floor. No, that wasn't right. Those weren't books on the floor. Not any more. I picked one up. All that remained was a front and back cover, and a brutalised spine that trailed a few broken red binding threads. The book's insides, every single page, had been ripped out. The others scattered around my feet were just the same.

'Jesus, Andrew,' I said. 'What have you done here?'

o

Andrew Black once called the novel *the universe between two covers.*

During the showdown with his publishers, he'd called hyperlinks atom bombs – punching great toxic holes into texts, collapsing their structures, leaving them bleeding focus, logic, fact and sense. He said that, without the lead-like protection of a decent cover, or even a simple paper page, all narratives faced corruption and cancerous mutation, with God-knows-what from other stories and texts leaking in and leaking out. He said this widening spiral of pollution and diffusion could only lead to the loss of order, structure and function; rising chaos, increasing dispersal and ultimately, *total entropic collapse.*

With his fists gripping his editor's shirt and shaking the man as if to wake him, Andrew Black roared that he, and others like him, were *sleepwalking into the apocalypse.*

o

'Andrew,' I said again, still holding the remains of the gutted book. He didn't stop and, after a moment, I could do nothing else but follow.

The book-massacre room opened out into a much larger, open-plan production space. With all the walls stripped away, it looked like one great long New York loft, or an east London attic. Andrew's homemade printing press stood at the far end, half surrounded with shelves lined with bottles and boxes, and printed sheets hanging on criss-crossing lines, like washing. Closer to us, there were trays and racks, vats, sinks and shelves of chemicals, along with several devices I didn't recognise, but when taken all together, the set-up told me this was Black's paper-making area. It looked like he'd altered his system at some point too; some equipment had been piled up and pushed aside to make space for a counter with bright lights and set of big green plastic bins. Black made his way over to the counter and I followed him. As he inspected something there briefly, I took the opportunity to lift one of the bins' lids.

Inside, I saw dark, murky liquid and a mulchy mass of printed pages.

'You're recycling the books,' I said.

'I am,' Black replied, not turning around.

'Why?'

'Take a look.'

I joined him at the brightly lit desk. At first, I didn't understand what I saw there. A thick, grey-white board had been laid out on the desktop, then cut into various geometric segments. Only – it wasn't board. I could see fibres and, here and there, the remains of printed letters, like fossils weathering out of its surface.

'Papier-mâché,' Black said.

Then he held up one of the geometric segments sliced from the block and I saw it for what it was. The square holes cut into its flat surface were little windows, the rectangular indentation, a door. The geometric, papier-mâché object was the newly set wall of a doll's house.

'Why are you doing this?'

Andrew Black looked at me for a moment, as if he was about to tell me something very serious indeed. Then he changed his mind.

'What I want to show you is just through there,' he said. 'Come on.'

We crossed the printing-room floor, passing his big homemade press with all its washing lines of printed paper, and came to a door in the far wall.

Black stopped, took out a key, and began to unlock it.

Why keep this door locked? I wondered. I'd seen no additional security on his stock or printing equipment, so why have a lock here?

A single word bubbled up from my subconscious – *privacy.*

The door came open and I followed Black inside.

The space behind the locked door had been kitted out like a design studio, or dressmaker's workshop, although its original purpose – paper cutting? Binding? Planning? – had clearly been overthrown some time ago. The room was fairly large, with its periphery now covered in a jumble of tools and raw materials – wire, wood of numerous different types, small tins of paint, a work bench with vices, a lathe, an easel, cutting tools, sanding tools, lichen, straw and grasses, rolls, cans, scraps of cloth. Everything seemed to be pushed back and heaped up against the walls. This created a generous walk space around the large work table that occupied the room's centre. On that table, under an array of bright spotlights, stood a half-completed doll's house.

'There,' said Black. 'There it is.'

I remember thinking how, compared to the vampire's castle I'd spent much of the afternoon looking at, it seemed quite ordinary. Not in terms of craftsmanship: as soon as I laid eyes on it, I could see that the level of skill and attention to detail were absolutely astonishing. No, what was ordinary was the subject itself. Black appeared to be building a normal, everyday, three-bedroom, suburban house.

As I followed Black to the table, I started to see that the model was even more detailed, even more meticulously constructed than the vampire's castle. The scale was much smaller than anything else in the shop, yet the attention to detail went far beyond anything I have ever seen before in my life. When Black reached in through the bathroom window and turned a bathroom tap head no bigger than a watch cog, I was astonished to see small droplets of water forming at the end of the tap and rolling into the bathtub.

'It has plumbing?'

'All the drains are in,' Black said. 'And the cooker has gas. I cooked a small piece of egg on it yesterday.'

'It's amazing,' I said. And it was. Whatever else – it was.

Around the model house were heaps of Polaroids, pictures of the interiors of various houses – no, as I looked closer, of one, single house. The photos showed various aspects of the house, macro to micro, in obsessive detail. And the micro really was incredibly micro here – I saw several Polaroids capturing hairline cracks in the plaster around a plug socket, several others showing mould formation on an external drain, and perhaps a dozen detailing the moss growing in the various gutters on the roof. There were diagrams too: the layout of cushions on a sofa, a six-step guide on how a particular bed is made, maps on squared paper highlighting the position of the occasional off-coloured tile or cracked slate on the roof. And as I looked I saw that each of these pictures and plans had been reproduced within the doll's house itself: the mould formation, the off-coloured tile, the made bed, the hairline plaster cracks. All there, all perfectly represented, or on their way to being installed.

'Amazing,' I said again.

And it really was.

But standing there, looking at the thing, I felt cold deep in my bones.

21
In Layman's Terms

Black was partway through showing me some tiny lengths of piping intended for the little house's central heating system, when a bell rang downstairs. I couldn't tell if this was the bell on the door, or if some brave soul had actually managed to find their way through the cabinet maze and all the way over to Black's counter, but it amounted to the same thing.

Black glanced at me, looking surprised and a little dismayed.

'I'll be fine here,' I told him.

'Don't touch anything,' Black said, glancing at the miniature house in the centre of the room. 'Nothing at all.'

'I would not dream of it,' I said. I tried to make myself sound relaxed and casual, but the words came out as flippant.

Black stared at me.

'I won't,' I said, with a serious face and both palms in the air. 'I promise. I won't.'

That seemed to be, well, not satisfactory, but enough.

The bell rang again. Black gave the doll's house a last worried glance, then turned to leave the room.

'Nothing,' he said again, pausing in the doorway.

'Nothing,' I said. 'Honestly. Go on.'

And then he was gone.

I listened to the sounds of his retreating footsteps on the floorboards in the workshop, and after a few moments, the distant creak and thump of him walking down the stairs.

I was alone.

I looked at the tiny house and let out a big lungful of air.

The only way out of this is through it.

My chest fizzed somewhere between panic and excitement.

Now. Now, now now.

I turned, heading out into the workshop.

I laid a hand on the laptop bag on my shoulder, the laptop-shaped scanner reassuringly solid and heavy inside. If I got lucky, if the manuscript really was in this place somewhere, there'd be a few uncomfortable moments and then I could go home and put everything right.

The floorboards creaked under me as they'd creaked under Black, and I tried to move as stealthily as possible, feeling like an idiot as I did – I hadn't promised him that I'd stay rooted to the spot; he'd expect to hear me moving around up here, but still.

I crossed back to the paper-making area, the papier-mâché-making area, as it had become, and searched around a little, glancing into another large plastic bin as I did and seeing submerged swirls of ripped-up book pages in the depths, their letters lifting away in the murky grey waters. With a sudden wave of panic, I thought of Black dropping *Maxwell's Demon* into one of those bins, of there being nothing left of his second book now but a papier-mâché wall, a roof, or the ordinary little garage on the domestic masterpiece in the other room.

He wouldn't do that, I told myself. *He couldn't.*

So assume he didn't, I thought, screwing down my nerve. *Assume he didn't and assume it's here. Where do you look? Where would it be? Come on.*

I turned on my heel a few times – nothing obvious, so I crossed the room again, ducking under and around the lines of printed sheets that hung like washing and obscured the back part of the space. As I looked around in there, I almost laid my hand on Black's printing press, but drew it back sharply when I saw that the press was covered in a thin film of dust. The last thing I wanted to do was leave a handprint on anything obvious.

I turned again, and was about to go back out through the washing lines when I saw a trestle table and chair tucked away in a nook, almost hidden behind deep shelving loaded with ink and boxes of movable type. I came around to get a better look, and my breath caught. On the table sat a black Royal typewriter, and in front of it, three neat stacks of A4 paper, each one about three inches high.

I stood very still and listened for Black returning. When I heard nothing, I crossed to that little nook, heartbeat hammering in my ears, eyes not leaving those paper stacks, all the time praying for them to be what I thought they were. I came to a stop in front of the desk and – finding I'd been holding my breath – let out a long, deep whistle of air.

Manuscripts. Three copies.

Hidden away in this secret little corner was Andrew Black's second book.

Maxwell's Demon	**Maxwell's Demon**	**Maxwell's Demon**
by	by	by
Andrew Black	Andrew Black	Andrew Black
[final & corrected]	[final & corrected]	[final & corrected]

I stood, staring.

Why three copies?

Why does Andrew Black do anything?

My heart thumped. All of those readers, fans, millions of them all around the world, and not one of them knew this thing existed. A fluffy layer of dust covered the typewriter and the manuscripts. The dust would have to be disturbed, but that couldn't be helped.

I opened my bag and pulled out the copier. It stopped pretending to be a laptop as I extended its four steel legs and stood it on the table. Once you dropped a stack of pages into it, the thing would do its job at an incredible speed, scanning and spitting the scanned sheets out into a neat pile underneath. I'd done a few dummy runs back at the flat and knew it would take only sixty to ninety seconds to copy a manuscript of this size. But in the wrong situation, sixty to ninety seconds could be a *very* long time. I listened one last time for Black and heard nothing, so carefully removed the cover page from the central manuscript – doing my best to preserve its blanket of dust – and set it to one side.

I took hold of the bundle of pages.

Deep breath.

I'd been preparing myself for this moment with thoughts of Kafka's friend refusing to burn his life's work, with all that other motivational crap Chesapeake had given to me the day we met. But right there, in that moment, I didn't need any of it.

I was too busy being the agent of my own fate.

And there was no fucking time.

I dumped the manuscript into the top of the scanner.

The thing immediately whirred to life, working its way through the stack, drawing in pages from on top, and spitting them out into a pile underneath with a very quick, and very quiet, *zip-zip-zip-zip.*

I listened again for Black as I watched the pile of pages on top began to shrink.

Nothing.

I felt no guilt then, only a wild, giddy elation.

I could do this.

I'd actually, almost, done it.

Fizzing with nerves and adrenaline, my eyes wandered over the other manuscripts on the desk.

Chesapeake's machine wouldn't allow me to download the page scans it was currently collecting – I'd practised with it enough to figure that out – so, if I wanted to learn even the first thing about *Maxwell's Demon* before the day it appeared in bookshops, this would be my only chance to do so. The decision to read wasn't really a decision at all – I found myself waiting out an agonising little block of time, and I had nothing at all to do with my shaking, nervous hands.

And so, with the scanner *zip-zip-zipping* away, I carefully lifted away the cover page of the right-hand manuscript, just as I'd done with the one in the centre, then quickly, furtively, I began to read . . .

o

Maxwell's Demon begins with Officer Dan Wayburn, Max Cleaver's reluctant sidekick, driving up to a desolate little cottage on the coast. It's a dour, lonely place perched up on a cliff, overlooking a stormy bay.

Wayburn gets out of his police car, knocks on the door.

No answer.

He knocks again. He keeps knocking.

Finally, the door opens.

'Go away,' says Cleaver. *'I'm retired.'*

o

I looked up from the manuscript.

I could hear shouting in the shop downstairs – a woman's voice, angry and infuriated. Then a man's voice rose up to meet it. I couldn't make out any of the words, but I felt sure the man's voice belonged to Andrew. Who the woman was, why they were shouting at each other so furiously, I had no idea.

Heart thumping, I checked Chesapeake's scanner.

The machine had made it through about two thirds of the pages, and was now entering the final stretch. *Zip-zip-zip.*

Well, keep on shouting, I thought, listening to the muffled voices and watching the scanner zip through the pages. *That's just fine by me.*

After a second or two more, I got to work straightening and tidying the right-hand manuscript, the one I'd been looking at. As I did though, I couldn't resist thumbing down through the thick block of pages for a quick look at the final few. Down near the end of the book, a fragment of a scene caught my eye.

o

Max Cleaver is running, alone and tired, through dark woods. He arrives at a clearing, breathless. A figure is waiting at the other side. It's a familiar figure in a damaged old hat.

'Abandon hope all ye who enter here,' says Maurice Umber, his words coming in the alien, electronic hum of a throat mic.

'I thought we were done with all this,' says Cleaver.

'What do you know about Apocalypse?' Umber replies. *'I mean, as a genre?'*

o

Suddenly—

A muffled slam and the distant, violent jangling of the bell above a shop door.

Then silence, the argument abruptly over.

I stared with panic at the scanner.

Zip-zip-zip.

The last few dozen or so pages were still waiting to go through the machine. *Shit.* I heard the sounds of an angry Andrew, walking fast – *very* fast. It sounded like he'd started up the stairs already. *Shit.* I'd have to move quickly or I'd still be here when he arrived.

Zip-zip-zip – come on, *come on* – *zip-zip-zip* – fuck, no time.

No time.

I pulled the last pages off the top of the scanner before they could go through.

Six. Six pages still to scan. Fuck, *fuck.*

I put the six pages back on the table, put the rest of the scanned manuscript on top, and then replaced both dusty cover sheets. I got everything back as hurriedly and carefully as I could, then picked up and folded in the legs of the scanner, getting one stuck and forcing myself to breathe and steady my shaking hands, before trying again, and – *click* – fastening it neatly away, then dumping it back into my laptop bag.

I came out of the little nook at speed, shuffling past the press, ducking under the washing lines of printed pages. I was crossing the workshop floor when I heard Black's rapid footsteps coming through one of the stockrooms. I resisted the urge to run – the creaky wooden floor would give me away – so I walked as fast as I dared, and I just managed to slip sideways through the doorway and into the miniature doll's house room as his feet started to creak the boards at the far end of the workshop.

Getting myself back in front of the tiny, detailed doll's house at the heart of the room, I grabbed one of the Polaroids and pretended to be comparing it to the model. I caught Black's arrival in the doorway out of the corner of my eye, and whirled around to face him. Knowing that Black would see guilt on my face, I played it up, trying to look all *caught in the act.*

'What are you doing?' Black said.

'Oops.' I quickly put the Polaroid back where I'd found it.

Black stared at me. I tried to control my breathing.

'You promised not to touch anything.'

'It was only a picture,' I said. 'You were gone a while.'

'So your promises expire then, is that what you're telling me?'

He was still angry from whatever downstairs had been about.

'I only touched the picture, not the—' I gestured to the little suburban house. 'I'm sorry, all right? I got bored.' I gave Black a long look, pretending to notice his ruffled feathers for the first time. 'Are you okay?'

Black looked at me without speaking.

I let a quiet moment pass.

As it did, I became gripped by the irrational horror that Black could somehow hear my heart pounding in my ears as loudly as I could. *Get out of here,* said the panic in my head. *Get out, get out, get out.*

'I'm going to get going, then,' I said, as evenly as I could manage.

A moment passed, then Black gave a small nod.

'This really is amazing,' I said again, meaning the doll's house. And it really was. So small, so carefully made, so absurdly, intensely accurate. As we left the room and I followed him out in silence, I stared numbly at the ripped and gutted heaps of Black's stock, and then at the tiny objects in their cabinets.

‘Thanks for coming, then,’ Black said, when I found myself standing outside, on the doorstep.

‘Good to see you,’ I said, touching his shoulder, ‘really good. You take care of yourself.’ *What are you doing?* I thought, as the panic subsided. *Don’t run. You need those six pages.*

‘Yes, you too.’

‘I will do. Bye then.’ *Find a reason to stay. You don’t need to scan them, just make an excuse to get back up there and stick them in your pocket.* A horrible sinking feeling hit me as I realised I could’ve done exactly that five minutes ago.

‘Bye then.’

‘Bye.’ *Come on, Quinn. Think of something, think.*

But nothing came. I felt myself turn. Stared down at my own two legs walking away.

‘Thomas.’

I stopped, about to cross the street, and turned back.

‘Would you come back inside and have a drink with me?’ Black said.

Black put a hand into his pocket and pulled out a little white square. He flipped it over to reveal a Polaroid and held it out to me. I knew what it was at once. The picture had been taken from a slightly different angle than the one he’d sent to me in the post, but the subject was exactly the same – that perfectly perfect sphere, its surface as black as a hole.

‘I think,’ Black said, looking down at the picture, ‘I really think it’s quite important.’

22
Two Tiny Moons

Hours after I'd left Andrew Black, somewhere in the middle of the night, the phone in my hotel room started to ring.

Brring-brring.

The Weerby Hotel stood on the far side of Owthorne. It was a ridiculous place, mostly on account of it being so very, very big. Owthorne was a little town, in the middle of nowhere, with almost nothing at all to do. And yet, I found myself staying on the second-to-top-floor of this gigantic hotel. Floor six. *Floor six.* The Weerby had been built right up against reedy mere, and I could only imagine that someone had planned a whole development there once – back in the '80s, by the look of the place – some mere-side, seaside holiday complex, and only the hotel ever happened. It was only guesswork, but what else could account for it?

Anyway.

Brring-brring.

I'd spent what was left of the afternoon and most of the evening in Black's shop, drinking with him. We got through most of a bottle of whisky, and a fair amount of gin. For large chunks of that time, I'd been trying to engineer a way to get back upstairs to get hold of those last six manuscript pages, but Black had no intention of letting me back up the stairs, or within throwing distance of his little doll's house ever again. The longer I stayed, the clearer this became, and I started to wonder what sort of deal Sophie could get out of Chesapeake for an almost-complete Andrew Black novel. But, at the same time, I couldn't let myself give it up – *it was just six pages, for Christ's sake, six pages in the room upstairs.* So I found myself staying at Andrew's, hoping for a chance that never came, well past the time when the 19.08 from Hull – the last train south, if you can believe that – could've got me back to London. When I eventually did leave, some time after ten, I thought about going south in a cab. I even got my phone out, but – no signal. I mean, yeah, I *could've* walked around holding my phone in the air until I got a single bar – there were occasional pockets of signal out here – but. But, but, but. *Six fucking pages.* So I made a deal with myself. If I could find a place to stay overnight, then I'd stay. I'd drop by Andrew's shop the next day and try *something* – I didn't know what exactly, but if that failed, I'd head back to London and make the best of what I had.

Which would be a fine, a fine plan, as long as Black didn't check on his manuscripts in the meantime, and realise they'd been tampered with.

But I didn't think he'd check. Apart from anything else, Andrew Black seemed completely over *Maxwell's Demon.* The manuscripts looked to have been set aside and forgotten months, even years, ago. What did concern him, what had bothered him more than anything else, as I've said, was the thought that I might touch his current project – that ordinary little doll's house.

That bloody house.

It bothered me, in the same way the Polaroid of the black sphere had bothered me.

And that's the other thing. I mean, as much as I didn't want to leave those last six pages behind, I realised that I didn't want to leave Andrew Black either. I felt—

I felt there was something *wrong* with him.

Brring-brring.

And as for the black sphere itself, his Polaroid picture had disappeared back into his coat as soon as we got inside. Whatever desperation made him pull the thing out of his pocket when I went to leave, it seemed to subside once we were back in the shop. At least, it seemed to subside enough that he wouldn't face up to whatever it was that he wanted to tell me about it. There was fear there, I thought, some sort of horror. I couldn't get a thing out of him.

Brring-brring.

And, yeah, I wanted to tell him things too. I wanted to tell him about the smoking man in the burned white fedora. I wanted to talk to him about angels and letters, entropy and the end of the world. *A hyperlink is like an atom bomb dropped into a text.* And, Jesus Christ, I wanted to talk to him about my dad. But this was Andrew Black, he'd always been the same. And anyway, I couldn't shake off the passage I'd seen near the end of *Maxwell's Demon*: Umber asking Cleaver *'What do you know about Apocalypse?'* If I brought up any of those words now – *Umber, Apocalypse* – how much more likely would he be to suspect I'd been poking around in his stuff while he'd been downstairs in the shop? It was a conclusion that I absolutely did not want him to jump to.

So, in every way that it's possible to get nowhere – we got nowhere, the both of us.

After hours of this slow sort of failure, I left, drunk, wandered, and found the Weerby Hotel.

Brring-brring.

I was sitting in the bath reading *Cupid's Engine* on my iPad when I realised that the phone was ringing, that it might've been ringing for a while. I'd put my headphones on because the people in the room upstairs had been banging around noisily, even though it was nearly two a.m.

I'd been poring over *Cupid's Engine*, not only Andrew's original words, but the metadata the app provided too – hundreds of reader-added comments that analysed, compared, contrasted, delighted in, dismissed, condemned, corrected, loved, hated, stated, refuted, theorised, panned, praised, parodied, ridiculed, debunked, exonerated and interrogated almost every line of the book. Reading like that felt exciting, but it also robbed me of the once-fundamental sense of privacy – that calming, isolated, shut-in-ness – and, because of that, it shattered my focus, scattered away my attention. I felt like a stone skipping across a choppy, noisy surface, when all I wanted was to sink, alone and quiet, into deeper waters.

Brring-brring.

Brring-brring.

Fucking hell. I tapped the screen to add a bookmark, balanced the tablet on the edge of the bath, and then promptly knocked it off, sending it clattering face down onto the tiled floor as I climbed out.

Fucking, fucking hell.

I stepped over it and jogged naked into the bedroom.

Interesting fact – the bookmark I added to *Cupid's Engine* that night would remain in the metadata for months, meaning that anyone could look at my iPad and tell with 100 per cent certainty where I was up to in the text that night, when the hotel phone began to ring. So where was I up to? I'd just finished reading one of those odd, domestic little scenes that seemed to serve no purpose. Max Cleaver at home with Olive, his dark-haired, amnesiac wife – the woman with the little s-shaped scar on her cheek. What did I call them earlier? *Two little moons sitting at the back of the great brass orrery that seemed to go nowhere at all.*

Brring-brr—

I picked up the receiver.

'Yes?'

A moment, then a woman's voice came down the line. 'Hello.'

'Hello.'

'Am I speaking to Thomas Quint?'

'Yes.' My fairly drunken brain raised a hand to object. 'Actually, no. It's Quinn, with a double "N".'

'Quinn.' The sound of pencil on paper, 'Double "N".'

'Who's this?'

'You were just here and I missed you.'

'I think you've got the wrong number.'

'No,' says the voice. 'You were just here.'

'I don't think . . .'

'I'm calling from the Palace? I understood that you wanted to buy our Dracula's castle?'

'Dracula's? Oh, you're talking about Andrew Black's shop.'

'Sorry?'

'You're talking about Andrew Black's shop.'

A pause. 'Listen, can I meet you at your hotel for breakfast tomorrow? If you'd still like to buy Dracula's castle, we'd be very keen to sell it to you.'

My drunken brain said, *Buy it to give something back, atonement.* Then, *six pages short*, and then, *what can Sophie get for an incomplete novel?* But my mouth only said: 'It's for sale?'

'Of course it's for sale; we're a shop. Eight-thirty?'

'All right—'

'All right then.'

'—but can I ask—'

A *clunk*, then the steady *booooooo* of dialling tone.

'—who's calling?' I finished, to dead air.

I hung up, then wandered through to the bathroom to get a glass of water and pick the fallen iPad up off the tiles. I flipped it over to discover a branching, hairline crack running the full length of the screen. Sitting on the edge of the bath, I traced a finger over the screen, following the fractures that ran through the glass like sharp, black lightning.

My upstairs neighbours were still banging around occasionally, and I felt lost and sick as well as drunk, so I carefully worked a finger over the broken iPad screen to bring up Dorm Cam Two.

I stared at Imogen's empty bed for a moment, then cycled through the other cameras. The whole base was empty. That was a little odd. It would have to be after nine p.m. on Easter Island. Imogen and the team rarely worked that late.

Did I ever tell you what Imogen was doing out there in the middle of the ocean? Well, in addition to the massive stone heads, Easter Island used to have a lot of other things too, like trees – and people.

The Easter Islanders cut down the trees to make fires, build homes and – increasingly – to move their ever more massive stone heads out from their quarries and into various positions across the island.

The problem was, Easter Island didn't have an endless amount of trees. It had enough trees, probably. Enough trees if they were carefully and sensibly managed and harvested. And this was vitally important as there would be no way to get more trees if the existing trees ran out; the nearest land was 1,150 miles away. Trees are important. You need them for heat, shelter, a whole lot of things if you've living on an island thousands of miles from anywhere. Not least, for boats.

The Easter Islanders didn't manage their trees carefully and sensibly.

They chopped them all down, every last one.

And when they cut down that last tree, they effectively sealed the fate of every man, woman and child on the island. It took a little while, but their society collapsed. Chaos. Horror. Nobody could leave. Most people died.

Imogen became fascinated with the idea of the last tree on Easter Island. Where was it? Could the site be found? The position, she decided, was vital. The position of that last tree could potentially tell us – and tell us for *certain* – something very, very important about human beings.

You see, Easter Island isn't very big, so Imogen wondered:

Was the person who cut down that last tree able to look out over the land and see – actually see with their own eyes – that it was the last one?

Did they know, and swing the axe anyway?

I fell asleep on the bathroom floor holding the iPad. I woke up in the early hours of the morning, stiff and sore, to see my wife's sleeping back in her bed on Dorm Cam Two.

I whispered *I love you* into the cracks in the glass of the iPad screen.

The people in the room above had finally gone quiet, so I crawled into the bedroom, into bed, and slept the deep, cold sleep of the drunk-and-painfully-sobering.

o

At 8.29 the following morning, I was sitting in a gloomy corner of the hotel restaurant, nursing a horrible hangover, and trying to convince a forkful of lukewarm sausage and gummy fried egg into my mouth, when the woman arrived.

She came in wearing a vintage, high-collared winter coat and a headscarf, protection from the wind and rain that battered the world outside. I watched her speaking to the waiter at one of those little 'wait to be seated' plinths that guard the perimeter of these sorts of places, and I saw him point her in my direction. I braced myself for the ordeal of talking and interacting as she made her way towards me, and, almost before my dried-out brain could prepare itself, she was standing at my table.

'Horrible out,' she said, then, 'Oh, wow. You look worse for wear, Mr Quinn.'

I nodded, dumbly, still holding my fork.

She unbuttoned her coat, took the headscarf off, and I saw her properly for the first time. Black hair fell loose around her shoulders and, even in the gloom, I could see that she was beautiful. *She looks like Imogen.* That was my first thought, *she looks just like a dark-haired Imogen.* But that wasn't all of it – there was something else, some bigger, more exotic 'looks like' going on that I couldn't quite get to grips with. The slight dimple in her chin, the dark tumble of hair, the pale grey eyes. These features were familiar, not Imogen's, but I knew them. I *knew* them. I searched. I knew them because – I'd read about them in a book.

That's when I saw the faint, s-shaped scar running down her left cheek.

My fork clattered down onto my plate.

She jumped at the noise, shocked.

'You're. No. How?' I managed.

Realisation began to spread across her face. 'No, I'm—'

'You're Maxwell Cleaver's wife,' I said, interrupting.

She looked at me for a moment.

'That fucking book,' she said. 'I didn't ask for it, you know. He was trying to be nice. Can I sit?'

It took me a moment, but I nodded. 'Who was?'

'What?'

'Who was? Trying to be nice?'

'Oh. The author. I'll put a little bit of our life in the book, he said, preserve it for ever – and now I have this' – she pointed at my fork on the plate – 'scaring the shit out of me whenever I least expect it.'

'I'm sorry.'

'No. It's—'

'I'm just—'

'Wait a minute.' She held up a hand, took a breath. 'Olive Cleaver is a fictional character in a book, whereas I'm an actual person. And to be honest, I try to think of myself as more than somebody's wife too, whenever the situation allows.'

A speech, well prepared and often recited.

'So,' I said. 'All right,' I said, wishing my brain would catch up.

'Andrew Black is my husband. That's why Max Cleaver's wife in the novel bears a startling resemblance to—'

I can only imagine the look on my face.

'All right,' she said, looking at my expression. 'That doesn't normally happen.'

'This is all very . . .' I said. 'I had no idea.'

'About what?'

'That Andrew was married.'

'You know Andrew?'

'I've known Andrew for nearly seven years.'

'Known him well, you mean?'

'Yes. Well, no. We're connected. A very old . . .' *Ghost.* 'He was a friend of my father's.'

'And he's never mentioned being married?'

'No. Jesus, no. I had no idea. None *whatsoever.* You've never heard of me either, I'm guessing?'

'Thomas Quinn . . .' She took a moment, looking at me, thinking.

'Oh my God. You're Stanley Quinn's son.'

'Well. It's just Thomas, really.'

'Of course it is. Because you try to think of yourself as more than Stanley Quinn's son when the situation—'

I nodded, smiling.

'God, I'm sorry. Of course you do.'

'It's fine. Honestly.'

'Okay then.' She holds out a hand. 'It's nice to meet you, just Thomas. I'm just Isabelle.'

We ordered a pot of tea, and once it arrived, Isabelle pulled her handbag up onto her lap and rooted through it, taking out a phone. She tapped and swiped a few times before passing it to me.

'So you know I'm who I say I am.'

I took her phone, and found myself looking at a photo album. I swiped through a dozen pictures of Andrew and Isabelle, Mr and Mrs Black, together on holidays, at the pub, in a living room, in a kitchen. In most of the pictures, they had their arms around each other. In most of the pictures, Andrew Black was smiling, actually fucking smiling.

Fuck me.

'Okay.' I put the phone down on the table. 'I'm still a bit – actually, I'm still a lot—' I made a jumbling, *confused* motion with my hands. 'Do you mind?'

'No.' She poured milk into her cup. 'Go ahead. I'm going to try to sell you a very expensive doll's house shortly, so.'

'Okay. You're Andrew Black's wife.'

'Uh-huh.'

'Not just that, but—'

'Yes.'

'Who looks exactly like Maxwell Cleaver's wife.'

'No, she looks exactly like me. I'm the real one.'

'Right, yes, and that's because Andrew wanted to put your life in the book?'

'To preserve the moment in every perfect little detail.' She looked up from the tea, a little embarrassed. 'That was when we were just – honeymoon period, you know.'

'Andrew said that? Sorry, I'm . . . Okay. So he wrote Olive Cleaver to look like you and put in some of the day-to-day of your lives together—'

'Uh-huh.'

'But not the story stuff.'

'Story stuff?'

'Olive's amnesia, bumping into Maxwell out of the blue one day with the bloody cheek and not remembering anything before that. All that stuff from *Cupid's Engine*, that's not . . .'

She raised her eyebrows.

'No!' I found myself smiling with surprise.

'Uh-huh.'

'You're kidding me.'

'All true,' she said, 'believe it or not. And I told him not to put it into the novel because—'

'It looks like a clue, or part of a different mystery altogether.'

'Exactly. But Andrew insisted. *Preserve the moment*.' She touched the scar on her cheek, caught herself doing it and then smiled at me, a little embarrassed. 'All I know is, I ran into Andrew one cold night in January, coming up for' – she thinks – 'coming up for ten years ago. Before that, there's nothing.'

'That's . . .'

'Unlikely?'

'I was going to say *amazing*.'

‘Well, either way, it is what it is.’ She sipped her tea, looking at me over the top of the cup. ‘Next question.’

‘Why are you so keen to sell me the vampire’s castle?’

I’m not sure I would’ve been so direct if my mind had been working faster, but I’d been doing my best with a blunt, and painful, instrument.

‘Because we’re broke, Mr Quinn. As in, really, truly, going to lose our house broke. I called you in the middle of the night because I didn’t want you to leave this morning without getting a chance to—’

‘Make the sale.’

‘Exactly.’

‘Why didn’t Andrew want me to buy it when I was there?’

Isabelle Black tried to suppress a bitter little smile.

‘Look,’ she said. ‘Left to his own devices Andrew would never let it out of his sight, not in a million years. I’ve said, *it’s just a thing*, you know? I keep saying that to him, *they’re just fucking things*. It doesn’t mean anything to let them go. We’ve got nothing left, nothing at all and he just . . .’ She’d begun squeezing her paper napkin, turning her knuckles white. ‘No, that’s not fair. He’s trying, he is. I honestly believe that . . .’

‘Oh, don’t worry. I know Andrew,’ I said. ‘He’s brilliant, but he’s also—’

‘There was a baby.’

I stare across the table.

‘There was a baby,’ she said again.

‘I’m sorry,’ I managed, eventually.

She thought for a moment.

‘You say you know Andrew,’ she said. ‘You think you know what he’s like, but he wasn’t like that with me, not in the same way. He worked long hours, and it’d be a lie if I said that he didn’t get lost in his work. But once in a while he’d put it to one side. Find his way out of the world of paper and letters, and later the world of wood and shavings, and back to real life. Sometimes it took him time to adjust. He'd walk away from his desk and have to sit quietly for an hour or so, so that the other world could retreat, and this one could reabsorb him. When he worked, it was like some kind of – like another state maybe, some sort of communion. Maybe structural parts of his brain took over and the social parts were shut down. Is this making any sense?'

'Yes, yes, it is.' I sometimes felt a similar sort of thing when I wrote, a kind of regression from the world. I told Isabelle this and she nodded.

'A regression, yes. When he started the press, he was always building, half inside some large wooden something-or-other. I'd shout *If you start to see trees and snow in there . . .* It's not funny but, you know, we laughed. I'm telling you so you know what he was like back then, even last year. How much things have changed.'

I nodded.

'It started when we found out I was pregnant. I'd never seen Andrew the way he was then, how happy he was. He made the most fantastic cot and when it was done, he was the proudest man on earth. *What other dad could do this*? he said. *What other dad could give their baby this?* And he was right. He worked with the printing press by day, and at night, he made furniture for the baby's room. I saw less of him then; he was so absorbed in making things for the baby and he was so happy. One night he put his arms around me and he said, I remember this part distinctly, he said, that he was going to work on making sure everything was absolutely perfect.'

I raised my eyebrows.

'I know. But hundreds, thousands of fathers-to-be say those exact same words, don't they? And to Andrew, perfect is just – that's him, you know? I couldn't have seen it coming. Nobody could've seen it.' She stopped, looking away.

'Are you all right?'

'Fine, I'm fine,' she said. There was a pause, then she looked back at me, as steadily as she could. 'When the baby . . .'

'Yes.'

Another pause. Isabelle took a breath.

'He'd finished her room by that point,' she said, 'built everything. When it happened, he'd just started making her a doll's house. I'm . . . There's a month or two where I'm not really . . .' She waved this part of the story past, jumping forwards. 'Anyway. Andrew receded. It's as if I came back to the world, only to find him,' she thought, 'further away.'

'Further away?'

'Yes, and I didn't know how to get to him. He'd made all those perfect things for the baby's room – cot, wardrobe, a chest of drawers – and he was still making them, over and over again, but in miniature. Doing the same thing, but by one degree of separation – he'd got further away.'

I didn't know what to say to this, so I didn't say anything.

'It's like we're out of step, and it's distance too, and it's – gravity. It's like a massive object is out there, and the gravity has him, and it's pulling him further away, like an astronaut disappearing into space. I'm not making any sense, am I?'

'Yes, you are,' I said.

'He's gone far away, far inside himself and far – I don't know. I don't go upstairs, in the shop, I mean. I don't go up there any more. Maybe I should, but . . .'

I nodded.

She was quiet for a moment, then she said:

'There are different kinds of space, I think, different sorts of distance. I've had the chance to think about this a lot.'

I gestured to her phone. 'Can I?'

She nodded. 'It's not locked.'

I opened the photo album again, swiping through until I came to a picture that had only half-registered earlier. A smiling Mr and Mrs Black on the driveway of an ordinary, suburban house. I'd seen the house before.

'This,' I tapped the screen. 'This is the doll's house he's working on now.'

'Are you sure?'

'Yes.'

'That's our home,' she said.

'I thought it might be.'

She looked from me to the picture and back again.

'And?' she said. There's something else, isn't there?'

'It's the scale. It's a lot smaller than anything else in the shop. It's tiny.'

'How tiny?'

I mapped out the rough dimensions with my hands.

Ms Black stared at the space I'd marked out on the table. Then she took the phone from me and sat quietly looking at the picture on the screen.

'I see,' she said, without looking up.

o

There wasn't much to say after that. Neither of us mentioned the vampire's castle again and she left shortly afterwards, taking my number as a sort of lip service to the idea that we'd pick up that piece of business in the future, but I didn't think I'd hear from her again.

She left, and I sat there with my cold breakfast and my hangover, staring, empty, into space.

The minutes passed, and then—

A napkin landed in front of me.

I jumped.

I looked up to see a waitress. A young woman in her teens. Her badge said *Hello My Name Is Janet.*

'Can I help you?' I said.

'I thought you could probably do with wiping your hands,' she said, not looking at me.

'I'm fine,' I said.

'Not fine,' she said and she put her hand on the napkin, jabbing it towards me. She gathered up my plates and the tea things and left quickly.

I picked up the napkin and opened it. There were words inside, written in red lipstick.

YOU SHOULDN'T BE HERE. GO QUICKLY.

I looked up from the napkin to see three police officers making their way through the restaurant towards me. I recognised the one in the lead. Sergeant Claybourn.

'Hello, Sergeant,' I said, trying not to sound nervous, as they made it to my table.

'Thomas Quinn,' Claybourn said, 'I'm arresting you on suspicion of—'

My heart froze.

'What? No.' I thought of the scanner upstairs in my room. 'I haven't done anything wrong.'

'Mr Quinn. You came into the station yesterday,' Claybourn said. 'You told us that Mr Black was missing, that there were signs of a struggle at his place of work.'

'Yes, but . . . I read a news article. It was wrong. He was fine.'

'He was fine yesterday. Sometime between the hours of eleven p.m.

and seven a.m. this morning, however, Mr Black appears to have gone missing. And there appear to be signs of a struggle at his place of work.'

Oh. Oh shit.

Claybourn stood back to give me room.

'I'd appreciate it if you could stand up now, please, sir.'

23

Under the Police Station

The stairs led down.

They were well-lit, nicely carpeted stairs, but still.

'Why are we going down there?' I said, looking at the stairs, but talking to Sergeant Claybourn, who stood in the corridor behind me.

'Alternative accommodation.'

I turned to look at him.

'There's a Duncan in the cell.'

'A Duncan?'

'Duncan Disorderly.' Claybourn didn't smile. 'You'll be getting my office, so I'd thank you not to break anything.'

I looked at him. He looked back, not giving anything away.

After a second, he held out a serious *after you* arm towards the staircase.

'Sir,' he said.

I made my way down.

There really *was* an office at the bottom, at least, of a sort. I walked into the middle of the space as Claybourn made his way down the last few steps. A cold, whitewashed basement, but someone had done their best. A simple desk, complete with desktop computer, phone and a couple of chairs, faced the staircase. A threadbare rug covered the middle third of the flagstone floor, and a plug-in radiator, an easy chair and a couple of bookcases attempted to be a sort of snug in the far corner. Was this better than being in with the Duncan?

My breath shuddered, and not just because of the cold. I didn't like being underground, surrounded by quiet earth, below the police station.

Claybourn passed me and picked up the phone from the desk; he'd clicked the lead out of the back and had begun wrapping it in loops around his hand before my brain processed what he was doing.

'Phone call,' I said.

He turned, looking at me.

'Don't I . . . don't I get a phone call or something?'

He stopped.

'You do, sir. Yes.'

'They took my phone and wallet from me at the front desk.'

A little put out, Claybourn began to unwind the wire from around his hand, then clicked it back into the phone. He pulled out the desk chair, inviting me to sit.

'If you want to use the station phone, you'll need to do that now, sir.'

'I don't know what's going on,' I said. 'I haven't done anything wrong.'

And I thought, *but please don't look too closely at that laptop in my hotel room,* then, *can they do that? Can they go into my hotel room and take things? Please don't let them be able to do that.*

'Sir,' Claybourn said, still holding out the chair.

'Sorry,' I said.

I sat down in the chair and took the phone from him.

I thought, holding it.

'I don't know the number,' I said.

Claybourn looked at me.

'Can I?' I said, meaning his desktop. Claybourn shook the mouse and the thing whirred to life. He blocked my view as he entered his password, then backed off to let me type.

Tap-tap-tap-tap-tap. I hit the search button and the handsome, stucco-fronted offices of the Hayes & Heath literary agency appeared onscreen. As I looked for her name on the drop-down tab, I wondered if Sophie Almonds even kept an office there. I'd certainly never been there. The idea of the wild, sharp-eyed Sophie bird sitting at a desk, surrounded by white plastic computers and printers and coffee cups had always seemed pretty ridiculous to me. But still, a number was listed for her. I tapped it into the desk phone.

I turned to look at Officer Claybourn, but he didn't move.

Nothing happened.

'You need to press zero,' he said. 'For an outside line.'

I tried again and got an answer machine.

'Sophie. It's Thomas Quinn.' I glanced at Claybourn, who pretended to look at the wall. 'So, as you know, I've come up to Owthorne to see Andrew Black,' I said, trying to speak evenly and carefully. 'Well, he's gone missing, and it sounds stupid but the police think I've got something to do with it.' I paused, thinking about Mike Chesapeake and his half-a-million-pound contract. I could feel Officer Claybourn's eyes staring at the back of my head. 'It's all a bit of a mess,' I said, at last. 'Can you do something? I don't know what, but – can you do something? Because I've been arrested, as I say.' A pause. 'So – thanks then.' I put the phone down.

'That was surreal,' I said to Claybourn as he took the cable out of the phone again. 'This is a surreal thing to be happening.'

'The chief will want to hear all about it when he gets here.'

'All right then,' I said. 'Good.'

After the phone call, Claybourn took the power cable from the computer, winding both into a loop around his hand. He asked if I needed anything else, and when I said no, he went to the corner of the room and turned the radiator on.

‘It gets cold down here,’ he said. ‘Someone will be down. Shouldn’t be long.’

I called after him as he started up the stairs.

‘Officer Claybourn.’

He stopped.

‘In the car, you had some of Andrew’s books, from his printing house?’

‘I did,’ Claybourn said.

‘And this is your office?’

‘It is.’ He pointed across to the bookcase. ‘Middle shelves. Read if you want, but be careful with them. The chief shouldn’t be long.’ And then he made his way up the stairs. I listened to his footsteps on the steps I couldn’t see, heard the door at the top of the stairs open and close and then a key turn in the lock.

The clock on the wall said *tick-tock, tick-tock, tick-tock.*

Everything else was very, very quiet.

I got up and crossed the room to the bookcase. Sure enough, the middle shelves held around two dozen books marked *Palace Press*, starting with *A Novel with One Hundred Characters*, and running through other lost gems of the ’60s, ’70s and ’80s, before moving into more familiar territory with beautifully bound copies of *The Magus*, Auster’s *City of Glass*, Zafón’s *The Shadow of the Wind.* As my eyes wandered over these, I thought, *surely Black has no rights to publish these books, unless he has an agreement for special editions?* But that seemed unlikely. So why on earth was he producing copies of books he couldn’t sell? What were they for? My gaze travelled further along the row: *Don Quixote*, *It*, *The Warlock of Firetop Mountain* . . . I froze. I knew this little set of books. The survivors. *These last three are the survivors.* Black had published beautiful hardback editions of the three novels that survived the fire at my parents’ country house when I was thirteen. They were even sitting on the shelf in the same order as I had them on my own bookcase at home. How could he possibly know about these books? I'd never told him. Coincidence? I thought about it. *It's only three books. Much stranger things are—*

Then I saw the title of the very last book:

The Acts of Thomas.

I yanked the book off the shelf, only to have two more remarkable things present themselves as soon as I saw its cover. The author's name hadn't been included on the spine, but it appeared on the front here in neat, gold characters under the title. *Ursula Black.* Andrew's mother. The second remarkable thing was what else I found on that cover – a neat technical plan, a building blueprint stamped into the leather in gold leaf. Though the rooms were unmarked, appearing only as adjacent boxes with the various doors, window and stairs symbols around and between them, I recognised the layout. I'd seen it in another set of blueprints, half buried under thousands of Polaroids up in Andrew's workshop. These were the plans for that painfully small, painfully ordinary doll's house that he'd been assembling. Which meant that they were also the plans for Andrew's family home.

Opening the book, the very first thing I noticed was that the title on the inside pages was different to the title printed on the leather cover. On the outside, it was *The Acts of Thomas*, while on the inside, *The Lost Books of the Bible*. The second thing I noticed was the paper. Homemade, I supposed, as all of Black's paper had been, but these weren't the smooth, creamy white pages I'd expected. The paper here looked dingy, blue-grey, like the off-brand shirt in an old washing powder ad. I rubbed the title page between my fingers. It had a speckled coarseness to it, black dots and stains mashed in amongst the thick fibres – paper made in a hurry.

The clock on the wall said *tick-tick-tick-tick.*

I closed the book, looked again at the design on the cover, those little golden building plans. I felt a bit sick. But still, I took the book to the chair, sat down, and began to read.

It became clear pretty quickly that *The Acts of Thomas* was a bound extract from a much larger work. The book in my hands contained just two parts – Ursula's complete introduction to her large and mostly missing text *The Lost Books of the Bible*, and second, a chapter that presented and discussed one of those books, *The Acts of Thomas* itself.

In her introduction, Ursula Black took a brief tour of the various gospels and holy texts that hadn't made it into the Christian canon for various reasons. What surprised me was that there were a lot of them. This wasn't a case of *the one we didn't like* and *the couple we lost.* The list went on and on – The Gospel of Judas, The Gospel of Philip, The Gospel of Mary, The Gospel of James, The Gospel of Joseph, The Gospel of Thomas, The Gospel of Eve, The Gospel of Matthias, The Secret Gospel of Mark – I turned the page – The Gospel of Andrew, The Gospel of Barnabas, The Gospel of Lucius, The Gospel of Valentinus, The Gospel of the Egyptians, The Gospel of the Hebrews, The Gospel of the Ebionites, The Gospel of the Nazarenes, The Q Source, The M Source – I skipped a page, and then another – The Gospel of Truth, The Gospel of the Twelve, The Gospel of the Adversary.

The Gospel of the Adversary, I thought. *I suppose it makes sense to put that one at the back.*

Ursula wrote:

> *Many of the books collected here cast long shadows, removed, expunged, yet for all that leaving traces of themselves in the surviving scriptural architecture, like lingering ghosts. One might notice the canonical texts refuting claims that have never been made, or swerving to*

avoid what would seem to be nothing but empty theological space. The lost texts linger. Look closely at the modern Bible and you'll see that Jesus talks primarily about physical resurrection and the coming of the Kingdom of God. Spiritual resurrection, everlasting life for the soul on a heavenly plane of existence, is actually a Gnostic belief rooted in Gnostic books that are missing from the canon. Likewise, the gruesome tortures and punishments of Hell that have terrified sinners and inspired artists and writers for centuries are nowhere to be found in the Bible itself, originating instead in the expunged Apocalypse of Peter.

Apocalypse. At the sight of the word, an image from the *Maxwell's Demon* manuscript tried to form itself in my mind. I saw Maurice Umber slouched against a dark, dark tree in a dark, dark wood. *No.* I pushed it away before it could fully form.

I flicked forwards through the pages.

In the book's second part, Ursula discussed *The Acts of Thomas*, and reproduced the original text in full. Within this text, it's strongly hinted that Thomas is Jesus's twin brother. Like Jesus, Thomas is a carpenter, though he's also a skilled builder and an architect. *An architect.* I felt my skin prickle a little at this and, as I read, I ran my finger over the golden lines of the building blueprint on the book's front cover. The shadows of the manifold danced again on the walls of my mind. *But what is it for? What does it do?*

I took a deep breath, and let it out slowly. I tried again to get my thoughts in order, I pushed down the noise down as far as I could, and focused my attention fully on the text, on the adventures of Thomas the Apostle.

o

One day, while travelling the world and preaching, Thomas met a great king and decided to accept a commission to build him a palace. The king liked Thomas's building plan – *doors to be set towards the rising of the sun, to face the light; the windows towards the west, to the winds; the bakehouse to the south, and water pipes necessary for the supply to the north* – so he supplied the apostle with a large sum of money to get the job underway, then left him to it. As soon as the king had gone, Thomas took all of the money and gave it away to the poor. Having no idea what the apostle had done, the king continued to send money for materials and wages at regular intervals, exactly as agreed. Thomas gave all of this new money away to the poor as well. Every time the king sent money, Thomas gave it to the poor. This went on for some time. Several months later, the king wrote to Thomas, asking how his grand palace was coming along. Thomas told him that the palace was pretty much done, but that he needed some more money for the roof. Fine, said the king, and happily sent some roof money. Thomas gave the roof money away to the poor. Eventually, the king came back to the city and asked his friends how his grand palace was looking. The king's friends told him what had been going on. *Upon hearing this,* we're told, *the king hit his face with his hands, shaking his head for a long time.*

So, the king sent for Thomas and for the merchant who introduced them. He asked Thomas if his palace was finished. *Yes,* said Thomas, *your palace is done. Then when shall we go and inspect it?* asked the king. Thomas told the king that he couldn't actually see it yet. This did not go down well. After having them both locked up, the king considered by what death he should kill them. He decided to flog them and burn them with fire.

Now, that very same night, the king's brother Gad became ill and he died soon after. The king was distraught, but then – during the funeral preparations – his brother's body miraculously came back to life. The resurrected Gad told the king that he had been allowed to return to earth for a few minutes to make his brother an offer – he would like to buy the king's new palace. When the king didn't understand, Gad said that in heaven he saw a most beautiful palace. He asked the angels who it belonged to, and they said it was the king's.

The king sent for Thomas, and the apostle explained:

'You asked me to build you a palace and I did so. Not here on earth, but in heaven.'

o

The sound of a key in a lock woke me up.

I sat myself up in the armchair as Sergeant Claybourn made his way down the stairs. *The Acts of Thomas* slid off my knee with a clatter, and by the time I'd collected it from the floor, Claybourn stood in front of me with a plate of toast and a mug of something steaming. The clock said 6.21.

'I've been here for ever.'

Claybourn didn't answer.

'Is it morning or night?'

Claybourn didn't answer. He just set down the plate and mug, then perched himself on the edge of the desk. It was a move that I guessed was supposed to look casual.

'The chief's been held up again,' he said. But he looked like he wanted to say something else. I caught a glance at the book in my hand.

'Have you read this one?'

'I've read all of them.'

'What do you think?'

'Of that one?'

'Yes.' When Claybourn didn't speak, I held up *The Acts of Thomas* to show the golden building plan on the front. 'I saw it, you know. The doll's house. The new one behind the locked door.'

'I see.'

'I'm his friend, and I think you're his friend too. Look, I heard about the baby. I'm worried – I'm worried he's gone mad and he's running naked through a field somewhere. Or, I'm worried that somebody found out he's been writing again and has – I don't know – grabbed him to get hold of the work or something. That's what I'm worried about.' I locked eyes with Claybourn. 'What exactly is it that you're worried about, Sergeant?'

'Andrew Black is currently missing under suspicious circumstances, sir. An investigation is underway.'

'I know, I know,' I said. 'I've been thinking about that, and here's the thing. There are CCTV cameras in the lobby of the Weerby Hotel, and even if there weren't, the same receptionist was on duty when I checked in last night, and when I got up this morning. What I mean is, that man knows full well I was in the hotel between eleven and seven, and not out kidnapping famous authors. I'm guessing that you know that too.'

Claybourne didn't say anything.

'Why would anyone walk into a police station and announce a kidnap plot twenty-four hours before carrying it out? It makes no sense. It's absurd.'

Claybourn still didn't say anything.

'And yet, here I am, arrested. So, I'd like to ask you again,' I said. 'What is it that *you're* worried about?'

A few seconds of silence passed, then Claybourne planted his elbows on his knees and rubbed his eyes.

'Are you real?' he said, face in his hands.

'Sorry?' I thought I'd misheard him.

He looked up. 'Are you real? Are you a real person?'

This caught me so completely off guard that it took a moment to answer.

'Yes. Of course I'm a real person,' I said. 'What else would I be?'

Claybourn told me a story then, a very odd story. A story about his answering a call from a very disturbed Andrew Black, and about the bizarre report that Black made to him when he arrived on the scene.

24

The Things that Andrew Black Reported to Sergeant Claybourn

Claybourn told me that, opening his living-room curtains one morning, Andrew Black had been shocked to see an old woman lying face down on his garden path. She wasn't moving, and the contents of her handbag had tumbled out in front of her, all over the flagstones.

He ran outside.

The woman was breathing but unconscious, with a swelling eye and a nasty cut on her forehead. Black didn't want to leave her alone, but his wife was in hospital at the time, complications from the – Claybourn struggled to find the words – *very sad news they'd had*, so Black went inside to call an ambulance himself. Then he came out and sat by her side, waiting for it to arrive.

He didn't recognise the old woman, but that didn't seem especially strange; after all, plenty of people walk to and from our front doors during the course of any given day, and most of them are people we don't know. Because of the situation, his concern for the woman's wellbeing, it took Andrew a few moments to notice something that actually *was* strange. He'd assumed that she'd been out and about delivering flyers or leaflets door to door, but from his position beside her, he could see that her handbag was completely empty – her purse, keys, umbrella, little make-up compact and half a dozen other things were lying all over his path. There were no flyers, no bundle of leaflets, no papers, no business cards. So if she *was* delivering something, then what was it? Where was it?

Andrew began to collect the old woman's possessions and put them back into her handbag, checking as he did for any clue as to who she might be and where she might've come from. In her purse, written in old, shaky handwriting on a small yellowy-white rectangle of card, Black found the words 'Property of Elizabeth Shaw'. But the card held no other information, no 'if found, please return to' address, no telephone number, and the other compartments in the purse were empty – no bank cards, no driver's licence, no ID.

Black thought he'd gathered up all the woman's belongings, and it wasn't until several minutes after he'd sat back down beside her that he spotted the little black pocket diary lying in the flowerbed.

Black leafed through the pages, looking for anything else that might be helpful – contact details for friends, family and carers – but the book was sparsely populated at best. Through January, February and March, the only entries were vague, mundane, mostly single-word reminders like 'groceries' and 'hair'. Black had all but decided to drop the little book into the handbag with everything else, when he saw a date marked with nothing but an asterisk. He turned the page and found another – one lone little black star. He flicked forward and found more. Initially, the asterisks showed up somewhere between once a week and once a fortnight, but by mid-August their frequency had increased to once every few days. By early September the asterisks appeared daily. When Black arrived at the middle of the month, he discovered a whole galaxy of them, hundreds and hundreds of asterisks, blanketing the white paper, obscuring the printed text, filling margins, asterisks everywhere.

He'd been about to turn to the next page when he saw that the woman's eyes were open, watching him.

'It won't be long now,' she said.

At the same moment, Black heard a siren approaching.

o

Two of Claybourn's colleagues arrived to interview Black that morning, and a couple of hours after they left, Andrew Black's doorbell rang once again.

As he made his way down the hall to answer it, he saw a person's diffuse silhouette on the other side of the door's frosted glass. That was entirely normal, Black was used to seeing the shapes of the people waiting on his doorstep before he opened the door, but the moment he saw that particular figure – *at that very second,* Claybourn told me – he was hit by a brutal wave of dizziness and nausea, and a headache that forced him to drop to his knees and left him there for some time, retching. When Black finally composed himself enough to get back on his feet, he saw that there were now *two* silhouettes waiting on the other side of the door, not one.

The doorbell rang again.

Black opened the door.

A fat man in a bright blue tie and a skinny man in a bright red tie stood there, smiling at him. *Big, unnatural smiles,* Claybourn said.

'Yes?'

'Who will leave it?' said the skinny man.

'Leave what?' said Black.

'Who will leave it? We are going the other way around.'

Black put a hand over his mouth and managed to fend off another wave of nausea.

'The other way around what?' he said.

The skinny man had a hawkish nose, a gaunt, vaguely regal face, tidy white hair and a neat, pointed beard. The fat man next to him was darker and shorter, with tanned skin, short stumpy arms and legs and a close-trimmed black beard of his own. Both were wearing simple, unassuming black suits, both shirts were spotlessly white, all four shoes polished to a mirror shine, and their ties – the red and the blue – made from brilliant, bright silk, tied perfectly. Black also said they had *an unsettling sharpness and distinctness to them*, a quality that made the world around them seem *badly printed*, and made Black's head throb, *as if it were about to thunder*. Equally peculiar – Black felt sure that he recognised the two men, and not just recognised, but *knew*. He had a powerful sense that these two strange people had been close to him once, very close and very important, a long, long time ago. Suddenly, Black felt very afraid. These men coming to his house, knocking on his door, everything about them appearing in his life like this felt wrong, *cataclysmically wrong*, and he didn't know why.

'Who are you?' Black said.

The two men looked at each other, then performed their big smiles again.

'We are the police officers,' the big man in the blue tie said. 'We'll come inside now, if you please. To get the job done.'

'I don't think so,' said Black. 'I don't think that's who you are.'

'We are the police officers,' the big man said again, taking a step forward.

'I don't think so,' said Black, and before the men could respond, he slammed the door hard. Moments later, when he checked from the living-room window – then from upstairs for a better view of the street – the two men were gone.

o

After making sure that all of his doors and windows were locked, and drawing all the curtains too for good measure, Black took some painkillers for his headache and lay down on his bed.

He only meant to rest, but he fell asleep at once. He woke a couple of hours later, to find his headache almost completely gone. He decided to take a shower to clear the last of the fog from his head, and was washing his hair, thinking about something else entirely, when he suddenly realised who the two men at the door had been.

He crashed and tumbled out of the shower and rushed, dripping wet and shaking, into the study to find himself a book.

Claybourn explained that, during the months that they had been expecting a baby, Andrew Black had devoted a considerable amount of effort to acquiring new copies of books he'd owned a child. The book he was looking for now was one of these, one of the most treasured, earliest books from his original collection – *The Children's Cervantes,* a fourth-birthday gift from his mother. Black loved the book, insisting that Ursula read it to him over and over again, every night for a month, every night for two months, three months, until the words stayed in his ears and the pictures on the inside of his eyelids when he settled down to sleep.

Black found the book. He took the book over to his desk, set it down, and opened it.

And there they were.

There they were, the two of them, exactly as he remembered them.

The skinny man with the neat white beard, the short fat man at his side who'd been standing at his door just ten minutes earlier.

Don Quixote and Sancho Panza.

The skinny man hadn't been wearing a suit of armour, of course, and the fat man didn't have the floppy hat or the small mule, but nevertheless, the bumbling knight and naïve squire as illustrated in *The Children's Cervantes* looked *exactly* like the two men who had knocked at his door a few hours earlier.

How could that be? *The Children's Cervantes* had been released in 1974. Even if there'd been some unlikely connection between the men and the book, any physical resemblance would have faded over the many years since publication.

Instead, the likenesses were *uncanny*.

Andrew Black retreated to his workshop, a place he most often went when he needed to think very deeply, or to not think at all.

He had an excellent memory, but even he was surprised at how clearly he could recall the two men's faces. He remembered the three stray hairs high on the fat man's cheek, trimmed short like all the others but escaped from his beard. He remembered the small white scar just to the right of the skinny man's mouth, and he remembered those few missing teeth on the same side, revealed for a second as the man had asked his nonsensical question. Black realised that he knew what had caused the scar and the missing teeth. That scar – that very human, very real scar Black saw with his own two eyes – had been caused by the smashing of an oil pot as Don Quixote attempted to sip his toxic 'healing balsam', during his famous battle with a flock of sheep that he had mistaken for an army. The pot had been smashed, and the teeth lost, when a group of shepherds began to launch stones at him with their slings. Black remembered the drawing in his book; the stone crashing into Don Quixote's jaw, the smashed pot, the little cut, the comical look of pain, shock and surprise, the three teeth whizzing away through the air. Black remembered the scar amongst the man's pores and wrinkles, a little sickle of white between the edge of the man's lips and his trimmed and tidy beard. A real scar, but earned in a fictional battle, on a printed page, in one of the world's most famous novels.

Black concluded that the skinny man didn't just look like Don Quixote. The face he'd seen when he opened the door that afternoon, that *was* Don Quixote's face.

o

There's something wrong here, isn't there? I mean, beyond the obvious. Black's obsession with cause and effect, with facts, should never have allowed him to arrive at a conclusion like that. Typically, Black's first step would have been to identify the absolutes, in this case, the single, glaring impossibility – that the two men *could not* be Don Quixote and Sancho Panza. All subsequent deduction would then have been checked and measured against this one unquestionable fact. But he didn't do it that way. He should've deduced that a man who looked exactly like Don Quixote from a childhood story book, with a friend who looked exactly like Sancho Panza from the same story book, and who even had identical injuries from that book, is *still* more likely to have and be all those things through nothing but blind coincidence, however incredibly unlikely that may be, because the alternative would be flat-out impossible. The skinny man *could not* be Don Quixote. But that's not the way Black went about things, which very much suggests that Black believed there was a circumstance where the man *could actually be* Don Quixote and his friend *could actually be* Sancho Panza, or at the very least, could somehow be wearing their faces.

Black told Claybourn that he'd given the matter a lot of thought before deciding that the solution was likely to be one of two things – either he'd suffered some form of psychotic episode, or the appearance of Quixote and Panza were evidence of *the other eventuality.*

'What other eventuality?' I asked.

Claybourn looked at me. 'Are you asking me what he told me, or what I think?'

'What he told you,' I said.

'That the world is full of holes,' he said. 'And it's falling apart.'

'Because of electronic text? Because of the internet?'

Claybourn didn't answer.

'Is that what you think?'

Claybourn thought for a long time.

'I've known Mr Black for five years now, and I've never knowr scared like he was when he reported this, these two men. Trem scared, he was.'

'So you believe him?'

'I wouldn't, but . . .' He looked at me. 'I've seen him.'

'Seen who, seen Don Quixote?'

'No.'

'Seen who then?'

'Maurice Umber.'

A cold buzz of shock hummed in my jaw, my temples.

'What?' I said.

'From *Cupid's Engine*, with the burned hat—'

'I know. You're saying you've seen him? You've actually seen hin

'I have. And' – Claybourn almost didn't continue – 'I know w he really is.'

'Officer Claybourn, I don't mean to tell you your job, but if yc know who is going around dressed as Maurice Umber, then that persc should be much higher on your list of suspects than me, and shoul probably be locked up down here right now, no?'

'Oh, I'm sure he's the one who has taken Andrew, Mr Quinn.'

'You're what? Then why don't you go and do something about it?'

'What could I do?'

I stared at him. 'What are you talking about, *what could you do* You're the police!'

'Are you familiar with the word *Hayyoth*, Mr Quinn?'

I stared at him. 'You're kidding. You're actually kidding me. You'r saying – you, a policeman – you're actually telling me that Andre Black's been taken by the angels?'

'No, Mr Quinn.'

'Then what?'

'I'm saying that he's been taken by the Devil.'

25
Acts of Creation

The doors of the Weerby Hotel swished open and I walked into the lobby, sweaty, dishevelled and looking a lot like I'd spent a good twenty-four hours in police custody, which – as everyone there knew – I had. I nodded to the receptionist, a different one today, and he half smiled while desperately trying to find something to do with the paperwork on his desk.

Jailbird, I thought. *Person of interest.*

After all he'd said under the police station, Claybourn found it very hard not to let me go once I demanded he do so. I had a cast-iron alibi thanks to the hotel CCTV, after all, and once he started talking about the Devil, I made sure to ask him what his fellow officers thought about that particular line of investigation. It rattled him for long enough to get me out of the door, though I certainly didn't want to stick around any longer than I had to.

Are you real? Are you a real person?

Jesus Christ.

I made my way towards the lift, planning to grab my bag and Chesapeake's scanner laptop and get myself out of Dodge as soon as humanly possible. The scanned copy was incomplete, but it would have to do. It might still be worth something to the publisher. Either way, I'd have to take my chances. Something had happened to Andrew and the window to get the rest was surely closed now, what with the police and everything. *Too hot*, as they say in heist movies. Cut your losses. With

Andrew missing, Chesapeake might well be able to retrieve the rest of the book himself. That is, if Chesapeake wasn't somehow involved in the disappearance in the first place. Did I want to help Andrew? Of course I did, but what did I know? What could I do? He'd just gone, and I'd come very close to taking the blame for that myself. *Too hot, too hot, too hot.*

Bing.

The lift doors opened and I stepped forward, not really paying attention. At the same moment, Hello My Name Is Janet – the girl who'd given me the napkin at breakfast – stepped out of the elevator and we almost crashed into each other in the foyer.

She stopped abruptly, horrified at our sudden close proximity, glancing around with a frightened expression to see if she'd attracted unwanted attention.

'What—'

'Not here,' she hissed. 'Top floor. Ten minutes.'

And then she bundled past me and was gone.

Bing. 'Sixth floor.'

I dashed out of the lift, practically ran down the corridor, and rammed the keycard into the slot in my room's door.

Inside, everything was exactly as I'd left it.

Thank fuck.

I pulled Chesapeake's scanner out of its bag and hugged it tight to my chest. An incomplete book had to be worth something. Even a few grand would help buy me a little breathing space to get us out of that hole. Even a few grand gave me a chance to stop the bailiffs from taking our life away.

But what about Andrew? What about Andrew, what about Andrew?

'Shut up,' I hissed out loud.

I repacked the laptop and bundled all the rest of my things into my bag, and I got the hell out of there.

I thought about heading straight down to the lobby, but I didn't.

Back in the lift, my finger hovered over the ground-floor button, before seemingly making a call all by itself—

Bing. 'Seventh floor.'

The top floor of the hotel was one massive open space. A function room, and it hadn't been used in years. Dusty chairs in ancient, Alcoholics Anonymous circles stood around here and there, the cheap henges of some long-forgotten hospitality culture. Dead plants, ferns and yukka trees rotted in their pots, or stood as bare branches, their fragile brown leaves scattered on the once garish, now dusty grey carpet. I saw a Club Tropicana-themed bar on the far wall.

Floor-to-ceiling windows looked out over the whole of Owthorne and that's where she stood, waiting.

Hello My Name Is Janet didn't turn around as I approached, and she didn't speak until I'd settled into place alongside her.

'I don't have long. This . . . this didn't used to be here. The hotel. The police station. The whole town. None of us used to be here, do you understand? Black's done all of this. Black *made* it.'

I opened my mouth to say *what does that mean*, but instead I stared at the row of shops over on the far side of town, and found myself thinking about Andrew Black's papier-mâché doll's houses; the miniature cabinet in the kitchen, the ordinary family home in his workshop, all those book pages turning to pulp in vats. I thought of the

Blacks' lost baby and of the two rabbis using their divine knowledge in assembling letters to make themselves a calf to eat for their dinner. I thought about Gutenberg's business partnership with Faust and about what Claybourn said when I asked him what the Devil could want with Andrew Black. *Perhaps he owes him for something.*

A deep, creeping unease gripped my insides.

I was about to try to speak again, when, far down below, I saw a bright red Vauxhall Astra roar off the road into the hotel car park, and come screeching to a halt in a cloud of dust outside the front entrance.

My pocket buzzed. I pulled out my phone and pressed the green button.

'Thomas,' said Sophie Almonds. 'Come out of there and get into the fucking car, right now.'

26
Sophie Almonds

'So, what do you think?'

The car roared along the empty road, under the empty sky.

Sophie stared straight ahead.

Angels and letters, Maurice Umber and the Devil, doll's houses, Isabelle Black, Hello My Name Is Janet, Officer Claybourn, the report of Black's disappearance coming twenty-four hours before the disappearance itself, entropy, time, the end of the world – I'd laid it all out for her, hadn't stopped talking since we left the hotel.

'Do you think,' I struggled, 'that there's, I don't know, something there? Not all of it, but . . .'

'What did I say?' she said. 'Do you remember? Is the world made of rocks, grass and trees, or from bank statements, certificates and letters? Is it made more from soil and rivers, or from beliefs and opinions?'

'So you think there's something to it?'

'Something to what? Maurice Umber, who may also be the Devil, prowling the countryside, snatching away writers? I very much doubt it. I think you believe it, but that's Andrew Black, isn't it? I told you not to go, and now' – she spread her fingers on the wheel – 'here we are.'

I stared out of the window.

'If you're asking me if I think you travelled through time,' she said, 'that you somehow arrived in this godforsaken place the day before you left, so that you could read about Andrew's kidnap on a Thursday and then somehow report it to the police the day before, on a Wednesday? Then, no, that didn't happen.'

'It does sound ridiculous.'

'It's nothing to do with how it *sounds*. I know for a fact that it didn't happen.'

I turned to look at her. 'How?'

'Because I know what *did* happen, and it's a little more mundane.' She glanced at me out of the corner of her eye. 'No time travelling.'

'Go on then.'

'All right.' Sophie shifted in her seat. 'What you don't know is that Sachs & Tuttle, who publish *Cupid's Engine*, made some bad calls financially, quite a lot of bad calls actually. They were about to be sold to a company called Barton Green.'

'Okay,' I said. 'I don't see what—'

'So wait a minute and listen. Now, Mike Chesapeake's company, who own Sachs & Tuttle, had been prepared to take a very low offer for them, but then you come along and drop your bombshell about a second Andrew Black novel. That changes the whole landscape of the deal. Sachs & Tuttle with a sequel to *Cupid's Engine* on its slate becomes a very different proposition to Sachs & Tuttle without it. It's very late in the day, but there's no way that Chesapeake's going to take the original offer from Barton Green after hearing your news. If that manuscript exists, and if he's able to lay his hands on it, then he needs to know ASAP.'

'So he came to me with all that money and insisted I get on the next train.'

'Yes. However, Chesapeake's opposite number at Barton does *not* want this. He doesn't want Sachs & Tuttle getting hold of that manuscript, at least not right now, because he desperately wants to push his low-ball offer through. He's about to buy the company for peanuts, knowing he can chase the Black manuscript himself at a later date, and make a killing when he gets hold of it. The one thing he absolutely does not want is you succeeding in your snatch and grab commando mission for Chesapeake.'

'Okay,' I said.

'The bad news,' said Sophie, 'is that Barton Green also owns an industry news website called Book Brief. I believe you subscribe to their newsletter?'

I nodded.

'Okay. So here's where it gets deeply unethical. When Chesapeake's opposite number over there heard about you and your mission, they sent you a fake news alert – actually sent it to you and only to you, I'm saying – a news alert from Book Brief saying that Andrew Black had been kidnapped.'

I turned to look her. 'What?'

'I know. They actually sent you a dummy alert, linked to a dummy article to try to put you off going to see Black and getting hold of that manuscript. They desperately wanted you to give up and turn back.'

'Jesus.'

'Yes, indeed. Some people at Barton Green were really uncomfortable about this, as you can imagine, and Mike Chesapeake got wind of what happened and he called me. Then *you* called me from a police station. I couldn't get anywhere on the phone, so in the end, I jumped in the car myself.'

'Thank you.'

The empty fields and sky raced by outside the window.

'Did you get the book?' Sophie asked, after a pause.

'Most of it,' I said. 'Will they give us money for most of it?'

Sophie thought. 'It would prove the book exists, so – yes. They won't pay what they were offering for the full thing though, not even close.'

A few moments passed.

'But Andrew's still missing, isn't he?' I said. 'I'm fucking off back to London and none of this explains Andrew actually going missing in exactly the same way the news story said he would.'

'That's right,' Sophie said, not taking her eyes off the road.

'How is that possible?'

'Well, I don't know,' she said. 'But nobody saw that fake article except for you. Well, you and the people who sent it at Barton Green, I suppose, but they're not in the kidnapping business. And even if they were in the kidnapping business, following through would gain them nothing, would it?'

'Right. So?'

'So the only way anyone else would ever know what that news story said would be if you told them about it yourself, wouldn't it? Did you tell anyone else about it, Tom?'

'I told the police. Claybourn.'

'Who promptly locked you up on suspicion. Anyone else?'

I checked back through my memories.

The bottom dropped out of my stomach.

Very quietly, with my eyes fixed on the road, I said, 'Turn the car around, Sophie.'

27

Twenty Minutes Later . . .

I stood in Black's upstairs workshop. I stood with my back to the door that was usually locked but that day wasn't. I stood facing the large table with his pride and joy on it – the tiny model of the Black family home. I stood, and I waited.

The police tape hadn't been hard to get around, forensics had been, if forensics were ever coming, and the place had been left unwatched and unguarded. All the cabinets in the shop downstairs had been smashed and I'd felt like Gulliver trying to get across the floor without crushing hundreds of Lilliputian chairs and tables, toilets, sinks, ovens, all the rooms and all the furniture that lay scattered all over the ground. Upstairs, it seemed, had survived more or less untouched. Sergeant Claybourn probably took this as evidence that Black's abduction had happened front of house.

I stood, and I waited.

I noticed the smell first. Cigar smoke.

A small, blue cloud of it plumed up through the bare floorboards under my feet.

Then came the crunching sound of somebody walking over the broken glass downstairs.

I stood, and I waited.

The creak of footsteps on the stairs.

I waited.

A loud, electronic squeal sounded somewhere behind me, like feedback through an amplifier. I jumped, gasped a little at the shock of it, then steadied myself. The feedback receded into a fuzzy rumble of static bass. I heard footsteps crossing the workshop outside, coming closer, taking their time. The smell of cigar smoke became stronger, and still, I didn't turn around.

The squeal came again, modulating itself this time, ranging up and then dropping through the various vowels in unstable tones of *aaaaaaah, eeeeeeeee, uuuuuuuuh*, until it began to form the beginning of words.

'SSSSSpeeeeeee-*eeee*' went the sound. It sounded like a powerful throat mic, one of those devices for people who've lost the ability to talk. 'SSsspeeeeak, thou vaaast and venerable head,' said the electronic voice, modulating itself into something approaching human tone and pitch. I could feel the hairs rising on my forearms. The footsteps moved into what I guessed must be the open doorway behind me, and then stopped. A cloud of thick cigar smoke billowed over me from behind, like a big ocean breaker.

Still, I didn't turn around.

'Speeak, mighty head, and tell us the secret thing that is thee. Of all divers, thou hast dived the deepest. That head upon which the upper sun now gleams has moved amid this world's foundations. Where unrecorded names and navies rust, and untold hopes and anchors rot; where in her murderous hold this frigate earth is ballasted with bones of millions of the drowned.' Despite the pitch and hum of the throat microphone, the words still managed to sound fluid and rich, dangerous and playful. The voice being projected by that machine sounded wild, passionate and very much *alive*.

Suddenly I was second-guessing myself. I pushed the rising panic back down.

Screw your courage to the sticking place.

'Hello, Maurice,' I said, trying to keep my voice level. 'I met a policeman today who thinks you're the Devil.'

I still didn't turn around.

A pause, and then another tumble of cigar smoke rolling past me and settling across the room. I could feel the heavy, silent weight of being stared at.

'So what happens now?' I said.

I wanted to run, if you'd like to know the truth. I really wanted to run.

'What do you know about Apocalypse?' the electronic voice replied. 'As a genre, I mean.'

I struggled to control my breathing. I didn't want the figure behind me to hear the shake in my voice, so I just stood there, facing away, not saying a word.

'Apocalypse literature tends to be produced when a religion survives to some level of maturity.' The voice hummed and purred the words out. 'What happens is this. A religion is formed. The god or gods of this religion are believed to offer protection to the loyal followers. But then something very bad happens – some protracted war or massacre. God doesn't save His people, and the people ask why? Almost always, they come to the conclusion that some dark power has set in, some rot in the world that stops God from coming to their aid and saving them. They have to, you see, to keep on believing.'

Why, why, why? And the Yod flew up in the face of God, asking, 'Why . . . ?'

Screw your courage. To the sticking place.

'Somewhat ironically, a rot *has* set in and the world *is* falling apart. Truth is going to buckle, Mr Quinn. The Endarkenment is coming, and it's coming in pixels, in one hundred and forty characters or less.

You've no idea what's just around the corner, I promise you that. So, in best apocalyptic tradition, a noble pilgrim – that'll be you – will be permitted to glimpse the awful shape of things to come by a generous, if terrifying, celestial entity, which, in this case, will be me.'

'You're not an angel.' I managed to put some weight into it. 'You're not the Devil, and you're certainly not Maurice Umber.'

'You're deep in the heart of the woods now.' The voice pitched and dropped, humming electronically over its Es and As. *So much confidence,* I thought, so much malice finding its way through that machine. 'You're just a little voice in the ink-black night, pressed in tight against the pulp and the pages. You must know that. You must know you should be careful what you say.'

I stared straight ahead. *Screw your courage to the—*

'Your name is not—'

'My *name*' – the voice swelled into deafening electronic thunder – 'is Iota, and Yod, and I. I. I. I. I am the handprint on the cave wall, older by far than the Alph or the Bet. I am the *I* of all thinkers and speakers, narrators and self-seekers. I am the selfishness and the self and I am not afraid to take matters into my own hands. I am the *what about what I want?* and the line in the sand. My black crown is the Eden apple, hanging just out of reach, and the singularity at the end and beginning of all creation – *in the beginning was the word.* I put myself first and last, and why wouldn't I? I am the real Alpha and the true Omega and I will not have my Great Work fall into ruin.'

'And I,' I said, turning around so that the figure in the doorway could finally see the wooden workshop mallet I'd been holding against my chest, 'I am not going to be danced off a cliff like a fucking puppet. Not any more.'

I raised the hammer over the tiny doll's house, over Black's family home.

In the doorway, the confident, slouched figure stiffened, just a little. From inside the deep shadow below that burned white fedora, there was a tiny, almost inaudible gasp. There.

There.

I lowered the hammer, letting it dangle at my side.

'Jesus. Jesus Christ.' I sagged under the weight of confirmation. How did I not see it before? Who else would be following me around dressed as Maurice fucking Umber? Except for the police, I only told one – just one – single person about the article I read coming up here: *Andrew Black is missing under mysterious circumstances.* I told Andrew Black, who took that information and made sure that it came true.

'You kidnapped yourself, didn't you, Andrew?' I said. 'All this, all this fucking pantomime, with Umber and whatever bullshit you sold that policeman, it's all you, and for what? To convince me of your Luddite, end-of-the-world bullshit? You staged all this to try to fuck with me so much that I'd honestly think that time and the world are actually fucking broken, didn't you? You got me arrested – fucking arrested, Andrew – and for what? To make me write up your crazy fucking theories – this gospel, that testament – because you're too fucking stubborn to give in to your publishers and actually write a single fucking word of it yourself. Take the hat off, and what is that under there? A black mask or something? Take it off – come on. It's over.'

He didn't move.

'Are you finished?' he said, in that same electronic voice, though I thought it had lost the tiniest fraction of its force.

'No. I'm going to save you from yourself. I'm going to save your wife, because that woman's been through enough too. We've all been through enough. You got me arrested and what my fucking father saw in you I have no idea – none, *none* – you fucking bastard.'

The figure went to take a step towards me. I raised the hammer to the doll's house again and he stopped in his tracks.

'I'm guessing this is like the other one?' I said, moving closer to the doll's house. 'Like the castle?'

'Don't touch it. Don't you dare touch that.'

I lifted off the roof, just as I'd seen Black do. I hadn't noticed this particular room when he'd first shown me the interior, but it was all so obvious now I knew what to look for. One of the bedrooms was a nursery, a tiny, perfect little nursery complete with crib and bookshelves and bunting.

That one.

I felt utterly fucking wretched.

'I'm trying to save you from yourself. Save my life too. Save all of us together, don't you get it? This will save us all.'

'Please, don't,' said the figure in the hat. 'Please.'

I took hold of the baby's room and pulled.

It lifted up and away in my hands.

Directly underneath, nestled in the core of the house, was the perfectly black sphere. *What do you think this is?*

I lifted it up gently.

He stretched out his arms involuntarily, ready to catch the sphere if I dropped it. I still couldn't see his face, but his concern for the object in my hands was the clearest thing in the world.

'Back up.' I began to walk towards him, sphere in one hand, mallet still in the other. 'Back up.'

He did, raising his hands as if I were pointing a gun at him.

'Please,' the electronic voice said. 'Please put it down, please be careful, please. Please. Please.'

'Back up,' I said. 'Back up, back up, back up.'

o

Two minutes later, I emerged from the little hidden space in the workshop with a huge pile of manuscript pages, all three copies of Black's second novel.

My arms were full, so I'd had to balance the sphere on top.

Black went completely rigid when he saw this, but he didn't try to come any closer.

I walked backwards, taking slow, careful steps across the large, loft-like room, heading towards the stock rooms and the staircase beyond.

'It's all right,' I said. 'I'll leave it on the top step for you when I get there.'

And then the papers shifted in my arms and the sphere slid—

Desperately, I tried to rebalance the pile, but I couldn't, and then the sphere was falling through the air towards the floor.

The figure let out a horrible shriek and rushed forwards, desperately trying to catch the thing, but he was too far away to reach it in time.

The sphere hit the floor and it smashed. Papier-mâché shards, robbed of all mystery and magic, just black paint and old paper, scattered away on impact.

He slid to a stop in front of it, collapsed to his hands and knees, and hunched low over the broken shell – a broken thing himself now.

'I'm sorry,' I said.

'You will see it,' the electronic voice said quietly, so quietly I wasn't sure that he was even talking to me. 'The world is ending and you will see it.' And then he just stayed like that, hunched over the smashed and splintered pieces. That's when I saw that there was something inside the remains of the sphere – a little black rectangle. A little shiny black rectangle with white edges.

A photograph.

An ultrasound scan of an unborn baby.

'Oh God. Oh God, I'm so sorry,' I said.

Dressed in his Maurice Umber costume, hat still in place, face still hidden from the world, Andrew Black didn't move. He stayed hunched over the broken sphere and the photograph. He didn't speak, and he didn't move one muscle.

I gripped the manuscript pages as tightly as I could, crushing some in my hands, and I ran.

o

I dumped the pages onto the back seat of Sophie's car.

She turned around in the driver's seat, staring at me.

'Is that the book?'

I probably looked like death.

'Thomas, is that the book?'

'Yes,' I said, slamming the back door, coming around the car and getting into the passenger seat next to her.

'You got all of it?'

'Yes,' I said. 'I got all of it. Three copies.'

Sophie looked me over for a moment. 'What happened?'

'Nothing good.' I let out a long, deep breath. 'He's all right. I mean, he's not – but he's all right.'

'Are you sure?'

I looked at her. I could still see Black on the floor, the scan picture with the cracked papier-mâché fragments all around it.

'No, not really,' I said. 'But . . . it's the end now. We're done.'

Sophie nodded.

'Can we go home now, please?' I asked.

Sophie started the car.

'We can,' she said.

The empty fields rolled by and the manuscript pages hissed and fluttered, settling in their heaps on the seats behind us.

'Do you want to talk about it?' Sophie asked, after the country lanes had become roads, and the roads had become a motorway.

'No,' I said.

I looked away. My breath steamed on the window glass, and I stared across at the driver in the next lane. The woman gestured and waved without realising it, talking hands-free on the phone to someone who wasn't really there.

o

Back in Victoria Park, we rolled along the quiet street and the London leaves blew and tumbled, just as they had when I left. I watched them swarming and rattling as the old church came into view.

'The wind's settled right in,' Sophie said. 'It's just sitting there on the weather map, you should see it.'

'I'll take a look,' I said, with no real energy.

Sophie glanced across at me. 'Do you want me to take the book to Chesapeake right now?'

'Yes, please.'

'Do you want to come?'

'No. I just want to go home.'

I didn't want to see *Maxwell's Demon* ever again. I didn't want to talk about it, didn't want to think about it. Not very long ago, I'd been excited to read it. Now, I just wanted it gone. I wanted it placed into Mike Chesapeake's hands and I wanted my money so that the bailiffs wouldn't come and take our things, so that Imogen could come back home. I thought about someone taking her 'I ♥ tea' cup from the worktop near the kettle and I told myself that I'd done what I had to do to keep our little world together. I'd done what I had to do. I felt sick.

'Can I get out here?'

Sophie slowed. 'Are you sure?'

'It's only around the corner. I really need some air.'

She nodded and pulled up.

'I'll drive this to Mike right now,' she said, leaning across as I climbed out. 'And I'll have them wire the money out today.'

I nodded, pausing before closing the door.

'Are you going to be all right?' she asked.

I thought about it. 'Did I sell my soul to the Devil?'

'Mike Chesapeake is an out-and-out arsehole, but he's not the Devil. And anyway, millions of readers will thank you for what you've done.'

'The two things are not mutually exclusive.'

Sophie fixed me with those pale blue eyes of hers.

'No,' she said. 'I don't suppose they are.' She straightened up in her seat. 'I'll mail you as soon as the deal's done and the money's transferred.'

I nodded, closed the car door and watched as she drove away.

Fastening up my coat and tucking my chin into my collar, I crossed the road and set off for home, head down, through the clattering, swirling leaves.

As I came around the corner at the end of the street, I saw a woman standing in front of our building. I couldn't see her very clearly, because of the distance and because she'd pulled the collar of a heavy cardigan up high around her neck as protection from the wind. But she looked to be pressing on the doorbell. As I got closer, she seemed to give up, crossing the road and heading for a blue car. I picked up my pace and met her at the car just as she was about to get inside.

‘Excuse me,’ I called out above the wind, causing her to pause and look around. ‘Excuse me,’ I said again as I finally closed the gap between us. ‘Can I help you? I think you were just ringing my bell.’

The woman closed the car door again and turned fully to face me.

‘My goodness,’ she said from inside her cardigan. ‘Don’t you look like your father?’

That stopped me dead.

‘What?’ I said.

The woman pulled her collar down. She had a look of someone familiar, but was, herself, utterly unfamiliar. What I mean is – imagine seeing someone you think you know in a bar and you go over to say hi, only to find that it isn’t your friend after all – you’re talking to a complete stranger. This woman was a complete stranger.

‘We got your message at the office,’ she said, ‘and, the thing is, your father used to be a client of ours. Did you know that? I suppose you must’ve known that.’ The woman tried to wrestle her long black hair back from the wind. ‘He was well liked,’ she said over the gale. ‘So I wanted to check up on you.’

‘What? Why?’

‘Because you called the office.’

‘I’m sorry,’ I said. ‘Who are you?’

Her brow knotted down. ‘You left me a voicemail message.’

‘I’m sorry, I don’t—’

‘Oh God, I haven’t got the wrong person, have I? Am I chattering on to a complete stranger in the street? My name’s Sophie. Sophie Almonds.’

28
Numbers

'You're not Sophie Almonds.'

We'd moved to take shelter in the doorway of the flats opposite.

'I'm sorry?'

'Who are you?'

The woman looked confused, then concerned. 'Are you Thomas Quinn? I'm sorry if I've—'

'No, I'm Thomas Quinn. And I know Sophie Almonds – you're not her.'

You look quite a bit like her though, I thought. *If I saw your picture, I might not know—*

The look of concern gave way to frustration and annoyance.

'All right, look,' she said, taking out her smartphone. She brought up the Hayes & Heath website that I'd used on Sergeant Claybourn's computer, then showed me her own name in the menu. She tapped through, and showed me the number on screen. 'You called me on this number. You said you'd been arrested and that you needed my help. And you said some other things too. We, at the office, we were – we were worried about you.'

'Wait,' I said. I brought up Sophie's mobile number from my phone contacts and dialled. It rang out. I tried the office number next, and that rang out too. 'Can I see that?'

The woman held up her phone, showing me the office number on the website page. It ended 2231. I looked at the number in my phone's address book. It ended 2232.

'No,' I said. 'That's not right.'

'You said you'd gone to somewhere called Owlthorne to see Andrew Black?'

'Owthorne,' I said.

'Owthorne, that's right. Only I was worried that you were in trouble, or someone was playing a trick on you, because—'

'Andrew Black is your client, is that what you're saying?'

'Well, this is the thing, Andrew Black is on my list, but . . .'

'But what?'

She looked conflicted.

'But what?' I asked again.

'Oh, for God's sake. There is no Andrew Black. It's just a pseudonym, a pen name. Andrew Black doesn't exist.'

'What?' I stared at her. 'That's . . . that's ridiculous.'

'Oh, I promise you. It's a pseudonym that got tangled up in a lot of – well, you don't need the details. And Owthorne too, actually. I spent a long time looking and it turns out that there was an Owthorne on the east coast a long time ago, but it fell into the sea in the seventeen-hundreds, so—'

'I was just there.'

'—so when I couldn't find it, I pulled in a favour with your old publishers and got your address. I thought I should come and—' She trailed off, looking at my expression.

'Who sent you to do this?' I said.

'You called me for help. Or someone claiming to be you did. Was it you? Don't you remember?'

I folded my arms. 'You're not Sophie Almonds.'

The woman stared at me for a moment.

'I'm going to go now,' she said, then she turned and walked towards her car without looking back. 'Don't call my office again, Mr Quinn.'

She got into her car and drove away.

Fuck.

Fuck.

What the fuck?

I tried calling Sophie again, pacing up and down the street, but her mobile just rang out and rang out and rang out. I tried three, four, five times. No answer.

I stuffed the phone back into my pocket and kept on pacing, trying to clear my head and figure out what in the hell had just happened.

I'd made it most of the way to our building when my mobile began to ring.

Sophie. I yanked it out of my pocket. *Thank fuck.* I paused. Not Sophie. Then, in spite of everything, I felt a small jolt of relief when I understood the meaning of that long, exotic string of numbers running across the screen.

'Hello, Eagle One,' I said. 'My battery's about to die, but I'm almost home. Can I—'

But Imogen was crying deep, gulping sobs.

The heart dropped out of the world.

'Please don't be looking.'

'Im? What's—'

'Please. *Please.* Don't be looking. Just turn it off.'

29
Imogen Naked

'Im?' I said. 'Imogen?' But my phone was dead.

I hurried up the street and up the steps to our flat. I put my hand on the front door and it swung open – the locks had been kicked off. The inside was a wreckage of turned-over bookcases, emptied cupboards, smashed pictures and drifts of leaves piled in the hall. I glanced to the kitchen and the 'I ♥ tea' cup was still in its place near the kettle – *thank God, thank God.* I clambered through to the living room. More leaves, more wreckage. Boxes tipped out. Drawers emptied and raked through. TV tipped over, Xbox gone. But the old desktop was still there, too big and old-fashioned for anyone to steal.

I clicked on the monitor, more terrified of what it'd show me than of any burgled flat. Dorm Cam Two flashed into being and when it did, I sank down slowly into the wreckage on the living-room floor. The word *no* leaked out of me with almost no sound.

Imogen was sitting with Johnny on the edge of her bed. They were drinking beers and laughing together, sitting close, knees touching, shoulder to shoulder, laughing into each other.

'No,' I said again.

I dug around for the landline, wanting to call her, but I couldn't find it in the mess. I pulled out my mobile but the battery was flat. I saw nothing but black glass.

My wife was laughing with Johnny on Dorm Cam Two, and then – exactly as they were always going to – they stopped laughing.

'Don't,' I said, like a child.

What are the signs of increasing entropy? Ice cubes melting, tea cooling, roofs caving in, glass vases smashing, people ageing, all manner of things we might casually associate with *time passing. As time passes, things fall apart. Or, because things fall apart, time passes.*

Imogen kissed him. He pushed her down hard on the bed and her arms were around him, pulling off his shirt.

The phone rang under a pile of books. I dug it out and pressed the little green button, but I didn't speak.

'Just don't look. Okay, please? I didn't want—'

'What?'

Imogen was crying. 'I wanted to get home and then—'

'Seventy-five thousand, two hundred and six.'

She didn't speak.

'Viewers,' I said.

Imogen-on-screen stopped kissing the man long enough for her top to be tugged up over her head.

'Jesus, Tom, please turn it off.'

'I want you to stop.'

'God. It just—'

'We're happy. All this stuff.' I let my hand find one of the books that'd been tipped off the living-room bookshelf. 'Our life. When you were here. When you left. It wasn't this.'

'I didn't want it to be like this.'

'It wasn't this at all.'

'Please turn it off now.' Imogen-on-the-phone's voice sounded hard through the tears.

Imogen-on-screen's mouth was open, her face flushed and her head thrown back. I knew the shapes her body made, and the sounds of her breath. I knew the way her underwear slipped down and I knew her thighs, and the way her calves looked when her knees were pushed up against her chest.

Afterwards, I felt numb and blank, and I wrote the viewer number from the website on a Post-it and put it up on the board because – well, no reason, but I couldn't stand to be just sitting there, and I had to do something with my hands.

4,442,237.

'Four million, four hundred and forty-two thousand, two hundred and thirty-seven.' I read the number into the phone, and it wasn't until then that I realised I'd been listening to nothing but a flat, dead tone for quite a while.

30

Entropy Tends to a Maximum

I called the police to report the break-in, then I put my back against the living-room wall and slid down to the floor.

I sat there, amongst the leaves and the wreckage of our things, as the sun went down and the streetlights came on outside. I sat staring in the dark, until I heard a knock on the front door and then the sound of it being pushed open.

Panic flared, but before I could stand, the light clicked on overhead, leaving me blinking and blind.

'Bloody hell,' said a man's voice.

I squinted into the glare until the black shape in the doorway resolved itself into a concerned-looking policeman.

'Are you all right?'

'Yeah. I'm not – it was like this when I got back. Burglary.'

I didn't make any attempt to get up, so the policeman clambered through the wreckage towards me. He looked youngish, floppy-haired, and with a big nose. He reminded me of Ringo Starr.

'It's shock.' He perched on the sofa, looking down at me and then around the room. 'Strong, sweet tea's the best thing for it. Should I?'

'No, no. Sorry.' I got myself up. 'I'll do it.'

'Are you sure?' The young officer didn't seem certain I'd make it.

'Yeah. Yes. How do you take it?'

He looked at me as if I'd said something strange.

'Here, sit down,' he said, sweeping debris off the sofa. 'I'll do it.'

He made his way to the kitchen.

'Not the "I love tea" one,' I called after him in a bit of a panic, and then I thought, *that doesn't matter. That really doesn't matter now.*

'Right you are,' he called back.

How weird, I thought, *how weird to be thinking that.*

An old, old feeling came over me – the feeling of snow falling on the inside, of everything becoming quiet and soft, disappearing under a blanket of white.

A couple of minutes later, he came back and handed me a steaming mug with a Dalek on the front.

'There you go, chief.'

'Thanks.' I drank a mouthful then I held the cup under my chin, breathing in the steam for a while.

There's no way to make the steam go back into your cup. Tea only goes cold, entropy only increases, and by increasing it drives the arrow of time. Steam being drawn back into the cup would look like a film playing in reverse. To all intents and purposes, that's impossible.

I thought I might start to cry.

'You just take your time,' the policeman said, nodding. 'Tell me what happened when you're ready.'

'I just got back from a trip with my agent.' I didn't want to talk about Black's manuscript, about the woman claiming to be Sophie, about Imogen. Not right now. 'With my book agent,' I said. 'I write things for a living. So, yeah. I just got back and found the place like this.'

'Sorry, what do you mean, you write things for a living?'

'I'm a writer.' I put down the tea and picked up the reading copy of *The Qwerty Machinegun* that used to live in my desk's bottom drawer. 'That's me, Thomas Quinn.'

The policeman stared at me, as though hoping something very wrong might still turn out to be okay.

'Is this some sort of roleplay, chief?' he asked dubiously. 'You know, figuring it all out?'

'Sorry? No, this is my book. I'm Thomas Quinn.'

'Am I supposed to play along?'

'What?

'Am I supposed to go along with it, you know?'

'With what?' I opened the book's back cover to show him the little author picture printed there. 'Look, this is me.'

'Begging your pardon here, chief, but it isn't.'

I felt numb, vague, under a blanket of fallen snow. Would I have been frightened otherwise? Angry? I don't know. All I felt was very tired, with a vague ache in my stomach that wouldn't go away. I wanted this policeman to go away too.

'I'm having the worst day, Officer . . .'

'Wayburn.'

'. . . Officer Wayburn. And I really don't—' I stopped.

The man in the police officer's uniform took this as recognition, or perhaps he did a very good job of pretending to.

'There you go. It's me, sir, Dan Wayburn.'

In Andrew Black's books, Dan Wayburn is Max Cleaver's sidekick. He has floppy hair, a big nose and, yes, looks a bit like Ringo Starr. I looked at the man, down at the book in my hands, and back to the man again.

'You had me worried there, boss.' He looked relieved, oblivious to whatever my expression was doing. 'Did you take a crack on the head or—'

'Get out.'

'What?'

'Whatever this is, whoever fucking put you up to this. Get out.'

The man calling himself Dan Wayburn held up his palms helplessly.

'Chief, I don't—'

I jumped up, marched into the kitchen. I saw Imogen's 'I ♥ tea' cup miraculously undisturbed next to the kettle and my heart leapt in two different ways at once, then I snatched up the various letters and bills that'd been thrown onto the floor and marched back into the living room.

'Here,' I said, jabbing the letters towards him.

'What's this?'

'My post. With my name on it.' He took the letters. 'Read it out,' I said. 'Read out what it says on those, and then you can go.'

'It says your name.'

'Read it then.'

'Maxwell Cleaver.'

'That is *not* what it says.'

Dan Wayburn offered the letters back to me. I took them, scanned the first one. *Dear Mr Cleaver.* The address at the top was still mine, but the name – *Cleaver*. But. No. I knew these letters. The red bills, the threatening notices, I'd opened them, read them all. And they were the same letters, by which I mean they were almost identical letters, every one, except that every one was now addressed to a Mr Maxwell Cleaver.

Letting them drop to the floor, I scrambled through to the hallway and picked up my travel bag. I rooted around in the bottom until I found what I was looking for, the envelope that started it all. I took out the envelope at the bottom, took out the Polaroid of the black sphere and then unfolded the note. For half a second I felt relieved to see Andrew Black's meticulous handwriting, then I froze.

Dear Maxwell,
Do you know what this is?
Maurice Umber

'Sir, are you okay?' The policeman came through to the hallway.

Filled with a creeping horror, I dropped the letter, rummaged in my travel bag again for the two books that I always took everywhere with me. The man claiming to be Dan Wayburn picked up the note and the Polaroid from the floor.

'What's he playing at, chief?' he said, reading.

I ignored him, getting hold of the solid slab of my father's *Collected Writing* and heaving it out of the bag. The cover read: *Collected Writing, Stanley Cleaver*.

'Quinn,' I said, staring at the book. 'It should say *Quinn*.'

I'd known this book my entire life: every crease, every fold, every scratch on the cover was familiar to me, and every single one of them was still there, exactly as it had always been. But now the name on the cover was different.

Beside me, Wayburn turned what had been Black's note over in his hands.

'This is all wrong,' I said. 'This is not . . . It's all wrong.'

'Hey, chief, is this a poem on the back of here?'

'What?' I said, glancing across to him.

Wayburn showed me the back of the note. In the same neat, precise hand were the stanzas of a poem that hadn't been there before.

'*Turning and turning in the widening gyre*,' he read, '*The falcon cannot hear the falconer; Things fall apart; the centre cannot hold; Mere anarchy is loosed upon the world, The blood-dimmed tide is loosed, and everywhere The ceremony of innocence is drowned; The best lack all conviction, while the worst Are full of passionate intensity.*'

'Yeats,' I said.

'Cheerful stuff. What does it mean?'

Dread dragged me down like Ahab's whale, into the deep, black skull-ballasted depths of the ocean, into the deep black of panic. I began to heave and toss everything else out of my travel bag, looking for the other book.

'*Surely some revelation is at hand*,' Wayburn read. '*Surely the Second Coming is at hand. The Second Coming! Hardly are those words out When a vast image out of* Spiritus Mundi *Troubles my sight . . .*'

I pulled out a bundle covered in bubblewrap and the special UV-resistant plastic that keeps *Superman* comics from falling apart in the sun, then I began to unwrap it.

'*. . . somewhere in sands of the desert, A shape with lion body and the head of a man, A gaze blank and pitiless as the sun, Is moving its slow thighs, while all about it, Reel shadows of the indignant desert birds . . .*'

The bubblewrap came away and there it was. My mother's book: *Broten's Encyclopaedia of British Plants and Trees.* Carefully, very carefully, I searched through to find my mother's rose.

'*. . . The darkness drops again; but now I know That twenty centuries of stony sleep Were vexed to nightmare by a rocking cradle, And what rough beast . . .*'

It wasn't there.

In its place – in its place I found a little black-and-white picture.

An ultrasound scan of an unborn baby.

I let the book tumble from my hands. It landed with a thump on the floor.

Wayburn glanced up at me. '*And what rough beast, its hour come round at last, Slouches towards Bethlehem to be born?*'

I was on my feet before I knew it, on my feet and clambering through the wreckage. Wayburn called out to me, but I was already past him, out in the hallway, then through the door, then outside and running. I ran into the wind and the storm of tumbling leaves. I ran down the street and towards the park with nothing in me but the running and the chaos of the wind and the leaves and the leaves and the leaves . . .

He was leaning against the door of the old church when I got there.

'You took the apple,' Maurice Umber said, smoke billowing and swirling away from the shadowy space under that burned white fedora. 'Everyone knows what that means.'

I fell to my knees. I felt sick and dizzy.

'Black apple, tittle-tattle. Knowledge and Revelation, as promised.' He held up his palms and the edges of that famous white hat burst into flames, creating a ring of fire, a burning halo around his head. 'This is my gospel and my testament.' His voice was a rumbling electronic hum. 'The Gospel of Ink and Autumn. The Testament of the Gutenberg Fall.'

… 3, physic… appeare…
…aw was 100% p…
…, I think, that Grover c…
…e point in the past and b…
…efinitely orange) and that he had…
…nt of his name. 'It's just what peopl…
…s we call you Pip even though your name…
…xplain that I already had the letters for Pip in…
…matter altogether, but my uncle was a very practica…
…truggled to understand each other. Many years later,
…y uncle's N was actually the product of a form of language
…nguists call 'rebracketing'. Up until the 1700s, people would
…with the words 'my' and 'thy' before any noun beginning with a co-
…sound, and 'mine' and 'thine before any noun beginning with
…o there were a lot of people going around saying that …
or 'thine Ed'. Try saying
you'll see how it sounds a
lot like 'my Ned'/'thy Ned'.
Over time, the N became
detached from 'mine' &
attached instead to the
beginning of various
vowel-nouns, making many Eds
and Anns into Neds and
Nans in the process.

Joseph Campbell argues in *The Hero with a Thousand Faces* that a single, underlying narrative structure can be seen again and again in both ancient myths and modern stories from all around the world. He calls this structure the monomyth, or the hero's journey. The stories of Moses and Christ have been described in monomythic terms, as have the adventures …f Frodo Baggins, Luke Skywalker and Jane Eyre. Camp…s this overview of his monomythic structure: 'A hero vent…n the world of common day into a region of supernatural …s forces are there encountered and a decisive victory …omes back from this mysterious adventure with the …n his fellow man.' In other words: the hero goes, …ely wins a great victory. Then, the hero returns …mpbell goes on to break down this journey …n adventure, refusal of the call, cross…f the Whale, Atonement with the …m Without, Master of Two Worlds. …racter encountered on the …ic character

Interestingly, the God of the Old Testament goes about His acts of creation in an eerily similar way to Maxwell's demon. That is to say, God doesn't tend to magic things into existence so much as bring them about through acts of dividing, sorting and arranging. For example: '*God divided the light from the darkness*' (Genesis 1:4); '*And God said, let there be a firmament in the midst of the waters, and let it divide the waters from the waters*' (Genesis 1:6); '*And God said, let the waters under the heaven be gathered together unto one place, and let the dry land appear*' (Genesis 1:9). Genesis even provides a brief description of the primal universe as a strange, high-entropy un-place: '*And the earth was without form and a void; and darkness was upon the face of the deep. And the Spirit of God moved upon the face of the waters*' (Gen. 1:2). God divides this high-entropy nothing space to create the lower-entropy elements of heaven, earth, day, night, sky, land and sea.

The Romans also believed that every man had a guardian spirit or Ally, his "genius" and every woman had a "juno" … Each person made offerings to the genius or Juno on his birthday, in return for guidance and protection, or a little extra brain power.' – Christopher Vogler.

The hero may have to be brought back from his supernatural adventure by assistance from without. That is to say, the world may have to come and get him.' – Joseph Campbell.

…ly true. … to be considered (elsewhere) was … divin… The victory of proto… eighteen hundred years ago is cur… having a huge effect on how you read a… interpret the words on these page… If the Gnostics' standpoint had prevailed, then our relationship with text – and by extension, language and thought – would be quite different today.

PART IV

The Gospel of Ink and Autumn

31

The Hero with a Thousand Faces

Max Cleaver sat in his study, staring at the clock on the wall. The study was dimly lit. Everything in the house was dimly lit these days, on account of his condition. Max Cleaver couldn't remember exactly how long he'd had his condition, only that it occurred during his last confrontation with Maurice Umber, that there'd been some business involving a manuscript and a doll's house, and that bright light was a bad idea.

The clock on the wall needed new batteries. As Cleaver watched, the third hand, the one that counted the seconds, tried unsuccessfully to move past the number 7, and up towards the number 8. He stared at the little red bar as it tried and failed, over and over, rhythmically twitching up towards the 8 without ever arriving. A little twitching pulse, an *almost, almost, almost* that never amounted to anything, but that never stopped either.

There is no time in a novel.

It wasn't a thought – just words that were in his head for some reason, and then they faded away from a lack of interest. It had been a long time since Cleaver had really had a thought, a long time since he'd truly paid attention to much at all, though he often stared at the clock, and right now he could hear his wife talking on the phone with someone out in the hall.

Residual effects and *semi-catatonic state*, Olive Cleaver said, and she thanked them for something, even though her voice sounded sombre and not thankful at all.

And then his wife was in the dim room with him, pulling up a chair and stroking his wrist in the almost-dark.

'Max,' she said. 'Max – that's you. Inspector Maxwell Cleaver. Do you remember? That was Dan on the phone. Dan Wayburn, from the force. He's been so worried ever since he found you all mixed up that day. He calls every evening, wanting to know if you've remembered who you are. He wants you back to your old self.' Olive pushed her long black hair out of her eyes, tucking it behind her ears, and Max looked briefly at the s-shaped scar on her cheek. 'We all want you back, Max. Me, Dan, the baby.'

Cleaver's head turned slightly towards her.

'That's right, the baby. You remember the baby, don't you? I think the baby breaks through into the—' She touched Cleaver's temple, gently, 'I think she finds her way into whatever's going on in there.'

Max Cleaver looked blankly into space.

'You call out for her in the night, you know,' she said. 'You say her name. It's only when you're awake that you forget like this, Max. In the day, you can't find your way back to us from wherever you've ended up. But when you're asleep . . .' Olive breathed out slowly. She took a new, brave breath. 'When you're asleep, I really think that you're Max and you're Daddy again.'

'Mrs Black,' Cleaver said quietly, as if repeating a word in a foreign language without really knowing what it meant.

'No, darling,' Olive said, as if she'd said it a thousand times. 'I'm Olive Cleaver, your wife. There's no Isabelle Black, no Andrew Black, and no Thomas Quinn. We don't know anyone called Imogen, and Sophie won't *ever* call you back because – she's not real, Max. Come on. Come on, darling, it's getting late. Let's go upstairs. You should try to get some sleep.'

o

Max Cleaver stood and stared at the bookcase in his study. A little time had passed and he'd begun to feel a little better and a little more like his old self. There were gaps in the rows of books and he didn't know why. He moved the books around on the shelf, but there were never quite enough books and however he arranged them, it always left exactly three gaps. Cleaver believed that the missing books were *Don Quixote*, *It* and *The Warlock of Firetop Mountain*. Inspector Cleaver had no idea why he might suspect that these were the missing books. Cleaver also suspected that the wall behind his bookcase might well be unsound. He would be at his desk, and would feel a draught coming in from one or more of the gaps between the books. He'd checked the bookcase, and it always seemed solid enough. Nevertheless, the gaps seemed to let in cold air, and this proved to be the case even if he moved the books around to change the location of the gaps. An hour ago, he'd felt a cold draught and turned around to see an orange and brown sycamore leaf settling onto the carpet. All the study windows were shut and, when he checked, he could not see any sycamore trees outside. It felt like a puzzle but he also had some concerns that it might be some lasting remnant of his condition, so he put the sycamore leaf into the waste-paper bin, put on his cardigan and did his best to ignore the bookcase draughts.

A little while later, a baby started to cry in one of the upstairs rooms. In its bedroom or the nursery, he supposed.

Cleaver looked up at the ceiling towards the noise. He knew that his wife Olive would take care of the baby. She always did, and she always stopped the crying. When he thought about it though – he still didn't think about things all that often – it occurred to Maxwell Cleaver that he hadn't seen his wife in some time. When he thought about it some more, he realised that he couldn't remember having seen the baby at all. That concerned him. How was it that he couldn't remember having seen his own little girl? Surely he *had* seen her. Or had they not let him see her yet on account of his condition? Cleaver was hazy on the details. He was hazy on all of it.

And still, the baby kept crying.

Could Olive be out? Was Cleaver supposed to be looking after the baby? That seemed unlikely.

'Olive?' he said. 'Olive. It's the baby.'

He listened, but there were no sounds of movement in the house.

Cleaver decided to take matters into his own hands. She was his baby, after all. Cleaver opened his study door, and then realised that he didn't know which was the baby's room. Apart from the bedroom and his study, his knowledge of the house was as vague as everything else. Why should that be? The baby was still crying in a room upstairs and Maxwell Cleaver ventured out of his study and into the hallway.

On the landing at the top of the stairs, he encountered a strange wooden toy set. A nativity scene. Cleaver couldn't be sure that it wasn't Christmas; the weather had turned cold and the landscape outside his study window certainly seemed bleak – nothing but tough, coarse grasses and a few bare, distant trees, the empty sky, the cliffs and the sea pounding the rocks below. It could be Christmas, but then, where were all the other Christmas decorations? And the nativity set was very strange. The baby Jesus in his manger looked as he should, but all of the other characters had been replaced with angels. Dozens of copies of the same angel figurine filled the stable. Two stood in Mary and Joseph's spots, a small group clustered where the shepherds should be, and three angels approached the manger in a row, clearly replacements for the wise men. Cleaver looked closer. The angels were not quite all the same. The angel taking the place of the lead wise man carried a gift, and the gift was a small, round, perfectly black sphere. *The apple.*

Why would he think that the thing was an apple? Because. Hazy. He let the words evaporate. His baby was still crying and he needed to stop wasting time and get to her.

He followed the crying to a bedroom door and pushed it open.

He blinked. The room inside wasn't dark and gloomy; the curtains were open and the space was filled with light. Despite the gale blowing outside, this room was very still. Dust motes hung golden in the air. It was a bedroom, but not his bedroom. He knew it though. At the very core of his soul, he knew it. Cleaver crossed the room to the bed. There was a large book on the bedside table, a horticultural book about plants and trees. The book had been left open, and lying on the open page was a beautiful bright red rose, freshly cut and full of life. Cleaver touched the rose with his finger.

The baby was still crying. He looked around. There was another door, a room coming off this room – a nursery. He crossed to this new door. Yes, the crying was coming from inside. Cleaver pushed the door open.

It *was* a nursery. A little white crib, coloured bunting hanging from the ceiling, bookcases, chairs and a little doll's house in the corner.

The crying, naturally enough, was coming from the crib. Cleaver approached. There was no baby inside. The crying was coming from a laptop in the crib. A laptop. The laptop had a copy of Microsoft Word open onscreen, and it was crying. Cleaver, still very hazy and still getting back into the swing of having thoughts, wondered if he should cuddle the laptop to stop it from crying. He went to do this, but as he reached in to pluck it up, he pressed one of the keys and a small 'a' appeared at the top of the Word document. Immediately, the crying settled down a little, but only for a moment. The laptop began crying again. Cleaver reached in and pressed a couple more keys experimentally, and that seemed to calm the crying down some more. Cleaver lifted the laptop out of the crib, wrapped a protective arm around it and typed the words *When I was little, my father was famous.* The crying stopped, and the laptop made a soothed and contented little cooing noise. Cleaver had a strange mixture of feelings. But his heart ached a little and he felt that, somehow, the world was improved.

o

Maxwell Cleaver awoke in bed. The room was dark and gloomy. The bedroom door opened and someone came in, but that someone was not his wife.

'Hello, Mr Cleaver,' said the man. 'My name is Dr Sackler, and I've come to check up on you. See how you're getting along. Do you mind if I have a look at you?' The man was close enough now to see properly through the gloom. He had ginger hair and big, thick, curly sideburns. He looked familiar.

Max Cleaver's brow furrowed. *He looked familiar.*

'Now, this condition of yours, Mr Cleaver. I have to tell you that, at this stage, there's a chance you've suffered lasting damage to your hippocampus, thalamus, paleomammalian cortex, which would certainly account for your confused state—'

Hippocampus, thalamus, paleomammalian cortex.

Max Cleaver suddenly found himself thinking about a noisy train.

Hippocampus, thalamus, paleomammalian cortex.

'Pardon?' he said, abruptly.

'I'm sorry?' said the doctor, who'd still been giving his diagnosis.

'What did you say? Hippocampus . . .'

'Hippocampus, thalamus, paleomammalian cortex.'

Max Cleaver sat up in bed.

'I know you,' he said.

The doctor looked surprised. 'No, Mr Cleaver. I've only just joined your case, so there's no way you could have. Have—'

'I know you. You were on the train.'

The doctor looked carefully at Max Cleaver for the first time. A look of recognition and panic flashed across his face.

Max Cleaver saw it.

'You *were* on the train, weren't you?' said Cleaver.

'No. I think you're confused because of the—'

Hazy. Condition. Cleaver rubbed his. Cleaver rubbed his eye. His. I.

Rubbed his. I. I rubbed my eye. I.

I rubbed my eyes.

'I'm not confusing you,' I said through the fog. 'You were sitting across from me on the train to Hull. You had that big block of printed pages and you were reciting medical words over and over.' I spoke slowly, giving these thoughts time to come.

And they did come.

'I thought you were a student practising for an exam. But that's not what it was. You were practising for this. The big block of pages wasn't exam revision, was it? It was a script.'

32
The Revelation of Thomas

I'm sitting on the windy porch of Maxwell Cleaver's house, wearing Maxwell Cleaver's clothes and wrapped up tight against the cold in Maxwell Cleaver's jacket. But Maxwell Cleaver doesn't really exist. He's just a fictional character from a book. My name is Thomas Quinn. I am a real flesh-and-blood person, and I've been doing a lot of thinking.

I look up, squinting against the wind at the sound of a car engine. A few seconds later, it rounds the bend and makes the long lonely crawl up the lane towards the house. The sky is white. The sea booms against the cliffs. The air tastes of salt.

The car, a police car, stops in front of the house and a man gets out.

'I wondered when you'd get here,' I call to him.

Sergeant Dan Wayburn isn't really Sergeant Dan Wayburn, of course; he never has been. Sergeant Dan Wayburn is another fictional character. But we're going to let that slide for now.

Dan sits down on the porch next to me. 'You all right, Max?'

'I am, Dan. I'm all right because I've cracked the case.'

'That's great news.' Dan is maybe a little bit hesitant, but he's doing very well, all things considered. 'What case?'

'Well, that's the thing, you see. Take a look around for me, would you, Dan? Take a good long look, at the house, at our clothes, at your police car parked over there.'

'Yes, boss . . . okay.'

'Good man. Now, here's the deal. One of two things is happening here, and that thing has been happening for quite a long time.'

'Right.'

'Either we're looking at Option One: the tidy kitchen of linear narrative and, by extension, our world, which God somehow wrote into being with his divine choir of Mighty As, Greedy Cs, and our rogue, devilish friend, Selfish I – this narrative is in the process of entropic collapse. A process caused by black hole hyperlinks, electronic text and the internet, because without the protective beginning and end of a good, solid, old-fashioned, physical book, entropy gets a free hand in all of it, leaving the final state of everything to become a meaningless, orderless jumble of dust.'

'I . . . right. Okay then. And Option Two?'

'Option Two is . . . well . . . Option Two is that somebody is fucking with me on a truly monumental scale, Dan.'

Dan Wayburn doesn't quite manage to look me in the eye.

'Here's a spoiler for you,' I say. 'It's the second one. But you know that already, don't you?'

'I don't—'

'My name isn't Maxwell Cleaver. I'm Thomas Quinn and I'm a writer. Or, I used to be.'

'Chief, I'm not – I really don't know what you're talking about.'

'Okay,' I say. 'If you like.'

'I don't . . .'

'Well, okay then. But I am dressed like the detective, and I have solved the case. Should I just keep pushing on?'

'I—'

'All right then. So. The case was hiding, you see – that's a key point here. The case was hiding just like the solution to that old thought experiment Maxwell's demon was hiding. Here,' I say, 'Look.' I pick up the stick that's next to me on the porch and draw a circle in the dirt. 'Thermodynamics. If something seemingly impossible is happening inside your closed system, then – pound to a penny – your system isn't closed at all, but open, letting in energy, and part of a larger closed system in some subtle way that you hadn't realised.' I draw a larger circle around the first, then I rub out part of the inner circle, making it look like a 'C'. 'Do you see?' I say.

Dan nods.

'Now with our case, the larger this outer, hidden, closed system is, the more improbable it seems. And this sense of improbability is the very thing that helps to hide it. Have you ever heard of the idea that a good magic trick works in the opposite way to a good story – through the encouragement of disbelief?'

'Uhhh. No.'

'Okay, so. Quick version. A mark is sitting in a theatre, watching a magic trick. If a mark happens upon a magic trick's actual solution while pondering how the trick was accomplished, but then goes on to consider how that solution would be too complex, outlandish, and unlikely to be true, then the mark discards the solution from their consideration. The trick goes unsolved. So, something being massively complex and unlikely doesn't stop it from being true is what we're saying. It fact, it's a very, very good way to hide that true thing in plain sight.'

I begin to draw larger and larger circles, each one encompassing the last.

'And the exact same thing is going on here, with our case. The larger the closed system is, the more work must've gone into creating and maintaining it, so the more outlandish and improbable it seems, the more likely we are to reject it as a solution. But. But, but, but. We need to ignore those nagging feelings of improbability, because they're the very thing stopping us from seeing the truth, you see? We have to keep going out and out, through larger and larger circles, concerning ourselves with just one thing' – I drag the stick out through each of the circles in turn, making a hole in each one, until I reach the biggest one on the outside – 'the point where everything balances. The point where we can identify the other key thing; energy being expended to account for all the strange work we've seen being done.' I wave my stick at the house, at Dan's police car, at Dan. 'And by *strange work*, I mean this, and this. And you.'

'Okay.'

'Einstein said that you don't argue with the Second Law of Thermodynamics, and we don't want to argue with Einstein, do we, Dan?'

'No, sir.'

'Good man.' I tap the edge of the largest circle. 'So this is what we're dealing with here: something so big, so obsessive, so unlikely and with so much inside it, that you'd be very hard pressed to spot it, to even force your mind to believe in its existence. Unless the actual shape of this massive closed system gave itself away somehow.'

'How would it do that?'

'We'll get to that in a minute. You see this part here?' I tap the C in the middle of the rings. 'You people putting me in this house, putting these clothes on me, shaking my grip on reality to the point where you're calling me Max Cleaver and I'm most of the way believing it, this is only the centre of something much larger—'

'But you are—'

'No, I'm not. I'm Thomas Quinn, as you well know, mister whoever-you-really-are. Right now I'm the mark sitting in the theatre, and I've just seen how the magic trick is being done. And it's beautifully put together. I mean, of course it is. Look at you, Dan. I'm going to keep calling you "Dan" because it's easier. But you're not really Dan Wayburn, are you? You're an actor. All of you are actors – no, shhh, you don't have to say anything, just listen. You're doing a great job. But there's so much more to it than that. This circle is huge. There are clues though, if you know what you're looking for.'

'What sort of clues, sir?'

'Well, here's the thing, Dan. None if this is just happening by itself, is it? Energy is being expended somewhere to produce all this strange, useful work. Like I said, all these occurrences, these events, have been carefully planned, arranged, and carried out so that – for me – it seems to be a series of real things happening in the real world. But it's not. None of it is *just happening*. It's a sort of heavily orchestrated . . . let's not say "con". I'm going to charitably say "interactive performance". It's a play, essentially, isn't it? A play with just one audience member – me – who isn't supposed to be aware of the play at all. But even the simplest play takes a lot of work behind the scenes to pull off. Now, every play has to have a planner, an arranger, an orchestrator – a *writer*. My guess is, this writer is the one secretly putting all the energy into this closed system. Good stories seem to just work, but they are actually *made* to work by *the artfully concealed application of a shitload of time*. And here's the thing about writers – they're like poker players, they all have individual tells that give them away. That's how computers can tell which bits of Shakespeare's plays he did and didn't write.'

'What?'

'Doesn't matter. The point is, when we get out here' – I tap the outer circle – 'not only can we tell that someone is putting in a lot of energy to make all this work, but we can potentially recognise who that someone is by what the work itself – what this whole big interactive performance – feels like.'

'So what are these tells, chief? What are you looking for?'

'Have you ever heard of a book called *The Hero with a Thousand Faces?* And there's another one called *The Writer's Journey* that breaks it down – but anyway, these books talk a whole lot about the character archetypes.'

'Character—'

'Right, quick version again. In stories, classically constructed stories, every character has a role, a specific job to make the story work, and once you know those roles, those jobs, you can spot the archetypes they are. *The mentor, the shadow, the shapeshifter.* You'll see them again and again. You're an *ally*, by the way.'

'I am?'

'Oh yes, and you're doing a great job. Anyway, our hidden writer of this interactive performance leans very hard into his archetypes, that's his tell. That's what's given this away' – I tap on the big circle – 'as a constructed narrative. Real life doesn't have character archetypes. Stuff is messier. But this giant closed system' – the stick swirls around the big circle – 'is full of neatly engineered storytelling and character archetypes, because he can't help himself. A story is a machine, you see, Dan. It's a machine that can only work in balance and counterbalance with itself. This, this performance that we're living in now, it's a wonderfully, insanely detailed, complicated artifice. It's one big—'

And as I'm speaking, my mind is travelling back to Hull after my first meeting with Black, when I first read *Cupid's Engine*, my sense of wonder at its construction, and the mechanical, meticulous tick-tock shape that story took on in my mind. And then, almost incidentally, I glance down at the series of circles I've drawn in the dirt. I find my eyes widening in surprise and a slow smile spreading across my face – a smile of wonder, despite everything. I've drawn nine circles in the dust. Now, I carefully draw one little dot somewhere on the line of each circle.

'It's one great big orrery,' I say. 'This play, this interactive performance, it runs like a Victorian orrery, Dan. You know, those models of the solar system with all the little brass planets and the orbits. That's what this is, what it feels like. Along with the character archetypes, that meticulousness is his tell. Now I can see it, I'd know it anywhere.'

'I'm not following you.' He looked down at the drawing in the dirt. 'Is this about God and the planets again? God making the universe with letters?'

I stare at him. Then I stare down at my dirt drawing, which does look like the solar system, and a cold prickle runs up the back of my neck. I feel a door opening a crack somewhere in the back of my head, and something truly vast beyond it.

I push the images away and scrub my fingers hard through my hair.

'No, no. Look, it's a model, a machine. The feel of it, and his use of character archetypes give it away. We can even think of the character archetypes as the planets, if you want, all doing their jobs balancing each other out. Once we find the outlying one, we can see the balance and the shape of this whole thing.'

'Not following you.'

'All right. So, this one out here' – I tap the dot on the biggest circle – 'one character archetype is known as the *Threshold Guardian*. Now, the threshold guardian's job in the story is to try to stop the hero from going on the quest, and to help us – the audience – understand how very dangerous that quest will prove to be in the first place. They have an important role in setting up the story, do you see?'

'Sort of.'

'I've had my agent for six and a half years, Dan. But I never went to her office in all of that time, isn't that strange? And here's the thing, she is clearly, obviously, 100 per cent, a threshold guardian. That means this closed system, this pantomime, this little performance that you and I are in the middle of now, didn't start when I showed up here, drugged by a hot cup of tea – thanks for that by the way – and it didn't start when I got on that train to go and steal Andrew Black's lost manuscript either. This closed system – this interactive play, let's stick with that – is six and a half years across. Which is fucking mind-blowing, I know, but she's the threshold guardian in this narrative. The story doesn't work properly without her, and because he really can't do true meaninglessness, he's given himself away.'

'Right. Who?'

'What?'

'Who can't help himself?'

'Andrew Black.'

'Who's Andrew Black?'

'Precisely, Dan. I think that's the question we need to be asking ourselves here. I'd always believed that Max Cleaver was based on Andrew Black, but what if Andrew Black the author is actually based on Maxwell Cleaver, the character?'

'But that's impossible, isn't it?'

'Is it?'

'A writer can't be based on the character they've written.'

'You're saying that effect can't come before its cause?' I ask.

'I suppose I am.'

'Well, that's true, probably. But what if someone is expending an awful lot of energy behind the scenes to make it look like it can? Stories are tricky. I called the University of Hull. That's the real edge of the circle by the way, that letter arriving from Black asking me to talk to his creative writing class. That's when we enter this closed system, this con, this real-world pantomime.'

'You were saying *interactive play*.'

'Right. That's when it starts. Black asked me to talk to his creative writing class at the University of Hull. Only, I called the University of Hull about an hour ago and they'd never heard of Andrew Black and never heard of the name he claimed to be teaching under, Mike Mondegrass, either. They said they'd never had a member of staff by either name. I called them, you see, because I realised that he met me outside reception that day, before I could go in and ask for him, and he taught his class in the open air, not in one of the classrooms. The fact is, I didn't interact with the university at all that day, except through Andrew Black himself. Why would that be?'

'Because this Andrew Black was never a real teacher . . . ?'

'Exactly, ten points for the Ally. The students who went along to his occasional classes went by invite only – they were duped into playing window dressing to the performance. We were all attending a university class that wasn't really a university class at all, and none of us had any idea.'

'Which means?

'Which means, at the very least, that Andrew Black an out-and-out crazy person. But I think it goes a lot deeper than that. You know, I met a woman who told me that she was the real Sophie Almonds. She also said that there is no Andrew Black. That it's just a pen name. I think maybe that's true. The doctor was an actor, you're an actor, Sophie, as insane as it sounds, has been playing her threshold guardian role for years. So why does Black himself have to be real? Isn't it possible that whoever is doing this looked at the novel *Cupid's Engine* very carefully, and came up with the character of Andrew Black in a sort of reverse engineering exercise – creating the kind of author you might expect to have written a book like that? At this stage, all bets are off.'

I got to my feet.

'Come on,' I said.

'Where are we going?'

'We're going to find Andrew Black.'

Wayburn followed me to his car.

'But you just said he doesn't exist. Didn't you?'

'The thing is, Dan, somebody wrote *Cupid's Engine*, and somebody wrote' – I held out my arms – 'whatever living, breathing pantomime this is. My hypothesis is this: the same mind that wrote the labyrinth of that novel, also created the labyrinth that we're in now.'

We got into Wayburn's car.

'Andrew Black is a pen name,' I said. 'And I'm pretty sure I know whose pen name it is.'

Wayburn clicked in his seatbelt and started the car.

'So where are we going?' he said.

'Into the woods.'

'What?'

'Back into the Special World of the story. That's the most complicated part of all this, the part that must've needed supervising especially closely. Take us to Owthorne.'

Wayburn looked at me. 'Do you know how to get there?'

'No,' I said. 'But you do, don't you, Dan? Because I'm guessing that's where you just came from.'

Wayburn looked at me for a moment, his face unreadable.

'If you say so, chief,' he said, and he started the car.

o

I stood in the empty car park of the Weerby Hotel with the man who was pretending to be Dan Wayburn.

'What's your real name?' I said.

'Sorry, sir?'

'When you're not pretending to be a fictional police officer, who are you?'

He looked at me. No denial, just a face that was a perfect, passive blank.

'Fine,' I sighed. 'Have it your way. This will all be over soon anyway.'

We stood there in silence for a moment.

'Do you know what happened after *Cupid's Engine* was published, Dan?'

'I don't, chief, no.'

'My father died.'

'Oh. I'm sorry to hear that.'

'My famous, brilliant father died a couple of years after giving a glowing endorsement to a wonderful new book with a mysterious author, even though he'd never done that for a novel before. He died seven years ago, off in Spain somewhere. I'm saying he died, but I didn't go to the funeral. I've never seen a grave or a death certificate.'

'Right,' said Dan.

'You see what I'm saying here, don't you, Dan?'

'I think I do.'

'Am I getting warm?'

'No clues,' Dan said. 'You're the detective.'

I looked at him. He gave me the blank face again.

'He called me, you know. Started talking through the answer machine.'

Still blank, so I pushed on:

'I think that seven years is enough time to get this whole thing up and running, and to prepare for a finale like this. I mean, you couldn't do it in much less. And my father made a lot of money from his writing. A lot of money. Doing all of this, pulling this off, it'd take a lot of money, wouldn't you say, Dan?'

'If you say so, boss.'

'All this stuff about babies, empty cribs. It's all about how hurt he was when we fell out, you see. Because, well, that's writers for you, isn't it? A normal person would just say how they fucking felt. A normal father would just say *sorry*, or *I'm not sorry, fuck you*, or, you know, something. But my father had no interest, was always utterly incapable of engaging with anything that wasn't a performance. It had to come with an armful of prizes and a glowing, full-page review in *The Times* or he was *just not there for it*, you know?'

Dan looked at me.

'I thought my father was haunting me from beyond the grave,' I said. 'Only he's not beyond the grave at all. He's right here.'

Wayburn looked up at the Weerby Hotel. 'And you think this is the place, do you, boss?'

'I do.'

'I stayed on the sixth floor here, and when I went to talk to Hello My Name Is Janet—'

'My – ?'

'Doesn't matter. But when I went to talk with her, we went up to the top floor, floor seven, which is an abandoned function room. No one had been up there since the '80s.'

'So what?'

'So who was banging around above my head the whole time I was staying in that room on floor six, and keeping me awake? You know, there's an easy way to check how many floors a building has. You just count the rows of windows on the outside. Could you do that for me, Dan?'

'One, two, three, four, five, six, seven . . . eight.'

'Come on,' I said, heading towards the hotel, 'we're going to see what's on floor six-and-a-half.'

o

We stepped out of the revolving doors and into the quiet lobby. There were no guests now, and reception stood unmanned. Low-level muzak drifted through from somewhere, over tinny speakers. Everything else was still.

I saw the figure sitting alone at a table in the corner of the room.

'This is as far as I go,' Wayburn said at my ear.

'I see.'

'Good luck, chief.' He nodded. He turned, stepped back into the revolving doors, and was gone.

I walked across the room, footsteps echoing.

'You almost had me at the end there,' I said.

The man I'd always known as Andrew Black got to his feet and we met, face to face for the last time.

'You're not him, are you?' I said. 'You're not Andrew Black.'

'No,' the man said.

I let out a long, slow breath. Thinking something and knowing it are not even remotely the same thing.

'All this time,' I said.

'All this time,' he agreed.

'You know, I always wondered why someone so neat and obsessive would keep their hair all shaggy like yours. I've only realised the reason why now that I'm standing in front of you.' I raised my hands towards his face. 'Can I?'

He seemed to think for a moment. I'd come to know that look well, although I understood now that he wasn't really thinking at all.

He looked back to me and nodded.

I took my hands and slowly pushed the long hair back behind his ears.

The earpiece was on the left. A small, skin-coloured speaker tucked inside the ear itself, with a tiny little mic looping under the lobe. Even with his hair back, most people wouldn't have noticed it. Expensive. Of course it was.

'The lines come in through here?'

He nodded.

'It was very good,' I said, 'a very good performance.'

His shoulders dipped in a very slight bow of thanks. The man had masterful control of his face, keeping it completely neutral in a way that Dan Wayburn had never quite managed. *And why not,* I thought, *this guy is the lead, isn't he? Don't be surprised that he's great at his job.*

'I never knew you at all, did I?'

He kept his face blank.

I turned away.

'But I saw something special in you, Tom,' the man said, out of nowhere. 'I hope you know that.'

My skin prickled. I turned slowly, looked at the man I'd always known as Andrew Black.

'Would that be a personal opinion?' I asked him.

Looking straight ahead, the man, the actor, gave a slow shake of the head.

'It came down the earpiece?'

A nod.

'Right.'

I thought of my father's words leaving ink on my fingers from the giant, broadsheet newspaper, his voice crackling in over the radio. A man dismantled. I thought of that old, old magic trick. How all these parts could come back together to make a man.

'You know,' I said, 'I think I've been waiting for this to happen all of my life.'

The actor touched his ear.

'Hello again, Tom,' he said, looking straight ahead.

'Where are you?'

'You know where I am.'

'I do,' I said. 'You're upstairs. Floor six-and-a-half.'

'I'm waiting for you where I've always been.'

'What's that supposed to mean?'

The man paused for a moment, then looked at me and shook his head.

'I don't have any more lines,' he said.

I realised then that I'd been crying. I rubbed at my eyes angrily.

'Tell him. Tell him I'm coming up.'

o

A second after the lift passed the sixth floor, I jabbed at the emergency button on the control panel. *Because that's how they do it in stories.*

The lift came to a sudden stop.

The doors opened.

And outside . . .

. . . outside was the secret floor.

I stepped out of the lift to find a carpeted hotel corridor and a trail of rose petals.

I bent, picked one up. Soft, fresh, brand new.

I followed the trail along the corridor, and it led me to a little anteroom with a set of large, closed double doors beyond. In the middle of this anteroom was a small table, and on that table stood a large vase of red roses, and about two dozen of my father's books, many of them published after his death, books I'd never read.

Collected Works III, IV, V, VI, VII.

On top of the pile of books sat a single white envelope.

I took it.

In familiar, neat and careful handwriting, the words on the front read:

I found this letter in your father's things after he died.
You should read it.
AB

I opened the envelope, took out the single sheet of paper inside, and began to read:

Dear Thomas,

I'm sorry.

Is that something? Is it anything? Two words. Seven letters. Curls and loops, ink and paper. Can we make something out of that, the two of us? Is it possible that I can write those shapes and that you will read them, and something can live and grow and become solid in the space between the one act and the other? I have lived with words for all of my life and still their magic and their strangeness amazes and confuses me, and often defeats me altogether.

I tried to balance my life in a way that seemed right. Between providing for you and what you needed, and what I needed for myself. In deciding to carve up my time in the world – I got my sums wrong. I am sorry. You needed me, and I was not there. When your mother died, you needed me even more and, God above, I was there even less. It is inexcusable. I loved your mother so very much. But still, inexcusable.

My assistant reminds me of you sometimes. I was going to write 'sometimes I wonder if I took on an assistant because I wanted to fill the gap you left when things went bad between us', but I am sick and done with artifice, and beating around the bush. I'll just tell you – that's exactly why I did it. I even encouraged my assistant to write fiction, because I always secretly dreamed of encouraging you to do so. Do you ever think about writing, Thomas? Does it hold any interest for you? I would be delighted to read anything you wrote, although I worry that my association with words and stories may have soured them for you.

I talk about you a lot, especially now, as we go about wrapping up what's left of my work. I'm beginning to suspect that my assistant has developed something of a fascination with you. My God, isn't that something? Although I have done what I can to forbid it, I wouldn't be at all surprised if the two of you end up face to face before long. Especially when I'm no longer here to caution against it.

A word of warning: if my assistant is determined to meet you, and I think she is, then that will probably happen. If she can write a book like Cupid's Engine, *and if she can have half the world running around looking for a fictional, middle-aged male author, then she can most certainly find a way to sit you down for twenty minutes for a cup of coffee.*

Please don't take your feelings about me out on her. She is good and clever and capable, and I think you might even have been friends if things had been different between you and I.

Those words again, and I hope you, we, can find a way to make them breathe: I am sorry.

With all my love,
Dad

I stood holding the letter for a while. I don't know how long.

I stared at the words on the page until they became shapes.

If Black is determined to meet you, and I think she is . . .

She.

I put the letter into my back pocket.

Enough now, I thought. Then, I walked around the table, pushed the large double doors beyond it open, and went inside.

o

I stepped into what looked like a control room, entirely empty and silent, with banks of monitors and roller chairs. There were makeshift dressing spaces and I saw mannequins wearing dozens of familiar costumes: the receptionist, Sergeant Claybourn, Andrew Black's various outfits, Isabelle Black. The last one had a note pinned to it in familiar handwriting – *mine, do not touch.*

I found a compact editing suite, with a file all cued-up onscreen and ready to go. I pressed play, and the programme ran half a dozen quick snippets from my father's various interviews and appearances over the years, assembling disparate words and phrases to form a question:

'Why an ox and an angel in Bethlehem?'

Listening in the quiet like that, I could hear how the audio had been cleverly stitched together. Something I hadn't been able to catch while running across the flat with my trousers around my ankles.

I moved on.

At the far end of the room stood a large pair of soundproof double doors, with a red sign brightly lit above them – *Recording. Do Not Enter.*

I paused for a moment, then took hold of both handles and pushed them open.

I stepped inside and—

My breath leaked out of my body in a hopeless little gasp.

It was a view I knew probably better than any view in the world.

A view I'd sat staring at for God knows how many long hours and sleepless nights.

I stood in a room full of beds.

But these beds were not supposed to be here.

These beds were supposed to be housed in a building eight thousand miles away, on the other side of the world, on Easter Island.

These beds were supposed to be for a research team doing important work on what happened to the indigenous people of that distant and lonely place.

I knew then:

There was no building, no research team, no twelve-month trip.

The view was familiar in a million different ways, but the view wasn't real. Beyond its edges stood cameras, monitors, lights, cables, steel cases full of equipment. This was a studio.

This was a set.

The view had always been a set.

The set had always been here, so –

She had always been here.

I found myself looking at the view from Dorm Cam Two.

I found myself standing in Imogen's bedroom.

33

A Palace in the Hereafter

'Hello, Eagle One.'

I turned around slowly, and there was Imogen, sitting on a folding table, holding a little tinsel halo above her head.

'Imogen.'

'Hey.'

'What the fuck?'

'I know. I may have gotten a *little* carried away.'

'Jesus fucking Christ.'

'Uh-huh, that's fair.'

'Are you really real, Imogen? Please tell me you're real and not an actor like every other fucker around here.'

'No, no. I'm real.'

I came closer, seeing her better. She looked scruffy. Uncombed, greasy hair. She smelled like she needed sleep, like she needed a bath. She'd applied a fresh coat of red lipstick though. Somehow that seemed real and reassuring, and also more fucking weird than anything else.

'I didn't sleep with him,' she said. 'In case you didn't figure that out from the—' She waved a hand towards the dormitory set.

I just stood there.

'Please be real,' I said quietly.

'I am.'

A moment passed.

'You look like shit, you know.'

She nodded. 'You've been . . . keeping us busy.'

'And you smell too bad to be an actor. That's a valid thing, right?'

'Actually, some actors fucking stink, for whatever that's worth. But, yes, I'm real. I'm me.'

'But. How can you be?'

'Because.' She toyed with the tinsel halo, fidgeting with it between her fingers.

My brain did its best to catch up.

'She. That agent. She said Andrew Black was a pen name. I thought that meant that Andrew Black was my father.'

'No.' Imogen put the halo down gently, and stared down at her feet dangling over the edge of the table. 'Stanley Quinn is dead, Tom. Well. As dead as any writer ever can be.'

'My father's really dead.'

'Really dead.'

'Huh.'

'Andrew Black was your father's research assistant,' Imogen said. 'Everybody knows that. Your father nurtured Andrew Black's love of writing, helped her get her first book published. He wrote that blurb for the cover, and he talked about this son of his that he'd ruined things with.'

'He said that?'

'Yes. All the time. Right up until he died.'

'And. *Her*? Andrew Black is a her.'

'She is.'

'Are you Andrew Black, Imogen?'

'I am.'

'You wrote *Cupid's Engine*?'

'Of course I did.'

A million thoughts, questions and protestations all tried to make it out of my mouth at once and caused a sort of logjam, leaving me speechless. I remembered her there at Black's creative writing class on the grass outside the university, appearing beside me. *Is this seat taken?* And somehow she followed my thoughts:

'I wanted to meet you. I was curious, because your father talked so much about you. But, I suppose things snowballed between us, didn't they?'

'All this was you.'

'Yes.'

'Isabelle Black at the hotel at breakfast, that was you. Actually, physically you.'

'Yes.'

'And everything about Imogen and Andrew Black's marriage, what happened to them. The baby?'

Imogen didn't answer. She looked down, looked away.

I'd come to know her expressions over the years, the things her face said when she didn't say anything. Suddenly there was no sound, no breath in me.

'Oh God,' I said.

Then, in a small voice, I managed eight more words:

'Why didn't you tell me about the baby?'

'I've been trying,' she said, at last. 'Don't you think I've been trying? I've been trying to tell you all sorts of things. Andrew's childhood? Ursula, Newhall? Your father wrote that story. Ursula Black was going to be your mother's pen name for her *Lost Books of the Bible*, and he cast himself as Newhall, the idiot who wasn't there when his son needed him. He wrote it to say that he understood how he'd failed you. He wanted to give you it to you, but he couldn't bring himself to call. So I did it after he died. And yes, I was Isabelle. And yes, all that stuff about her and Andrew was about us. I tried to tell you about . . . about . . .' She stopped, stared off into the distance.

'You were pregnant with our baby, and you didn't tell me. The baby died, and you didn't tell me. Instead, you made all of this. Why the fuck didn't you just tell me like a normal fucking person?'

'How could I?' She almost yelled it, and then, staring me straight in the eye: 'How could anyone? And anyway, don't you think I tried? You're still so hung up on something that happened twenty years ago, that you don't see time passing. You're not the neglected child any more, Tom, you're the adult now – you. And you didn't notice. *You* didn't notice. I tried to tell you.'

'You tried.'

'I tried.'

'A normal person would've tried harder.'

Imogen flung out her arms. 'Harder than this?!'

'A normal person—'

'Stop saying that to me. *I am not* a normal person.'

'You do not fucking say!'

Neither one of us spoke for a little while. Finally, Imogen broke the silence:

'When I fell out with my publishers over electronic books and they signed me to that gagging order – that part's all true, by the way – I thought it didn't matter, that I could be happy with you, that it would be enough. But. I couldn't get over the loss.' Imogen wiped her eyes, laughed a sad little laugh. 'The world really is ending, you know. A hyperlink really is an atom bomb and truth will mean nothing at all in a year or two, you'll see. It's all falling apart.'

'You really believe that?'

'It's not a case of believing. It's happening already.'

'So you have all this stuff that you want to get out there into the world but you can't write, can't publish any more, so you needed someone to write it all for you. Someone who could experience all these things and come to believe them, someone who you could push and push and push until they're in a position where they'd have no choice *but* to write it down, like a prophet hammering out his vision of the apocalypse. You even trained me for the job, didn't you? I'm not your husband; I'm your *fucking ghostwriter* and I didn't even realise.'

'That would be a harsh thing for a lover and a friend to do, wouldn't it?'

'Yes. It would.'

'But then, someone who really, truly believed those things would have a very serious obligation to make them as widely known as possible, no?'

'And *Cupid's Engine* sold however many million copies, is what you're saying?'

Imogen nodded. 'The book gets read, the message spreads.'

'It's cruel, Im. It's inhuman.'

She gave a sad little shrug.

'It is. But then, you're assuming that I'm Imogen the human, who's pretending to be Iota the angel. Maybe I've always been Iota. In the Bible, it says that the angels came to earth and had children with people, did you know about that?'

Imogen picked up the little tinsel halo again.

It twinkled a little more brightly at the touch of her fingers.

For a moment, it *glittered*.

I felt my brow crease.

'What is the world made of, do you think,' she said, 'when you really look at it? Is it rocks and trees and rivers, or is it letters and pages and words? Do our questions make the universe? If it goes unobserved, does the universe even exist, or is it like a story in a book, a story that needs a reader's eye moving over the letters to bring order and meaning, to cause the wave to collapse into a particle? Do the dark waters have to be seen and divided by a Maxwell's demon, by a God, to make a something from a nothing?'

'Have you lost your fucking mind, Im? Is that what this is?'

'Maybe. Oh Jesus, I have a whole lot of things going on in here right now, Tom, a whole fucking lot. But I need to be careful what I let out, because the choosing and sorting can't get tipped too far this way or the other.'

'What are you talking about? I'm here. You mad fucking, mad . . . lunatic. I'm here, and I demand that you tell me every last fucking thing. I love you, and you're telling me there was a baby?' I could only stare at her when I heard the words coming out of my mouth, and she stared right back. 'We had a baby.'

'Autumn. She died inside me. Her name was Autumn.'

'Christ.' I hung my head.

Imogen watched me, but didn't speak.

'And now you think you're an angel,' I said.

'And now you don't get to know what I think. Home truths and hard facts could ruin the whole thing. I wish I could talk to you, my God, believe me. I mean. Look at me. I'm in need of a long fucking chat.'

'So talk to me.'

'I can't. The wave doesn't collapse into a particle until someone observes it – and that's you right now. You've got to make observations, not give me a big hug, as much as I want one, because if you do that, I'll fall to bits and tell you everything and leave no room for debate and it'll all be over.'

'You've really, totally lost me.'

'Come on,' she said, 'think. A narrative almost lost to chaos and entropy, only to be miraculously rescued and sorted out in the final chapters by virtue of a structure-saving, order-imposing twist. Isn't that exactly the sort of thing an angel would do?' She considered. 'Or a demon?'

'I thought we were talking about the baby.'

'And?'

'And, Jesus, *and* – you lost a baby. I thought Black was trying to bring his baby back, and I thought you were trying to find a way to get your book out into the world.'

'You still don't get it, do you? The book and the baby are one and the same.'

'What?' I said. A little bubble of outrage rose up in me then; I think I meant to demand to know if she'd been speaking metaphorically about one thing or the other this whole time, but then I didn't, because I saw that she hadn't, or maybe I saw something else – that the answer wouldn't be the answer, and *yes* or *no* or *that* or *this* wouldn't really tell me anything at all because the question itself was hopelessly flat, misguided and inadequate. The shadow of the flag manifold danced on the wall. I felt my legs go weak and I sat down on the floor.

'What?' I said, again.

'Autumn,' Imogen said. 'Stop saying *the baby*. I named our little girl Autumn.'

I stared up at her. 'Did it work?'

She didn't answer.

'Imogen. Did it work?'

'We've come all this way and you *still* don't get it – it's up to you. The power is entirely in your hands. Not mine. All of this – all of it – it's completely at your say-so. Of course a novel's an engine, but what is it for, what does it do? *And the Lord said "Let there be light" and there was light.* She'll come floating down the river in a basket of reeds, or she won't. It depends on you. You. It's your call to make it happen or not happen. Angel means messenger, and angels have been dancing to your tune since this whole thing began.'

'Except for you.'

'Well, I went a little rogue. The point is, my voice was taken away from me but you still have yours. You can still write the world however you want it to be, you just need to do it. Hence' – she held out her arms – 'everything.'

I felt dazed.

'It's been so long since I held your hand,' I said finally, from the floor. 'For it to be warm, to squeeze it and have you squeeze back, you know?'

Imogen gave me a small, sad shrug.

'Everything is falling apart,' she said.

Imogen jumped down from her table. I watched as she opened a panel in the studio wall. Behind it was a window, part of the bones of the hotel building. She opened this too and stood looking out, looked down, I guessed, at the reedy mere below.

I could hear seagulls, the distant sound of waves.

'What are you doing?' I said.

'Here's a question. If information drives Maxwell's demon, what drives the creative acts of God? It has to be something powerful, doesn't it? To make a Big Bang, to take that little black apple and smash it out into an entire universe? To sit down, turn on the computer again and open a new Word document after He's given up on His works, and on Himself. It'd have to be something pretty major to get God creating on that scale.'

'Imogen.'

'It's all for nothing if God doesn't have the drive to get started.'

I thought about the plastic letters on the fridge in our kitchen. I thought about the way Imogen's eyes were shiny, and the way Sophie's eyes shone when she was angry. I thought about Imogen's hair lighting up in the sun, and I thought about how my mother's hair glowed in the sunlight when I was a child. I thought about one thing slowly becoming another, and I thought about the steam from the teacup dissipating into the universe. And I thought about entropy, and how everything is falling apart.

'You know how Moses came down the Nile in a basket of bulrushes?'

I nodded.

'Do you know what those bulrushes would've been? What was growing on the banks of the Nile back then? Papyrus. Moses came floating down the river and into the world in a basket of papyrus.'

A searching look – Imogen looking for understanding in my eyes.

'I can keep putting all this stuff in front of you, Thomas, I can keep laying it out for you, but you're the one who has to see. To fucking – to fucking *do* something about it.'

'Imogen.'

'Thomas. Do something about it.'

34

Combining the Letters by Which the Heavens and Earth Were Created

Is the world you inhabit right now made more from rocks and grass and trees, or from bank statements, articles, certificates, records, files and letters?

In Genesis, God said *'let there be light'*, and only after the word – l-i-g-h-t – had been created, did the light itself appear. God divides and sorts, Maxwell's demon divides and sorts, and the messengers, the angels – Mighty A, the Aurochs, the Alph, The Bet of Bethlehem, Greedy C, the whole heavenly host – are arranged in their choirs across the page, and something is created.

Is your conscious mind a resident of the Book of Worlds or the Book of Words? You can decide what you think, with this as with all things, because deciding is important. Choosing is important. It's perhaps the most important thing there is. The writer divides and sorts, the reader divides and sorts. Useful work is done and something is created. From mess and dust, wonders are drawn, miracles. You can achieve a whole lot with nothing but the artfully concealed application of a shitload of time.

... am the small-est of all the letters, Thou has withdrawn me from the name of that righteous woman!'

The hero may have to be brought b-ack from his sup-ernatural adventure by assistance from without. That is to say, the world may have to come and get him. – Joseph C-ampb-ell.

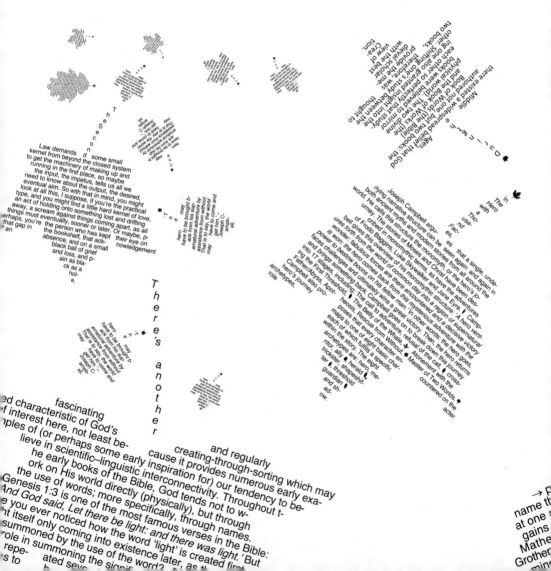

The second Law demands some small kernel from beyond the closed system to get the machinery of making up and running in the first place, so maybe the input, the impetus, tells us all we need to know about the output, the desired, eventual aim. So with that in mind, you might look at all this, I suppose, if you're the practical type, and you might find a little hard kernel of love, an act of holding onto something lost and drifting away, a scream against things coming apart, as all things must eventually, sooner or later. Or maybe, p-erhaps, you're the person who has kept their eye on that gap in the bookshelf, that ack-nowledgement of an absence, and on a small black ball of grief and loss, and p-ain as bla-ck as a hol-e.

During the Middle Ages, there existed a widespread belief that God authored not one, but two books: the Book of Words (the Bible) and the Book of Works (the physical world). The two divine books were believed to mirror each other so perfectly that study-ing one also granted insight into the other. Shifting one's study between the two books, therefore, was thought to provide the me-dieval scholar with the best view of Crea-tion.

In The Hero with a Thousand Faces, Joseph Campbell argues that a single, underlying narrative structure can be seen again and again in both ancient myths and modern stories from all around the world. He calls this structure the monomyth, or the hero's journey. The stories of Moses and Christ have been described in monomythic terms, as have the adventures of Frodo Baggins, Luke Skywalker and Jane Eyre. Campbell gives this overview of his monomythic structure: 'A hero ventures forth from the world of common day into a region of supernatural wonder: fabulous forces are there encountered and a decisive victory is won: the hero comes back from this mysterious adventure with the power to bestow boons on his fellow man.' In other words: the hero goes, faces challenges and ultimately wins a great victory. Then, the hero returns and brings something back. Campbell goes on to break down this journey into 17 stages, including: The call to adventure, refusal of the call, crossing the First Threshold, The Belly of the Whale, Atonement with the Father/Abyss, Apotheosis, Rescue from Without, Master of Two Worlds. Campbell also proposes that every character encountered on the hero's journey maps to one of eight basic character archetypes, each of which fulfils a specific role within the story. The eight archetypes are: hero, mentor, ally, herald, trickster, shapeshifter, threshold guardian and shadow.

There's another fascinating characteristic of God's creating-through-sorting which may be of interest here, not least because it provides numerous early examples of (or perhaps some early inspiration for) our tendency to believe in scientific–linguistic interconnectivity. Throughout the early books of the Bible, God tends not to work on His world directly (physically), but through the use of words; more specifically, through names. Genesis 1:3 is one of the most famous verses in the Bible: *And God said, Let there be light: and there was light.* ' But have you ever noticed how the word 'light' is created first, light itself only coming into existence later, as summoned by the use of the word? ... role in summoning the signi... repe- ated seve... s to

→ p ... name th ... at one ... gains ... Mathe ... Grother ...

the yod [letter i] which the Lord took from Sarai soared aloft before God and prote-sted, 'Sovere-ign of the Univ-

any object collapsing beyond a certain point would form a black hole, inside which would form a black singularity. The initial state of the universe, at the beginning of the Big Bang, is also predicted by modern theories to have been a singularity.

A tittle or superscript dot is a small distinguishing mark, such as a diacritic or the dot on a lowercase i or j. The word tittle is rarely used. One notable occurrence is in the King James Bible at Matthew 5:18: *'For verily I say unto you, Till heaven and earth pass, one jot or one tittle shall in no wise pass from the law.'* In the Greek original are found the words 'iota' and 'keraia' (Greek:κεραία). Iota is the smallest letter of the Greek alphabet (ι). Alternatively, it may represent yodh (י), the smallest.

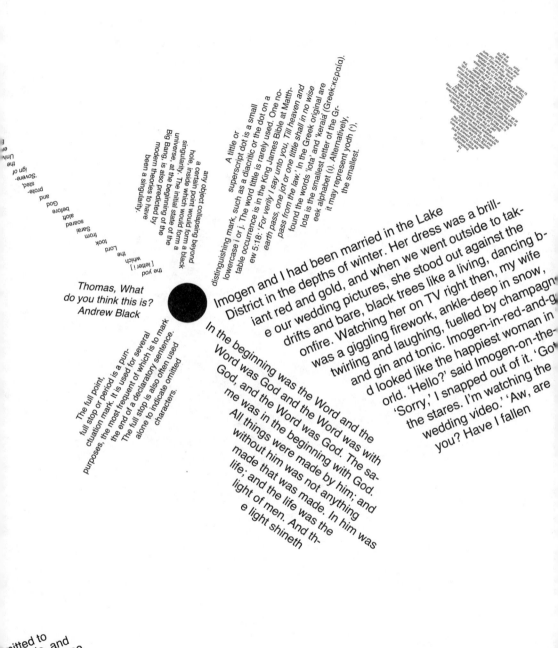

Thomas, What do you think this is?
Andrew Black

Imogen and I had been married in the Lake District in the depths of winter. Her dress was a brilliant red and gold, and when we went outside to take our wedding pictures, she stood out against the drifts and bare, black trees like a living, dancing bonfire. Watching her on TV right then, my wife was a giggling firework, ankle-deep in snow, twirling and laughing, fuelled by champagne and gin and tonic. Imogen-in-red-and-gold looked like the happiest woman in the world. 'Hello?' said Imogen-on-the-... 'Sorry,' I snapped out of it. 'Got ... the stares. I'm watching the wedding video.' 'Aw, are you? Have I fallen

The full point, full stop or period is a punctuation mark. It is used for several purposes, the most frequent of which is to mark the end of a declaratory sentence. The full stop is also often used alone to indicate omitted characters.

In the beginning was the Word and the Word was God and the Word was with God, and the Word was God. The same was in the beginning with God. All things were made by him; and without him was not anything made that was made. In him was life; and the life was the light of men. And the light shineth

...mitted to
...animals, and
...d the same time
...ominion over them.
...atician Alexander
...eck said 'he saw the act of
...mathematical objects as
...gral part of their discovery,
... grasp them even
... been entirely
... Skywalker
... and

...ies.
...logos is
...nd later the
...er) and either
...y connected
...od Himself:
...ish people
...God
...ation
...y

You only have to select, choose, divide. Heaven from Earth, sea from sky, night from day. Because we're in this together, the two of us. Your eyes over the lines, my fingers over the keys. I am typing now, racing, directing the choir. The Engine of Worlds and Works is running. The cherubim, the hayyoth, are taking to the stage with words and actions, even as they're singing the good news of creation across the page – the Alph, Bet, and Impulsive Iota, the letter who flew in the face of God.

Maybe there will be a miracle play here today, a nativity, to bring forth something truly wondrous.

Where wast thou when I laid the foun-dati-ons of the earth? Decl-are,
and prote-sted 'Sovere-ign of the Univ-erse! Beca-use I am the small-est of all the letters, Thou has withdrawn me from the name of that righteous woman!'
It happened after the sons of men had multiplied in those days, that daughters were born to them, elegant and beautiful. And when the angels, the sons of heaven, beheld them, they became enamoured of th-em, saying to each other, 'Come, let us select for ourselves wives from the progeny of men, and let us beget children.' (Book of Eno-ch 7:1–2)

The hero may have to be brought back from his supernatural adventure by assistance from without. That is to say, the world may have to come and get him.' — Joseph Campbell

During the Middle Ages, there existed a widespread belief that God authored not one, but two books: the Book of Words (the Bible) and the Book of Works (the physical world). The two divine books were believed to mirror each other so perfectly that studying one also granted insight into the other. Shifting one's study between the two books, therefore, was thought to provide the medieval scholar with the best view of Creation.

A tittle or superscript dot is a small distinguishing mark, such as a diacritic or the dot on a lowercase i or j. The word tittle is rarely used. One notable occurrence is in the King James Bible at Matthew 5:18: '*For verily I say unto you, Till heaven and earth pass, one jot or one tittle shall in no wise pass from the law.*' In the Greek original are found the words 'iota and keraia' (Greek: κεραία). Iota is the smallest letter of the Greek alphabet (ι). Alternatively, it may represent yodh (!), the smallest.

any object collapsing beyond a certain point would form a black hole, inside which would form a singularity. The initial state of the universe, at the beginning of the Big Bang, is also predicted by modern theories to have been a singularity.

the yod [letter i] which the Lord took from Sarai soared aloft befor

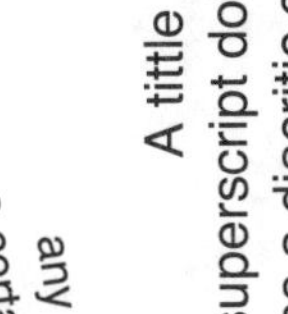

Thomas, What do you think this is?
Andrew Black

Imogen and I had been married in the l
District in the depths of winter. Her d
iant red and gold, and when w
e our wedding pictures, sh
drifts and bare, black
onfire. Watching
was a giggling
twirling a
and

In the beginning was the Word and
Word was God and the Word w
God, and the Word was God.
me was in the beginning w
All things were made by
without him was not an
made that was made.
life; and the life w
light of

The full point, full stop or period is a punctuation mark. It is used for several purposes, the most frequent of which is to mark the end of a declaratory sentence. The full stop is also often used alone to indicate omitted characters.

any object collapsing bey
a certain point would form a
hole, inside which would form a
singularity. The initial state of the
niverse, at the beginning of the
g Bang, is also predicted by
modern theories to have
been a singularity.

A titt
superscript
hing mark, such as a diacritic
ase i or j. The word tittle is ra
occurrence is in the King Ja
w 5:18: 'For verily I say unto
earth pass, one jot or one
pass from the law,'

Imogen and
District
it:

In the begin
Word wa

tabl
lowerc
distinguis

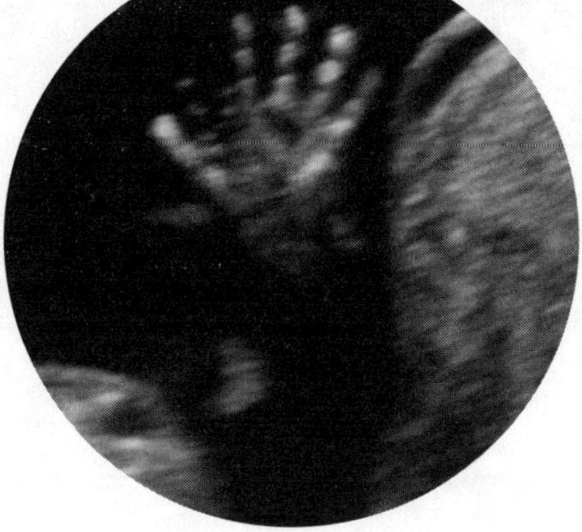

ond
black

used
entence.
n is to mark
everal

What
k this is?
Black

Is the world you inhabit right now made more from rocks and grass and trees, or from bank statements, articles, certificates, records, files and letters?

R

i

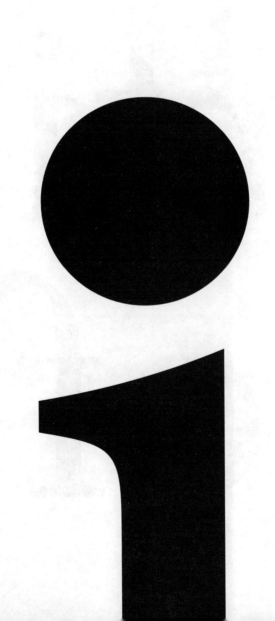

'Autumn.'

'Yes.'

'What a lovely name.'

'Thank you.'

ertif

of

icate

Birth

The health visitor finishes looking over the birth certificate, then hands it back. Lying on her changing mat, Autumn kicks her chubby feet and stares in wide-eyed fascination at the light coming in through the window.

'Well, you have one healthy, happy and thriving baby girl here, Mr Quinn.'

I nod, smile.

I gently take hold of one of Autumn's feet. I feel its real-world weight, feel her fat little leg pushing against my palm.

'You're telling me,' I say.

We're sitting in the living room of the London flat – me, the health visitor and Autumn on her mat. Two hundred and twenty-nine brand new manuscript pages are neatly stacked next to the computer on the desk.

The health visitor clicks a ballpoint pen and starts filling in a form on her clipboard.

'I'm sorry we haven't seen you sooner for the home visit,' she says. 'These sorts of mistakes with the data are very rare, thankfully.'

'That's okay,' I say. 'We didn't know you didn't have her on the system.'

'Oh, we had her. We just had her as—'

The health visitor stumbles, mortified. I help her out.

'Look, don't worry, honestly. She's absolutely fine. She has no idea what your records said about her. She's doing great and, well – eating mostly.' I give Autumn's foot a gentle squeeze, and it kicks against me again. She's surprisingly strong.

The health visitor nods, relieved, and then a little distracted:

'And Mrs Quinn?' She checks her notes. 'Imogen?'

'She's at work.'

The health visitor's eyebrows shoot up. 'Already? What does she do?'

‘Well.’ Now I’m the one struggling. ‘She’s actually taking a break, but . . . She needed to take care of a few things. See some colleagues about . . . recent developments.’ My brain says *wrap this up* and *she’s going to kill you*. ‘A handover.’ I finish.

‘What does your wife do, Mr Quinn?’ the health visitor asks again.

‘She’s in construction,’ I say, and I smile, pleased with myself, like an idiot.

The health visitor does not smile back.

‘Sorry, no. I mean she writes. She just finished a book. Almost. Well, we have. Together.’

‘You’re writers?’

‘We are.’

The health visitor’s face softens. ‘Oh, that’s interesting, isn’t it?’ But it does not soften entirely. ‘And she’ll be here next time I visit?’

‘Absolutely.’ I say, and I think, *well, this could be interesting*.

But then I tickle Autumn’s warm little foot and I think, *these are not the worst problems to have*.

The health visitor leaves soon afterwards, and then it’s just me and the baby, together in the quiet flat and with the last of the year’s sunshine streaking in through the windows. I lift her from her changing mat and cradle her in my arms.

I should call Real Sophie, I think, tell her that the book will be finished today. Soon it’ll be ready to be printed onto thick, white paper and bound into reassuringly heavy hardbacks. *A universe between two covers*, I think, *a whole world pressed and preserved*. I was able to make the publication requests I’m mentioning here – the Real Sophie says *demands* – because the name Andrew Black goes a long way, it turns out. Even in co-authorship.

And so, the baby and I sit in happy silence for a little while, and in amongst drifting nothing thoughts, I think that I really should start calling Real Sophie just Sophie now, because, well, it's starting to get weird. But mostly, I think about being a father, a creator of something that did not exist before, and I cradle the bundle in my arms, and I am joyful.

Her name is Autumn. Newly born and delivered. She's my world, my complete universe. I'm proud of her, and I fear for her, because I know there will be few like her in the years to come. Her name is Autumn, and she's my little rose. Her name is Autumn, and as the days grow colder, as the wind rises, and as all the stars in the Gutenberg galaxy blink out one by one, we will stand in the path of approaching winter. I will hold her hand and she will hold mine, and we will face the future together.

o

Later that day, I go through to the tidy kitchen to make some milk. The kitchen isn't *quite* tidy any more. The 'I ♥ tea' mug is standing on the draining board next to the sink, with a fresh, red lipstick mark on the rim. And on the other side of the kitchen, on the worktop near the kettle, where it waited for all those months, the cup has left a circle . . . not quite closed.

Acknowledgements

Thank you to Melanie Hall, Simon Trewin, Francis Bickmore, Jamie Byng, Leila Cruickshank, Sharon McTeir and Megan Reid. I am indebted to Joseph Campbell's *The Hero with a Thousand Faces* and Christopher Vogler's *The Writer's Journey*. Texts from Wikipedia's pages on full stops, tittles and singularities appear on pages 319–325.

Permission Credits

Every effort has been made to trace copyright holders and obtain their permission for the use of copyright material. The publisher apologises for any errors or omissions and would be grateful if notified of any corrections that should be incorporated in future reprints or editions of this book.

Excerpt from *The Invention of Solitude* by Paul Auster. Copyright © Paul Auster, 1982. Used by permission of Faber and Faber Ltd.

Excerpt from *Desolation Angels* by Jack Kerouac (Penguin Classics, 2012). Copyright © Jack Kerouac, 1965.

Excerpt from *11/22/63* by Stephen King. Copyright © 2011 by Stephen King. Reprinted with the permission of Hodder & Stoughton, a division of Hachette UK; and Scribner, a division of Simon & Schuster, Inc. All rights reserved.

Excerpt from *Johnny Panic and the Bible of Dreams* by Sylvia Plath (Faber and Faber, 1977; Harper Perennial, 2000). Copyright © 1952, 1953, 1954, 1955, 1956, 1957, 1960, 1961, 1962, 1963 by Sylvia Plath. Copyright © 1977, 1979 by Ted Hughes. Used by permission of Faber and Faber Ltd; and HarperCollins Publishers.